THE THEFT
OF THE
AYN NOOR

THE THEFT
OF THE
AYN NOOR

CHARLES L.M.
LARTIGUE

Published by One & Twenty Books, Midcoast Maine
theftoftheaynnoor.com

Edited and designed by Girl Friday Productions
www.girlfridayproductions.com

Cover, interior, and map design: Paul Barrett
Cover illustration: Chris Beatrice
Logo design: Dave Horowitz
Project management: Sara Spees Addicott
Editorial: Tiffany Taing, Leah Tracosas-Jenness

ISBN (paperback): 978-1-7352687-0-5
ISBN (ebook): 978-1-7352687-1-2

Library of Congress Control Number: 2020914949
Printed in the United States of America

This book is dedicated to the beautiful and courageous people of Haiti and Tibet.

KINGDOM OF ILYRIA

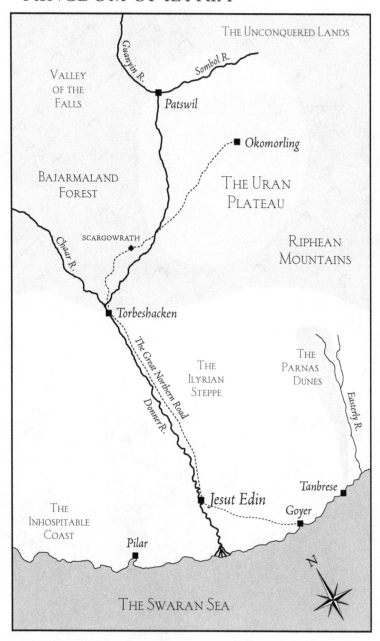

"Even a tiny pebble casts a long shadow."

—Pagani proverb

PROLOGUE

Marius found himself not so much listening to what Lieutenant Peter Griswald was shouting about but rather observing the deep furrows set between his brows and his dark, strained eyes. *"What... if... the... rope... slips!"* yelled Peter, attempting to be heard over the falls. Marius doubted the knots were faulty, but to appease him, he pulled on the rope tied about his boots. *"They're fine!"* he shouted back. In truth, the rope was too tight. Peter should have had more concern for the circulation to his feet. But there was no time to set it right; a fattened August moon was about to rise—its light was all they were waiting for.

Earlier that day, in the cover of the forest, they had cut and delimbed trees, designing a structure that could not only span the river but hold a log across the front of the waterfall, which Marius would use to descend to the pool below. Fortunately, the roar of the water cloaked the sound of their axes and the whinnying of their horses, keeping their presence hidden, for they were deep in enemy territory. Coaxing fresh-cut trees over boulders and stumps in the dark had been its own battle—and nearly their demise. Much of their clothing was torn, the blisters on their hands had burst, and their shins were bloodied and bruised by the time they had the timber gathered at the river's edge.

The apparatus itself was simple enough. The two heaviest logs were set parallel to the river on either bank and secured to rocks and trees with rope. Between them, smaller logs were strapped across the river, making a platform upon which Corporal Caleb Sturgis could sit. With a stack of rope coiled at his feet, Sturgis would lower Marius to the pool in search of Colette's mystical diamond.

In the summer, a chill circulated in the high mountains after sunset, but they did not dare make a fire. Gathered on the bank, waiting for the moon, the three of them ate, chewing dried venison and cracking flatbread between their teeth, too tired to talk. When a faint glow of silver began to dust the horizon, Sturgis took his post on the wooden platform, while Marius and Peter departed for the log positioned out over the falls.

After tying Marius' feet—too tight—Peter walked the extra cordage back to Sturgis, taking all slack out of the line. Returning to Marius' side, Peter stood, head downcast. By now Marius knew the habits of Peter's mind. A question would be forthcoming. Peter looked up, his eyes ablaze. *"What if . . . you . . . don't come . . . back?"* he bellowed. But Marius had already told him—and Sturgis—in no uncertain terms, if something went wrong to cut the rope. They were to unburden the horses, abandon all equipment, and ride like the wind toward the Sombol River. Once across, they should either go upriver to the garrison town of Patswil or ride southeast over the plateau to the city of Okomorling, the seat of the Ilyrian Empire in the north. Of one thing Marius was certain: shouting back and forth was futile. With a vigorous jut of his chin, Marius motioned in the direction of Peter's post. Peter started to turn but then stopped. Marius quickly lowered his gaze and fiddled with his boots. *"Good luck, Marius!"* hollered Peter. Marius kept his head down. When he did chance a peek, he was relieved to see Peter walking toward his post.

Sitting with his feet tied and his back to the precipice, Marius struck the log with his palm. There was not a hint of vibration. Marius pushed down until his arms straightened. He pressed the weight of his body through his hands and lifted his butt and bound legs into the air. He then began to shimmy sideways along the trunk like a crab. Going a few inches at a time, he passed over the edge of the cliff. The brisk thump of his heart made his chest feel hollow. He wasn't so much afraid of heights, but the thundering cataract and the dark, half-veiled pool two hundred feet below made him uneasy.

Through the darkness, he could just make out a shadowed silhouette, the colossal outline of Caleb Sturgis, his feet braced against the timber frame. He was a bearlike man with rounded shoulders. Marius felt confident that Sturgis would be able to lower him and, with help from Lieutenant Griswald, pull him back up. As he neared the middle, the trunk began to bounce slightly. He kept his vision firmly on the lip of the river and lowered himself to sitting. He was less than six feet from the rushing water. It coursed toward him as smooth as porcelain; the only imperfection was where the rope dipped slightly into the river. Just then a gust of river wind burst upon him, filling his face and hair.

Over his shoulder, the rising moon was just visible. Marius peered into the semidarkness to see if he could locate Peter—he could not. Peter's post was farther along the cliff, where he could observe both the pool and Sturgis. He was to signal when to stop lowering Marius and when to pull him back up.

When Marius found himself staring at the gibbous moon floating in the inky complexion of the evening sky, he waved at Sturgis, who gestured back. It was time. Marius dropped backward off the log.

Upside-down, he began to spin. One moment Marius could see a solid wall of water rushing past him . . . and the next an open bowl, formed by the curve of the surrounding cliffs. His shirt hung slightly over his chin, but he could still make out the sky beyond his feet, where a few glimmering stars could be seen. It was a perfect, cloudless night! For all he knew Colette had planned this too. His sister's insight, as with most things, was uncanny. Perhaps she had divined it from her ancient map, the culprit that had set this lunacy in motion.

Marius remembered the day well: the sunlight drizzled upon the parquet floor of the palace, the footmen with their long blue coats and tall white stockings standing on either side of the gilded doors, and the click-clack of officers' boots, muted only by the cloth-covered walls with their floral patterns. Marius hadn't gone but ten steps past the footmen when Colette seized his arm and pulled him to one side. Her hands were trembling. "I found it!" she gasped. From behind the tousled strands of raven hair shone her piercing blue eyes. Colette looked wild, as if she hadn't slept in days. If he hadn't known his sister, he might have thought she was mad.

"I found it!" she repeated.

"Found what?" asked Marius, coming out of his private aversion to her appearance.

"*The Ayn Noor!*" she said firmly. "I can't believe it." Her voice quieted. Her fingers wandered to her lips as her eyes cast downward. "The Ayn Noor!" she repeated, as if to herself.

"I have no idea what you're talking about," said Marius, unmoved.

Dropping her hand, her eyes seared into his. "What do you *do* in meetings all day? The Ayn Noor! The Pagani's talisman. It's there on the map . . . Apparently, nobody can see it but *me!*"

Marius noticed some officers and courtiers lingering, talking in half conversations so as to bend their ears toward the siblings. "Quietly, Colette," he urged, turning his broad back and wedging himself between her and them. Colette proceeded to ramble on about the Pagani fleeing the underworld with the Ayn Noor at the beginning of time. Marius listened for as long as he could, but none of what she said made any sense. Then it occurred to him.

"Why are you telling me this?"

Colette's eyes became small and her lips tightened.

"Just tell me!" Marius demanded. "What do you want?"

"*No!*" said Colette. "Forget it! I'm not going to tell you. Just go back to whatever you're doing. Obviously, it is *very* important." And she dug her elbow into his ribs to push past him. Gently but firmly taking her shoulders with his hands, he positioned himself in front of her. Colette folded her arms and glared back. It was now a matter of who would budge first.

Colette's hand shot upward, pinching his ear. Pulling his head down, she began to whisper. When he had heard enough, he took her wrist and freed himself. "Colette, I don't care if it's the mother of all diamonds . . . Going that far into Pagani territory . . . to steal the . . . whatever you call it, is insane!"

"But don't you see?" she said, her eyes imploring his. "You've always wanted to do something valiant. Don't you see? This is *it*! This is your chance!"

Marius shook his head. "There is a thin line between a heroic act and a stupid one, Colette. What you ask leaves no room for doubt." Looking around at those lingering, he was certain Colette's outburst had not gone unheard. "I've got to get back to the garrison; we'll talk later." With this, he moved to kiss her cheek, but she quickly turned her head and crossed her arms, warding him off.

If it had ended there, that would have been fine with him. However, a dim phosphoric light began to hover behind his eyes. It wasn't particularly bright, but it never went away, not even when he shut his eyes at night. A few days later when he told Colette, she rebuked him. "What do you expect when you ignore your destiny?" The word "destiny" made him laugh, but Colette shrugged—it was her turn to walk away. The light persisted until the day he consented to go. Thus, one year and five months on he was in the high mountains, beyond the border of the Ilyrian Empire, going headfirst down a waterfall in search of Colette's outlandish stone.

As Marius neared the bottom, the thunder of the cataract was the sound of the river being obliterated, a million particles exploding in every direction. It was as if he had fallen face-first into a patch of stinging nettles. What's more, his head was throbbing. He could barely see, for streamlets kept running into his eyes. To prevent this, he tied his shirt around his neck. When he came to a halt, just a foot above the water, Marius stopped himself from spinning by using his hands as paddles. The cold water made his fingers ache. Through the mist he could see large boulders sticking out of the black broth like the broken teeth of a giant.

It was then he realized that this was the extent of their plans. All Colette had said was that otherworldly creatures— luminescent crabs—held the crystal. When the moon illuminated the pool, the crabs rose from the depths, bringing the diamond to the surface to align it with the celestial bodies. Not that he believed any of that. Mostly, he hoped he wouldn't have to cut the rope and dive into the pool to search for the jewel—there was no point in coming this far and not doing a thorough investigation. As tentacles of moonlight began to creep down the edges of the pool, Marius strained to see past the churning water. Searching right . . . then left . . . he could make out nothing. A whole minute passed before a hearty guffaw sprung from his mouth. If he had been in a tavern, he would have jumped on top of the table and danced. It was only now, after coming all this way, hanging upside down, that he could see how foolish he was! Once more, he had gotten lured into one of Colette's childish fantasies! And he, a captain in the Ilyrian army no less!

Yet even as the bitter irony turned his stomach, he noticed a flicker of light. And before he could determine if he had actually seen something, it disappeared . . . until another twinkle sparkled from below. Feverishly wiping the water off his face, Marius squinted. But the effort was unnecessary, for a fiery white light began spiraling upward, circling out of the depths of the pool, growing larger and larger. Marius closed his eyes and reopened them, fully expecting the mirage to be gone. Instead, he found himself ensconced in an opalescent aureole, the arc of which extended well beyond his body. He was uncertain where the center of the light was located due to the churning water, but it seemed to be emanating from a point just below the surface. Marius raised his arm to shield his eyes—for the light was too bright. Surely, all of this was just an illusion. It had to be some bizarre interplay of the moon and the frothing water. Peeking beneath his arm, Marius found the light had diminished . . . or his eyes had adjusted. Either way, the intensity was just bearable.

Without warning, Marius was no longer hanging upside down. There was no rope around his feet . . . and no waterfall. He was standing in a chapel of finely cut limestone. Looking down at his legs, then at his hands, then back at his legs, he kept wondering where the rope had gone. He patted his shirt and chest only to discover that his clothes were bone dry. Marius searched about for the chapel door but found none. The light was coming from stained-glass windows high above. As he walked up the aisle, he noticed an ornately carved sarcophagus sitting in the crossing. Closer to the tomb, he could see that the seal had been broken and the topping stone pushed aside. Marius leaned over, peering into the chamber. The sarcophagus was empty except for a crumpled, dust-ridden tunic. Marius swiveled his head around, half expecting to see the dweller of the tomb standing behind him. Resting his hand on the edge, Marius skimmed his fingers along the top as he walked to the far side. Toward the back of the chapel, an arched colonnade formed a semicircle. Once he had passed beneath it, he came to an opening with stairs that led down into an impenetrable blackness. Marius could feel the faint tug of a chilly draft. Moist air permeated his nostrils along with the aroma of the subterranean realm. He unbuckled his knife and held it tight in his hand. Taking measured steps, he descended slowly. The fine-cut stone turned to rough-hewn rock until the walls became mere dirt and loam, crumbly to the touch.

The stairs ended on even ground. Before him was a large cavern. Long crepuscular shafts of light streaked down from an invisible source above. Marius found it strange there was light at all given that he was so far underground. The slanting beams settled upon an object at the far end of the grotto. Marius considered it might be an altar of sorts. Once across the cavern, he discovered it was not an altar but a calcified spring, a protuberance standing waist high. Clear water bubbled out of the top of the cone and seeped down a velvety green layer of algae and moss interspersed with tiny white blossoms.

A sudden realization, an intuition, dawned upon him— that a person of great spiritual importance was about to appear. Marius' hands began to shake and his fingers opened. His knife dropped helplessly to the ground. As Marius' knees buckled, he fell onto them, clasping his hands together in prayer.

◆ ◆ ◆

Peter was beside himself. He could not understand why Marius did not just reach for the diamond or whatever it was that was shining so brightly before him. Not long after the moon had touched the water, it had been set aglow. Surely, all Marius had to do was reach down and take it. But as of yet, he hadn't moved!

"Come on, Marius," grumbled Peter. "What are you waiting for? Grab it and let's go!" But as more and more time passed, he presumed that Marius had fainted—perhaps from hanging upside down for too long. Reluctantly, Peter abandoned his post. Crouching low, he scurried across the cliff. When he came upon Sturgis, he explained what was happening. They agreed that Sturgis should give the rope a good shake, and if Marius didn't respond, they would have no choice but to pull him back up—with or without the jewel.

♦ ♦ ♦

Suddenly, the cave disappeared. Once again, Marius was hanging upside down before the falls, delirious and cold . . . and gravely disappointed for the missed encounter. The pool was supremely calm—there was not a blemish or disruption anywhere. What's more, the luminous jewel was hovering before him, suspended, just below the surface. It was still too resplendent for him to locate its edges, but he presumed by its brightness that it was large. Gazing into what seemed to be the source of the light, he found himself traveling into it as if pulled by an invisible force. Advancing past the prism bars of the rainbow, he journeyed between the multicolored walls of the ordinary. For the first time in his adult life, he didn't know what to do. All he knew was that he was being drawn deeper and deeper into the scintillating orb. And the farther he traveled, the less he knew of himself. He was being stripped of all physicality, losing all reference points to the material world. Only with great mental effort was Marius able to stop himself. But when he did, he was immediately catapulted out of the crystal. Once again, he, Captain Marius Proudst, and the jewel were two distinct objects. And for a moment, its radiance diminished; he could now make out its edges. It was clearly a large diamond. He had a sudden, overwhelming impression that it was being offered to him. Did he dare take it? But to come all this way, risk so much, and not make an attempt to seize it seemed absurd. Besides, what would he tell Colette?

Firming his resolve, he wiggled his fingers to limber them up. He directed his eyes just above the diamond to account for the deception of the water, just as one does when spear fishing. Most likely, he would have only one chance, especially if there were otherworldly beings protecting the gem . . . which at this point he did not doubt. Marius raised himself to gain leverage by arching his back before thrusting both arms into the ice-cold water. Immediately, his hands became luminous, as if they were not made of flesh but of spirit. Hesitating for an instant, he pushed deeper. As he grasped the diamond Marius was flung mercilessly into a realm of unshakable darkness.

1

Jesut Edin, the Capital of Ilyria

"No good to lie in the dark," said Pola, as she stepped into the room carrying a lamp. Brill turned his head just in time to see shadows leaping across the wall like spirits in a primeval forest. As Pola glided past the foot of his bed, Brill imagined she was queen of the faeries, the only one who could keep the woodland imps from misbehaving.

Pola had been the family's governess since before he could remember. His first memory was of her bathing him beneath the bright sun in the courtyard. On hot nights Pola would bring him a wet cloth to cool his head, and on cold winter nights, a warm pan to heat his bed. She was thin as a broom handle—and hard as one too. She didn't waddle from side to side like Sisal the cook, or "seesaw" as his older brother Nikolas liked to chide.

"I see you haven't washed," Pola said flatly.

"No, not yet," answered Brill.

"Let me see your teeth," she said, holding the lantern up to his face. Brill opened his mouth wide. "Put on your nightclothes while I go fetch some water."

"Yes, Pola," replied Brill, sitting up.

"Oh . . ." she said, stopping at the door, "and say your prayers! I'll be back before you can say, 'A hoary sight to behold the ornery mustache of old Mister Calabash.'"

Brill was sitting cross-legged on the end of his bed when Pola returned. Putting down the pitcher of water, she pulled back his sheet, fluffed his pillow, and tapped it lightly. Brill waited for her to turn around before springing back. When he looked up, Pola's face remained unmoved, giving no indication that she was surprised to see him under the covers. Dipping the cloth in the stoneware, she wrung it out. Brill listened to the chime of the water droplets. Leaning forward, she made a quick swipe across his face, taking away what dirt he had missed. Dipping the cloth again, Pola set it on his forehead. The cold felt immense.

Brill waited for her to ask him about his day, but instead, she slumped into the upholstered chair beside his bed and closed her eyes. *"Today,"* Brill started, "Costa said that the Pagani are burning villages in the north."

"So I've heard," said Pola, her eyes remaining shut.

"You're Pagani, aren't you, Pola?"

"I am . . . but I didn't burn any villages today," she said, opening one eye to give him a curious gander.

Brill grimaced shyly. "Some other boys were saying that the wells in the city are going to run dry—and the Donner River will soon stop flowing. Then everyone will have to leave Jesut Edin."

"Boys! Always trying to scare each other, aren't they? See who's bravest." Pola used the arms of the chair to push herself forward. Leaning over him, she removed the cloth from his forehead. After giving it another few dunks and a squeeze, she returned it. This time it didn't feel as cold.

"Is it true, Pola?" he asked.

"Some say great winds of change are upon us."

"Are you scared, Po?"

"Me? Noooo!" she said, shaking her head. "I am too old for that. But what about you, Brill? Are you scared?"

"A little . . . maybe."

"Don't worry yourself too much about the affairs of men, not yet anyway."

"But I will soon be a man," he said, removing the cloth and handing it to her. "I'm almost fourteen."

"You have a few months to go yet," said Pola, taking the cloth and draping it over the pitcher. "Do you know what the poet Rafeet said?" Brill shook his head. "'Only in the spirit of the unfettered boy will a man ever know true happiness.'"

"What does that mean, Pola?"

"It means . . . just be a boy . . . for as long as you can." And with this, she reached forward and dusted his brown curls. He watched her closely. The crescents under her eyes seemed darker than usual. He knew she was working longer days now that his mother had let two more servants go. Even so, Pola didn't have affable features—bristly gray whiskers on a sharp chin, hardened lips, and indistinct gray eyes. If she were a stranger and Brill were meeting her for the first time, he might have thought she was mean.

"Pola, tell me a story," said Brill. Her face remained unmoved. Brill promptly asked a question that had been on his mind. "Is it true what Liis said—that you never went to school?"

"Where I grew up, there were no schools," answered Pola.

"Then how did you learn?" he inquired, turning onto his side to see her better.

"We just kept our heads about us. You know, some say life is a pretty good teacher."

"I wish I didn't have to go to school."

"Schools are the way of your people," she stated.

"But what if I fail my test?" he asked.

"Then your mother will decide what's best for you."

"She'll send me to seminary!"

"Then study hard and pass your exams," asserted Pola.

"It doesn't matter how hard I study, when the teacher says, 'Begin!' I can't put my thoughts into words."

"What do you do?"

"I look out the window."

"I've never taken a test in my life," confided Pola. "So I don't know about such things."

"Never?" inquired Brill.

"Never," repeated Pola. "But perhaps, if you lie very still, I will tell you a story." Brill spun onto his back and pulled his arms straight against his body. "How about 'The Good Samaritan,'" started Pola. "Or 'Joseph and the Colored Robe'? I know you like that one."

"Nooo," said Brill, shaking his head vigorously. "Tell me one of the other stories . . . you know . . ."

Pola raised an eyebrow at him. "I don't need to remind you that your mother forbids them."

"My father didn't," he said as he pushed himself onto his elbows.

Pola squinted. "I suppose you think that because you mentioned your father, I will feel sorry for you?"

"No, it's just that I like those stories better."

Pola wiped her hands on her apron. Leaning back in the chair, she spoke. "My grandmother was the most wonderful storyteller. In the winter, when snow was filling up the woods, we would gather around the fire to listen to her tell stories. Everyone came—my cousins, my aunts and uncles, my parents. The small children would sit in someone's lap or on the floor about my grandmother's feet. In the beginning, her words were slow as tree sap, but it wasn't long before they were flying about our heads like swallows. Sometimes I became so enchanted I would forget to breathe.

"I don't recall ever telling you the story about Asharvin and the witch Ufansil." Brill shook his head. Pola shifted slightly and leaned back before closing her eyes. Brill liked to watch her closely before she began a story. Her face seemed to change. For an instant he could see the little girl she had once been. But not today. Today she remained old and haggard . . . and her eyes stayed shut for a long time. At first, Brill figured she was gathering the threads of a great story, but then he began to wonder if she hadn't fallen asleep. He was about to reach over and nudge her when her eyelids eased back. There was a faraway look in them as if she were gazing down a trail rising out of a mist-laden valley. Perhaps Pola was watching someone approach her, maybe even her grandmother.

"A long, long time ago," began Pola, "before there were proper roads in Bajarmaland, when the northern forests were thick and impassable, a young huntsman named Asharvin lived with his mother and little sister, Talitha, deep in the woods.

"But these were hard times, for pestilence and disease had spread throughout the land—there wasn't a corner that death's bony finger didn't come to. Kings and paupers were taken in equal measure. Even in remote regions the black death came, taking people away in the windowless carriage drawn by six ash-white stallions."

"Where did the horses take them?" asked Brill.

"Bardo Fey," replied Pola.

"Wha-what's Bardo Fey?"

"The Land of the Dreaming Dead," she answered flatly. Brill sank lower, pulling his sheet up above his nose. "What's more," continued Pola, "the terrible sickness had seized Talitha . . . and there was none that Asharvin loved more dearly than his little sister. Desperate, Asharvin sought a mountain sha- man, a diviner, who told him the only thing that could save her was the Ayn Noor."

"Tell me, Pola," said Brill, drawing the covers down from his mouth. "What is the Ayn Noor?"

"I've told you before, Brill."

"Tell me again."

"Well . . . it's hard to put it into Ilyrian . . . but if I must, one might say . . . it's a crystal of sorts," Pola explained.

"But what *kind* of crystal?" inquired Brill.

"Some say it shines too bright to know. Few have gazed into it long enough, but it's rumored to be a diamond. From the Ayn Noor all things arise . . . and in the end, all things return."

"Is it the diamond people are talking about?"

"Perhaps," said Pola. "They *say* that if a person touches it, one of two things will happen: they will either gaze upon the bright shores of eternity, or they will be cast into the dark corridors of madness."

"Do you believe that, Pola?" asked Brill in a hushed tone.

"It doesn't matter what I believe, Brill. What matters is what *you* believe."

"I believe it!" he stated with an earnest nod of his head.

"That was fast," said Pola, betraying a smile.

"Where does the Ayn Noor come from?"

"Brill," said Pola sternly, "which story do you want to hear tonight? I cannot tell you *both*."

"I'm not tired," he pleaded, opening his eyes wide so Pola could see how awake he was.

"You may not be, but I am."

After a short silence, Brill spoke. "Tell me about the Ayn Noor . . . then tomorrow you can tell me about Asharvin."

"We'll see about that," said Pola, shaking her head. Brill flipped onto his side and pulled his pillow tight under his head. "The Ayn Noor . . . comes from the realm below this one, before it was the Land of the Dreaming Dead. Back then, it was a beautiful garden world, ripe with fruits and flowers and plenty to eat. All creatures spoke the same language, the language of the gods. It is unclear why changes took place. Some say the gods themselves were to blame, for instead of taking pleasure in what they had created, they found it increasingly tiresome. Retreating to their castle nestled amidst the clouds, they mingled amongst themselves, eating and drinking in their sun-drenched halls, drifting in and out of sleep and dreams.

"Instead of bringing rain to the pastures, they left the sun shining upon the fields for days. In these regions, the earth became very dry, and the plants grew hollow and brittle. Even the slightest breeze would snap them in half."

"Like here in Jesut Edin," said Brill.

Ignoring him, Pola continued. "Dust storms swept across the earth, leaving houses scattered like empty shells in the sand. But in other regions, the gods forgot to blow the rain clouds away! Weeks of downpour left rivers swollen, and when rivers swell, they spill their banks. Rivers joined rivers until they became lakes, and lakes became seas. In the far north, snow fell uninterrupted for months, and sheets of ice began to creep south. People and animals had to search farther and farther for less and less food, often fighting each other for mere carcasses and bones.

"But there was one, a goddess, who didn't care for feasting. Her name was Iana. What she cared for were the streams and meadows, the harvest and the small animals. She loved filling the air with fragrance and the grasses with dewdrops. She gave the world many gifts, like the cherry blossom and the honeybee. Seeing all the destruction made her very sad. One day, while journeying across the skies, Iana spied a young woman. Queemquesh was her name. Iana could plainly see that Queemquesh was not only strong and brave, but fair and honest. So that night, Iana opened her palms and blew Queemquesh a dream about another world, a better one, above. It was a bountiful realm with a bright yellow sun and a great many stars. It even had its very own moon. There were deep blue oceans and rolling fields. But to reach it, one had to travel up the Spiral Path, a passage that wound around itself like a vine, stretching so high that the end vanished into the blue of sky.

"When Queemquesh woke, she immediately told her brother, Kurul, about her dream. Convinced it was a vision, Kurul insisted they seek the Spiral Path. After all, he was tired of being hungry. She agreed they should at least try, so Queemquesh gathered the people and the animals and told them about the world above. With newfound hope, many followed. After several weeks of travel, they came to a ridge overlooking a lush valley. At the center of the valley rose the Spiral Path, shimmering like a silver wand, going around and around itself. Although marvelous to behold, upon seeing it, the people and animals fell silent. Their hearts were anxious, for it looked far too dangerous to climb. Where was the end? And how long would it take to reach the next world? they wondered. And what would happen when it became night? What would keep them from falling? Unsure what to do, the people began to bicker and quarrel amongst themselves. Seeing their despair, Queemquesh set off into the wilderness in search of another vision.

"Iana, who was watching, knew that sometimes even gods had to be bold. So off she flew to gather the Ayn Noor, the Light of the Inner World, which resided on the island in the lake beneath the mountain. Arriving, Iana scooped the Ayn Noor out from its crystalline hollow and sped away as fast as she could, for she knew its disappearance would not go unnoticed for long.

"Queemquesh was greatly humbled when Iana appeared before her. 'Queemquesh,' said Iana, 'take the Ayn Noor and use it to guide the people and animals up the Spiral Path. But I warn you, once you pass the threshold, you must throw it back, for it does not belong in the upperworld.' Besides, Iana knew that the gods were jealous gods, and once they woke to discover its absence, they would grow bitter and vengeful. Vowing to return it, Queemquesh accepted the Ayn Noor from Iana.

"Returning from the wilderness, Queemquesh held the Ayn Noor high above her head for all to behold. Upon seeing the shining crystal, radiant as the morning star, the people and animals took heart. As Queemquesh began to climb the Spiral Path, they bravely followed behind. But progress was slow. When night came, they slept uneasily, huddled together away from the edge, for the fall was mighty. On the morning of the seventh day they began to see a glimmer far above—the opening between worlds. But by this time, the lower realm had grown dim, and the gods woke fretfully from bad dreams of theft and betrayal, which to their astonishment were all true, for they could see a great exodus of creatures being led up the Spiral Path with the Ayn Noor in their grubby little hands! Furious, they roared and stomped their feet in rage and sent Bardor, the god of the abyss, to destroy them. He began filling the lower realm with a storm the likes of which had never been seen. The waters rose as fast as a thousand tidal waves. But Queemquesh's heart was stout, and she led the creatures onward, shouting for them to hurry.

"Birds were the first to pass into the blue skies of the upperworld, filling the four corners with their songs. The four-legged animals, such as the red deer and the horse, were next. Seeing the tall grasses, they bounded through the opening with the lions, wolves, and bears close at their heels. The magical beings were soon to follow. But the tortoise and other small creatures like the mole, the mouse, and the snail, whose legs—if there were any at all—were tiny, lagged far behind. The cold, lashing winds that surge ahead of great storms fell hard upon them, and their progress came to a halt.

"Realizing they were not going to make it, Queemquesh spun to face Kurul, who was standing with her at the edge of the opening. 'Wait for me,' she bellowed.

"Kurul shook his head. 'Leave them. They're too slow!'

"'No!' Queemquesh shouted back. 'We cannot leave anyone.' She handed the Ayn Noor to Kurul and pushed her way against the gale-force winds and stinging rain down the Spiral Path. Reaching the littlest creatures, she ushered the smallest ones onto the tortoise's shell and hoisted the lot above her head. By now, the black abyss was swirling about her feet, and lightning cracked like a bullwhip above her head. Bardor's booming voice could be heard skirting the tops of the breaking waves. Through the hole above, Kurul yelled for Queemquesh to hurry, but his words were lost in the roar of the raging sea. But Queemquesh's sturdy knees were strong, and she beat the ground with her swift feet. Up, up, up the Spiral Path she raced. With eddies around her waist, Queemquesh plunged through the opening. 'Throw back the Ayn Noor!' she cried, as she dropped the tortoise to the ground.

"As Kurul lifted his arm, the frothing waters churned around the hole. '*Why? Why* should we return it?' he shouted, lowering his hand.

"'Because it does not belong here. It's the Light of the Inner World!' yelled Queemquesh, pushing herself to her feet. But a darkness had already descended over Kurul. He remembered how neglectful the gods had been, how much his people had suffered. He resented them for it. Besides, he had something they wanted, and that pleased him. Kurul turned his back to Queemquesh. And just as he did, Bardor grabbed her by the ankle. With a solitary scream, Queemquesh was gone.

"Bardor's storm would have poured through the opening, flooding the upperworld, if it had not been for Iana, who smote it closed, sealing the underworld from the upper, trapping Queemquesh below. All that was left of her were the deep grooves her fingers had made upon the earth as she was pulled down. These became the valleys and mountains of Bajarmaland."

"That's horrible!" said Brill, sitting up.

"I know," said Pola, shaking her head. "I used to cry when my grandmother told us this story."

"Is that the end?"

"End? Is there ever really an end, Brill?"

"So . . . so what happened to Queemquesh?" he asked.

"She remains trapped," said Pola, her face drawn long. "After Bardor's flood, the underworld became the desolate realm of Bardo Fey, the Land of the Dreaming Dead. And Queemquesh will stay there until the Ayn Noor is returned. Legend has it that one day the gates will open. If the Ayn Noor is returned by the hand of Kurul's descendants, Queemquesh can rejoin her people, and the world will be made whole once more."

"Gates! What gates?"

"The place where Iana closed the opening between the two worlds. It is the only place where a person, in blood and flesh, can walk into Bardo Fey."

Brill shivered. "What about Kurul? What happened to him?"

"Kurul became hardened. He convinced himself that he had done right. And many Pagani followed him, for they thought he was a great chieftain. Kurul's people became known as the Red Bow Clan. They are fierce warriors, but they never feel they have enough—and are forever restless.

"But not all Pagani followed Kurul. Some could see he was no great leader, and they formed their own clan, the Turtle Clan. It was the Turtle Clan that built the beautiful temple city of Okomorling—and their city became a bright light of hope in the upperworld, a reminder of what could be.

"After many, many years, Kurul grew old and sick, and although he possessed the Ayn Noor, he could not heal himself, for his eyes were covered by his own ignorance. To him, the Ayn Noor was merely something to be possessed. Even before his death the Red Bow Clan began to fight among themselves. After all, who would get to keep it—they trusted no one, least of all each other. And rightly so, for deep down they knew their own greedy hearts. Unable to decide what to do, they quarreled and made secret deals. It was only when Ufansil came to them and promised to protect it that they hushed long enough to listen. She told them that she alone could keep it safe; after all, the upperworld now had its fair share of sorcerers and evil enchantresses. 'And who,' she declared, 'is more powerful than me?' To this, they agreed, and like fools they gave the Ayn Noor to a witch for safekeeping!

"They weren't even finished patting themselves on the back when Ufansil vanished. They searched high and low, but they could not find her anywhere, for she had disguised herself as a kindly babushka. Tucking the Ayn Noor into her apron, hiding it among roots and herbs, she hobbled through the country-side where villagers took pity on her, giving her apples, bread, and cheese to eat. And like so, she snuck back to her dreadful castle, where she wrapped the Ayn Noor in a thick hide of festering bearskin, all but extinguishing its bright light from the upperworld.

"Thus began a second terrible age, but this time, in the new world. People huddled in their caves and huts, shivering in the bitter cold. Sickness returned with a vengeance. Once more, the people lost hope. They began praying to Iana and Queemquesh to save them—but their pleas could not be heard.

"But it is in hard times that heroes are born. Having learned from the shaman that only the Ayn Noor could heal his sister, Asharvin knew that he had but one choice—to find the witch's lair and win the diamond back. But as you might have guessed, Ufansil was no ordinary witch."

"Does Asharvin kill her?" inquired Brill, clenching his fists.

"Noooo, you cannot kill Ufansil," answered Pola, shaking her head.

"Somebody must be able to," he implored.

"Nobody," said Pola, disconsolately. "Perhaps she can lose her powers, but that's a story for another time."

"*Nooo . . . Pola! Pleeease!*" Brill entreated.

"Sorry, Brill!" she said, shaking her head slowly. "You chose . . . remember?"

Brill buried his face in his sheets. When he looked up, he found Pola with her eyes closed. She was leaning back in the chair. He wanted to protest further, but she looked frail and much older than he could ever remember; it was as if she herself had just been pulled into the underworld. With great restraint, he said nothing more and lay back. When Pola opened her eyes, he quickly shut his. Brill waited for her to leave his room before moving.

Sleep did not come easy that night. Flipping from one side to the other, he couldn't stop thinking of Queemquesh, Kurul, and the underworld. Of one thing he was certain, if it had been him, he would have thrown the Ayn Noor back.

2

THE ANCIENT TEMPLE CITY
OF OKOMORLING

Emhet Turan tapped the side of the litter, signaling the porters to set the carriage down. Pushing the curtains aside, he estimated the landing was thirty feet across. Poking one foot out, then the other, he wriggled his hips free from the door of the lacquered sedan. His legs felt thick and heavy, as if they had been cast in a vat of wet mortar. Straightening his back, he took a deep breath. He could see they had come a long way, as they had already crossed over the section called "the bridge," a seemingly unending stone walkway with hundreds of steps that connected to the city below.

As Emhet stood there, a gypsy wind whipped about the landing. He sheltered his face. After it receded, he lowered his arm and turned the other way to have a glimpse of the old sanctuary sitting atop a barren spur of rock that struck out of the Uran Plateau like a white flame. The temple city was now the governor's palace, the seat of the Ilyrian government in the north—his destination.

Craning his neck beyond the familiar toward the unnatural, he could barely make out the top. It was said that in the old days pine trees grew among the shrines and temples on the upper terraces, their spicular branches extending beyond the gilded eaves. From where he stood, Emhet could not see any trees, although he could make out the steep tiled roofs with their curving tips that ushered back skyward. He admired what he saw; even a couple centuries of Ilyrian rule hadn't diminished its allure.

To Emhet, Okomorling appeared more like a citadel than a place of worship, with thick inward-sloping walls built to hold back the winds that raced brazenly across the Uran Plateau. Instead of moats, there was a symphony of finely orchestrated stairs, and instead of turrets, tall windows that journeyed in stately rows along the powder-white facade. Even so, a lump of resentment stuck in Emhet's throat; there were still hundreds, if not thousands, of steps left to climb. Taking a deep breath, he scrutinized what remained. Not much farther, the stairs split, going in opposite directions toward the outer edges of the mountain where they began zigzagging in mirrored symmetry until they turned back toward the center. Emhet assumed where they met at the top of the mountain had to be the location of the entrance. He was no romantic, but he did find himself searching for the temple's famous jade doors—to no avail. He scowled.

Every aspect of his journey had been horrendous. Bajarmaland was the farthest, most remote region of the kingdom, the "shit stall" of the empire, as he overheard the foot soldiers calling it. The city of Okomorling was at the very end of the Great Northern Road, which went from one side of Ilyria to the other—from the seaport of Goyer, to the capital city of Jesut Edin situated on the steppes, to Torbeshacken at the foot of the Riphean Mountains, where the road began its final ascent up to the Uran Plateau, where it concluded at the gates of the city.

The first part of his journey from Jesut Edin had been mostly routine. Aside from the occasional rise of a hill or a slight drop into a valley, his four-horse coach sped easily across the flat, drought-stricken lands in the south, and all would have been fine, were it not for the dust. Two weeks of grit in the eyes, ears, and nose was maddening enough, but the grinding sand in his teeth with every meal approached inhumane.

Torbeshacken, the third-largest city in Ilyria, was an old outpost built to transport farm goods as well as timber on barges down the Donner River to Jesut Edin and beyond. Gradually, it became an Ilyrian stronghold. Many a morning, while waiting for his team to resupply, he walked the ramparts, scrutinizing the bucolic hills and the occasional Hutsu farm. He enjoyed tracing the road as it wound its way over hillocks before vanishing into verdant hollows, only to be reborn a couple of hilltops away. A week later, upon recommencing his trip, Emhet discovered the beauty was only skin deep. With every hundred feet of elevation, the nubile fields, with their green coverlets, stretched thinner, exposing the white-knuckled stones embedded in the earth's red clay flesh. With each passing mile, the little holes became bigger holes, causing the very joinery of Emhet's carriage to sway and creak like some antiquated seafaring ship. The farther they traveled, the towns became villages, and villages became hamlets, and hamlets became

whitewashed cottages that dotted the steep valleys whose ter-
raced farms clung to the mountainsides like babies clutching
their mothers' shirts—the only arable land that hadn't already
slid into the cleavage of the boulder-strewn gorges.

After the trading post of Scargowrath, the road became
near impassable. The late spring thaw and accompanying
squalls left quagmires around every bend. Amidst ruts and
swilling bogs of mud, the trip slowed to a rollicky crawl. The
passage either weaved between the legs of giant Bajarmaland
pines, or drew straight and taut as snakeskin traversing ver-
tiginous bluffs. How *this* could be the Great Northern Road
was beyond Emhet's comprehension. Days of brain-sloshing
and belly-jostling travel had all but ruined his appetite. Emhet
paid for the journey with his own flesh. Every mile cost him an
ounce . . . and each morsel of fat he lost meant one less ounce of
cushion for his rump. He simply could not bear the thought of
the return trip, no matter how much he would rather be home.

Emhet pulled his shoulders back and attempted to stand
straight, but in doing so, a pain shot down his leg. "This diamond better be worth it," he grumbled. Seeking respite, he
turned away from the innumerable stairs. The view before him
did something to mitigate the transgression of the journey.
An even blue sky spread like turquoise cream from horizon to
horizon. Spring was nigh upon the north. The whitewashed,
mud-brick houses of Okomorling were built one on top of the
other, stacked neat as rice cakes, like offerings at the feet of
their master. He marveled at how far the porters had already
carried him.

Emhet's eyes swept past the city and its fortified walls.
Skimming across the plateau, his vision came to a halt on the
incisors of the Riphean peaks. He likened their jagged white

tops to a wolf's fangs. Beneath the snarling white teeth, a much softer world was laid bare. A patchwork of greens blanketed the earth. There were the cultivated lands, the long, thin strips of bright green barley fields, unfurling like bolts of emerald cloth, and just past their edges were the muted greens of the native flora, which eventually gave way to the rambling borders of the dark green conifers as they commenced their march up the mountains, thick as a beard. As Emhet looked upon it all, for a moment it felt as if he were soaring high above the earth, but that impression lasted only until he caught sight of two raptors, not much bigger than dots, riding wind currents far overhead. For the duration of a streaking comet, he felt oddly humbled.

Emhet Turan wasn't a tall man, but his neck and shoulders were solid as a bull's. Nevertheless, they were gradually rounding forward. Lately, when he happened to see his reflection, he noted with more than a little trepidation that his head seemed to be slipping off its pedestal—he was beginning to look the way he remembered his father had in old age. But unlike his father, he was a prosperous businessman, perhaps the most well-known diamond merchant in all of Ilyria. Crown Prince himself had sent him north to evaluate the diamond that awaited him in the governor's keep.

Not yet ready to submit to his seat, Emhet studied the porters. There were seven in all, four to carry the litter, two to haul his baggage, and one boss. Two of the porters were already sitting on *his* trunk. He could not understand their language, but their fevered exchange sounded to him like a couple of seagulls squawking over sardines. Six were obviously of Pagani descent—blond hair, thick bones, pale eyes, and freckled skin. Their hair was much longer than any Ilyrian's, but it seemed well-enough looked after. A few had tails with the ends wrapped in leather, and a couple of the men had tattoos covering large portions of their faces—but for their roving eyes, he might have mistaken their faces for masks.

For hundreds of years, before the Ilyrian conquest, Okomorling remained a city unto itself, protected by its sheer inaccessibility. In the south, its existence was mere rumor, a faint whisper upon the tongues of the few, for only the most resilient explorers had ever reached it. The high, hardscrabble mountain passes, the harsh winters, and the savage Pagani were more than enough to deter all but the most persistent. Thus, for centuries, the Gnos priests lived in peace on the Uran Plateau, the highest plateau in the world.

The explorers who managed to return from the temple palace talked about its wealth with veneration. They reported gold statues so large they nearly touched the lofty rafters and carved jade columns supporting the open temples overlooking rooftop ponds. But the adventurers who saw the world in terms of reverence described wooden temples filled with butter candles and the bluish haze of incense that mingled below the tapestries and paintings of saints, bigger than houses, which hung on the walls above the shaven heads of chanting monks. These wayfarers spoke of the simplicity and the joy of the mountain priests, and referred to the temple of Okomorling as "the master's mountain."

When King Anastopheles' army came north, he did not come for wisdom—he came for conquest and for Okomorling's reputed treasures. The Pagani were little more than obstacles that existed between him and his prize. To reach the city, one had to cross their lands. The Ilyrians were never able to attack the Pagani outright, for they would abandon their villages before the cavalry would arrive. When pressed, the Pagani simply disappeared, vanishing into the void of the woods.

As Emhet gazed out, he imagined the Ilyrian army advancing all those years ago, the cavalry with their streaming red-and-white banners, the long lines of foot soldiers with their shields gleaming in the sun and the steady beat of their marching boots. Even amidst snow flurries, King Anastopheles' men must have taken strength, for there is nothing like the nearness of plunder to revive a soldier's weary limbs. Emhet felt his chest swell with pride. Even now, he thought he could hear panicked voices in the wind shouting from above. He could only imagine what must have ensued in the great temple. Oh, the stories these walls could tell!

With Okomorling at King Anastopheles' feet, a horde of Pagani warriors clad in leather and fur appeared out of the forests wielding swords, battle axes, and bows and arrows—no modern army. Their regard for the Gnos must have been high, for they were finally willing to give King Anastopheles a proper battle. But if engaging in the forest was natural for the Pagani, fighting in the open would prove the opposite. The barbarians did not know how to organize themselves into formations and had no understanding of the strategies of open-field warfare. King Anastopheles outmaneuvered them with ease, and before nightfall, he had routed the Pagani. By moonrise they had ransacked the city, looted the temples, pillaged the shrines, slashed the tapestries and scrolls, burned the books, and tossed any defiant monk over the edge. The priests who didn't die that day would do so either as slaves building the Great Northern Road or in the dungeons of Grebald. But if the Gnos had disappeared in a puff of smoke, the Pagani were like weeds—nearly impossible to eradicate. Emhet was certain the

Pagani would have to be totally annihilated before they would cede any more territory to Ilyria.

His imagination leaping off the pages of Ilyrian history books did much to ameliorate Emhet's foul mood. It was the first time since he had left Jesut Edin that he wished Costa, his son, was with him. He hoped that someday he, too, would look out over the plateau and gaze into its storied past. But there had been no question of Costa coming on this trip, for he had to sit for his exams. Emhet was confident that Costa would pass on his own merit, but just in case, he had invited the dean of students, Mr. Sardashkin, to the house before departing north. Some things could not be left to chance, certainly not something as important as acceptance into the Lyceum of Jesut Edin. Emhet laughed out loud. He had reacted like the meddling, overprotective father that he was—Costa was many things, but no dullard.

With a smile still on his face, Emhet hobbled forward and leaned out to sneak a peek over the side. The boulders below looked like mere pebbles, and the trees, no more than shrubs. The porters frantically waved their arms, beckoning him to come away from the edge. A draft of dizziness came over him, and Emhet tipped sideways just as a gust of wind caught him from behind. Luckily, he was a heavy man and managed to stumble backward. From then on, he stayed to the middle of the path.

What Emhet found most bemusing, perplexing really, was how easily Okomorling could have been defended. Why had the Gnos priests refused to do so? At the very least they could have destroyed the bridge or built a wall around the lower city to protect themselves. Surely, they must have considered the threat of invasion. Were the Gnos naive? Did they believe their god would come to their rescue? Or were they counting on the combative Pagani to save them?

Emhet himself didn't care so much about the fate of priests. Mostly, he was fascinated by the mistakes that caused once powerful cultures to crumble. Even if the Gnos did not believe in violence, surely a protective wall would have been morally permissible. Doing nothing was just plain hubris. Had pride been their undoing? In the end, there are always consequences for one's beliefs—and sometimes, savage ones.

Emhet's own religion was mixed on the subject of violence. The Old Testament was full of carnage. God himself was a retributive warlord who dealt out healthy portions of punishment and death. But then there was the New Testament, and Christ's message was abundantly clear. "Turn thy cheek," "love thy neighbor," precepts coming from the very son of God. But maybe that was it, he was the Son, not the Father. For better or worse, Ilyrians were father-fearing realists, not son-loving pacifists. And if any claimed otherwise, surely their arguments were only a perfunctory dressing, a subterfuge for the deeper, more abiding instinct of Ilyrian self-preservation.

Fittingly, the first thing Ilyrians did upon conquering Okomorling was build a defensive wall around the city. It was a wise action, for ramparts save lives! They had saved the Ilyrians during the Great Uprising forty years before, and only eight months prior had saved the bastard prince. It was reported that Marius had come riding across the plateau, half-naked, with the infamous diamond in his outstretched hand, pursued by a feral pack of female warriors.

The theft of the jewel had sparked another revolt in the highlands. The Pagani were rebelling with a ferocity that had not been seen since the Great Uprising. Settlers had begun arriving in Jesut Edin in droves, leaving their farms for the protection of the city. Apparently, the diamond was endowed with supernatural powers. Even in Jesut Edin people were talking about it, whether in parlors or on street corners. But Emhet had never met a diamond that had magical abilities, other than the ability to cause a woman's soul to bleed and the resultant ripple that forced her husband to nervously seek his fifth, and most secret, pocket.

Emhet certainly did not believe in magic. He was a businessman and partial to science. He enjoyed attending lectures at the University of Jesut Edin, to listen to learned men. What Emhet appreciated most about science was that it depended on quantifiable data. Science did not rely on legend. There was no room for superstition. Emhet was certain that the so-called Ayn Noor was nothing more than a gem made by the hand of a skilled craftsman, definitely *not* given to the Pagani by some goddess. Of one thing he was certain, no diamond ever came out of the earth precut. Once Emhet had a chance to inspect it, he would know from where it came. After all, he knew all ancient and modern cuts. Only by the skilled hand of a master cutter did a stone become a jewel. And he would always treat this diamond as such, as a product of man. But first, he had to see it for himself, and avoid, at all cost, getting caught up in conjecture and mob speculation. After all, the essence of his job was to stay level headed.

Emhet had witnessed the army preparing in Torbeshacken. Two regiments were being readied. If necessary, they would come north to put down the rebellion. Emhet had gone ahead, escorted by thirty cavalry. His mission was most pressing. Crown Prince Julian went to great lengths to explain that if the diamond was anything but exceptional, Emhet should advise the governor to humbly return it—sending regiments north would be costly.

Going to war over a diamond might seem foolhardy to many, but not to Emhet. He understood that a diamond could be many things, from an emblem of prestige associated with a ruling dynasty to a betrothal gift of the most persuasive kind—and Julian was, as of yet, unmarried. A great diamond was at the very least a substantial makeweight in all political negotiations. Helvatian financiers were known to pay large sums for such prizes. And what with the drought worsening by the day, surely Julian was accumulating assets. Jewels, after all, were not burdensome. A large diamond could slip easily into a pocket yet was worth more than a ship full of gold.

From the corner of his eye, Emhet noticed the porters were shifting from leg to leg, picking up packages and placing them down. They were desperate to deliver him to the waiting governor. The sooner they finished their work, the sooner they could return to the taverns below. But their desires did not concern him; only the grumble in his belly prompted him to take his seat.

3

Deep in the Forests of Bajarmaland

Roan spied Surl blundering across the meadow like a recal-
citrant bear. Surl's gait was unmistakable, for her legs were
thick as tree trunks, and every step seemed to require one leg
to circumambulate the other. Roan and Tieg had been comb-
ing the nearby hills, culling saplings and stripping them of
their branches to shape into cavalry spikes for defense against
Ilyrian horsemen. Since the theft of the Ayn Noor the previous
summer, in the year of the three dead snakes, the Red Bow
Clan had been burning Ilyrian settlements across the plateau.
Their actions were inevitably drawing other clans into their
rebellion, for the Ilyrians would not discriminate among the
Pagani tribes. It was reported that two, maybe three, regiments
were being prepared in Torbeshacken.

There were seven Yatu tsiks spread throughout
Bajarmaland, each tsik consisting of roughly three hundred
female warriors. All tsiks were now in wartime preparation,

reinforcing armor, sharpening swords, making arrows, and storing food. All the necessary arrangements were underway.

From the very first day Roan arrived at her tsik, at the age of eleven, Surl had bullied her, from small things like tripping her as she walked past or stealing her practice arrows, to more obvious transgressions like spitting on her or calling her names in front of the other novices. Surl's two favorite names to call her were "southerner" and "breeder." The first name implied Roan was Ilyrian. There was some truth in this accusation, for Roan's family lived south of the Sombol and Guanyin Rivers. And to make matters worse, Roan's father was of Ilyrian descent. But Roan's mother had been a Yatu warrior herself, one who had left the warrior's path to raise a family. It was a disgrace for a warrior to marry and have children, thus, the second name "breeder." Surl particularly enjoyed saying, "Go make Ilyrian babies with your mother."

For the first few years, Surl's dominance was easily achieved, especially since Roan was so much smaller. Even so, Roan was not idle. She paid close attention in hand-to-hand combat training, learning everything she could from the older warriors—for even a hand lock, if used properly, could immobilize a much larger opponent. Eventually, Roan grew a woman's body too. And although she would never be as large as Surl, she was strong. But more than anything she was agile and quick . . . and thanks to Surl, resilient. Now, after all the bruises, scrapes, and bloody noses, they were evenly matched. In their last bout, Roan had simply kicked Surl's foot out from under her and dropped her to the ground like a lump of clay.

When she reached the bottom of the incline, Surl yelled up to them. Roan was being summoned by Ruus, their new leader. Tieg, who always took an interest in Roan's welfare, descended the hill—with Roan close behind. They pressed Surl for details, but she would only say that two men, "traders," had come asking for Roan. The thought of men, other than her father and brothers, knowing her whereabouts seemed incomprehensible. Sweat began to prickle under Roan's brow. Concerns unknown to her seconds before started to surface. Surl had already turned back when Tieg shook Roan out of her thoughts. "Hurry," she said, "unless you want to spend two days standing in the rain."

Ruus hailed from the northernmost tsik, where they lived in yurts on the open plateau. They were remarkable on horseback . . . and hardy, for they were exposed to strong winds that swept across the high plateau eight months of the year. Their reputation was that of being severely disciplined. Any sign of weakness was purged from the girls by depriving them of food and forcing them to stand in inclement weather for hours, sometimes days. Ferja, Ruus' predecessor, had been a more tolerant leader, especially with the novice warriors—more emphasis was placed on skills training.

Surl was already a good ways ahead when Roan began running after her. She followed Surl up the Valley of the Falls. Roan figured she was being led to one of two places, either to Ruus' lodge or to the Pukka. The lodge could mean anything, but going to the Pukka meant one thing, a meeting of importance.

Crossing the footbridge near the big fork, Roan noticed a couple of saddled horses, a gray speckled mare and a chestnut-brown gelding, and two mules. The gray stood tallest. Roan suspected these must be the mounts of the men who came asking for her, but instead of going toward them, Surl kept walking. Roan could see Ussuri speaking to a trader next to an open crate. She held a shiny flintlock in her hands. This in itself was strange. The Pagani had chosen not to fight with firearms, refusing any weapon that they could not make themselves. The chieftains felt it would weaken the tribes by creating dependence on the Ilyrians. Roan's belly twisted into a knot.

The trader had the characteristics of a Hutsu: tall, with a thin face and mangy auburn hair. On a number of occasions, Roan would observe Hutsu traders as they led their mule trains up the Great Northern Road. She would never let them see her, but surely they sensed the forest was watching them. The traders usually avoided Yatu territory, their reputation for being man haters was renowned.

Eorl and Jannicka were standing nearby, lording over another wooden crate—presumably full of muskets as well. It was then Roan noticed a second trader sitting on a rock farther back. He was camouflaged in the speckled shade cast by the trees but was watching the proceedings closely. His musket was resting next to him, and the man's fawn-colored hair was as unkempt as his besmirched buckskins. His appearance made her wonder if the Hutsus did not teach their children to wash and bathe and enjoy the pleasures of water. Roan did not trust the first trader, but much less this one.

The Ilyrians were crossing the confluence of the Sombol and Guanyin Rivers more and more frequently, venturing into the unconquered lands. Regardless of the treaty signed by Teufel, King of Ilyria, after the Great Uprising, the settlers kept pushing north in pursuit of the yellow metal that drove them mad with lust. And there was much of it in Bajarmaland. The traders were never far behind the settlers, selling them goods, including the nefarious lubjok. The elders warned the Pagani youths against coveting Ilyrian merchandise, especially lubjok. They said it was a poison drink, stronger even than one's bond to clan. Even worse, it was known to destroy the umbilicus to spirit. Roan suspected this was of little concern to the traders.

If they had come asking for her, Roan wondered, why was Surl leading her past them? It was all very confusing. As Eorl and Jannicka looked up, she sent them a friendly hand gesture, but their gazes remained hard, even though Roan was certain they had seen her greeting. Jannicka worked between the tannery and forge making armor, and Eorl taught hand-to-hand combat. Eorl knew every pin and hand lock and could execute them with ease. She had short, cropped hair, and muscular arms. In the great hall, she often sat at the center, spinning stories with crass exaggerations. She had always been friendly toward Roan, but Droogie, Roan's best friend, went to great lengths to show her that it wasn't just friendliness but flat-out favoritism. There was no such warmth today, however. Roan was greatly relieved when they were out of sight. After passing the turn to the chieftain's lodge, Roan felt her chest tighten and her heart beat faster—they were headed for the Pukka.

Soon the valley cleaved the mountain in half. The trail narrowed, funneling into a couloir pressed by steep sides that forced them against the rushing water. As they climbed over boulders, the chatty river spit and nipped at their heels. When at last they crested the hill, they found themselves in a large treeless bowl. The surrounding walls were a peppered-gray stone with the occasional embedded tree that eked a living from a mere crack. The ground about the bowl was littered with boulders, large chunks of stone that had fallen from the cliffs. Tufts of brilliant green grass pushed their way out from underneath them. But as spectacular as the bowl was, nothing compared to the bellowing falls. The water surged over the rim. From below it appeared to pour out of the very sky itself.

As it fell, the overlapping sheets of falling water seemed to slow to a crawl. On sunny days there were rainbows, but every day gray mist wafted out over the pool. As Roan admired the sight, the sweat on her shirt began to cool in the ubiquitous vapors. She shivered.

Surl led her to the right, away from the pandemonium, up a hidden trail that wound through the rocky scree. Coursing their way between the boulders, they went ever upward until stairs appeared. Once over the last step, they arrived at the outlook, the old guard post—now abandoned. Surl continued down the stairs on the far side while Roan paused. She hadn't been in the bowl since the theft and was curious to have a look. She wondered if she would be able to tell the difference now that the Ayn Noor was gone. Not even Farwah claimed to have ever seen it. Only shamans like Issa were known to have looked upon the talisman or its caretakers, the Garbadine crabs that held the Ayn Noor under the falls—but they were said to have returned to the spirit world.

The outer edges of the pool appeared as she remembered—calm—sequestered from the core of churning water. A trinity of blues shimmered in the shallows. Roan had seen the falls from the guard post only a couple of times. Gazing upon the scene below, she could not see a difference but still did not doubt what they said was true—the Ayn Noor was gone.

When she looked over her shoulder, Surl was glowering up at her. Skipping down the stairs, Roan smirked. Surl shook her head and carried on toward the Pukka—the grass-covered tumulus that rested against the cliff. At the end of the pathway were two gray stones that bowed outward, pushing aside the darkness. This was the sacred giob, the entrance to the Pukka. Roan always dreaded going inside. Her wariness wasn't because

of the damp air or the formidable darkness, for as one journeyed deeper, the stone walls began to glow feebly, warmed
by an occasional torch. What Roan dreaded most was that the
passage never traveled straight. It always curved, sometimes
veering right, sometimes left, but always conspiring to turn
one way or the other. It was disorienting, and invariably, Roan
would lose all sense of direction. She hurried to catch up with
Surl, but just as she thought she had caught sight of her foot,
it would disappear, leaving Roan wondering if she had seen it
at all.

The passage ended in the Room of the Guardians.
Megaliths carved with ancient symbols stood on their ends.
Even the smallest stone was three times Roan's height. Roan
walked cautiously amidst them. Surl was nowhere to be seen—
only the crunching of her feet kept her company. And just
when Roan began to wonder if this wasn't one of her tricks,
Surl stepped out from behind a guardian and growled, "Keep
up, Roan!"

Surl led her to the outer wall where two torches burned.
Years of fire had left tall black streaks on the stone. At the very
base of the wall was a small hole about two feet across. Even
a person with knowledge of the Pukka would have difficulty
finding it. It was only large enough for one person to pass at
a time. Surl motioned for her to go in first. Roan lowered herself onto her hands and knees and began to crawl forward.
When Roan sensed there was no more stone, she stood up. The
air was tinged with the acrid aroma of burning wood. As she
brushed the pebbles off her knees, she caught sight of a fire
in the distance. Next to it was a person bundled in fur. Roan
knew this would be Ruus. It would be considered improper to

approach the fire without Surl, so Roan waited, noting the cold
moisture of the cave camping on her upper lip.

The Pukka was built up against a cave that descended into
the heart of the mountain. It was here that the most sacred
ceremonies took place. Sometimes one could hear a faint
howl, like the sound of wind blowing in a distant realm. Some
Yatu said that the cave went all the way down to the opening
between worlds, where Queemquesh had passed the Ayn Noor
to Kurul at the beginning of time. But Farwah said this was not
so, that the ancient opening was much farther south, in the old
country.

As Roan stood there waiting, she began to hear a faint
clack. It was oddly familiar. If she wasn't mistaken, it was the
sound of wood striking against wood. Roan looked toward the
fire. Ruus remained as she was, unmoving. Suddenly, memories buried in the shadows of her mind began to surface. They
had been there all along, biding their time, but now they came
crashing over her like a rogue wave. As the water drew back,
a plethora of images and feelings remained. The clacking was
the unmistakable sound of the Three Sisters' loom! Before her
were the sights and sounds from her naming ceremony! The
memories were as fresh and vivid as a first snowfall.

◆ ◆ ◆

They had been gathered around the very same fire but with
Issa, the shaman. She had just passed Roan a gourd, half-full
of a bitter liquid. Roan had taken a couple of swigs, which was
then followed by a long, enduring silence. She waited for someone to talk, but no one did. Issa began to sing. They listened
to the old woman's creaky voice—until the roof of the cave

disappeared and the night sky came crashing down, filling
Roan's eyes with starlight.

It was soon thereafter that the Three Sisters appeared.
They were gathered, side by side, on a rustic bench in front of a
gigantic loom. Each had long hair that spilled across the floor
into the beyond. They didn't seem to notice Roan. Although
their backs were toward her, somehow Roan could see their
faces. One was as wrinkled as the bark of an old tree, another's
was soft and youthful, while the third sister's face was firm, her
shoulders enduring and her breasts tumescent and full. Their
fingers worked nimbly, and with great assuredness they passed
the tools between themselves, moving the yarn in unison.
Their tapestry extended past the cave walls, stretching across
time and space.

Issa pointed to each sister in turn. "Dolorous," she said,
pointing to the old crone. "Her name means 'wisdom that
comes with pain.'" Roan remembered repeating the name out
loud. "Aradavai," said Issa, pointing to the woman with the
powerful shoulders. "Her name means 'confidence that comes
with maturity.'" Then she pointed to the third. "That is Juve,
her name means 'youthfulness and the pleasure of newness.'
Together they weave the tapestry of life."

Issa explained that from out of eternity come two threads,
the vertical threads and the horizontal threads. The vertical
runs up and down the loom—transcendent fibers birthed from
the unchanging realm. Roan could see the warp yarns, the silver strands shining with perpetual light. Horizontal threads,
the weft yarns, wove over and around the vertical threads, covering the luminous filaments with all the colors and patterns
of the physical world, leaving the transcendent realm invisible
to the naked eye.

Roan closely examined the tapestry. The harder she looked, the deeper her vision went, until she entered the mélange of existence. She saw the first star explode at the beginning of time. She watched lightning strike a blackened sea and the ensuing life that began bubbling forth. Then came swarms of infinitesimal creatures, until little ones morphed into bigger ones. Soon there were proper fish and plants and ultimately the great pine trees of Bajarmaland that Roan so loved.

Gradually, the Three Sisters faded. Roan found herself walking alone, through a dense forest. She had her bow in hand—she was hunting. As she came to an open clearing, a large buck crashed through the trees. Dropping to one knee, she reached for an arrow. The stag sprung forward bounding to the far side of the meadow. There it turned to face her. Steam came pouring out of its nostrils, its white mane glistening. In all her years, she had never seen such a formidable buck. Its rack bore many points. Crouching, Roan moved her feet slowly over the ground, inching ever closer. But just as she began to raise her bow, her foot snagged. For a precious moment she lost her balance, and when she looked up, the buck was gone. She tossed her head back, lamenting her misfortune with a groan. Frustrated, she searched the ground for the root or log that had caused her to trip. But the culprit was neither. It was a giant snake, lying thick and straight, stretched across her path. Roan froze. But seeing it did not move, Roan reached out her foot and nudged it. The snake was rigid with death. She put her arrow back in the quiver and squatted to inspect. There were no visible wounds. Roan rolled the serpent over, where she found a long gash running straight along its flaxen under-belly. The forest floor was dark with blood. It appeared to be the slash of a sword.

Just then Roan heard galloping horses coming from afar. Ilyrian cavalry riding from the south! A wickedness was coming! Alarmed, Roan sprang to her feet. She must warn her tsik! But from the corner of her eye, she noticed movement. Looking closer, she caught sight of the tiniest snake twisting in a ball among the blood and leaves. Roan reached down and scooped up the motherless creature. It had bright, defiant eyes and radiant blue skin. When she held it up to her face, the snake's red forked tongue struck out toward her nose. Roan instinctively felt that the little snake was in danger. She carefully put the baby snake in her satchel, tucking it amongst her kindling and flint.

Suddenly, the clearing vanished! The woods were gone, and Roan found herself sitting cross-legged inside what appeared to be a luminous egg. Issa was on her left, and a man she had never seen was seated on her right—their eyes were closed. They were equidistant from one another, forming a triangle. Roan had a fleeting impression that they were dreaming her. The absurdity of it all made Roan feel nervous. None of this made any sense. Roan laughed out loud; it was too preposterous. More and more laughter spilled out of her mouth. Nothing was particularly funny; she just felt weightless and giddy. Roan looked at Issa, then at the man. Their eyes remained closed, which only made Roan laugh even harder.

When she finally stopped, Roan found herself lying on the ground in the Pukka. The luminous egg was gone. Tieg and Farwah were wiping sweat off her face. Roan tried to sit up, but she couldn't. She collapsed in Tieg's arms, exhausted. When she did manage to sit, Issa, who sat across from her, spoke from out of the black hole of her mouth. The words came drifting toward Roan, hovering in the air like cold breath. Slowly they formed into meaning. "Papa Para Keet Magento," she said. "Your name is Protector of Little Blue Snake."

The name meant nothing to Roan as the walls of her mind floated apart. It wasn't until the beatific face of her mother appeared large before her that the expansion came to a halt. *Everything* was now her mother's face. It was the bright face of youth, with full cheeks and alert blue eyes. Roan somehow knew that she was seeing her mother before she was born, perhaps even before she had been conceived. She herself was a faceless soul, a seed consciousness, passing through the shadowy realm of Bardo Fey, looking in. Her mother was singing as she hung clothes to dry. Her voice was as clear as birdsong.

Roan then noticed a dark, indistinct figure approaching her mother. At first, Roan feared for her, but then she noticed her welcoming smile. The two embraced. Roan realized it must be her father! Soon thereafter, Roan felt an irresistible urge, the physical desire for life—to pass through the veil and join them. She found herself entering the damp cave of her mother's womb.

Once more, the vision changed. Roan now saw herself as an old woman, sitting under the long arm of the evening sun. She had lived her entire life—a satisfying life, but one burdened with loss. She had buried her parents, her wife, and countless others. It was now her turn to die, and she was alone. In fact, she had just taken her last breath. Before the final exhale, Roan saw herself not much older than she was now, lying facedown in a puddle. But it was not water; it was her own blood. Her life force was spilling onto the dirty streets of an unknown city. Her blood was pooling faster than the thirsty dust could lap it up. There was a lot of commotion around her. Roan realized that it was a battle, and she watched her own bloodied fingers scrape the ground.

Just then cold water was splashed onto her face. Tieg was standing over her. Roan could feel her body twisting wildly. She felt out of control. Eventually, Roan heard herself protesting, "No, no, no!" She was back in the Pukka with Tieg and Farwah. But even as she protested, she was unsure what she was protesting. Roan began to sob. When she was able to gather herself, she felt drained and deflated. After an unknown amount of time, Tieg assisted her to sitting. Roan wiped her face, then looked at Issa. "That's not what's going to happen to me, is it?" she asked.

"You mean die?" inquired Issa.

"Yes . . . no! I mean"—she couldn't think straight—"no . . . I mean, yes . . . die like that!" she said, attempting to straighten her thoughts. She felt so very weak.

"You saw two possible deaths," said Issa. "Why do you hold on to only one vision?" Roan shook her head hopelessly. Another wave of sadness came over her. "What is it, Roan?" asked Issa.

"I don't know," said Roan, wiping her eyes with her sleeve. "I don't want to bury everyone I love."

"Life is cruel . . . No one here would argue that. There is much sorrow . . . much sorrow." Roan couldn't seem to bring her thoughts together; they were all flying so fast, bouncing off each other. Issa spoke to her with great care. "Before a spark leaves the fire, it *is* the fire. But then, there is a crack, and a spark breaks free. Perhaps, if the spark is very hot, it will rise high above into the night sky. Sometimes it goes past even the tallest tree. A soul is like a spark, released for a time, free to travel its own path . . . but it is still born of the fire. Accepting the spark that you are is all that matters. How long will you burn? You do not know. Nobody knows. Do not think too much about what will happen to you, or how you will die. Instead, think about what you will do while your little spark still burns."

Roan considered all Issa was saying. She repeated the name. "Protector of Little Blue Snake. What is a Blue Snake?"

"Blue Snakes are Gnos priests, souls that have chosen to return."

"How could that be my name? You must be wrong!"

"I merely interpret what spirit shows me," replied Issa.

"Then spirit must be wrong," said Roan. "It makes no sense."

"Spirit does not make mistakes. From the perfect springs the perfect!" said Issa, and with this she beamed her wide toothless smile. "Do not try too hard to understand," she said, patting Roan's hand. "What you have seen today, you will forget . . . until it's time to remember." With this, Issa passed her ancient hand across Roan's face.

◆ ◆ ◆

"Move it, Roan," snapped Surl. Her gruff voice was so unexpected that Roan jumped forward. She was back in the cavern. She had never left! Roan must have been standing there for less than a minute. It was as if eternity had been compressed onto the head of a pin. Her body felt big, clumsy, and more than a tad unreal. Her face was wet. Reaching up, she wiped warm tears from her cheeks. She was glad Surl could not see them. All the memories from her naming ceremony had come upon her so fast. Perhaps it was as Issa said, "Until it's time to remember."

But why now? Wouldn't it have been more prudent to come to her some other time when she had a moment to consider? It was certainly not helpful before her meeting with Ruus! Surl pushed her from behind. "Stop playing games, Roan!" growled Surl. Roan stumbled toward the fire. Just then, she heard a loud crack. She looked up as a gush of red sparks erupted, rising into the dark cavern—so many souls!

Stepping nearer to the fire, Roan felt her mind become extraordinarily sharp and focused. Surl stopped her just outside the ring of light. Roan desired to sit down next to the burning logs and contemplate all that she had just seen. Instead she remained standing, waiting for Ruus to speak. Ruus' coarse hair fell to the sides of her face; only a thin trace of her nose was visible. She didn't look up to acknowledge Roan, but then, Roan had not expected her to.

Just then, Ruus jerked her head to dismiss Surl. Roan sensed the faintest stiffening in Surl's neck. She hadn't expected to be told to leave.

"Go!" barked Ruus. As Surl trudged away, Roan felt happy Surl would not be privy to their conversation. The less Surl knew the better. Ruus turned her head to follow Surl's slow progress away. It was then Roan caught sight of Ruus' face and the thick ink markings around her eyes.

"Sit down, girl," she commanded. Roan stepped closer to the fire but sat down a good distance from Ruus. She crossed her legs. "Do you know the Noumenos Clan?" Ruus inquired. Everyone in Bajarmaland knew of them. Roan nodded. "Do you know of the one called Minol?" Ruus continued.

"I do not know him, but I know of him," answered Roan.

"He sent guns for you."

"For me?" Roan's voice squeaked inadvertently.

"That's what I said. Three crates! A mighty sum for a girl . . ."

"But . . . we don't use guns," said Roan.

"That's not for you to decide!" countered Ruus.

"No, but I am not a slave. I cannot be traded like one."

"I did not trade you, girl!" Ruus snarled. "I agreed to send you to him, that's all. He wants to talk with you."

"Three crates of guns just to speak with me?"

"I agree. It's a lot."

"What does he want?"

"He wouldn't say; that was part of the agreement. You must go tomorrow. Take no horse, and no road; no one is to know where you are going. He requests that you come without being seen. And he said for you to come quick."

"That's a strange request," said Roan, finding her mouth had almost gone dry.

"Yes, it is. But he's clever, sending guns! He knows our need. But he is only a small creek, and we are a big mountain. The creek has to find its way around the mountain."

"If he wants a warrior, why not send for Ussuri or Eorl?"

"That is my question too. What could you possibly do for him?" Ruus studied Roan's face. "Tell me, what do you know of the Noumenos Clan?"

"I know they are outcasts."

"Go on!"

"They are a family of healers. Minol is a shaman, but Ule, the grandfather, was a skywalker."

"Never mind him, what do you know of Patrig?" With the mention of his name, Ruus spit into the fire. Roan watched her spittle blacken a piece of coal.

"Patrig . . . is . . . Minol's father. It was he who betrayed the Pagani at the Battle of Hidden Ridge."

"What else?"

"Skadje and the Red Bows cut Patrig's eyes out and left him to be eaten by wild animals."

"And?"

"That's all I know."

"When Patrig was no more," added Ruus, "his wife, the conniving Katriyana, converted to Christianity. Minol, the youngest of her two boys—the only Noumenos left—sent for you. Why?"

"I don't know," repeated Roan.

"Do you know where he lives?"

"He lives beyond the Guanyin and Sombol confluence, just north of Patswil. My father took me there once."

"What was your father's business with him?"

"My father was a builder, he helped construct the chapel for Katriyana."

"Your mother was Yatu?" Roan nodded, but her eyes found the ground. "Just as well," said Ruus. "She was weak!" Roan said nothing.

"I don't trust Minol," Ruus went on. Her stare was unrelenting. "The Noumenos are traitors, and once a traitor, always a traitor. You must come see me as soon as you return. Even before going to your lodge. Do you hear me?"

Roan nodded.

"I want to know what he wants from you. I want to know everything. Do you understand?"

Roan looked up to gaze into the middle of the fire. The hottest embers were glowing orange. Again, she heard Issa's voice. "Until it's time to remember!"

"Do you understand?" repeated Ruus.

"Yes!" declared Roan, nodding her head briskly.

4

The Royal Palace, Jesut Edin

"Ewww, a cockroach! Get it, Clarise!"

"*Me?* Why me?"

"'Cause I said so . . . and besides, you're younger."

Clarise crossed her arms and gazed in amazement at Poule, who was at most a year older. "Oh, come on, fatty," derided Clarise, "you can move too."

Friel, the washerwoman who was standing nearby, promptly lifted her apron and skirt and darted forward. Crack! came the sound from underneath her shoe. The two house-maids recoiled. Friel grimaced and walked stoically back to the linen table. Their eyes followed her every step of the way. Once there, she turned and glared back at them. "What? Haven't you killed a cockroach before?"

"I killed *seven* yesterday," said Poule, her eyes opening wide as she spoke. "Now clean it up, Friel," she demanded, putting her hands on her hips.

"Cleaning the floors is not my job," Friel replied. "Linens are *my* job."

"Clean it *up!*" Poule's voice peaked.

"What's the commotion," demanded Madam Twombly, stepping into the room.

"Friel just mashed a cockroach into the floor," answered Poule, pointing at the crushed insect.

"They were too 'fraid to kill it, madam," said Friel.

"Yesterday, I killed seven," claimed Poule. "Ilam was there, he'll tell you."

"I just found dozens in the pantry," said Madam Twombly, shaking her head.

"Where are they coming from?" asked Clarise.

"From below," came Maenska's smoky voice. Poule, Clarise, and Madam Twombly turned toward the old woman. The huge pile of linens lumped on the table before her made her look tiny. Poule could not remember ever hearing her speak. Maenska stood hunched, her spine as rounded as a waterwheel. Her hand moved the iron steadily over the white linen. Friel placed a fresh iron on the holder next to her. Maenska took it without so much as a glance, while Friel returned the used one to the stove.

"What do you mean, 'from below'?" asked Madam Twombly.

"From below, the gates will open."

"Old woman, are you suggesting the cockroaches are part of some Hutsu prophecy?"

The washerwoman did not answer. Madam Twombly clucked her tongue and shook her head. "I don't know about prophecies, but it would sure be nice if they would go back to where they came from."

"Maybe what she means," said Poule, "is they are coming from the lower level, below the palace. Have you ever seen the door?" Clarise shook her head nervously. "You have to go all the way down, past the water room, past the guards, and even then it's locked," added Poule. "Supposedly, only the queen and the chamberlain have keys."

"Where does it lead?" asked Clarise.

"To the slain wives of King Anastopheles!" said Poule, her eyes widening again. "And their ladies-in-waiting," she quickly added.

"Oh, shush, Poule," admonished Madam Twombly, giving her a monstrous look, but Clarise's hand was already cupped over her own mouth. "That's how daft rumors get started."

"Sounds like a mooking," stated Friel, loading a basket with creased and folded sheets.

Clarise lowered her hand. "'A mooking'? What's that?"

Seeing Friel was not going to provide an explanation, Madam Twombly obliged. "A mooking is a Hutsu gathering where they slaughter a herd of pigs . . . It's a festival of sorts."

"Hutsus are vulgar," declared Poule. Friel kept her eyes down and continued folding, but there was a faint glint of satisfaction upon her face. "Besides," she added, "nobody invited you into this conversation."

Clarise chirped, "Maybe . . . that's where they put the crown jewels."

"No, the jewels are placed atop the garrison tower in Grebald, with an entire regiment to protect them, Clarise," countered Madam Twombly. "Now stop gabbing you two, and get back to your chores." Her patience with the two girls was wearing thin.

"Maybe there's nothing down there," said Clarise, too nervous to heed Madam Twombly's redirection.

"You don't lock nothing," declared Poule.

"From the bowels of the earth, destruction and ruin will come," the old woman spoke again. They watched Maenska in silence. Steam rose from the table where the iron was deftly maneuvered . . . Fifty years of ironing could do no better.

"'Bowels of the earth'?" repeated Clarise. Her voice came slowly, but her tone betrayed her fascination.

"Well, I reckon Maenska might be right about one thing," said Madam Twombly. "The cockroaches could be coming from underneath the door. I will inquire with the Chamberlain of the House. Now move, you two." She began urging them onward with her palms open as one might shoo a couple of chickens in the yard. "Go, go . . . go!"

Just then a well-dressed man stepped into the linen room. "Mister Balzar," said Madam Twombly, startled. The girls stopped and bowed slightly.

"Who is responsible for cleaning Prince Julian's quarters today?" he asked.

"Poule and Clarise," replied Madam Twombly.

"They must wait until I tell them to go in. The queen is visiting."

"Yes, sir," said Poule and Clarise in unison.

• • •

"Go . . . *a-way!*" shouted Julian for the third time, but the banging simply would not desist. Scrambling over arms and legs to get to the side of the bed, he sat up. Reflexively, Julian leaned over his knees and clasped his throbbing head. He vaguely recalled a dreamscape that had morphed with the banging at his door. A large egg-shaped figure dressed in a black hood with only holes for eyes burst into his room, shattering his door into splinters. Spinning like a whirling dervish, the executioner stopped on point directly in front of him and positioned an outstretched finger accusingly at his face. "Guilty," they pronounced.

"Who are you?" Julian demanded, but there was no reply. Reaching up, he yanked off the hood only to find himself eye to eye with the queen—his mother.

The incessant banging on the door brought him back from his reminiscing. "Bastard!" growled Julian. "I'm going to kill that son of a bitch!" he exclaimed, pouncing toward the assorted piles of clothes on the floor. He located his scabbard and pulled out his sword. Standing, he took a moment as the room swayed. Julian attempted to shout, but his weak lips struggled to break the seal of sticky white foam at the corners just as a surge of nausea rose to his mouth. Gazing back at the bed, he considered retreat. He had never been a good sailor. He reached down his throat with his finger, triggering an exodus, then wiped his mouth with the back of his hand.

But for his smallish, pouty mouth, Julian had an altogether attractive face, due mostly to a strong jawline. People often commented on how much he resembled his father, the Duke of Marmar, in his youth. They must have hoped that mentioning the similarities might give him a paternal connection, but Julian never pined for a father he couldn't remember. In fact, there were distinct advantages to not having one—certainly one less parent to interfere with his lifestyle.

With sword in hand, Julian whipped his head toward the door. His thick black hair fell over his eyes, momentarily shielding his already-challenged vision. Nonetheless, he could make out the archeological footprint from the night before, the artifacts, a rubbish trove of bottles and clothes spread in irreconcilable order around his feet. Leaning forward, Julian grabbed hold of the nearest bottle. He held it up to the light of day, then tilted it toward his mouth for maximum pour, but nothing came. He tossed it and groped for another one. A splash of liquor remained, its feisty contents were hot. The smell provoked a slew of mostly regrettable memories, but the liquid fire did bring a modicum of moisture to his throat, enough to strengthen his voice. "Who the hell is . . . banging?" he barked.

Any other day he would have recognized Woefus' voice, chief of the Black Coats, but his mental faculties were bobbing through the liminal waters of his still-intoxicated brain. Tightening his grip around his sword, Julian willed himself forward. He walked to the door. As he unlocked it, the door inched open. A face appeared in the crack. "Good day, Julian."

"*Woefus!*" he bellowed.

"None other," said Woefus, pushing the door wider. He entered with his sword ready. He knocked Julian's blade aside as the point proceeded feebly toward his belly.

"Put it back before you skewer yourself," reprimanded Woefus.

"Of all people, *you* should know better than to wake me!"

"You will thank me later—your mother is on her way."

"Then I'll slay her, too . . . get it over with," he declared, squaring up to the door.

"Naked, Julian? Really?"

"Why doesn't she arrange a meeting like *everyone* else?" he exclaimed, waving the tip toward the open doorway.

"She says you never respond to her requests."

"I'm a busy man," replied Julian, returning to the pile of clothing. He found it every bit as confounding as it had been a minute before. After locating his britches, he collapsed into a chair. "Ughhh, my fucking head," he griped. He shoved a leg into one hole and pulled, but he quickly realized they were backward. "Help me, Woefus," he moaned while he struggled to get his foot out.

"I refuse to help you put your pants on," replied Woefus, frowning as he studied the occupants in the bed. It was hard to figure out which leg or arm belonged to which head.

"Not with my pants, you idiot," hollered Julian. "Find me a bottle with something to drink!" Woefus moved to the bed and grabbed the top blanket with his free hand, then yanked the cover off. Groans ensued. "Rise and shine, darlings," he quipped. "The queen will be here any minute. I suggest all you little rats disappear if you want to remain in her good graces." The bodies slowly levitated like lead balloons. Woefus directed them toward the lavatory.

Julian yanked his pants up to his waist and then buttoned them before collapsing back on the chair. "That's enough work for one day," he proclaimed.

Woefus grabbed a white shirt from the floor and flung it toward Julian. Pulling it over his head, Julian noticed a red stain spilled across the front. "It will have to do," said Woefus. Julian's fingers shook as they fumbled for the holes. Woefus then picked up a half-empty bottle from the table and handed it to him. Julian's lips fastened to it like a calf's to its mother's teat.

Just then a footman stepped through the door. "Her Majesty, the queen," he announced.

Six porters carried the queen upon an open sedan chair. In the middle of the room they set her down. "Where are they?" Queen Beatrice demanded.

"Who, Mother?" asked Julian, not bothering to look up.

"My courtiers . . . and whomever else you enlist in your debauchery."

"There's no one here," he answered plaintively, motioning to the empty room.

The queen waved her guards forward. "I want everyone out." Soon a line of semiclothed bodies was being ushered out of the bathroom, their heads down, and their hands covering their privates. "Is that Lilleth Hamsted?" declared the queen. "Oh, Julian, her father and mother would be . . ." Julian's eyelids descended to half-mast, and he gave her a look of feigned disinterest. "Get him out of here as well," said the queen, waving off Lucius, who had managed to appear fully dressed—although his inner shirt and sleeves were badly misplaced.

"Lucius is my personal assistant," protested Julian. "You know that."

"Perhaps in matters of depravity, but not in the affairs of state," said the queen. Lucius stomped toward the door like a spoiled child. "No, wait." The queen waved him back. "I've changed my mind; Julian will need someone to remind him of our conversation."

"Sounds ominous." Julian's voice trailed off.

"For you, I believe the choral bells of heaven would sound ominous."

"Is there a point to this, Mother?"

"Beware, the point is sharp, Julian."

"How sharp could it be?"

"People are asking me for a succession plan."

"And . . ."

"Many doubt your readiness to be king."

"They've been grumbling about me for years."

"It's getting louder."

"Who *are* these people?" asked Julian, his eyes flashing.

"When your grandfather Teufel was king, royalty could do as they pleased. This is no longer the case. Spotted fever is worsening by the day. The Hutsus are flocking to the city; their herds are dying, and their fields lay barren. They come hoping to find work and food, but find no such thing. To make matters worse, the granaries are at an all-time low. And now there are rumblings of another rebellion in the north, due to this . . . this . . . *diamond*."

"Blame Marius for that."

"You could have returned it, as you were advised."

"When did we start pandering to savages?" bleated Julian, adjusting himself.

"*Subjects*, Julian. *sub*-jects! But only as long as we have power over them."

"And soon we will. I am sending two legions north. Their ill-advised rebellion will be over in a month."

"Sending two legions will be expensive."

"That is precisely why this diamond is important! If it's everything I've heard, it is worth all the gold in Grebald."

"Who will buy it?" asked the queen.

"The Helvats, a Sulkid prince, what does it matter?"

"If they sense you are desperate, you will be in no position to negotiate. They will offer you half its value. One has to stand in a position of power to demand top price."

"Diplomacy lessons from a queen who never fought a battle in her life."

"The greatest battles are not fought with weapons, Julian . . . but in meeting rooms. Sometimes with your closest advisors and at times even with your own children! Power is like water in the hand; you have to be very careful, for it can easily slip through your fingers. And yes, that *is* another lesson for you."

"You woke me up just to argue about the fine points of ruling?"

"No, there's more. I will not live much longer. The aristocracy is rightly nervous. Quite frankly, you scare them. They forgave you when you were in your twenties. 'He's young, he will grow up,' they said. Now you are thirty-two, and they are beginning to doubt you ever will."

"For God's sake, Mother. One last time, who is *they*?" he snapped. "Give me some names!"

"'They' is *everyone*, including me!"

Julian stood up and strode over to the doors that looked out over the palace gardens. He put both hands against the frame and gazed out beyond the sculpted hedges. "Who do *they* want?" he asked. "Marius? Is that who they want?" he said, turning back to face her. "Is that what this is about?"

"No, silly boy. The crown is still yours to lose, but you had better make some good choices. Which brings me to my point."

"A point?" Julian threw his hands up. "Great. I have yet to hear one."

"Marriage!" announced the queen, her chin lifted, face stoic.

"*Marriage!*" Julian repeated. His face went flat. "What a repugnant notion!"

"If you marry, the aristocracy will consider it a step toward maturity . . . It would make you appear a little more

. . . respectable. And to appease the commoners, I propose you marry one."

"A commoner! Are you out of your mind? No Proudst has *ever* stooped so low."

"I said commoner, but I did not say milkmaid. She can be of noble ancestry."

"If I marry," declared Julian, beginning to pace, "there is only one I would marry."

"But she will not marry you, and quite frankly, I would not sanction that marriage."

"If I am going to marry, that's who I want."

"Colette's your first cousin! It's simply out of the question."

"Such marriages have been arranged before. Besides, she *is* a commoner."

"Half a commoner," added the queen. "And the other half came straight from your uncle's loins. Regardless, you would not survive a marriage with Colette . . . and I doubt I would either. The person I have in mind is more mild mannered."

"Ahhh, you've been plotting, I see. Is she beautiful? She has to be beautiful," said Julian.

"So they say."

"Then I must know her," he said, focusing intently on the queen. "I know all of them. Who is it?"

"Liis Hoffe!" stated the queen, squaring her shoulders.

Julian shook his head vigorously. "Beautiful, yes . . . I give you that. But a more prudish, boring do-gooder could not be found anywhere in the kingdom."

"Precisely."

"She's a cold fish, Mother. I thought there had to be . . . What do you call them? Progeny!" he declared, snapping his fingers. Lucius giggled. "I can't imagine her in bed!" Julian began to pace again. "She does nothing for my loins," he added. "There could be no children of this union."

"Your loins could use some restraint. People think very highly of her. Somewhere in her mother's line are Proudst, so there *is* nobility. She would bring some goodwill to the crown."

Julian passed his fingers quickly through his thick hair. "I wonder," he said, stopping abruptly. "She probably brings books with her to bed. Do you know if she's a virgin? I hate virgins!"

"Julian!" The queen's voice rose, her tone reprimanding. "I am serious."

"But it's important!" he said with a half smile.

"My reports are that her interests are mostly scholarly if that answers your question."

"I doubt I could manage with her."

"I am sure you can muster at least one child . . . I did."

"No need to overshare, Mother. So, has she agreed to marry me?"

"No! Though Monsignor Iraneous has her mother's ear. I don't see why an agreement couldn't be reached."

"I see, I see; you and the archbishop have been scheming."

"He looks out for our interests."

"Our interests . . . or *his*?"

"The crown and the church are two wings of the same bird. You need both to fly."

"What does the archbishop ask of us in return?" Julian's eyes squinted.

"You are not to support the sciences."

"Nothing bores me more. So the matter is settled?"

"No!" said the queen. "That is my one stipulation: you must make an effort this time. And I strongly suggest you make a good impression on her. For in the end, if she doesn't agree to marry you, I will appoint another heir; this I swear."

"You would not!"

"I would," she answered, nodding her head in the affirmative. "Maybe even Marius."

Julian's cheek twitched. "Well, congratulations, Mother, you have become a tyrant in your old age."

"Just make an *effort*, Julian . . . for once!"

"How?"

"There are ways to ingratiate oneself."

"How awfully boring!"

"Get used to it. Being a king *is* boring. But this I promise: she is not going to agree to marry a whoring drunkard."

Lucius snickered. Julian spun around, his eyes burning into him. "Shut up," he scolded.

"So moody this morning!" declared Lucius, rolling his eyes.

"So I should start reading books?" asked Julian sarcastically.

"You don't have to go to extremes. Just show some interest in her affairs. Maybe she will begin to think you are not as bad as your reputation."

Julian looked toward the ceiling and raised his hands. "Ass-kiss the commoners. Is that what the crown has come to?" Half turning to Lucius, he spoke under his breath. "Perhaps with enough booze, anything is possible."

"Marriage or give up the crown," declared the queen.

"Those are my only two options?" He shot her a mean glare.

"I believe so . . . yes."

"I thought negotiation was the highest art of diplomacy."

"With you, negotiation would be foolish," continued the queen.

"Mother . . . this is all happening too fast . . . I need more time!"

"You don't have time, Julian. People are desperate. A fight broke out yesterday during bread distribution. Leadership is needed. Everything is happening much faster than I antici- pated. Perhaps I even waited too long to come to this decision."

"Stop the self-pity, Mother; it makes you doting and old," grumbled Julian. "So have the Hutsus been making demands?" he asked, picking up a bottle.

"No, but Woefus here says they are gathering."

"'Gathering'? What does that mean?"

"Coming together to talk."

"*Talk!* Where do they *talk*?" he asked.

"In their homes! In the streets . . . I don't know."

"Why should we fear them? What are they going to fight us with? Kitchen knives?"

"A thousand Hutsus with wooden spoons can do more damage than you think. Besides, do I need to remind you, the Hutsus comprise over a third of our foot soldiers. It would be wise not to alienate them. In fact, if you have forgotten, Woefus here is Hutsu."

"I can barely stand Woefus." Julian smirked over at him.

"This conversation has only increased my worry."

"Why, Mother? Why?"

"Why what?"

"Why is everyone speaking badly about me!"

"You don't see any of this," she said, motioning to his room. "*You're oblivious!* You don't demonstrate right and proper instincts! You have little feeling for anyone other than your- self!" The queen's face was red. She waved for a courtier to come fan her. After a short minute, she took a deep inhale.

"But people *do* love a royal wedding. It might appease them. Besides, there is a lot of goodwill toward Liis. She may save you."

"Save *me*? She's supposed to be *my* savior?" demanded Julian. "I don't think so!" he said, wagging his finger at his mother. "Marrying me would be her lucky day! Her family is in need of a benefactor if I recall."

"At this point, Julian, I think you need her more than she needs you. Listen to me. The moment people don't believe in the crown, the crown is nothing. Belief . . . and perhaps fear, are the foundations upon which every ruler stands. But make no mistake, the crown and your head can part ways!"

"Fine, Mother, get me that girl, and . . . and I . . . I can't even say the word."

Queen Beatrice shook her head. "I have spoken to the archbishop, but that's all I am going to do. This time, you will have to make an effort." The queen turned toward Woefus. "He has so much to learn!"

"Aye, my queen," replied Woefus.

With a wave of her hand, the porters lifted the queen's sedan. When they were all gone, Julian lifted a bottle and took a long swig. Sitting back down, he closed his eyes and imagined a deep valley within an unruly forest. At the lowest point, under the trees and among the rocks and leaves, was a small cave. The entrance was blocked by a sturdy door that was locked and chained. In front of the door, two hungry lions paced back and forth. Julian only vaguely suspected what was inside, but one thing he was certain of, the door should never be opened.

Springing to his feet, he announced, "If I have to marry the Hoffe girl, I *swear* I will have Colette first." With this, he raised the bottle in a toast toward the departed queen.

5

The Hoffe Residence, Jesut Edin

Brill listened to the ticktock of the clock in the hall—its steady rhythm interrupted only by a clang of pots coming from the kitchen. It was approaching noon. Liis and Pola were seated beside him at the dining room table. They were waiting for the sound of the clapper. Today was the day—and about the time—when exam results would be delivered to students' homes. A passing score was guaranteed acceptance into the Lyceum of Jesut Edin.

Under the dining room table, Liis squeezed Brill's hand. Whenever he happened to look over at her, she sent him a hopeful smile. Liis was twenty-one years of age, eight years older than him. And Nikolas was another two years older than her. When people heard they were siblings, no one believed them. Nikolas was tall, with blond Pagani-like hair but darker Ilyrian skin. Liis not only had the same straw-blond hair, inherited from their father, but she also had Alber's fair skin.

Their mother with her black hair, black eyes, and full cheeks was classic Ilyrian. Brill, on the other hand—with his brown, curly locks—looked like no one in the family.

When the brass rapper sounded on the front door, Pola scooted her chair back, pressed her dress down, and departed the dining room. A minute later she returned holding an envelope. Brill sprung to his feet, but Pola lifted it into the air above her head. "Your mother requested to see it first," she said.

"Why does everyone else get to see my results first?" he protested.

"I am sorry, Brill," said Pola, heading toward the arch in the dining room that led to his mother's quarters.

"Wait here," said Liis, and with this, she pursued Pola down the corridor.

Brill collapsed onto a chair and dropped his head onto the table. The house was suddenly all too quiet, even the clock seemed to have stopped ticking. Amidst the lull, Brill thought he heard a couple of faint clacks. It sounded as if someone was hitting the front door with a stick. Against his better judgment, he got up. He went through the foyer to the front door and opened it. On the stoop stood his cousin, Costa.

"Well?" said Costa, his head slightly bobbing.

"I don't *know*," answered Brill. "It's just arrived."

"Why is yours so late?" he asked, leaning forward on one of his crutches and frowning. "My results came over an hour ago!"

Brill shrugged. He had no idea. What he was certain of was that Costa was the last person he wanted to talk to about it. "Probably not the best day, Costa," said Brill, moving to shut the door.

Costa wedged his crutch between the door and the frame. "Don't you want to know?" he asked.

"I already *do*," stated Brill. "You passed . . . or you wouldn't be here."

"My father always said that acceptance into the lyceum would be my first step into manhood," said Costa, lurching forward and grabbing hold of the railing. Brill shook his head. The word "manhood" seemed like quite a leap.

Costa hauled himself up to the threshold of the door—very nearly knocking over a potted flower on his way. Brill yielded, stepping back to let him pass. "Let's go to my room," he conceded. Costa's crutches smacked against the frame as he hobbled into the foyer.

As he took the chair by his desk, Brill noticed that Costa had left the door open. No matter how many times he asked, he never closed it. For a long moment, he stared at Brill. Costa's eyes were black, like two inkwells, making it near impossible to distinguish pupil from iris. This made his eyes seem larger than normal and gave him the appearance of being supremely tender. But anyone acquainted with Costa knew this was only a trap, for after his eyes lured you in, he sowed his words like tiny grains of salt in your wounds. And he seemed to know exactly where the wounds were—perhaps because his were there for all to see. Costa's chest was disproportionately large compared to his misshapen legs. Brill had seen them in the flesh only once, but it had been enough to see that he would never walk properly and certainly never run and play like other boys. Costa used wooden crutches to get around, dragging his limbs along behind him, but he did so without complaint. "My father says," Costa started in, "that many of the teachers at the lyceum are also professors at the university."

"Is that so?" said Brill, sinking lower. Costa proceeded to tell him what classes he would be taking his first term and with whom. As Costa prattled on, Brill found his eyes getting ponderous. Sliding farther down the chair, his head went back, and his eyes found the crack in the ceiling, the one he went to when escaping his mother's lectures.

For Liis, school was the Holy Land. She was very much her father's daughter. Nikolas, on the other hand, had shown no proclivity for school and left home as soon as he could to join the navy. In this respect, Brill felt similar to Nikolas, but unlike Nikolas, becoming a sailor held little appeal. He would much rather wander the streets and watch people, or climb on the roof and look out over the city and think about things. In classrooms he felt stifled, shackled to a desk—never free. In the end, he was certain the lyceum would be preferable to seminary. Surely, if he didn't pass the exam, that's where his mother would send him. She had always wanted a priest in the family.

It was then Brill noticed Costa had stopped talking. His brows were scrunched together, and he was staring at Brill with a look of incredulity. "Just like in school!" he declared. "You weren't listening to anything I was saying." Brill vaguely recalled hearing something about a respected scholar on trade. "Oh, don't try to get away with it. Just admit it; you weren't listening," pressed Costa.

"I heard you! You were talking about a professor named . . . Hesse."

Costa's eyebrows furrowed. "Amazing how you always escape the noose!" Suddenly, his face opened up. "Want to hear something *really* interesting?" Brill wasn't sure that he did. Costa waited for him to reply, but seeing that Brill was not going to, he continued. "We received a letter from my father."

Brill stopped studying the ceiling long enough to turn and look over at him. "What did it say?"

"He said that someday he wants to take me up to Okomorling."

"Did he mention the diamond?" asked Brill.

Costa glared at him. "Of course he did!"

"So?" Brill sat up. It was all he wanted to hear about.

Costa leaned forward. "I'm not going to tell you unless you promise not to repeat it to anyone . . . not Liis, and *definitely* not Pola."

"Why not Pola?"

"She's a northerner! For all we know she could be a spy."

"A spy! Come on, Costa," said Brill, shaking his head.

"Promise, or I won't tell you."

"*Okaay*, okay, I promise!" said Brill.

Costa studied Brill's face until he was either satisfied with what he saw, or just unable to contain the news any longer. "My father says the diamond is the size of a goose egg!" He cupped his hands to demonstrate. "And a *large* one at that! He says it must be hundreds of carats. And he's *never* seen anything like it! He says it's the most perfect jewel he's ever laid eyes on. No flaws whatsoever! And the cut!" With this Costa's head went back. "The facets are perfectly arranged in exquisite balance. He says that looking into it is like entering an ocean of light . . . and those were his *exact* words."

"Did he touch it?" Brill asked, leaning forward.

"Why do you ask?" said Costa, his tone turning serious.

"Just curious."

"The governor wouldn't let him, not without gloves anyway."

"Why not?"

"He said there were some things that he couldn't write in a letter. But he's already done an appraisal for Julian."

"Appraisal? What's that?"

"That's what my father does! He determines what stones are worth."

"Your father's trying to sell it?"

"No . . . well . . . maybe. It's for Prince Julian! It's only natural for him to find out what it's worth."

"Who would he sell it to?" asked Brill.

"To the Helvats, to the Moohady . . . the Sulkids. It doesn't matter."

"He'd sell it to the Moohady? But they're our enemy, no?"

"In commerce, everyone is a friend. But no one will know who purchases it—that's the trick. That way, no 'rules' are broken."

"Pola thinks they should return it to the Pagani."

"Pola's a servant!" hammered Costa scornfully. "Besides, it's too late. My father's going to bring it home!" Suddenly, Costa's face became serene, almost angelic. He was probably considering his father's commission. "What my father would really like to know is how it ended up in Bajarmaland! He figures someone must have brought it from another land, someone that history has forgotten. He says the person would have to be a true master to cut such a stone."

"If it's the diamond Pola tells me about, it comes from the beginning of time," said Brill.

Costa rolled his eyes. "What other nonsense does she tell you?"

"She says that Queemquesh led the Pagani up the Spiral Path with the Ayn Noor. That's what they call it. It means 'divine light.' The Pagani believe that if a person touches it, they will either gaze into eternity or lose their minds completely."

"Well, I'm pretty sure my father touched it, and he hasn't become a raving lunatic."

"I thought you said the governor wouldn't let him."

"That's what I *said*, but I am sure he did."

"Well, maybe he's not open to the possibilities."

"'Open to the possibilities'! Of what, becoming a *madman*?"

"What I want to know is," asked Brill, ignoring Costa's question, "How did the Ilyrians come upon it?"

"Everybody knows that Julian's bastard cousin procured it," provided Costa.

"That's a funny word," said Brill.

"Bastard . . . yeah . . . that's kind of funny," agreed Costa with a smile.

"No, 'procured.'" said Brill. "It sounds so official."

"It just means he found it!"

"But why don't they ever tell us *how* or *where* they find things?"

"It doesn't matter *how*! . . . *or where*!" declared Costa with a scowl.

"It does too matter," retorted Brill.

"It does not!" replied Costa.

"Do you know the story 'The Woman and the Ring'?" asked Brill.

"Oh, here we go. Is this another one of Pola's stories?" Brill did not reply. "Go on, tell me. I know you're going to anyway."

"Just so you know, this is not one of Pola's stories."

Costa crossed his arms. "Fine."

"Two women go to the market to buy a fish . . ." started Brill.

"I thought you said, '*the* woman,'" interrupted Costa. "'*The*' implies one, not two."

"Well, I meant two."

"Are you making this up?" asked Costa, vigorously scratching his nose. "Is this what you do at school all day, make up stories?" Brill shrugged. "Well, go on, then. Let's get it over with!" said Costa.

"*Two* women go to the market to buy a fish," continued Brill.

"Did they go together?" asked Costa.

"No! *Alone!*"

"You just got to be clear," stated Costa. "If you want to tell a good story, that is . . ."

"The two ladies go to the market—*alone!*" belabored Brill. "After they choose a fish, each returns home. *Alone.* While cleaning the fish, the first woman discovers a gold ring inside its belly."

"The other woman is going to be *mad* she didn't buy that one," injected Costa.

"Holding the ring up, she recognizes it," Brill continued. "She is overcome with emotion, for she realizes it was a ring that she lost many years ago while washing her clothes down by the river. After all this time—and in such a strange manner—it came back to her!

"Now, the second woman is preparing her fish . . . and she, too, discovers a gold ring inside its belly. Immediately, she puts it on. It fits perfectly! She holds up her hand and admires it. She can't believe her good fortune and rushes out to tell the neighbors."

Costa looked at Brill blankly. "Go on," he said, waiting for Brill to finish.

"That's it," said Brill.

"Noooo!" Costa howled, his head shooting backward. "What's the point?"

"The point is that the second woman doesn't remember it was her ring, even though she lost it years ago."

"That's stupid! No woman would ever forget her ring."

"It's an allegory, like Father Bartholomew teaches. The first woman sees the miracle, but the second woman only sees it as luck and nothing more."

"So what exactly are you saying?" said Costa, his eyes narrowing suspiciously.

"All I'm saying is that it matters how the diamond was found. You either believe things happen for a reason, or you don't."

"All that interests me is whether *you* are the first or the second woman!" exclaimed Costa.

Brill glared at him, but before they could continue, Liis stepped through the door. "Morning," she said upon seeing Costa. "Arguing already I see."

"So . . . ?" said Costa, spinning so he could see Liis. "Did Brill pass?"

"Believe it or not, Costa, there are some things that are none of your business."

"He didn't pass—I knew it!" bellowed Costa gleefully.

"I didn't say that," snapped Liis. Brill watched her closely. If one didn't know her, one might not be able to distinguish the lines that formed on her brow when she was concentrating from the lines that formed on her brow when she was upset . . . and how when she *was* upset, her soft brown eyes became a smidgen hard. Costa was just opening his mouth to speak, but

Liis beat him to it. "Not everything is black and white, Costa. Consider that your first lesson from the lyceum."

Liis looked over at Brill. "Mother and I are off to see the monsignor. But I'll come find you as soon as I get home."

"The monsignor," chimed Costa. "Oh, Brill, it's seminary for you."

Liis turned and closed the door sharply behind her. For once, Brill wished the door had been left open.

6

The Archbishop's Manor, Jesut Edin

Father Mazarin was taken by the faintest smell of myrrh. The confines of the archbishop's carriage were both immaculate and luxurious. Purple velvet covered the interior walls of the post chaise; the plush fabric even curved over the edges of the benches. Mazarin searched inwardly but could not find one sensation of discomfort anywhere in his body—a stark contrast from his journey from Bajarmaland.

Over the course of his travels, he had grown accustomed to every sort of ache and pain. He had started on an old workhorse in Okomorling, but the poor beast collapsed halfway down the mountain. It had taken six weeks just to arrive in Scargowrath. There he boarded a rickety farm carriage with plank benches. Eventually he relinquished protocol and accepted the ensuing guilt, placing his leather satchel containing his finest cassock and liturgical surplice under him. In Torbeshacken, Father Mazarin boarded a four-horse carriage. The threadbare cushions were adequate, but the dust was awful! Once in Jesut Edin, it took him two washes to get the dust out of his clothes ... and three to get the dirt off his skin.

The spinning wheels of the archbishop's carriage met the crest of each cobblestone with the enthusiasm of a mason apprentice's hammer, eagerly chipping away at the streets with each rotation. Turning his attention to the man sitting across from him, Father Mazarin studied Monsignor Iraneous, whose eyes were closed. His cassock was lined with silk and accentuated with fuchsia piping and matching buttons going down the front of his vestment. He wore a black biretta. The monsignor's demeanor was the antithesis of joviality; his face portrayed a man who spent considerable hours in rigorous contemplation—with none of the benefits. His hands were crossed in his lap. Mazarin saw his thumb and forefinger were stained with ink. He was the archbishop's bookkeeper and envoy, all in one. It was then Mazarin noticed the archbishop's gold signet ring. The letter summoning him five months prior was imprinted with this very seal.

Looking up, Mazarin found the monsignor staring at him. The monsignor's eyes were as penetrating as they were hard. Both men gazed at one another until Iraneous' voice broke above the marcato clatter of the speeding carriage. "You were looking at the ring," he announced. Unsure how to respond, Mazarin held his tongue. "It's the archbishop's ring," continued the monsignor. "Nine times out of ten I write and sign his correspondence . . . but only with his permission of course." Father Mazarin realized the monsignor was suggesting how he should think about what he saw.

"An invitation to Archbishop Farfan's table," the monsignor went on, "is highly sought after. It is considered *the* most lavish repast in all of Jesut Edin. And here you are, a humble priest from a tiny parish, on his way to break bread with the archbishop."

"It *is* a great privilege to be summoned by His Eminence. Of this, I am most aware."

"I don't believe you understand me."

"Perhaps I do not," countered Father Mazarin.

"The archbishop takes only *one* meal a day, the afternoon meal, precisely at ten minutes past two. Marie Antonin is his personal chef. To eat her cuisine is . . . is nothing short of prayer." Seeing the light of understanding growing in Father Mazarin's eyes, the monsignor commented, "The queen wanted to hire Marie Antonin away from the archbishop, but she was unsuccessful."

"Unusual, no?" queried Father Mazarin.

The monsignor raised his shoulders slightly as if to say, *Maybe not.*

"Archbishop Farfan is the king of the Church of Ilyria. Even the queen cannot challenge his ecclesiastic jurisdiction. But this is irrelevant," stated the monsignor, pursing his lips. "Marie Antonin would never leave him."

"Not even for such a prestigious position?" inquired Father Mazarin.

"No," affirmed the monsignor, pulling the edges of his diminutive lips downward and negligibly shaking his head to emphasize his point. "With the archbishop, she has an unlimited budget, to which I can *personally* attest. Marie Antonin is an artist, and what do artists desire most, Father Mazarin?"

"I don't know, Monsignor."

"Freedom! The archbishop makes few demands. She has complete artistic control! Whereas the queen has many banquets, and many diplomats and guests to consider. The archbishop has visitors, yes, but one meal a day is all that she is required to prepare. Why would she leave? She wouldn't! It is as simple as that."

Father Mazarin nodded, wondering how much longer he could feign interest. "If the church is the body of Christ," said the monsignor, "and the Holy See is the heart, then the arch-bishop is its stomach."

Father Mazarin was not sure if this was meant to humor him. Regardless, he didn't laugh. "Seems a bit extravagant for a man of religion, no?" Father Mazarin could no longer help himself. Too much of this talk always provoked his fiery streak—which is how he ended up in a parish in the far north.

The monsignor lifted an eyebrow. "Ahh, yes, the idealistic country priest. In your parish, Father Mazarin . . . well, what's left of it . . . how many souls do you service?"

"One hundred and fifty, give or take."

"Do they bring you gifts?"

"On occasion . . . apple cider, bread, butter, mutton, some-times hunted game."

"Now imagine the archbishop. The entirety of Ilyria is his jurisdiction. Besides prayer and clerical duties, what do the monks and priests do?"

Father Mazarin shrugged.

"They are, as you know, erudite men of God. Thoughtful creatures . . . with no wives or children to indulge. So they devote their lives to mastering the culinary crafts, be they wines or cheeses or brews. A crock of apple cider and a lit-tle meat is . . . is *nothing*. Imagine receiving a thousand times that! I assure you, he is feted from all dioceses and monaster-ies throughout the empire—although I don't recall your parish ever sending anything?" Father Mazarin shook his head. The monsignor stared at him but did not indicate whether he noticed the guilt flushing Mazarin's face.

Father Mazarin only wished the conversation had never begun. In a mere fifteen minutes, the political machinations of the church had caught up to him, and with it the unwanted turbulence, the stirring pain that cut deeper than all the discomforts an arduous journey could ever bring. It was the kind of hurt that wakes one up at night and tosses the soul about like a small boat on a perilous sea. The emotions, the helplessness and anger, were the waves battering the gunwale. If helplessness was dominant, depression inevitably ensued. But if waves of anger dashed his boat, his mind marched toward the necessity to act and all the burdens such bravery entails. It had been four years since he was sent north. Father Mazarin found that the farther away from the center of the Ilyrian church he went, the calmer his internal seas became. The last four years had been the happiest he had ever known. That is, until the theft of the Ayn Noor.

"You see, Father, the archbishop sits near the top of an organization that has tendrils leading far beyond our borders."

"'Tendrils'?" repeated Father Mazarin with more than a hint of bewilderment.

"Yes. The archbishop is in constant exchange with bishops and cardinals from afar. The queen's table is without a doubt delightful, but the archbishop's table is unrivaled." Father Mazarin told himself to be patient. Surely, Monsignor Iraneous had more to say.

"I will tell you this once," the monsignor went on. "The archbishop's midday meal is sacrosanct. Prepare yourself. It will be a lot for a parish priest. Whatever you do, *do not* finish your plate before the archbishop. But also, keep up with him, eat as much as he eats, or at the very least, don't refuse anything. However long it takes him to eat is how long you eat. And mind you, one does not talk unless spoken to . . . as Father Vardy recently learned." And, as if on cue, the carriage slowed just as Monsignor Iraneous finished. Father Mazarin had the sudden impression this conversation was one he had with some frequency.

The sound of boots were followed by a coachman opening the carriage door. He assisted the monsignor down. Father Mazarin waved him off. Stepping upon the firm ground, the solid earth felt true. He tilted his head and looked up at the archbishop's residence. He had seen it many times as a seminary student, but this would be his first time setting foot inside.

At the door they were greeted by a maid in a black dress and a white apron. Beyond her, an enormous wooden cross hung in the foyer below the double staircase. Monsignor Iraneous crossed himself. Father Mazarin followed his lead. Marble flooring ended at the stairs with their curving balustrade. At the top they were met by a substantial man, the archbishop himself. Father Mazarin's eyes went to the gold Augustinian cross hanging from his neck. It rested prominently on his shoulder cape. Archbishop Farfan held out his amethyst ring for him to kiss. "Your Eminence," said Father Mazarin, kneeling on the top step.

"Welcome, Brother Mazarin," said the archbishop, dispensing with formality and position and touching his shoulder as if to say, *Rise.*

"Venerable brother," answered Mazarin as he stood, returning the gesture of intimacy.

"How was your journey south?" asked the archbishop.

"Very good, thank you," answered Mazarin. For a moment he was taken off guard by the tenderness the archbishop conveyed. His concern was disarming. Mazarin had only met the archbishop once, when he had graduated from Saint Peter's Seminary, and that was merely a formality. The impression he made at the time was not atypical of one in the church hierarchy, a large-bellied priest with graying hair. Up close, his girth was not to be denied, but his eyes were what stood out—they were particularly small, two mere cutouts at the base of an overly round forehead ceding acres of skin under a tiny silk skullcap.

"Modern travel," said the archbishop, "is nothing short of a miracle. When I was young, I crossed the empire in a donkey cart."

"The youth are spoiled, Your Eminence," added the monsignor.

"To a degree, to a degree," affirmed the archbishop. "But I doubt it is easy up north?" He pointed the comment at Father Mazarin as he led them farther into the house.

"In the service of our Lord, I am content," replied Mazarin.

Stopping rather abruptly, the archbishop turned partially, enough to glimpse Father Mazarin. "I hope all the travel has not ruined your appetite."

Father Mazarin noted the monsignor looking at him from the other side of the archbishop. "Indeed, not," he answered quickly.

"Good, good, then you will join me for my midday meal. It's the only one I allow myself."

Father Mazarin soon found himself in front of a long table. Its polish was so excellent that it reflected the light with almost equal brilliance of a window. Three chairs were positioned together toward one end, where the finest blue-and-white porcelain plates lay beautifully arranged with silverware aplenty. A man in a suit with a long-tailed jacket came forward and assisted the archbishop to his chair, then the monsignor. Father Mazarin managed for himself. Following the archbishop's lead, Mazarin removed his napkin from his plate and placed it on his lap as a second waiter came forward. He was dressed like the other and transported a silver tray with three small crystal flutes. After placing one in front of each priest, he disappeared. The archbishop picked his up, his pinky slightly flared, and tipped the drink. Both Monsignor Iraneous and Father Mazarin followed his lead. Mazarin felt an immediate warmth come over his belly—an anise-flavored aperitif.

The servant reentered with a platter of fruit, cheese, and cold meats, offering it to the archbishop first. Mazarin watched him take the silver spatula and go back and forth a couple of times. Then plucking a fresh fig between his plump fingers, he closed his lips around it and battened his eyes. They remained closed as he savored the fruit, while another server filled tall glasses with red wine. Father Mazarin gazed across at Monsignor Iraneous, who promptly lifted a soft hunk of melted brie and raised it toward Mazarin before placing it on his tongue. Father Mazarin figured he had better start, so he quickly took hold of a green olive.

After clearing the first plates, a servant returned with bowls. Out of a porcelain tureen, steaming soup was ladled into them. This was accompanied with fresh-baked bread and a side plate of buttered asparagus. Father Mazarin listened to the archbishop slurp as he ventured deep into his bowl. The sound reminded him of the paupers Mazarin used to feed in the back of his chapel in Bertold, except their soup was mostly barley and parsnips. And just as he considered what wonder he was consuming, the archbishop offered the answer: "Soup of tortoise."

"Ah," said Father Mazarin, "most delicious."

The archbishop mumbled in agreement as he refocused on his tongue's delight. Next came the triangle pastries, light and crispy. The archbishop reached for one, this time forgoing the serving pincers. As he bit into it, the crust broke apart, releasing steam from its innards. After they were done and the crumbs were swept up, small plates came, each with a single fried quail at the center of what looked like a halo of tiny halved eggs, their yolks of tender yellow radiance colored with a dash of red paprika and a sprinkle of parsley. "Don't be afraid of the bones," instructed the archbishop, taking a leg and crunching down on one to make his point.

When the plates held merely refuse, there was a pause in the eating as the table was cleared once more. Their glasses were filled with a drier red wine. Already, Father Mazarin's stomach felt distended—it was well beyond its known limit. He hoped they were done as he watched the archbishop dally with his wine, twirling and sipping alternately. To Mazarin's chagrin, when Farfan neared the bottom of his glass, another course arrived: veal, with a demi-glace of dry red sherry and bone-marrow gravy dripped over creamed potatoes. This time around, Father Mazarin did not wait for the archbishop, for he knew he had to eat faster in order to keep pace. And just when he doubted he could muster another bite, a servant, one whom Father Mazarin did not recognize, appeared with a silver tray full of desserts: chocolate mousse, layered white cake with raspberries, custard with sprinkled cinnamon, green pistachio cookies with roasted nuts and confectioner's sugar. As the waiters exchanged plates, the archbishop helped himself to a large slice of white cake. When Father Mazarin's turn came, he sought the smallest item. The butter biscuit half dipped in chocolate seemed least threatening. Shortly thereafter came the coffee. Only after his second cup did the archbishop stop. Leaning back in his chair, he placed his elbows on the armrests and interlaced his fingers above his belly.

After a long silence, the archbishop turned and stared at Father Mazarin without uttering a word. Father Mazarin was reminded of the games boys sometimes play—who would look away first? About the time Mazarin began to wonder if the archbishop was ever going to speak—he did. "It's been a long time since I heard a firsthand account of the north. Tell me about Bajarmaland."

"What would Your Eminence like to know?" asked Father Mazarin. "About our diaspora in Okomorling? Where we pray? I can tell you, Father Gabriel has been most accommodating."

"No," objected the archbishop, "tell me about the uprising! When did the Pagani attack?"

"Late fall. There had been rumors it might happen ever since the captain stole the diamond."

"Why do they care so much about this . . . jewel?"

"Their entire mythology revolves around it," answered Father Mazarin. "To them . . . it's akin to the Holy Grail, or the Crown of Thorns. First the Pagani attacked settlers and their homesteads, but then they became bolder and started attacking villages. I am sure you will have heard my town, Bertold, was razed to its timbers."

"I hear that you interceded with the savages and negotiated with them to save the lives of the townspeople."

"I only did what any priest would have done, Your Eminence."

"What was the exchange you offered them?"

"I offered them *everything*—for our souls and clothed bodies."

"Costly . . . but necessary, I suspect."

"Fortunately, the Lord shepherded his flock safely to Okomorling."

"Perhaps in the future there will be another appointment in the north for you . . . but first I want you to serve me here in Jesut Edin."

"How may I be of service, Archbishop?"

"I understand you speak Hutsu?"

"I was born in the foothills. I am of Hutsu descent, yes."

"Hutsu and Pagani are closely related, are they not?"

"Very similar language, dialects really. But as you know, we *are* Christian."

"Christian on the surface, anyway, Father Mazarin. The pagan is still far too near their hearts."

"It takes time to cast off the old superstitions, this is true, Archbishop."

"Sometimes I think the Hutsus cover themselves in Christianity simply to deceive us." Father Mazarin did not reply. "There is much unrest in Jesut Edin," the archbishop went on. "We could use a respected Hutsu priest to parlay with them. You not only speak their native tongue, but you obviously have considerable skill with diplomacy. If I have need, I will call on you. Until then, you will teach at the seminary. Monsignor Iraneous will provide you quarters. He will also instruct you in what you shall teach."

"As you wish, Archbishop," said Father Mazarin with a bow of his head.

"As God wishes," corrected the archbishop.

"Yes, as God wishes."

"Monsignor," said the archbishop, turning to Iraneous, "speaking of seminary, there is a small matter of the Hoffe family."

"Lisbeth Hoffe! Does she pester you as well? With me it's almost daily!"

"How are the boy's grades?"

"Poor."

"So unlike the father."

"Like night and day."

"But no, it's the queen. She has taken interest in the family."

"The *queen*!" The monsignor's eyes popped out of his head like a frog's. "She's interested in the Hoffe family?"

"Calm yourself, Iraneous," said the archbishop. Turning to Father Mazarin, he said, "The monsignor has never been able to forgive Alber Hoffe."

"A modern-day Judas Iscariot if there ever was one," said Iraneous.

"They have a long history, you see," explained the archbishop. "The monsignor and Alber were peers at the seminary." Father Mazarin looked across the table at Monsignor Iraneous, who managed to not betray his feelings any further as he listened to the archbishop relate the tale. "They were peers, but only in class. Alber Hoffe was by far the superior student; his intellect has never been surpassed by any to this day."

"I see," said Father Mazarin, nodding slowly.

"Do you know Father Groupon?" the archbishop asked.

"I have heard of him," answered Mazarin. "A radical libertarian priest from what I've been told."

"The thorn in my foot is my younger brother. And I don't mean brother figuratively, I mean it *literally*."

"I see," replied Father Mazarin.

"Like you, he was spreading the gospel in the far north . . . only, after the Pagani Uprising. As with most civil unrest, there is little food and much hunger. A widow begged Father Groupon to take her eldest boy, for not only was he precocious, but there simply were too many mouths to feed. That boy was Alber Hoffe, though Hoffe was his baptismal name. Groupon brought him to Jesut Edin where we clothed him, fed him, and gave him the best education. A beautiful boy, and as bright as clear light. Naturally, he outgrew the seminary. Perhaps our mistake was when we sent him to the University of Jesut Edin to further his studies. Unbeknownst to us, he was introduced to science. At first, he remained steadfast and faithful. But one day, he told us that he had fallen in love. Said student was Lisbeth Proudst, quite the capture for a Pagani orphan. Sure, we would have preferred him to become a priest, but a lay Christian we could accept. Had I known what was coming, I would never have condoned any of it."

"And what was that?"

"Marriage and children were just the beginning. Where it *ended* is the problem."

"Where it ended?" queried Mazarin.

"It ended badly . . . in pure blasphemy. He started to worship *reason* and *science*. God became a distant third. In full knowledge of his actions, Alber turned his back on the church. One day . . . to *my face*, he said, 'I no longer believe in God.' To *my face!*" The archbishop crossed himself, followed by the monsignor. Father Mazarin duly joined. "On many occasions I offered him the sacrament of reconciliation, and when he became ill, his wife, Lisbeth, begged him to receive it, but each time he refused. He said, 'I only believe what I can see with my eyes, or measure with my instruments.' And those were his exact words."

Monsignor Iraneous piled on. "I have never known a more self-righteous man."

"And for it he suffered greatly," countered the archbishop gruffly, his head nodding once to punctuate the tenor of his mood. "And God put disease and boils upon his skin . . ." he continued, but his voice softened. "Surely, he will now suffer the fiery torments of hell for all eternity. And *your* penance, Monsignor, is to pray for him," the archbishop reproached Iraneous, turning toward him. "It is only your pride, Iraneous, that denies him your forgiveness."

"Your Eminence," said the monsignor, bowing his head. Father Mazarin looked over at him to see if his affect was sincere. He could not tell. After a moment of contrition, Iraneous' eyes blazed upon the archbishop. "On what grounds does the queen interfere on the family's behalf?"

"It has to do with Julian."

"It is not possible!" The monsignor's disbelief was tangible. "The daughter?" he said, his voice sounding haunted.

"Yes," replied the archbishop, "but I assure you, Monsignor"—he raised his finger—"babies and royal duties will be the end of her scientific pursuits. As for the boy, I don't aspire to fill the seminary with dull-witted ones, but we will shoulder divine patience and accept him. After all, not all of God's designs do we see." He glanced at Father Mazarin. "His ways are mysterious, are they not?"

"Mysterious indeed," agreed Mazarin.

The archbishop's eyes remained upon him. "Tell me your opinion, Father—is spotted fever a religious concern, or is it a scientific one?"

"Can it not be both?" asked Mazarin.

"No!" bellowed the archbishop, pounding the table with his fist.

Startled by the outburst, Father Mazarin reeled back in his chair. For a fleeting second he imagined the archbishop as a marauding giant wielding a club. "Faith is the *only* foundation!" he proclaimed. "Every priest, every student, every parishioner . . . *must be taught.* They must understand this as deeply as the apostle Paul. Even the savage Pagani are nothing compared to the malediction of science. We must *never* allow it to erode the *via sancti fides.*"

7

Prince Heberdy's Quarters, the Royal Palace

Colette tapped her fingers against the doorframe, waiting for Jyacko. He was tall and gangly, and even when he hurried, he appeared slow. Jyacko insisted on bringing up the rear. Perhaps it was his natural position as he was the tallest and could see over everyone's heads. As he strode past, Colette kept her eyes on the corridor, listening for any hint or sign of them being followed. Colette had told the butler and maids to let the five of them come unattended, but that didn't mean they would. She was certain that Julian had the palace staff reporting her doings.

Without the faintest sound, Colette shut the doors. Inserting a brass key, she turned slowly until she heard a hard click. Depositing it into the pocket of her dress, Colette pivoted, and without the slightest glance up, she marched forward. The five parted.

The entry room was long and slender but spacious as a ballroom. Couches of differing shapes and sizes; rugs and runners; statuettes and busts of dead queens, duchesses, and unknown bald men; vases and dressers adorned with lace doilies; and various specimens of handcrafted furniture were all positioned in meticulous order. Tall, thin arched doors filled with square panes stood overlooking the palace lawns, dispersed symmetrically along the entire length of the room on either side. During lightning storms, Colette liked to fling them wide open—there was nothing quite like curtains blowing in a driving rain. Above, painted ceilings framed with gilded moldings rendered an array of pastoral scenes. To Colette, everything was perfect, and thus, perfectly dull. The room bothered her so much that she often covered the doors in black fabric, leaving the hall in a perpetual state of gloom.

Queen Beatrice hated when she did this and berated her for it. "A princess does not hide in the dark, Colette . . . nor does she act so morbid." But what the queen failed to realize was she was not hiding. She simply *preferred* the dark. In fact, her alterations made her inwardly ecstatic. What's more, what the queen said was false. If she *was* a princess, she was a princess without pedigree, which in plainspeak translated to "bastard." Worse than a bastard, though: Colette, and Marius for that matter, was a child of a courtesan, and the only difference between a courtesan and a street whore was the clientele—only the well-heeled sought the affections of Crespula.

Colette led the five into the smoking room where she had taken her renovations a step further. Normally, it was reserved for men to drink and smoke and discuss finances and affairs of the state. Marius never cared for such rituals, and since their father hadn't been seen in years, it was, in Colette's opinion, her prerogative to do with it as she pleased. Not only did she blanket the windows, she also veiled the royal portraits, including that of Prince Heberdy, their father. It was reported that he had only gone to the brothel to gather a friend, but upon seeing Crespula, became obsessed. For three years he would not allow her to see anyone besides himself. Heberdy's black heart had fallen into a pit from which only an aberrant, twisted form of love could grow. Many said Crespula was a sorceress and that she bewitched Heberdy. After all, she was Pagani, taken into captivity during the Great Uprising . . . which went a long way in explaining Colette's blue eyes.

Illegitimate children were not unheard of in the trials and tribulations of Jesut Edin royalty, but any courtesan who dared conceive one, let alone two, be forewarned! They were dealt with harshly by the Black Coats. Before fleeing Jesut Edin, Crespula made Heberdy promise to take Marius and Colette under his protection. He managed to honor his agreement, but went no further than abandoning them in his wing of the palace . . . before he himself disappeared across the Swaran Sea. But crying children are hard to ignore, and eventually Queen Beatrice took them into her care.

At the far end of the room was a giant painting of King Anastopheles' army crossing the Uran Plateau before the Battle of Okomorling. Colette lifted a burning candelabra off the table and walked up to the floor-to-ceiling canvas. She took hold of the frame and pulled. The entire painting swung outward, revealing the faint lines of a door. Glancing over her shoulder, she noticed Jyacko had picked up the second candlestick.

Four years prior, on his first day of lyceum, Jyacko had fumbled like a puppy under his long legs, going from one group to another, happy to be with everyone, not yet sure with whom he belonged. This phase didn't last but a couple of months until Jyacko found his niche, a cluster of boys, cadets, training to be officers. With one simple decision, Jyacko joined the single most powerful cabal of men—the military. And in doing so, he erased the most significant aspect of adolescent anxiety, social acceptance. For now, all Jyacko had to do was obey the rules of membership. The directives were simple enough: dress accordingly; be polite, particularly in high society; be courteous to women of equal or higher stature; stand for personal honor; temper one's emotions, especially vulnerable feelings; and most of all, follow orders! The requirements were uncomplicated. So instead of a goofy, loose-limbed boy, Jyacko became stiff as his worsted blue cadet coat. Marius found the new Jyacko charming, but then, Marius was himself a soldier. Colette was not impressed. She preferred the gangly puppy, but she did appreciate not having to remind him to help, unlike the others.

Feeling her way, Colette's fingers soon found the hidden lever. Seizing it, she released the door. A rampant smell of dust and cold was exhumed from behind the wall. The initial step was a bit high, but after that it was just a narrow stone corridor. All the residences in the palace had a means of escape. This particular one emptied into a private mausoleum in the cemetery, a short distance from the outer wall of the palace.

Soon the corridor echoed with shuffling feet. Colette often thought of herself as a ringmaster, leading a family of bears into a circus tent. A good way down the tunnel was a contingency armory that had been built into the passage. It was a sizable room, certainly plenty big for their purposes. She and Marius had removed all the ancient armor and swords and piled them in a heap in the auxiliary guardroom before closing its door, probably forever. Afterward they scoured the palace for furniture, making midnight raids into lonely corners and obscure halls, carting off tables and chairs whose disappearance would not be noticed. Around one of Queen Beatrice's priceless Madge rugs, they placed leather armchairs in a circle facing inward, furnishing the room in a manner befitting a secret society.

Colette moved around the chamber lighting candles until the room glowed bright. Setting her candelabra down, she turned to find four of them already seated. Only Jyacko remained standing. Colette pretended not to notice the unclaimed chair that would have been Marius'. She took note of Willian's tense face. His jaw seized tight. She knew he would come out fighting, but she could handle him. Colette took her seat, Jyacko promptly followed.

There was a moment of silence before Yelena began. "I call to order the twenty-seventh meeting of the Secret Society of Erebus," she said, her voice sullen. Yelena's idea of the occult meant that one had to be somber. "Those present," she said, as if she were introducing guests at a funeral, "Willian Delft, President. Lazar Quitt, Treasurer. Jyacko Cotswald, Secretary. Colette Proudst, Chief Scout, Linguist, and Cartographer. Martine Strout, Esotericist. Lastly, myself, Yelena Odin, Master of Ceremonies. Absent, Captain Marius Proudst, Master-at-Arms."

"Now let us take Don Anton's oath of the magi."

All the voices in the room incanted:

Seven rays upon the golden bower, seven
petals of the white flower, bound by one that
none can split asunder. Our intention noble,
our purpose clear, to enter the realm where
spirits roam. To pass through the veil is our
aim, for form is empty and emptiness is form.
Having consumed the apple, the gates of per-
ception were sealed, but none here shall rest
until we break the chains of mortal imprison-
ment and partake, once more, in the rapture
. . . and freedom . . . of the limitless.

As the echoing voices in the chamber silenced, Willian's voice rang out. "So, Colette, have you heard anything from Marius?"

"No, Willian, I haven't. All I know," Colette continued, keeping her eyes fixed upon his, "is that he succeeded . . . and that Marius alone survived." Everyone besides Willian kept their eyes planted firmly on the rug.

"The Pagani are taking up arms again!" said Lazar with a quick glance up.

"Obviously, the Ayn Noor is important to them."

"We had *no* idea this was going to be such a firestorm," prompted Willian. "If we had, surely, we wouldn't have . . ."

"*We?*" interjected Colette. "Or do you mean 'you'? You cannot speak for *everyone*, Willian!"

"Fine. *I* wouldn't have pursued the Ayn Noor if *I* had known people were going to *die*. Not to mention setting off another uprising."

"That's not our doing; it's merely an unfortunate conse-quence," replied Colette.

"But what if they track any of this back to us?" asked Lazar.

"Marius would never say anything. So, if none of you speak, we should be fine."

"But what now?" pleaded Martine. "The Ayn Noor is in the possession of the governor. All our efforts have been for nothing. Such a shame . . . How I wanted to hold it!" Martine pulled her hands to her chest as she closed her eyes.

"They'll bring it to Jesut Edin. Julian will be desperate to have it," stated Colette. "I say, let them bring it to us."

"We'll never see it! Julian will place it in the far reaches of Grebald," said Lazar.

"What are we, the Secret Society of Pessimists?" said Colette, looking around at each one of them. "Chins up! All is not lost. On the contrary, we should take heart."

"Explain . . ." said Yelena, tilting her head as she looked at Colette.

"Well, for one, now we know there *is* truth in the Pagani legends," answered Colette. "When Marius went north, we knew no such thing. We didn't even know, for certain, if the jewel existed. It appears that the myths are real, and now all you want to do is pull the covers over your heads!"

"Before this we were playing a game," countered Willian. "We tell our parents that we are going to meet each other for schoolwork, but instead we come here, or head to Grappa's to speak with spirits . . . but nothing ever really came of it."

"I swear I felt something touch my leg," said Martine. "And Yelena might have heard a man's voice."

"No, I definitely heard a man's voice," said Yelena, shuddering.

"Yeah, but what did he say?" asked Willian, reaching his hands out and waving his fingers at Yelena. "Luub-*jok*!"

"So what exactly are you trying to say?" demanded Yelena.

"Aside from a ghost that yearns for grain alcohol, no one else has ever heard anything!" grumbled Willian.

"It's not our fault you're not attuned," said Yelena.

"But it's always you two. Grappa makes a little suggestion, and both of you start trembling." Martine lowered her brow and scowled at him. "My main point is that no one was getting hurt. Now it's for real. People have died! And Marius could have been killed."

"Marius knew the risk he was taking," added Colette.

Willian folded his arms and shook his head. "This is not pretend anymore," he said, looking around at the other four, avoiding Colette.

"Then stop pretending," Colette rebuked.

Willian focused intently on Martine. "I know I'm not the only one! Martine, you told me yesterday that you were having doubts."

"But I still want to hear what Colette has to say," she answered, lifting her nose and turning her head away from him.

"I agree," added Yelena. "Colette, you said this would suggest other legends are true. What legends do you have in mind?"

Colette gazed at each one of them in turn, looking them in the eye. "Have any of you heard of the Gates of Hell?"

It was as if everyone stopped breathing, until Lazar finally managed to squeak, "Good God, Colette! Do you ever stop!"

"Don't be scared by the word *hell* if that's what you are afraid of, Lazar. It's a translation! Probably the best that the historian Elgin Walchower could manage back in his day given the limitations of the Ilyrian lexicon. As far as I am concerned, he could just as easily have called it Angel's Gate or the Gates of Heaven, for it is simply a passageway connecting the spirit world to ours—and angels exist in the spirit realm just the same as demons. It is written that there exists a gate that, when opened, allows a man . . . or woman to pass, body and soul, into the spirit world and arrive at the Chasm of Eternity in order to return what doesn't belong." There was a tremor in Colette's voice.

"What doesn't belong?" asked Martine.

"It isn't obvious?"

The others looked blankly around at each other. "No," said Yelena finally.

"The Ayn Noor!"

"The diamond that Marius just stole?" asked Yelena.

"Yes, dear," replied Colette sarcastically. "By the Pagani's response, it makes me believe it even more. See, the story goes back to the earliest of their myths." With this Colette suddenly lifted a little book that none of them had noticed before and waved it in the air. *"Jurgen Jasper's Fairy Tales for Children,"* said Colette.

Yelena raised her voice. "We have that book in our nursery back home . . . but no one reads it," she added, her voice trailing off.

"Apparently," stated Colette. "The book was written well over two centuries ago; it has long gone quite out of style. What people don't realize is that many of the stories are old Pagani folktales. There have been other publications, but his version is probably the closest to the original. What I find refreshing is that it's not overly pedantic. He's the only one who speaks of the goddess Iana and her role with the Ayn Noor. Let me read part of it for you."

When Colette was finished, she closed the book. A protracted silence followed until Willian grumbled, "That's *stupid*! A hole in the sky? A Spiral Path that leads people into a new world? It's . . . ridiculous!"

"Well, I think it's beautiful," countered Martine.

"What did Don Anton say in his treatise on the dark arts?" added Yelena.

"'Disbelief is the first step to believing.'" Willian rolled his eyes.

"Congratulations, Willian, there's hope for you yet," said Colette. "But let's not forget," she continued, "not so long ago, the mythical diamond seemed just as absurd to all of you."

"But what does all this have to do with the Gates of Hell?" asked Lazar.

"I've already told you!" Colette's eyes flashed as she looked at Lazar. "The gates," she emphasized, "are real! They're an actual place! Where one of us, or all of us, could step off this world . . . and enter the spirit realm!"

• • •

Willian noticed Colette's imperious blue eyes never seemed to waver. They were alluring and magnetic. All objects of lesser density seemed to get pulled into her orbit. Was it her beauty? Was it her coldness, or her unflinching hardness? Willian tried to remember if he had ever seen her smile.

Colette was slender, which made her look taller than she really was. She had high cheekbones, and the ends of her straight hair, which was parted down the middle, closed around her thin face like black curtains. From behind them, her eyes seemed to sparkle, alive as two icicles in the sunlight.

Colette's lips were not full, but delineated and sharp like her nose. Unlike a typical Ilyrian, her skin was pale, almost pasty.

Willian himself secretly disdained girls. Thus, Colette's enchantments did not work much on him. But others . . . they seemed to fawn over her, whether out of fear or some perverse wish for her approval—or simply to be in her sphere of influence. At times he just wanted to slap Martine and Yelena, knock them out of their trances. Just last night Martine swore up and down she wanted out, yet here she was ingratiating herself. Even the queen seemed to defer to Colette's wishes. Willian's father, Erol Balzar, the Chamberlain of the House, often came home ranting that she alone would destroy the Proudst name. He called her "the maniacal vesper" who was "a bigger threat to the empire than the Moohady!"

Prince Julian was even more obsessed. He insisted on knowing every detail of her life, from her whereabouts to her friends to what she was wearing. He often just wanted to hear about the secret society. Julian found their doings comical, and his snickers inevitably crescendoed into prolonged bouts of laughter. Afterward his mood seemed to lighten. Willian was certain Prince Julian would piss himself laughing when told about the Gates of Hell.

Willian himself hated the secret society. He felt as if he were in some kind of purgatory in which he was biding his time, sleepwalking through a meaningless game, and ultimately wasting his precious youth. His reward would come, though, but only when the queen died and King Julian bestowed a royal appointment upon him. Surely, it wouldn't be much longer, after which he never again would have to abide by Colette's nonsense.

◆ ◆ ◆

Jyacko watched Willian. He couldn't quite identify what bothered him, except that Willian never truly seemed interested in what they were doing. Jyacko turned his attention back to Colette. He didn't believe what people said, that she had no feelings. If anything, he felt sorry for her. Once, he had come to their quarters to speak with Marius, who had summoned him, and found Colette collapsed on a couch. She was barefoot—her feet were covered in cuts and dried blood. Her dress was torn and dirty, and her eyes were vacant. She was the saddest-looking creature he had ever seen. Marius had told him to not mind her, that "she is not herself today."

Jyacko's family were commoners, albeit wealthy ones. Colette and Marius were the outcome of a love union between a commoner and a prince. Thus the commoners considered them to be their own. If either ventured into the city, one would hear all about it—where they went, what they did. Sure, people would get dark pleasure from hearing about the extravagances and scurrilous adventures of Prince Julian and his entourage, but interest in the comings and goings of Marius and Colette bordered on religion. Jyacko's family were very proud of his relationship with them. Jyacko himself felt great dedication to both. What's more, Colette had personally invited him to join the Secret Society of Erebus. Unbeknownst to any of the other members, even before taking the vow of loyalty, he swore before God and queen to protect Colette. And it was Willian, not the Gates of Hell, that he was most concerned about.

◆ ◆ ◆

"Come. There's something I want to show you," said Colette, standing up. She turned and headed toward a large table where maps were scattered, intermixed with books and burning candles. Amidst all of these were various tools: a compass, a caliper, and several rulers. There was plenty of ink and quills and lots of papers—many with various notes, numbers, and mysterious symbols scribbled upon them.

"Where'd you get all these books?" asked Yelena, leaning her hip against the table.

"The royal archives, if you must know."

"I'm surprised they let you take them," said Yelena. Colette looked at her with a puzzled expression.

"She didn't ask," denounced Willian. "She *stole* them!"

"What do you mean 'stole'?" said Colette, turning toward him.

"Does anyone know you have them?" he asked, keeping her gaze.

"What matters is that I *use* them," she replied dismissively, returning her focus to the table. With her palm open, she passed her hand in a sweeping gesture over the pile. "These . . . precious tomes," she started, "were banished to the archives, or in other words, to the basement, where old books and charts apparently go to die. Honestly, I am not sure anyone even knows they exist. But for our purposes"—she touched the edge of a faded parchment—"this one is most important! Viktor Badstuber's map. Without it, none of these discoveries would have ever been possible."

"Is that what you used to find the Ayn Noor?" asked Martine.

Colette nodded. "After Marius captured the Ayn Noor, I studied the map in even more detail. Back when it was printed, there was no empire. The land was open and without modern borders. But there are things of interest," added Colette. "Anyone want to have a look?" She lifted up a hunk of convex glass for someone to take. Willian reached forward and took it from her hand. Colette pointed toward the bottom of the chart. Willian leaned over the table with the lens between his fingers.

After a moment, Yelena inquired, "Well . . . what do you see?"

"Nothing, really . . . just faded lines."

Colette frowned. She took the lens and plunked it back down. "Look right here!" she pronounced gruffly.

Dropping his head again, Willian studied it before declaring flatly, "All I see is a faded triangle. Is that what I'm supposed to see?"

"Yes, that's what you're *supposed* to see'!" responded Colette dryly. Willian gave the lens back. Martine stepped forward. Colette handed it to her, and she leaned in to have a look. After each of them had a turn, Colette spoke. "Even though the red mark is faded, it is distinct, so I assume the cartographer placed it there for a reason."

"It could have been wine or tomato sauce spilled from Viktor's supper," suggested Willian.

"You know, Willian, it's because of people like you that nothing is ever discovered! But what I can't figure out is why you make up these stories in the first place. Is it simply to be disagreeable, or to thwart progress?"

Willian shrugged. Yelena spoke in his place. "So if it was placed there on purpose, what does it signify?"

"*That's* the right question to ask!" said Colette. "Since there is no key explaining the triangle, I decided that I should find its approximate location on a modern map. Searching for topographical similarities, rivers, mountain ranges, and whatnot, I looked for anything that might give me a clue . . . and then I found this!" Colette traced her finger along a sharply curved line. She then went to the Badstuber map and traced the same line. "This is the one telltale landmark that matches both!" said Colette. "Do any of you recognize it?"

Willian's eyes got wider. "That's the Uroboros Loop, the big bend in the Donner, not far from Jesut Edin."

"Precisely. It's the river's defining turn. It is as unmistakable now as it was back then . . . and the triangle is just south of the big turn."

"But . . ." said Willian, his face showing a hint of concern, "that would be Jesut Edin!"

"Very good!" proclaimed Colette. "You're smarter than you look."

Willian glared at her.

"Now, I might remind you," Colette continued, "Viktor Badstuber created this map before the Ilyrians built Jesut Edin. He was King Demontagnac's official cartographer, given the task of mapping what was the new frontier. As you all know, way back then, the Ilyrians lived in various cities along the coast of the Swaran Sea."

"So what you are suggesting is the red triangle signifies something that was here before Jesut Edin existed?" said Yelena.

"Yes, but more than that, I am proposing that the red triangle signifies something important that *coincides* with the exact location of Jesut Edin."

"But what could it have been?" asked Martine.

"Grass," said Lazar, grinning at Willian.

"Lots of it," agreed Willian with a wink.

"What our history books conveniently forget to mention is that there were people here before us!"

Martine blurted out, "The Pagani!"

"There were twelve tribes, according to Viktor's field notes, that lived up and down the Donner. At first they welcomed us. It was only once they realized we wanted all of their land that they began to resist our presence."

"From the Swaran Sea to the Riphean Mountains," began Lazar in what was a common recitation, a history lesson from grammar school. "From the Parnas Dunes to the Inhospitable Coast and all the fertile land between. This is the covenant between God and the Ilyrians. This land is our divine right."

"At least that is *our* version," answered Colette, looking over at Lazar, clearly unimpressed. "But . . ." she continued, turning back to the others, "according to Viktor, not long after our arrival, eleven of the tribes retreated to the mountains."

"What about the twelfth?" asked Lazar. "You said there were twelve tribes."

"The twelfth tribe is what the Pagani call the Warsalay, or the Lost Tribe. Apparently, they did not leave. This point was made very clear."

"What happened to them?" asked Yelena.

Colette raised her brow as if to say, *Do I* really *need to tell you?*

"Oh," said Yelena, her face reddening. "But why would they stay, knowing they would be killed?"

"My theory is they stayed to protect something. The Warsalay chose to make a stand. Not because it was strategic, for it clearly was not, but because it was a sacred site. So sacred, in fact, that they were willing to die to protect it." Silence circulated through the room. Colette returned to her seat. The rest duly followed. Once everyone was seated, Colette continued, "There are a few reasons why cities rise. Most importantly they must have access to food and water, or at least the commerce to bring them such things. A lesser-known reason—not unheard of for a conquering people—is to build on top of the previous culture's most sacred site. It's a way of demoralizing them. After all, the conqueror's gods must be superior."

"What could be so sacred?" asked Martine.

"I believe it's the place where Queemquesh and the Pagani emerged from the underworld, which I suspect is ~~might also~~ be the Gates of Hell. To the Warsalay, this was worth dying for." /

"That's all conjecture," stated Willian.

Colette held up her finger. "For once, Willian, I agree with you. I wasn't satisfied with my suspicions either, so I went to the Grebald prison tower."

"You went to *Grebald* to visit a prisoner?" exclaimed Yelena, touching her hand to her chest.

Colette nodded. "Yes, to see the one they call Skadje. She was one of the leaders of the uprising forty years ago."

"She's still alive?" asked Martine.

"Very much so!"

"They say she's a Pagani witch!" added Yelena.

"They say," answered Colette.

"Why didn't you tell us any of this before?" asked Willian.

"I didn't want to scare you . . . or maybe I don't trust you."

"Funny, Colette," he said, shaking his head, but his voice sounded strained.

"What was it like in there?" asked Martine, whispering as she leaned toward Colette.

"I can tell you about the macabre of the dungeons; they are harrowing—but meeting Skadje is . . . not for the faint of heart."

"So what did she tell you?"

"Let's just say, she confirmed my suspicions. That the Ayn Noor was real and the gates are indeed below Jesut Edin! And the time will be soon upon us."

"What are you suggesting," asked Willian, "that we start digging?"

"It's well known there are caverns below the city," replied Colette. "So you'll be relieved to know there are other ways."

"The ravines," burst out Martine, her excitement unbridled. "We could go down the ravines!"

"But what about the Creepers?" protested Yelena. "You know what they say."

Colette's voice peaked. "Who are the Creepers anyway?"

"Rat people!" said Willian.

"Thieves!" added Lazar.

"Those are the things we tell ourselves, but who are they *really*?" stressed Colette. "Where do they sleep? Do they live by themselves, or in families? And if so, where? And what do they do during the day? We're all so afraid of them, but it's as if everyone is taking everyone else's word for it. Nobody finds out for themselves!"

No one said a word until Willian broke the silence. "My guess is that they come together at night and murder Ilyrians who wander too close to the ravines."

"Why are they so small?" asked Martine.

"Because they eat our trash!" said Lazar.

"All I know," said Yelena, "is it's common knowledge that the Creepers are dangerous."

"There might be another way," offered Colette, seeing the conversation was going nowhere, "but we'll need a boat."

"A *boat*! What kind of boat?"

"Preferably one that doesn't sink," quipped Lazar.

Ignoring Lazar, Martine queried, "Why do we need a boat?"

"To cross the lake."

"*Lake!* Where?"

"The one under Jesut Edin," said Colette, her voice calm. "It's well known," continued Colette, "there is a lake under the city . . . that the palace has its own supply of water. After all, why would its gardens be so lush and green when the rest of Jesut Edin is brown?"

Willian's face flashed red. "Colette, you are *never* to discuss such matters."

"The Secret Society of Erebus discusses whatever it wants to discuss." At that, Willian shook his head in disbelief while crossing his arms.

"My grandfather's got a rowboat he used for fishing on the Donner," offered Yelena.

"Can we use it?" asked Martine.

"I am pretty sure. It just sits in the yard, and he's way too old."

"Who's in?"

"I am!" said Jyacko, speaking for the first time.

Colette almost blushed; for a moment she actually felt moved. "Jyacko is coming. Who else?"

"I'm crazy scared," said Martine, "but I think we should at least try."

"Me too," added Yelena.

They all turned to look at Willian and Lazar. "So what about you *boys*?" asked Martine.

For as much as Colette didn't care for Willian, she knew that without Marius, he and Lazar would be needed. If it came to a fight, or carrying a heavy load, they would be vital. Lazar would certainly do whatever Willian decided.

"As president of this society," said Willian, drawing a deep breath, "I want it to be noted I am against this expedition. But I'll go *if* we get the necessary supplies, like muskets and dry powder."

"And sabers," added Lazar.

"We'll get those and more," said Colette, even as she cringed inwardly. The idea of walking through dim caverns with the two of them carrying loaded pistols was about as stupid a thing as she could imagine . . . but for now, it was a start.

"When do we go?" asked Martine.

"As soon as I get hold of the Ayn Noor," answered Colette. The five of them stared at her in disbelief. Colette held up a card with a large red dot in the middle. "Do you remember these?" They all nodded. "The day you receive this card, meet me at midnight at the mausoleum. You know the one." Again, they nodded. "You five will bring the boat, and I will supply the guns and powder and whatnot. Have your own clothes and provisions ready," said Colette. "Be ready to go at a moment's notice."

8

North of Patswil

Golden rays of sun filtered through the portals of the far-away canopy, illuminating a lone girl running through a sea of giant ferns. Between the earth and the lofty boughs, particles hung suspended in the shafts of light as if in their own celestial orbits. The conifers, the pillars of Bajarmaland with their colossal trunks and sturdy branches, held back the sun, protecting the streams and verdant mosses sequestered beneath the trees.

As Roan bounded forward, the turf below her feet felt soft and spongy from all the matted roots and needles thrown off the heads of the wind-scratched pines. She couldn't stop thinking about her visit to the Pukka, or the memories from her naming ceremony that had flooded her moments before her meeting with Ruus. Issa had warned her, "You will forget . . . until it's time to remember." But what strange timing! Of one thing Roan was certain—spirit may be mysterious, but frivolous it was not!

As Roan ducked the occasional branch and wove her way among the ferns, she considered Minol. Would he reveal the meaning of her name, Protector of Little Blue Snake? Roan had known the whereabouts of the Noumenos dwelling for years. It was not too far from where she had grown up. After the uprising, Katriyana had converted to Christianity and hired her grandfather to build a chapel. Roan considered this *might* be how Minol knew of her, but the possibility seemed remote, for she hadn't yet been born. Roan had never met any Noumenos in person, or at least, if she had, she was too young to remember. Regardless, he knew she existed, and shamans, like Issa, saw things that ordinary people did not.

Roan was known in the clan for her stamina, but what no one knew was her secret. It was simple—the beauty of the earth gave her feet wings. From the silky moss crowding the trickling brooks, to the tall grasses bowing in the wind, to the corcu's willowy song in the blue sky above the tree-barren peaks. Everything about Bajarmaland made Roan want to run. Often, she imagined herself a springing doe, or even a wolf attempting to round a herd of red deer. At times she had an urge to run faster and faster until she would either consume the world or collapse trying. The Yatu teachings counseled her not to go too hard. "Unless you are in danger, it is reckless to run too fast. Gasping air through the mouth is clumsy. This will only hasten your exhaustion."

As Roan drove onward, she scanned the ground for the subtle quality of openness. The arching fronds made the trail near impossible to locate. She knew she was headed in the right direction though, for she had kept the sun just above her right

shoulder, guiding her northeast. Soon she would arrive at Little
Guanyin Creek. Roan had some familiarity with the Guanyin
watershed. She had hunted here last autumn, but unlike then,
Roan had left her hunting bow and arrows behind. The only
weapon she brought with her was her knife, which would not
impede her movement.

She had risen while the day was as opaque as obsidian.
Everyone, except Tieg and Farwah, was still asleep. The distinct curve of Farwah's spine was easy to recognize. Tieg sat
close by, her head bowed between her knees as she blew on last
night's coals, coaxing them out of their ashen slumber. Roan
lay watching as a flame burst, throwing light to the four corners of the lodge.

Fire was the center of all things in the oikos, just as the sun
is the center and mother of all life. At night, putting out the
fire was the last thing they did, and in the morning, lighting
it the first. Around the fire pit all things important took place:
cooking, eating, storytelling, weaving bark, repairing clothes,
and sewing hides. Hanging over the firepit, from giant beams,
was a thick log with wooden pegs that held a smattering of
kitchen necessities: herbs, both medicinal and savory, dried
horse bladders for water storage, clay earthenware, utensils
and tools, and a variety of smoked meats.

There was only one door to any oikos. Traditionally it faced
east, where the sun rises on the equinox. All the lodges were
built with Bajarmaland pines—from the sturdy roofs with
their steep pitches made to support the heavy winter snows
to the soft mats woven from the inner bark. Along the outer
edges of the cabin were the sleeping platforms with animal
furs aplenty. The younger warriors and trainees shared bunks,
while the senior warriors had their own.

Each oikos had two leaders, the sun and the moon. Tieg was the sun. She led with the strength of her force, and her rules could not be bent. Farwah was the moon. She was the elder, and her rules ebbed and flowed with the needs of the moment. She led with her kindness and stories. Tieg and Farwah were the final authority on all matters in the oikos, just as Ruus, their chieftain, was the final authority on all matters in the tsik. Roan had never heard Tieg and Farwah argue. If they did, it was never done in front of the other warriors. In Roan's oikos there were sixteen women, ten warriors and six novices.

As she lay in bed that morning, Roan took a moment to listen to Gynn's untroubled breath. It was smooth and even, as breath is when unencumbered in sleep. Roan often thanked the goddess that Gynn was her bunkmate—Vera tossed and kicked ferociously in her sleep. Gynn, on the other hand, lay straight as a board. Even asleep she was reluctant to take up space. Gynn was only twelve and probably wouldn't wake for a few hours yet. She had joined their tsik two summers before, but had had great difficulty adjusting to life as a Yatu. Some girls knew from an early age they wanted nothing more than to be warriors, while others were given by their families—some because there were too many mouths to feed, others because it was an honor to have a Yatu in one's kin. There was a marked difference between those who chose to join and those who were given. Roan suspected that Gynn had been sent against her will. She was not a natural warrior, only a formidable sufferer.

Springing to her feet, Roan grabbed her suede leggings from a peg on the wall. She tied her belt snugly, then secured her knife. Next she pulled a strap of leather around her chest and laced it tight at the front. Her breasts were by no means large, but the garment made running much easier. After this, she took her leather top, the one with an open neck and put it on. She then grabbed her moccasins with the thick wapiti soles. They were best for long travel. Lacing them up, she sealed the straps with double knots. Lastly, from beneath her pillow, she took a pouch tied to a string and dropped it over her head. In it was a small figurine of the mother goddess, Oosh Oosh, given to her by her mother. From the reservoir of her enormous breasts, all animals were fed.

At the pit, Farwah handed her a steaming cup of broth. Roan held it to her nose—acasia root and plumkit. The plumkit was a calming herb, the acasia, stimulating. She would need both, for she had a long day ahead of her. Tieg and Farwah said nothing. Morning was a quiet time in the oikos, a time to reflect upon one's dreams and gather one's energy for the day. Both Farwah and Tieg occasionally glanced her way. Roan could sense the tension in their bodies—these were uneasy times.

Theirs was the southernmost Yatu tsik. But it was considered the most important in all Bajarmaland, for they had to bear the burden of protecting the Ayn Noor. Ever since the theft, life had changed drastically. The shame of losing the talisman was great. The weight of failure was still upon them, and many Yatu were done whispering. They had begun pointing fingers and blaming one another in broad daylight. Ruus, their new leader, had done nothing to stop this. It seemed she almost welcomed it. Emotions were burning hot as the repercussions from the theft were still rippling outward. The waves had rolled to the farthest reaches of Bajarmaland. On the previous full moon, chieftains from every Pagani tribe had descended upon their tsik. They had come to see if the rumors were true. Words, after all, are mostly air. By the end of the great council, Ferja, their beloved leader, was expelled to the wilds, to lead a solitary life, forever barring her from contact with other Pagani. A grim conviction, but many, particularly the Red Bow Clan, felt the council had been too lenient. Tieg had warned each of the girls not to draw unwanted attention to themselves. She was certain that the tribes would be seeking another scapegoat.

The Red Bows were burning Ilyrian villages up and down the Uran Plateau. Ruus had them preparing for war, for surely, the Ilyrians would not distinguish between tribes. Most of the Pagani had been resistant to another uprising; it had taken years to regain their strength from the last one. But the Red Bows were leaving them little choice. It was either fight as one or die alone. But unlike in the Great Uprising, the Pagani were using muskets this time. Even the Yatu were abandoning tradition, which is why Minol had sent three crates. Roan could still not fathom what Minol could possibly want from her. Why would he send so many muskets? She would soon have answers. If all went well, she would arrive at his house by evening.

Roan set down her empty bowl. Tieg and Farwah said nothing. Next to the front door, she lifted a bag she had packed the night before. It held an extra pullover, another pair of leggings, and a bow drill for starting a fire. As for food, there was a small pouch of dried berries, nuts, and smoked trout. Tying the satchel across her shoulder, she braced it snuggly against her body. This way it would not interfere with her running. Roan lifted the crossbar that locked the door at night. She set it carefully against the wall before slipping out of the lodge.

Roan inhaled the fresh air. She looked up at the morning light lining the edges of the faraway clouds in a coral pink, "mare's tails" as her father called these high clouds with frayed ends. A solitary bird began singing. Dawn was creeping northward, but it would be a while; light had yet to grace the tops of the trees, and the ground was still shrouded in darkness. But the lack of light did not deter Roan, for she knew the trails around the tsik. All she needed to navigate them was the subtlest hint of shade and shape. Roan began to run.

It was nearing midday when she first heard Little Guanyin Creek. There was no mistaking the sound of the stream. Roan slowed her pace. From up on a high bank, she caught a glimpse of it through the trees. She came to a halt—her heartbeat was strong. Arriving at an opening, she found herself with a view of a wide portion of open water. In the shadow of a young pine, a drop of sweat wriggled off her chin and fell onto her legging, where it was absorbed quickly by the suede. Roan scanned the far bank for any sign of movement. There was nothing unnatural, only the normal activities of river life: the lazy-making drone of insects, the occasional blow of the wind through the branches. Roan zigzagged through the trees to the edge of the stream and squatted behind a bush near the water. There she searched for any sign of movement, human *or* animal. Normally, the Pagani didn't hunt this far south; it was far too close to Ilyrian territory . . . but due to the Red Bow's aggression, it would be unlikely that she would come upon any Ilyrians either. The most sensible ones had already retreated to Okomorling, taking cover behind the high walls of the city, awaiting the arrival of troops.

On the far side, a raucous band of sparrows chased each other from bush to bush. Amidst their chatter, Tieg's voice came to her. "The forest has many eyes and ears. Heed them all. Even an insect can alert you to the presence of danger." Roan watched and listened but noticed nothing untoward. There was hardly a breeze on the creek. A fresh brood of mayflies were being carried downstream, buoyed by a puff of warm air. Their diaphanous wings shone bright in the sunlight. Among them, an iridescent dragonfly hovered, latching on to one portly treat after another. The only evidence of the midair feast were the inedible wings that came twirling down. As ravenous as the dragonfly was, the sheer number of them made the slaughter more or less insignificant. *Perhaps the Ilyrians are like mayflies,* thought Roan. *There are so many, maybe it doesn't matter how many the Pagani kill—more will always follow.*

Little Guanyin was a wide stream, although only a small tributary of the Guanyin River, which emptied into the great Sombol. But it was certainly big enough to warrant careful selection when crossing. Roan's eyes drifted over to a group of bushes whose white blossoms were beginning to cluster around the tops—the north was losing its faint grip on spring.

After locating a few suitable rocks, Roan bent low and sprang for a river stone, then another. She kept on until she reached the far side. Here she ducked behind one of the bushes. Crouching, Roan watched the side from whence she'd so recently left to see if she was being followed. Seeing nothing alarming, Roan squatted on a rock next to the river's edge. Dipping her fingers into the water, she swirled them around, creating small eddies. She touched her forehead and offered a prayer to the river spirit. Roan then scooped a couple of handfuls to cool her neck and a couple more to moisten her mouth. The water tasted sweet. With the sun's reflection on her face, she ate a handful of nuts and dried berries. While she chewed, Roan admired a pretty yellow stone that sparkled on the river bottom. She reached down and plucked it out of the

stream. Turning it over in her fingers, she admired its purity—
it seemed impervious to stain or blemish. It was the size of her
thumbnail, and heavy too. Roan suspected this was the amber
metal that the Ilyrians sought. She pulled her pouch out from
under her shirt, and she placed the stone beside Oosh Oosh.

Roan directed her attention back to the riverbank. The
water level had lowered since the high of spring runoff. New
mud always made for easy tracking. Roan could see that a raven
had walked there yesterday, perhaps looking for a meal of juve-
nile snakes. Scanning farther down, she came upon the prints
of a weasel a couple of days old. When she turned upstream,
she locked eyes upon two large fresh prints—the front paws of
a Bajarmaland lion. It must have come to the river that morning to drink. She could see that the top edges of the prints had
only begun to dry; they couldn't have been more than a couple of hours old. This lion was big, and probably male from
the size of its paws. Roan recalled the Yatu teaching. "When
prey flees, the predator attacks. Never run from a lion. If one
approaches, stand your ground. Look it straight in the eye.
Make noise, bang sticks, become a formidable adversary. If it
attacks . . . fight!" Roan felt the knife at her side. Most likely,
the cat had other food on its mind, for not long ago Roan had
seen fresh deer droppings. As she was considering all of this,
a yellow butterfly danced up and down, passing right in front
of her nose. She took this as an omen, a sign that the lion was
hunting elsewhere. Regardless, she was forewarned.

She returned to running, stopping occasionally to listen.
At no time did she sense danger, or smell anything adverse.
An hour later, the land began to angle downward. At one
point she spotted the rim of a slender gorge coming out of the
mountains and, beyond the gorge, the Guanyin River flowing

southwest out of the canyon, glistening like a silverfish. Roan wanted to stay in the cover of the trees, but the slope became too steep. It pulled her relentlessly downhill, forcing her onto the barren rim. Although her destination was on the plateau, she knew she had to continue upriver toward the narrows to find the crossing. Years ago, a log had been dropped over the gorge for traversing. Roan began to run faster. The sooner she got off the rim, the better—she was far too visible.

It wasn't long before the corridor became covered in shadow—afternoon was upon her. She did not recall the crossing being so far. She should have already arrived. But then a thought occurred to her. What if the Red Bows had pushed the log over the edge? Roan played out the repercussions in her mind. If so, she would have to backtrack, taking the western rim all the way to the plateau, which meant she would then have no choice but to use the bridge that crossed the Sombol River at the garrison town of Patswil, the northernmost fortress in Ilyrian territory. The garrison town was hated by the Pagani. It was a symbol of Ilyrian cruelty and domination, for many Pagani had been imprisoned and tortured there during the Great Uprising. The bridge was the only safe way across the river without a boat. Ilyrians kept track of all who passed. Her father and mother had a small farm outside of Patswil, though her mother had recently sent word that they had fled to Okomorling. Roan's mother bore no pretenses that the Red Bows would spare her family. In their eyes she would be considered Ilyrian, or worse, a traitor. As Roan contemplated her options, she caught sight of the felled tree. The old trunk was as it had always been, just wide enough for one person, or horse, to pass. Only the bravest horse could cross over it, and even then, it would have to be led. The bridge was used for foot travel, as the Pagani intended.

As Roan approached the crossing, she could hear the Guanyin River churning far below. She looked over the edge. She could see whitecaps unfurling among the boulders in the turbulent water. Roan had little fear of heights, but nonetheless, a slip would be fatal. Roan recalled a Yatu teaching. "The most powerful weapon the warrior has is her mind. Place your attention on your fear, and you will manifest fear, place your attention on your task, and fear will pass." She locked her eyes on the giant trunk.

Roan's legs carried her swiftly across. Once she reached the opposite bank, she turned east, toward the Uran Plateau. Soon she picked up the trail again. Nearing the lowlands, Roan began to make out the stone battlements of Patswil. Roan knew she would eventually intersect the settlers' road, for it hugged the western edge of the Uran Plateau. The road was no more than a narrow path among trees, but an invaluable landmark, a wagon trail used by Ilyrian frontiersmen that led to their illicit settlements farther north. After the uprising, the Ilyrians felt emboldened to renege on their treaties and push into the unconquered lands. Most Pagani stayed clear of the trail, choosing to travel through the woods alongside it. The Noumenos dwelling would not be far now.

As she journeyed, she thought more about her mother. She had lived in the same oikos as Tieg and Ferja when they were young. When Roan had asked her parents to let her join the Yatu, her mother conceded without argument, for she recognized the pull from her own youth. Her father was less amenable. In his culture, girls were to be married. Women were the keepers of the house and were valued as mothers. In due time, however, her father consented. After all, Roan had by no means been a "normal" girl. Unlike her sisters she had never shown the slightest interest in playing with dolls. The last time she had played with them she had cut off all their hair. From then on, she was forbidden to play with her sisters' belongings. So Roan began to follow her brothers. At first, they were rough with her. It wasn't uncommon for them to lock her in the smokehouse. But even this was preferable to dolls.

Eventually her resilience won out, or was it that they discovered she wasn't afraid of snakes or a little blood or that she would not tattle on them? Although they were better than her at archery, none of them were as good as their mother, who could still hit a target accurately from across the field. "Silly boys," she would chide with a wink toward Roan. "They always think they are so much better than girls, but they still can't outshoot a forty-year-old housewife!"

Every chance Roan got she would go foraging through the woods looking for edible mushrooms, berries, tubers, and nuts. Sometimes she would go on hunting expeditions with her brothers. The most important asset for a hunter—patience— few, if any, of the boys possessed. If they didn't hit the creature the first time . . . more often than not they gave up. But Roan would wait, long after the boys had moved on. She could outwait a marmot, staying patiently with the noose around its hole until it stuck its head back out again. Roan was the first to catch one, which immediately made her a proper hunter in her brothers' eyes. But Roan didn't stop there. The hunter in her had been woken. She began to carefully study the habits and behaviors of animals. Doing so, Roan learned many things: at what times of day certain animals moved . . . and to what locations, which animals were night animals and which ones preferred the day. She learned how animal behaviors changed with the seasons. She learned all the different things animals ate, from the beaver who consumed trees to the small birds who found the tiniest seeds among the grasses. She followed deer, discovering where they bedded down and how they positioned themselves according to the wind.

Her father's family had all been craftsmen, from the south. As more and more Ilyrians settled in Bajarmaland, more woodworkers and stone masons were needed. When her brothers reached a certain age, their father brought them to work alongside him. One by one, Roan lost her playmates. But eventually she, too, had to make her decision. One day she saw a band of Yatu pass through the woods near her house. In that instant, she knew that was the life she wanted.

Coming to a straight section of the wagon trail, Roan stepped out of the woods to spy in both directions. With stealth befitting a whisper, Roan slipped to the other side. The sun was now just grazing the tops of the trees. She recognized the huge grizzled pine, and next to it the trail overgrown with grass and low-hanging branches. Beyond she could make out a solitary horse path. It appeared to be used with some regularity. She followed it for a while until she came to a hilly meadow. At the crest, a stone manor loomed large. It looked more like an enormous cairn than a house. The abode was two stories high, with a steep slate roof and chimneys in abundance. It was a tribal dwelling unlike any Roan knew of, not single clansman lingered in the yard working. There were no kids, and even more peculiar, no animals. Only a single tuft of smoke from one of the many chimneys betrayed the presence of inhabitants.

The carriage road circled the meadow before approaching an oaken door . . . which was flung wide open. *Curious!* she thought. Roan could see no one. She decided to walk around the house and see if someone was in the yard before announcing herself. As she journeyed, Roan counted three entrances in all—the other two were closed. Roan passed a stone chapel with a slate roof and a pointy spire. Next to the chapel was a small fenced yard with a handful of gravestones. If Roan could have read, she was certain she would have found a stone belonging to the great Ule Noumenos. "Katriyana" would likely be on another. Nearby she spotted a well but still not a single person. She grabbed a bucket to pull up some water and drank and washed. She changed into her dry top, then rubbed her legs down. After great exertion it was best to do so, to keep one's muscles from stiffening.

As she rounded the front of the house, she contemplated whether she should step up to the door and knock or wait for someone to invite her inside.

9

BRILL'S DREAM

"Nikolas!" shouted Brill, sitting straight as a jackknife. His eyes were filled with darkness. It took a moment for him to realize he was in his own bed. His heart was pounding—if the door to its cage had been open, it would have flown. Dropping his head back, Brill exhaled. It had only been a dream! Hopping out of bed he fell face-first. Whack! His palms slapped the tile; his sheet had twisted around his leg. Kicking free, he hurried out of his room.

When he came to a tall door, Brill turned the brass handle and pushed inward. The muted hue of night was everywhere. Liis' hair spilled across the mattress like a moonlit delta. "Liis," he whispered.

She raised one arm overhead. "Brill?" she answered in a faraway-sounding voice.

"Yes . . . it's me," he replied.

"Another one of your dreams?" she asked, not yet able to pry open her eyes. Liis patted the top of the bed. Brill pushed the canopy aside and climbed in. Facing her, he crossed his legs. He was far too awake to sleep. Liis rolled onto her side and propped her head under her arm. "Do you want to tell me about it?" she asked, batting her eyes a couple of times.

Hoping for such an invitation, Brill started right in. "First, I dreamt about a blind old man."

"How did you know he was blind?" inquired Liis.

"Because his eyes were sunken and shriveled like dried prunes!"

"Interesting," she commented.

"He asked me, 'Why do you need your eyes to see, Brill?' I didn't know what to say, so I opened my eyes really big and told him, 'My eyes *are* open'—which made him laugh really hard. Before I could ask him why he was laughing, the dream changed, and I was standing outside in the dark. It was windy and cold. I didn't know where I was. I couldn't even see my feet, but there was a faint light on the horizon. It was like when we used to go to the farm in the early, early morning with Gasol and Father. I was trying to decide what I should do when I heard moaning. At first I thought it must be the wind, but then something grabbed my leg. I jumped back but bumped into something behind me. I didn't dare move again. I knew morning wasn't far off, so I decided to stay still until I could see better. But as I stood there I began to wonder if I hadn't just made it all up. I was about to start walking again when I noticed shapes moving past me. The morning light was stronger now, and I could see that they were men! They were all going in the same direction. But they didn't seem to notice me. Most of them were on their feet, although some were pulling themselves along the ground by their arms. I figured they must be wounded and that's what they were moaning about. I began to follow them. Soon they were all around me. It was crowded like Friday market. Then I noticed a little tree; we were passing right next to it. It was small, but I managed to grab hold of it. Climbing up, I stood on the lowest branch. I wanted to see where they were all going but I couldn't see very far. Just then I heard a bird. Looking up, a large black bird was sitting at the very top. The moment I saw it, it took flight . . . but as it did, it's like I became the bird, but I was also myself.

"At first we flew just over the men's heads. But soon we rose higher. They were coming from far away, from across the plain. They were all headed toward a curving line in the distance. Flying closer, I could see the line was actually a cliff, and the men were not even bothering to stop. They were falling over the edge into a massive pit. At the bottom I could see them squirming, like worms in a bucket. As we turned away, in the distance I saw mountain peaks shining in the morning sun. Among them was a sort of palace in the clouds. I knew that's where I was supposed to go, but just as I thought this, I fell.

"I landed on the ground very near the pit. I scrambled to stand, but a man rammed into my back, knocking me down. When I tried to get up, another man's leg hit my face, and I felt a sharp pain in my nose. I reached up to check if it was broken, and another man smashed into me. It was then I realized I was being pushed toward the edge! I reached for a little shrub to hold on to, but it ripped right out of the ground. I tried to push my way between the men's legs and was making a little progress when a man grabbed me by my shirt and lifted me up and said, 'Where are *you* going!'

"I told him, 'Mister, there's a pit over there! I don't want to fall into it . . . and neither should you!'

"He glared at me and said, 'This is what we do!' But then I saw Nikolas out of the corner of my eye. I turned my head and shouted for him. He looked toward me, but it's like he didn't recognize me, and he kept walking. I saw that he was about to step off the cliff. I screamed for him, and that's when I woke up."

Liis' eyes were open now. "My goodness, Brill," she said. "That *is* terrifying!"

Brill reached up and felt his nose. "It seemed so real."

"What do you make of it?"

"It was scary, that's all I know."

"Sleep here with me tonight, and we'll talk more about it tomorrow." With this she took his arm, and pulled him next to her.

When he woke up, sunlight was pouring from the court-yard window into her room. Liis was nowhere to be seen, but he found a note on her pillow.

Dear Brill,

I hope you slept well. I am off to Malador Hospital. Today, Papyri and I are going to Tripe Town to deliver care packages. I will come see you when I get home. I continue to speak with Mother on your behalf, regarding your wishes not to attend seminary. Perhaps we can propose an alternative that would work for both of you. Remember to stay off the roof!

Liis

p.s. Some exciting news—Doctor Oppensky
and I have found some of Father's penicillium
cultures! We are going to attempt to produce
more medicine.

Brill let his hand and letter fall to the bed. For a while he
tried to imagine what an "alternative" might look like, but he
was overtaken by the angular shape the sunlight made upon
Liis' wall. She had one tall window facing the courtyard.
This time of year, the sun crested the roof of the house early.
Already he could feel the nascent heat of the new day grafting
upon yesterday's memory.

Brill got up, went over to Liis' armoire, and pulled back
the doors. Liis kept all of her old school uniforms. They were
not only arranged by size, but by color—all were in impec-
cable condition. Brill pulled one out and held it up. Just then
he heard a door close. Brill quickly put the dress back. It was
probably Hanna going through the rooms collecting dirty linens—she was the last person he would want to find him going
through Liis' dresses. Brill put his ear up to the door. When he
was certain that no one was in the hall, he slipped quickly out
of the room. It was then he realized he was famished.

When he arrived in the kitchen, he saw Sisal standing at
the counter chopping meat with her back to him. She didn't
bother to say "good morning" or even attempt to be congenial,
although he knew she had heard him come in. Out of a boiling
pot stuck a cloven hoof. "Where is Pola?" he asked.

"Gone to market," she answered gruffly. Brill found a hunk
of dry bread in a covered basket.

"Is my mother up?"

"She is," Sisal replied, not bothering to stop what she was doing. "But she ain't feelin' well."

Brill understood this meant he was not welcome. He headed aimlessly down the hall, chewing the hard bread, and coincidentally, he ended up at the bottom of the stairs that led to his mother's room. He had half a mind to go visit her anyway. Instead, he turned right and wandered through a second set of doors that led to the inner courtyard. Unless one knew the architecture of these grand old houses, from the street, one would not suspect there was an inner yard. It was a decent size, too, with its own well . . . and chapel. Half of the courtyard was smoldering in a radiant ochre—the result of sun baking the tinted plaster walls. The other half of the courtyard was draped in blue-grays, the cold palette of shade.

Brill meandered up to the well. Putting his hands against the rim, he peered down to where a splash of sky, like a keyhole, was reflected below. He searched the ground, found a pebble, and dropped it in. A moment later he heard a plink, and the sky disappeared. Stuffing his hands back in his pockets, he walked away. He kicked a stone and watched it skip across the courtyard and strike the door of the chapel. He quickly looked behind him, he was relieved to see no one, especially Hanna. Two years ago she had come from the countryside to work for his family. If his mother ever wanted to know what he was up to, she would ask Hanna first. She tattled on him with the compulsion of a jealous sibling.

Against Liis' advice, he decided to go onto the roof. He went up the stairs, then took the ladder from behind the cistern and leaned it on the edge of the tiles. Before his father's death, he rarely managed to sneak onto the roof. He certainly was not permitted, given that it was a forty-foot drop to the cobbled streets below. But since his father's passing, the rules at home had become malleable. With his mother venturing out of her room less and less, and with Nikolas away in the navy, Liis and Pola were the only ones left to enforce the rules.

Taking a seat, Brill gazed out over an expanse of red-tiled roofs. There were no proper clouds today, only a few dreary ones like wool shags stretched far too thin across an empty slate of stale blue. He doubted they would amount to even a tiny bit of shade on the ground. In the days before the drought, mighty clouds used to accumulate on the horizon this time of year. Their puffy white heads rounded and full like the sails of great ships being blown over an ocean of grass. To Brill, they seemed to be the very buttresses of heaven itself. And if the downy tops were the hallowed grounds of angels, their dark underbellies scraped the earth, sinister and foreboding, bringing flashes of lightning and claps of thunder to the plains. But no more. The clouds these days were thin as the beasts that farmers once called horses.

Sitting atop the most prominent hill in Jesut Edin, the homes gathered close together, standing shoulder to shoulder around a park under the watchful gaze of the cathedral, as a congregation gathers under the watchful eye of a priest. The church anchored the entire eastern side of the park. Through the spindly branches of the dead jacolandi trees, Brill could make out its broad steps going up to the enormous arched doors. Tracing up the cathedral's facade, he skipped past the stained-glass window, going all the way up to the gilt cross. It was the highest point in Jesut Edin, higher than the pointy minarets of the palace, and even higher than the crenellated towers of Grebald.

Turning his head northward, Brill spied the Donner, the emaciated river on its way through the steppes. The hot nostrils of the sun were blowing flames upon the river like a smithy's forge. The circuitous vein of liquified gold wound through the steppes like an ornamental snake. Abandoned boats tilted sideways on the banks, stranded. Spring runoff had come and gone and had done nothing to lift them. Boulders and rocks proliferated the riverbed. The Donner River seeped forward with the same morbid vacuity of an old man's indecipherable last breath.

Only a few years before, the Donner passed into the city full and robust. The smooth water poured around the pillars of the northern bridge like molten glass. The sailing barges, coming down from Torbeshacken, full of sheep, timber, and grains, entered the city with their captains at the helm, their hands on the long tillers, steering their boats safely into the city. The pillars were now no more than bewildered masses of stone, anchored in the visible ledge, standing with their knobby knees over the river like lonely spectators. But no matter how feeble the river, a line of people, like ants, carrying clay pitchers and wooden buckets, went back and forth all day long.

By a small miracle, the well in their courtyard still bore water. But for how much longer? And when it did run dry, would he have to go down to the river to fetch water too? Surely, it would come to that, for recently their mother had let more servants go. Brill often wondered what people would do if the river ever went dry. Would they have to leave Jesut Edin? But where to? Southwest to the rugged, Inhospitable Coast? Or toward the Easterly River and the Parnas Dunes and beyond? Would they cross the sea to the land of the Sulkids or the Moohady? Would the Moohady, their old enemies, allow them onto their lands? Brill turned and gazed north. If it were up to him, he would go to Bajarmaland. Supposedly, it was an arduous trip, but that's where his father came from—and maybe there was still family that could help them.

On his mother's side, uncles, cousins, and aunts were plentiful, but they were all in Jesut Edin. Emhet Turan was married to his mother's sister. He was the only reason they continued to live as they had been accustomed. But his support was not freely given. According to Emhet himself, his assistance was nothing more than a loan. Every month he came with his ledger. He would open it on the dining room table and read aloud the new total while Sisal served him tea and biscuits. Already the sum was quite extraordinary. Nikolas was only a second lieutenant, and his rank did not warrant much pay, which was further reduced by his proclivity for drink and women. Liis did earn some coinage working for Dr. Oppensky, but she made only what the good doctor himself could tithe her from his own modest salary.

Brill stood up; the roof was getting hot. Going down the ladder, then the stairs, he headed straight to the well. Taking the ladle, he scooped water out of the bucket. A couple of drops ran down his chin. Wiping his mouth with his sleeve, he found himself gazing at the chapel doors. *It will be cool in there,* he thought.

Pushing back the doors, he was greeted by a reverberating silence, as when one enters a cellar. The walls were made of thick mud bricks covered in a smooth plaster. On the far side, candles flickered on the altar. His mother required the servants keep them burning at all times. The chapel was a relic from when the priests lived in the house while the cathedral was being constructed—it was a great source of pride for their mother. She always said they were lucky to live on consecrated ground.

Walking up the nave, Brill lit more candles until the flames burned brightly, illuminating the life-sized carving of Jesus and Mary on the wall above. As the burnished wood glowed, the creases and folds in Mary's robe seemed to melt into rivulets. Brill followed the current of her downcast nose and delicate eyes. Her sorrow poured out and over the limp body of her son with such tenderness. As he looked closer, he saw that it was not Jesus anymore, but he himself, lying in his mother's arms. Yet her eyes were shrouded. "Mama, what is it?" he asked. In that moment it was no longer him but Nikolas in her arms. Now his mother's tears flowed freely.

Collapsing on a bench, he thought back to his father's illness. He had come to the chapel every day to pray for him. But nothing had changed; his father had remained profoundly absent. And after his father died he began to doubt himself—perhaps he had not prayed hard enough. As days became weeks, his thoughts and prayers became as directionless as hunted birds—flying every which way.

As he sat there, Brill remembered his dream and the blind man. "Why do you need your eyes to see?" he had asked. *Everyone needs their eyes to see,* thought Brill. He imagined the pit and the men falling into it. Pressing his fingers into his temples, he attempted to make the image go away. When he opened his eyes, to his astonishment, a priest in a long black cassock stood, facing the altar. Brill was surprised he hadn't heard the door open.

"Who is more arrogant than man?" came a deep quivering voice. "He mocks you, Lord. He makes you in his image and destroys in your name. He writes his own laws but calls them yours. Man desecrates your temple. He leaves ruin upon everything thou hath built . . . but you do nothing . . . nothing!" Brill sensed anger as his speech quickened and voice rose in pitch. "Thou hath given him good land, clean air, and the sweetest water, but he treats everything with disdain. Because of my love and devotion, I will punish him. I will treat man as he treats you. My wrath will come like fire into his eyes, and when he begs for mercy, I will show none. Between the altar and the throne my son and daughters hang slaughtered, their white fur runs crimson . . . sacrificed by their wicked swords. O Father, you will be the testament to my oath. The sacrificer will become the sacrificed."

Brill knew that one should never leave during a priest's sermon, but he shot to his feet, knocking over the kneeling bench. It clattered to the ground as he dashed up the aisle. He barged through the doors and ran until he reached the far wall of the courtyard—only then did he dare to look back. Clasping his chest, he tried to catch his breath. He stared at the chapel doors and waited for the priest to appear, but it was only Hanna who approached him from inside the house. "What are you doing?" she demanded. "You *know* you're not supposed to be in your mother's herb garden!"

Brill looked down to see his errant path and all the crippled plants left in his wake. "Have you gone into the chapel this morning, Hanna?" he asked, not bothering to defend himself.

"Not yet. Why?"

"Has . . . has a . . . priest come to the house today?"

"Nobody has come to the house."

"But . . . there's a priest in the chapel."

"Nuh-uh," she said, putting her hands on her hips, giving him a vexed look.

"Go see for yourself," he implored.

"You're a lost cause, Brill."

"I promise! Go look!"

Brill watched her march toward the chapel. Swinging the doors open, she disappeared. After a couple of minutes, Brill approached. And just as he reached forward to pull the door open, Hanna burst past him. She ran and ducked behind the well. *"See!"* he said, hustling to catch up to her. But as he came around the well, he could see she was doubled over laughing— laughing so hard she could barely speak. Brill turned away. He grabbed a crushed lavender plant and headed straight for the kitchen. He could still hear her cackling as he entered the house. In the kitchen, he took a knife and cut off the root before wrapping the lavender with twine, making a posy. Bringing the bundle up to his nose, he found the aroma soothing. Sometimes Pola made them for him.

Going up the stairs toward his mother's room, he caught sight of Sisal just as she was making her way inside, holding a tray. Brill hurried to follow her in, but when he arrived at the door, he found Sisal's substantial body blocking the doorway. "I *told* you, your mother is not feeling well."

"But . . . I need to speak with her!" he declared.

"She doesn't want to be disturbed."

Brill gazed at the ground searching for an excuse, but he could find none. Placing the posy on the tray, he said, "Give this to her . . . Tell her it's from me. And tell her I will be outside waiting to see her."

Sisal grunted before disappearing behind the red-and-black-checkered door. Brill strolled farther down the hallway. Tall windows opened out onto the courtyard, dousing large portions of the wall and much of the floor in sunlight. Brill positioned himself in the centermost point and sat down. An immense pressure had been growing in his head. Reaching up, he pressed his skull with both hands. It did something to relieve the pain, but the moment he let go, the pain rushed back. He leaned back and began to slide down until only his head was propped up against the wall. The rest of him was lying flat on the hard tile, his wing bones angling sharply into the floor. With his eyes remaining closed, he listened. He could hear the high-pitched calls of the vendors on the street, the distant caterwaul of cicadas from the park, and the faraway clatter of carriages. As he lay there with his eyes closed, the sunshine filled his vision with all-encompassing orange. It was then he noticed the pressure in his head had dissipated, replaced with a sensation of floating weightlessly on a sea of color.

Until a shadow passed over him. A gruff voice rumbled from above. "Your mother will see you now." By the time Brill forced his eyes open, Sisal was nowhere to be seen.

His parents' bedroom had always bewildered him; it seemed he had to walk forever just to reach their bed. To his left, windows faced the backstreet—not that one could tell, these days the shutters were never open. A bear hide with out-stretched claws lay splayed at the foot of his parents' bed, its long incisors bared as if still battling the hunters. It was a ves-tige of his father's secret past. Brill had always given it a wide berth.

His mother was propped up against an array of pillows with a cloth poultice over her eyes. Brown leaves protruded from under it. He stopped at the foot of the bed. His father's side remained unruffled. His mother stayed to her side as duti-fully as a martyr. Brill couldn't imagine him having ever slept there. Looking around the room, he searched for the usual evidence—his hat, his books. Even his britches were still hanging over the chair.

Facing his mother, he announced himself: "Hello, Mother." Although he could see the posy of lavender on the dresser, he asked anyway, "Did you get the lavender I sent you?" Lisbeth's lips rose slightly before she reached out with her hand. Brill walked over to her side to take it. "Join me," she prompted. "'The Lord is my shepherd. I shall not want. He lays me down in green pastures, and leads me beside the still waters.'" Lisbeth abruptly stopped. "I can't hear you, Brill."

"Sorry, Mother."

Her voice rose once more. "'He lays me down . . .'"

Brill joined in. "'In green pastures, and leads me beside the still waters. Though I walk through the valley of the shadow of death, I will fear no evil. For you are with me, Lord.'"

As soon as they were done reciting, Lisbeth spoke. "I have some good news for you." Brill felt a tightening in his belly. After a moment of silence, she asked, "Don't you want to hear what I have to tell you?"

"Of course, Mother," he answered obsequiously.

"Come, sit."

Brill did so.

"I have been speaking with the monsignor . . . and he is strongly considering you for the seminary."

Brill fiddled with the fabric on the arm of the chair but then abruptly looked up at her. "But, Mother . . ."

"What? What's the matter? Are you not happy?"

"I don't want to—"

"Brill," interrupted Lisbeth, her voice hardening. "You did not get accepted into the lyceum. What do you suppose you are going to do?"

"Why do I have to go to school at all? Pola didn't go to school."

"Pola's a *servant*, Brill. You're not!"

"Isn't there another alternative?" he asked.

"Who have you been talking to . . . Liis?"

Brill sunk lower in the chair and gazed up at the massive rafters. "Have I told you"—his mother's voice lightened—"that when your father was young, he was the most devout Christian in all of Jesut Edin." Brill had heard this so many times, he knew exactly what she was going to say next. "He prayed like no one I had ever seen before!" Her face softened as if she was remembering something beatific.

The only memories Brill had of his father's Christian past were his parents arguing, his mother admonishing Alber for refusing to go to church, and him telling her to stop berating him for not. "So what happened?" asked Brill.

His mother's jaw tightened. "He lost his way . . . I fear for his soul. And for Liis', for that matter. I am afraid she will follow in his footsteps . . . but you, you can right the wrong."

"What wrong?"

"The sins of this family."

Brill opened his mouth to protest, but no sound came out. "Go," she said, pointing to her bureau. "Read to me." Brill stared at the giant tome. "Go on," her tone soft, supplicating.

Brill got up. His legs felt heavy. With both hands, he hauled the Bible off its perch. Back in the chair, he dropped the giant book onto his lap. "What shall I read?"

"There's nothing bad in its entirety," she stated. "Start anywhere."

He cleaved it open, the sides thumping against his legs. He raised his forefinger and randomly put it down. Summoning the little bit of moisture that was left in his mouth, he began to read. "Then I saw between the altar and the throne the slaughtered creature, a cloven ram hanging with blood dripping down its white fur."

"Brill!" Lisbeth interrupted, her voice shrill. "What passage is this?"

"I don't know," Brill answered as he rubbed his eyes and tried to focus them.

"Well, go on, then."

"Having seven horns and seven eyes," he continued but then abruptly stopped. "I can't read anymore, Mother." With this, he closed the book.

"What's the matter with you?"

"Did you know there was a priest in the chapel this morning?"

"There was not. They always ask before coming to the house."

"I swear there was a priest!"

"Don't swear, Brill."

"Sorry."

"Maybe you mistook Gasol for a priest?"

"Mother, may I ask you something?"

"Of course, you can ask me anything."

"Is the devil real?"

"Is the *devil real*!" Lisbeth gasped. Momentarily, she pulled up the compress and brought one eye to bear upon him.

"You said I could ask you anything."

"But what kind of question is that!"

"Well, I just wanted to know. Is he real?"

Moving her head back, she adjusted the poultice before speaking. "I did say you could ask me anything. If you must know, then my answer is yes."

"Who is he, Mother?" pursued Brill.

"Satan is Lucifer, a fallen angel . . . a jealous angel who was so proud he sought to be as powerful as God, and as such was cast out of heaven. Bitter, he tempts mankind, pulling people into sin."

"Can people see Satan? Like Monsignor Iraneous, has he *seen* him?"

"People don't actually see Satan, Brill. Well, I guess some might. Perhaps he visits certain people to test them."

"But why?" Brill pleaded. "If God loves us, and we are obedient, why do we need to be tested?"

"God has reasons we cannot presume to know. A truly faithful person doesn't question God's designs! When Satan tested Job, he sent disease upon him and took all his possessions. He put festering boils upon his skin, but Job never blamed or cursed God. In the end God rewarded him for his unwavering faith. He gave him great wealth and many wives."

"Why did Job need so many wives?"

"That's not the point, Brill! The point *is* . . . he did not lose his faith. Soon you will learn to ask the right questions. The priests at Saint Peter's Seminary are learned men. They will teach you. No question will be too much for them." Brill bowed his head disconsolately. "I must rest now," said Lisbeth. "I told Sisal to prepare food for you."

Brill set the Bible on her nightstand. He moved to the foot of the bed and waited for his mother to say something. She did not. He walked the length of the room and closed the door quietly behind him. Following the corridor to the right, he came to the top of the stairs where he stopped. He couldn't help but wonder, If God was all-powerful, why would he allow Satan to terrify mere children? That did not seem fatherly at all! He waited to be punished for this thought. The truth is, he would have welcomed punishment . . . Any response from God would be better than his eternal silence. But the only punishment he received were the plebeian sounds coming off the street, the barking vendors and the clomp of shod horses.

10

Fifth Ward, Malador Hospital

Hands rough as farm gloves held the reins of the wagon with the tenderness of a seasoned spinner. Two-story houses pressed up against the road, crowding the wagon as it twisted and wound its way through the labyrinth of Jesut Edin. The temple of the moon was about to close shop, while the sun readied its wares.

Turning into an alley, the wagon shuddered, its back wheel finding the same hole with unfailing loyalty. Sandwiched between crumbling walls, the lane, lined with ancient trees three-quarters dead, rambled on interminably in the dusky clapboard of dawn. An edifice gradually emerged above the wagon and driver. Mercurial morning light endeavored to make its way around the sharp edges of the mansard roof whose missing tiles and battened windows, like sad eyes, augmented the melancholies and spurned splendor of the old mansion—befitting the present-day inhabitants of Malador Hospital's fifth ward.

Pinching the straps under his thumb and fingers, Papyri pulled upon the reins and uttered a low "Whoooaa, Jutta. Whooaaa." Soon thereafter, a flickering lantern outlined the contours of a full-bellied man passing through the gate. "You're late," growled Loffa.

After pulling the wagon lock, Papyri looped the leather straps around the peg on the foreboard, just as a shadowy figure slipped past Loffa. Soon Timothy appeared below Papyri—his big unblinking eyes complementing his unhinged jaw, his mouth resigned to hang open in perpetuity. The last of his rotten teeth were stranded like a couple of bats in an exposed cave.

"Hiya, Timmy," said Papyri.

"What took you so long?" grumbled Loffa, striding up to the wagon, his keys jingling on his belt halfway hidden by his prodigious belly.

"Long lines," replied Papyri turning toward the warden. Timothy tittered sheepishly as he scraped horse manure off Papyri's boot.

"More lines by the day," said Loffa. "People are hungry. What are they to do if there's no work?"

"Don't forget the poor," said Papyri, attempting to parrot one of Loffa's favorite sayings.

"'*Ignore* the poor at your own peril,'" corrected Loffa, holding the lamp over the side to take a look into the wagon. His eyes widened. "Is that all! That won't last but a couple of weeks!" The warden set the lantern in the bed before securing one foot on a spoke and throwing his other leg over the sidewall. Loffa was surprisingly agile for being such a big man. The wagon leaned until he positioned himself in the middle. Noticing that

Timothy and Papyri hadn't moved, he hollered, "What? You buzzards jus' gonna sit there? Come 'ere and give me a hand."

Papyri stayed as he was, admiring the morning star hovering over Loffa's hairless pate. He had been following its progress throughout the night. "Pretty!" said Papyri.

"'Pretty'? What's pretty?" demanded Loffa.

"You!" answered Papyri. Spittle blew out of Timothy's mouth, which was always a precursor to a burst of giggles.

"Don't get 'im started," warned Loffa. "Come 'ere, Timmy!" he growled. Lowering his head, Timothy trudged toward the back of the wagon. Timothy had been in the fifth ward longer than any cook, warden, or supervisor. Agewise, he wasn't the oldest resident, but he certainly was the most amenable. No one really knew when he first came, for his records had gotten lost—perhaps they never existed. No family came to visit. No one had ever claimed him as their own. Timothy had seen the comings and goings of a myriad of directors; however, the most current, Dr. Oppensky, was by far his favorite. He said nice things to him, like, "Timmy, you cannot keep a lid on a pot of boiling water, you must let the laughter out!"

Loffa himself had served eight directors. To him, there had never been one as disagreeable as Dr. Oppensky. He was the direct appointee of Queen Beatrice, who lavished him with conspicuous favor. Dr. Oppensky and the late superintendent, Alber Hoffe, had introduced a new policy for patient care that they termed "moral treatment." The staff was now required to behave in a respectful manner toward the loonies, showering them with kindness and patience at every turn. They were only permitted to shackle them when they were violent and at risk of harming themselves or others. What's more, the staff were now supposed to take the residents on walks around the grounds as if they were taking a lady's pet dogs for a stroll! The older attendants hated the new policy. They felt as if they were treating the lunatics to some seaside holiday. Loffa missed the days when all he had to do was make sure the inmates took their medicine and keep them from wandering too far from their rooms. Sometimes, when Dr. Oppensky was away, Loffa reverted to treating the patients in the manner he was accustomed.

To Loffa's chagrin, Dr. Oppensky outlasted everyone—four years and counting. Few directors were good for more than two. Being assigned to the fifth ward, the ward for the incurables, was considered a nudge toward retirement. And now with spotted fever becoming an epidemic, all reasonable physicians kept their distance.

Timothy shuffled his way to the back of the wagon. Loffa was readying the first sack. "What would happen, Timmy"—his voice rang out—"if the hospital ran out of flour?" Timothy said nothing. He never thought about such things. Being a ward of the state, he had no choice in the matter, and such questions, by their very nature, suggested a plurality of options. Likes and dislikes, good or bad, were the privileges—and burdens—of free men. Timothy simply accepted what was in front of him.

A morsel of air escaped Loffa's throat as he hoisted the fifty-pound sack onto Timothy's shoulder. Timmy stutter-stepped backward. "Go on," commanded Loffa, waving his hand in the direction of the gate. "Take it to the kitchen," said Loffa as he followed Timothy's wayward progress with his gaze. He considered it a strong possibility that he might not find the gate.

"Loffa!" said Papyri loudly.

Startled, Loffa shouted back at him. "What!"

"Imagine holding a diamond!" said Papyri, cupping his hand.

Loffa scowled. "If you want to be taken seriously, Papyri, talk about *real* things."

"What is real?" asked Papyri, getting out of the wagon and coming around to the back.

Loffa hauled the next sack of flour and lifted it. "This . . . is real," stated Loffa, hoisting it onto Papyri's shoulder. Papyri didn't budge. Grabbing the next sack, Loffa added it to the first. "And *this* . . . is real!"

Papyri stood firm. Loffa glanced back at Timothy. "The other way, you dimwit," he yelled.

"Diamonds are real," said Papyri.

"Diamonds are real, but only to kings and queens, not to imbeciles!" countered Loffa, throwing his head back and expelling a hearty laugh. He only wished another attendant were there to share his joke.

"To blue giants, diamonds are real, Loffa," explained Papyri.

"Blue giants!" Loffa repeated, managing to lift the third sack on top of Papyri's load. Papyri had always insisted he was not just a giant, but a blue giant—which meant nothing to anyone. Granted, Papyri wasn't short, and his build wasn't scant, but Loffa had known bigger men. Dr. Oppensky was always quick to point out that none of this mattered, that patients' beliefs were irrationally locked in their heads. He often reminded staff, "Remember, our patients wear their delusions like winter coats. If we take their coats from them, they will freeze. It's better to show them that it's warm outside—then perhaps they will realize that they don't need them at all."

"Fine," groused Loffa, gripping the fourth sack by the tail. Heaving it upward, he let it fall roughly. "There you go, my little blue giant!" He waited for Papyri to stagger, but Papyri took the fourth with the same aplomb as he had taken the first. Pulling a handkerchief out of his pocket, Loffa wiped his brow. Squinting, he studied Papyri more closely. He was expecting at least a wobble, but Papyri did not so much as shift a foot. One half of Loffa's mouth raised in bemusement. "Why are you talking about diamonds anyway? Is it because of this *jewel* people are talking about? The one they found in the mountains?" Papyri remained suspiciously quiet, so Loffa continued. "Forget it, Papyri," he said, shaking his head. "You'll never see that diamond, or *any* jewel, for that matter. But you are king when it comes to carrying flour, I'll give you that." Loffa had seen much larger men stop at three. "I thought giants were supposed to be *big*," he continued.

"Where I come from . . . I *am* big," answered Papyri.

"Give 'im an inch, and he'll take a mile," mumbled Loffa, dragging the last sack from the back of the wagon. "Let's see if you can handle one more!" He had never known anyone to carry five. As Loffa struggled to lift it high enough, Papyri obliged him by squatting lower. Bringing it to the top of the pile, Loffa waited—then clapped his hands like a child at a puppet show. Wistfully glancing around to the back of the wagon, Loffa wished there were more. He wondered just how many sacks Papyri *could* carry. "Damn, Papyri," he exclaimed.

Of one thing Loffa was certain, he would fit right in at a circus—for a more foolish-looking fellow could not be found. He had big doughy eyes and a round baby face with large front teeth. What's more, his right eye drifted, while the other seemed to angle slightly inward, making it near impossible to know which one to look at when speaking to him. Papyri's black coat was too big, but he insisted on wearing it, and his black pants were too short. His legs were always visible above his boots. A large round hat with an undersized brim topped it off. Loffa had not seen him without it since before the days of moral treatment.

Before the arrival of Dr. Oppensky, Papyri had been the most difficult patient in the fifth ward. Loffa had seen up close the damage he could do. Back then, the only way to deal with Papyri was to give him enough laudanum, the molasses, opium, and lubjok mixture they gave to the patients—and sometimes snuck for themselves. The "sauce," as it was referred to by the attendants, kept Papyri and the like sedated. But that was all before moral treatment. The sauce was forbidden now. What's more, Dr. Oppensky had Papyri running errands for the hospital.

Loffa was surprised that Papyri was allowed out to mingle among the good folk of Jesut Edin. He had read Papyri's chart. He knew why he had been admitted to the fifth ward—Papyri had killed two men—albeit in self-defense. But surely running errands was a step beyond moral treatment. Loffa wondered at the recklessness of Dr. Oppensky. He was convinced that in the director's eagerness to prove his techniques, he had lost all medical objectivity.

Yet children were irrevocably drawn to Papyri. They gathered around him like moths around a streetlamp. Whenever schoolboys caught sight of Papyri, they would run alongside his wagon. At first, they heckled him, pretending to be idiots, plodding around knocking into one another, trying to outdo the others' antics. But to Papyri, they might as well have been songbirds chortling sweetly in his ears. Inevitably, one of the boys would climb aboard his wagon to ask him questions. They sensed an otherworldliness in Papyri that only kids can. He always told them the same thing, that he was a blue giant. And more than that, the very *last* of the blue giants!

"But you're not blue!" they would point out.

"You can't see the blue," Papyri would explain. This of course made no sense, but it was curious, and curiosity is the native language of children. "I rode with Papyri the blue giant!" they would later brag to their friends. Somewhere along the way, doing so became a childhood rite of passage.

Loffa held his hands on his hips and looked down at him. "Five sacks of flour, Pap! An' you're not even wobbling! I wonder how many more you could carry?" There was the slightest hint of admiration in his voice. "I tell you what, we should go to market and take bets. Make a little money—what do you say?"

Papyri looked blankly at Loffa. "Go on!" said Loffa, motioning him away with a flick of his wrist. He watched Papyri go, then shepherded Timmy through the gate. "After you take those to the kitchen, put Jutta in the stable!" he called out. Then placing one hand on the sidewall, he leapt to the ground as lightly as a dancer. After picking up the lamp, he passed through the gate before latching it.

◆ ◆ ◆

Klempt rolled onto his left side in an attempt to give his right hip a break. The wooden planks bored into his bones, and a measly, threadbare blanket did little to assuage them. Next to him, his father was sleeping restlessly. Occasionally, he would grumble as if he were in an argument. His mother, on the other hand, slept as if she were a corpse—no movement, no sounds, hardly even a breath. She worked as a washerwoman all day, thus the moment her head touched the planks, it was as if she had fallen into the deepest, darkest pit of Tartarus. Penelope, Klempt's older sister, snored. She had been staying out late and coming home in the early hours of the morning stinking of perfume. Klempt had spent most of the night caring for Clara, his five-year-old sister. His vigilance had cost him any rest of his own. He resigned himself to listening to the others. Clara was very sick. She had had a fever for two days running, often waking throughout the night with her shirt soaking wet and her hair caked to her face. Klempt would wipe her down with a cool cloth and console her until she was ready to sleep again. They were all worried. Tripe Town had seen too many deaths lately. People said it started with a couple of red spots, then a sore throat, and after that, an incurable fever.

Klempt sat up. He sensed the nearing of the sun as all farmers can. If Clara woke now, their mother would take her. Klempt crept into the next room of their house, if you could call a domicile with two rooms, no yard, no kitchen, no well, and shared walls on three sides a house. He sat on one of the frayed wicker chairs they had brought from the farm, one of the few items they hadn't sold. He resisted lighting a candle; they were too costly to burn. Putting his elbows on the table, he leaned his chin on his hands. He wanted to look but knew it would be a wasted effort—there was nothing in the cupboard.

Life in Jesut Edin had not been what they expected. For every story of success that reached the Hutsu villages, there were thousands of failures—only the failures were never talked about. In the old days, before the drought, people took secret pleasure in hearing about the failings of others, especially those who moved to the big city. But now, there was too much misery; even the sweetness of gossip could not be afforded. The Hutsus were desperate. To crush another's hope was to crush their soul. The dream, the belief that their lives might get better was what kept them going. But the truth was this: Jesut Edin was a locked door. The only Hutsus that were successful were the ones making money off other Hutsus—particularly the new arrivals. Those who had come earliest were now selling goods to the newcomers at inflated prices. As they said in Tripe Town, it was: "Eat or be eaten."

It had been two years since his family had moved down from the foothills. They were only a few copper klats away from being beggars. As farmers, they could at least scratch the earth for food, or hunt birds and squirrels, or fish the streams. In the country, good air was plentiful and allowed one to properly think. Here, rubbish and squalor spilled into the streets. Everything disgusting to the eyes and nose congregated just outside one's door. The side corners of houses reeked with the stench of urine. There were brave rats and half-starved dogs rummaging around piles of trash as flies buzzed about.

If one was lucky, one had enough money to rent a second-floor apartment and escape the putrescence. But even so, nobody was above the noise. If the neighbors fought, it was as if your own family were fighting. Secrets were a thing of the past, gone with the farms, and with the farms also went one's self-respect. Death was as commonplace as birth, only now you pitied the newborns and felt a certain jealousy for those who passed on, released from the hell that was Tripe Town.

Klempt's family were what the people of Jesut Edin called "bottom feeders" after the sucker fish with long whiskers and giant pouty mouths that ate the river waste. Only the scorned Creepers, the pint-sized vagrants that lived in the ravines, were viewed less favorably.

Klempt's father could only find a job as a dung farmer, someone who harvested animal manure off the city streets. But even this job was not guaranteed. There were just too many people seeking work, each man willing to do the job for less. Klempt watched as his father slowly collapsed. His shoulders and head drooped lower and lower for the effort required to keep his head up equaled his despair. At noon, he was often still in bed. There was no going back to the foothills, even if they had the money to purchase a wagon and a decent horse; they had sold the family farm. Their fate was inextricably tied to Jesut Edin and all the other miserable Hutsu souls therein.

Their mother made a few copper klats scrubbing the stains out of the bedsheets of proper Ilyrian families. She beat their linens until her sinews were ragged and the skin of her hands raw from the lye. Her gaunt face and faraway eyes offered little hope for either Klempt or Penelope. Neither of them wanted anything to do with washing. The long days seemed endless. In their opinion, it would only lead to an ignominious end, a beggar's unmarked grave. Besides, they were still young, young enough to hope for more. They scavenged Jesut Edin looking for other ways to make money. The city had many moods and wanted many things. There were a few professions open to bottom feeders. Thieving and prostitution were two of them. Perhaps not noble professions, but the poorest didn't judge— only those with the luxury of choice seemed to point fingers.

The life of a thief certainly had risks, but Deetmar was a great teacher. If it hadn't been for him and the Clan of Gilbert, Klempt's family would have starved their first winter in Jesut Edin. Deetmar had taken Klempt under his wing, giving him a few terkels here and there. He called them "advances." Klempt suspected the advances were akin to down payments, for loyalty and future services rendered.

Standing up, Klempt peered through the crack in the shutter. Morning had arrived. Klempt grabbed the boots he had pilfered from a soldier two nights before. The fool had passed out drunk in the street. Deetmar had kept watch while he pulled them off his feet. Klempt chuckled, imagining what it must have been like to stumble home in his socks—surely, to his neighbors' delight and his wife's fury. The boots were a touch too nice. Deetmar was always telling him that a thief must go unnoticed. Klempt tried to give them to his father, but he refused them. He would not accept an "ill-gotten gift." Yet his father ate the food Klempt brought home. It seemed a tad hypocritical that he would judge one item and turn a blind eye to the other.

Sleep was very much still in people's faces as they headed toward the river. Even at this hour, there were lines going down to the Donner. People were trying to beat the crowds to the best water holes. For Klempt, every step away from Tripe Town made him happier. As he walked, he caught a glimpse of the morning star floating above it all.

Klempt followed the river upstream. The farther out of the city one was willing to walk, the better the water became. After passing underneath the northern bridge, Klempt found a small pool in which to splash himself clean. He took a couple of drinks. To the east, streaks of pink and gold seared across the sky like dragon breath.

When Klempt returned to his house, he found Penelope with Clara at the table. Walking over, he kissed Clara upon her clammy forehead. She managed a feeble smile. Penelope looked up. "We're out of bread," she stated.

"Didn't Mother bring any home?" he asked, though he already knew the answer.

"How?" asked Penelope.

"Didn't she make any money yesterday?"

"She had to pay for Clara's tincture."

"What about you? Did you make anything last night?"

"No," said Penelope. "What are we going to do? I'm hungry . . . and Clara's hungry."

"I'm hungry too!" said Klempt. "What do you expect me to do . . . turn water into wine?"

Just then there was a knock at the door. Klempt was in no mood for visitors, especially not the likes of Turner, who had a habit of coming by to talk about the "revolution." He would go on and on about how the poor were going to rise up and overthrow the monarchy. "'A revolution with forks and brooms,'" Klempt liked to chide him.

Go away, Turner, he was about to shout but stopped. Yelling at him from behind a closed door would have less effect than yelling in his face. Klempt pounced for the handle. He swung the door wide open, but instead of Turner's possum-like snout, he found himself gazing into a pair of kindly brown eyes. Klempt suddenly felt defenseless. The eyes belonged to a young lady with blond hair that was carefully tied in a braid. She seemed to be just as surprised by the abruptness of *his* appearance. In that moment he forgot he was standing in his own doorway. He could have been standing in some fancy boutique or at the doorstep of an Ilyrian aristocrat but for the brown dress with the insignia of a cross. It was a nurse's uniform.

"Good morning," she said, no longer waiting for Klempt to be cordial.

"Who is it, Klempt?" barked Penelope.

"Uh . . . I think I'm dreaming, Pen," he replied, and he reached forward to touch the woman's arm.

Intercepting his hand, she diverted it back. "You're not dreaming," she answered with a faint smile.

"Who did you say you were?" asked Klempt.

"My name is Liis. I come from Malador Hospital. My assistant and I are going door to door taking a census, among other things."

"'Census'? What is that?"

"Uh . . . Well, we're counting the sick. But also giving tips on disease prevention," she added quickly.

Klempt could see no one behind her. He then looked at Liis more closely. "Are you Hutsu?" he asked.

"Hutsu?" Liis repeated, surprised by the question.

"Yeah, you don't look . . ."

"Ilyrian? No, my phenotype is certainly not of Ilyrian origin."

"Feno . . . What?"

"I am Ilyrian," explained Liis. "But my father was Pagani." Klempt knew the Pagani and the Hutsus were related, even their language was similar, but it was surprising to hear she was of Pagani heritage, for they were a crude and uncultured people who adhered to a barbaric view of life, where spirits embodied trees, water—even rocks. But it was their belief in the afterlife that Klempt found most bizarre. Upon death, the souls of the dead were nothing more than visitors, passing through a weightless realm on their way to rebirth. There was no heaven . . . but then, no hell either. When Klempt used to ride into the high mountains with his father to hunt, they would come across shiny objects hanging from branches, or find Pagani shrines at the mouths of springs. This girl was far too well dressed to be Pagani. She looked as if she would be more familiar with reading books than tanning deer hides. Her clothes had been recently washed and pressed, and Klempt doubted very much by her own hand. If her father was Pagani, he had done well for himself.

"Is there anyone in your house who is sick?" she asked. Just then Klempt saw a man with an odd hat and an assortment of bags and satchels and whatnots over his shoulders. Klempt turned his head. "Clara, come quick!" he shouted back into the house. "It's Papyri, the blue giant!"

The sound of a chair scraping could be heard inside, followed by the patter of feet. Looking back at Liis, he apologized. "Clara has always wanted to meet Papyri." Clara squeezed next to Klempt, taking hold of his leg. *"Where?"* she asked, with as much excitement as the feverish girl could muster.

"Right there," said Klempt, pointing.

"Ohhh," said Liis, nodding her head. Kneeling down, she asked, "Clara, would you like to meet Papyri?" Clara nodded. "Can I lift you up?" Again, Clara nodded. Liis scooped her up and turned sideways. "Clara, this is Papyri," she said. Clara dropped her gaze, but only for a moment, for her desire to meet him outweighed her shyness. All the children in the neighborhood had heard of Papyri, and every day when Klempt came home, the first thing she asked was if he had seen him. If he had, she wanted to know what he was wearing, which never changed, where he was going, which he never knew, and anything else she could possibly think to ask. "You're a blue giant," she said. Liis and Klempt glanced at one another. Papyri nodded. "The very last," he said, bowing slightly.

"What happened to the others?"

"You don't want to know," he said, shaking his head.

"But I do," insisted Clara.

"Ufansil, the witch, threw them into the Chasm of Eternity."

"All of them?" asked Clara. Papyri nodded. "I'm sorry!" she said.

Liis turned toward Klempt. "Clara feels *hot*! Has she been sick?"

Klempt nodded. "She's had a fever for two days."

"Are you not feeling well, Clara?" asked Liis, looking into her eyes.

Clara shook her head no. "Can I see your throat?" asked Liis. Clara opened her mouth. "Does it hurt?" Clara nodded solemnly.

"We're afraid she has what's been going around," said Klempt.

"Do you mind if I look at her skin?"

"Please."

Liis set Clara on her feet. "Can you lift your dress for me?" asked Liis. Clara pulled it up, exposing her thin belly. Liis inspected around her armpits. There were telltale red spots developing. Liis felt for her lymph nodes at her neck and groin. They were swollen tight. "Thanks, Clara," she said, giving her belly a gentle rub. Clara lowered her dress.

Liis stood back up and caught Klempt's eyes. He interpreted her gaze. "What can we do?" he asked. Liis shrugged and tilted her head. Klempt leaned forward and picked Clara up in his arms before speaking. "Yesterday, my mother bought some of Dr. Phinny's Remedy."

"You would be better off saving your money," replied Liis.

"But . . . they told us . . ."

"Trust me, it will do nothing."

"What about the hospital? I heard there is a man who cures people."

"That . . . probably would have been my late father," said Liis.

"Oh," said Klempt. There was a look of surprise.

"Dr. Oppensky and I are trying to isolate the mold that he used—but we only have limited knowledge . . . and cultures."

"Mold!" declared Klempt.

"I know," confessed Liis, "it sounds strange. But we might still have enough of his medicine for someone as small as Clara. If you want, bring her to the fifth ward. Ask for me, Liis Hoffe."

Just then Clara turned and whispered in Klempt's ear. "Don't say that, Clara," he answered.

"Why not?" she said in a plaintive voice.

"You're not going to, besides, it's . . . it's not polite to talk like that."

"But I want to know," she persisted.

Klempt softened his stance. "Well then, ask Papyri yourself," he said. "He's right there."

Clara's voice squeaked. "Papyri, if I die, will I meet other blue giants?"

"More beautiful creatures in Bardo Fey than blue giants," he answered. Papyri reached up to the rim of his hat and, to everyone's amazement, produced a tiny white flower. Taking it, Clara dropped her face onto Klempt's shoulder.

"Is Clara the only one in your family that is sick?" asked Liis.

"My father is, but it's a different kind of sick."

"How so?"

"He's unable to find work. He sleeps most of the day."

"We do have care packages for families in need, would you like one?"

Penelope, who had been watching from the background, stepped forward, edging Klempt aside. "We'll take one," she interjected, before Klempt had a chance to answer. Speaking to Penelope, Liis said, "It's not much. There's some bread, hard sausage, cheese, a bit of tea, soap, and a few candles . . . but it's something." Penelope mumbled an imperceptible thank-you as she took the box from Papyri.

Klempt's face turned red. "We really appreciate it," he said, loud enough to be heard.

"You should really thank the League of Christian Ladies, they're the ones who put these together," said Liis.

"Then I'll thank them at church on Sunday," said Klempt.

"You won't exactly see them, you know," answered Liis.

"Why? Don't they go to church?"

"Of course they attend church, but you won't know who they are."

"He doesn't go to church anyway," said Penelope. "He's just trying to impress you." And with this, she disappeared back into the house with the box. Klempt's face flushed brighter.

"Don't worry," said Liis. "I have two brothers."

"I bet they're not as difficult as Pen!" he said.

"Brill's pretty easy, although he does like to put on my old uniforms . . . and climb onto the roof."

"You mean he climbs onto the roof with dresses on?"

Liis put her finger up. "I had never thought of that."

"Do you worry about him?"

Liis' eyes narrowed, and her head angled to one side. "You mean, worry about him wearing dresses? Or worry about him falling off the roof?"

By her question, he could tell she didn't think much about the dresses, so he opted for the latter. "I mean worry about him falling."

"Of course I worry about that."

"What about your other brother?"

"Nikolas? He goes out of his way to irritate me. But he's not home much anymore, and I guess that's just as well!"

"Where is he?"

"Wherever the royal navy sails. But listen, we're also handing out pots for boiling water." Liis turned to Papyri to have him retrieve one, but he already had a pot in hand. "Thank you, Papyri," she said, taking the container.

"For boiling water?" Klempt asked, looking perplexed.

"Ideally, you must boil water for three minutes before drinking."

"Three minutes!" exclaimed Klempt.

"Yes, it appears that the animalcules can survive for quite some time."

"Never heard of boiling drinking water to kill things, unless of course one is boiling meat, but no one can afford meat around here. But we never use muddy water. We always let the dirt settle."

"You can't see the animalcules with your eyes. Even clear water can be full of them. This was my father's discovery. He believed that impure water might be the cause of dysenterus. So have your family wash their hands when preparing food, and preferably, after they go to the bathroom."

"I'll tell them, but I doubt they will. We barely have enough kindling for cooking food, let alone for boiling water."

"Try, that is all we can ask. Oh, and do bring Clara to the hospital," said Liis. "I might have enough medicine for her."

"I will," said Klempt.

"Will Papyri be there?" asked Clara.

"Yes, my little albu," said Papyri.

"What's that?" asked Clara.

"The name of the pretty flower," he said, pointing to the one in her hand.

"Al-bu," repeated Clara shyly. Klempt hadn't seen such a big smile in days.

Liis waved goodbye. "Okay then, until we see you at the hospital." With this she turned away.

Klempt leaned slightly against the door and watched them cross the street. Clara spoke first. "You should marry *her*," she said.

"Marry! Marry who?" he asked.

"She's very pretty," said Clara.

"What makes you think she'd marry me?" asked Klempt. Clara shrugged. "I'll marry her if you marry Papyri," Klempt offered.

Clara pushed the white flower toward Klempt's nose. "Okay," she said.

Klempt shook his head. "Oh, come on my little albu, let's get you some food!"

11

Minol's House, Bajarmaland

Moving through the tall grass, Roan brought each foot down with the single-minded focus of a hunting feline, occasionally stopping to listen. The Pagani preferred the woods or at the very least bushes. Arriving at the steps, she saw that the door remained open. Roan listened but could hear no sound coming from inside. Easing up the first steps, she called out, "Hello!" There was no answer.

Taking the next step, she called out louder, "Helllooo!" Still no reply. Was Minol not home? Maybe he did not think she would come? Reaching the top step, Roan peeked around the doorframe and found herself looking down a dimly lit hallway. As her eyes adjusted, they focused on what appeared to be a large dog on the runner about fifteen feet away. Sitting on its belly and haunches, the dog had its front paws stretched out toward her. Roan withheld the impulse to reach for her knife; after all, it hadn't growled or bared its fangs. As she studied it,

Roan realized this was no dog—but a wolf. She knew wolves from watching them hunt caribou on the plateau. A few times, she had even come upon them in the woods. Its ears were up and positioned toward her, but none of the hair on its back was raised.

What kind of person is Minol if he keeps company with wolves? Maybe he is the wolf, she thought to herself. Roan had heard of warlocks that could change into animals, but she had never heard that Minol was one such person. After a few seconds of eye contact, the wolf stood up. It turned and sauntered deeper into the house, then stopped and looked back at her as if saying, *Are you coming?* Roan's inclination was to wait for her host, but what if the wolf *was* her host?

Unsure what to do, Roan's eyes fell upon the wide planks that ran lengthwise down the hall. The grain of the wood seemed to beckon, tugging her forward. As she stepped into the house, the wood floor creaked underfoot. There would be no concealing her whereabouts. Passing a score of empty pegs, she noticed two coats. The first was a wool coat whose patches were in need of patching. The second coat was of soft leather and stained with years of grease and soot. The hood and sleeves were lined with fur. Many years ago, it must have been a handsome brown. On both sides of the hallway, thick beams were left exposed in the walls, sparking memories of her grandfather's home. But it was the odor that truly brought her back—the faint scent flowing on imperceptible currents that exude from cupboards and cabinets in old houses, spinning off invisible eddies rising out of the still waters of infrequently visited closets whose secret coffers emit an almost sweet fragrance, one so particular and true to these ancient abodes that, surely, there could be no cause of the smell other than its own independent origination.

About halfway down the corridor, a dust-filled shaft of light seeped halfheartedly into the passage from the left. It was then Roan realized she had lost sight of the wolf. Arriving at the doorway, she turned to find herself looking into a great hall. About fifty feet away, at the far end, the wolf stood . . . again with its head turned back toward her. Once making eye contact, the wolf continued onward, but this time it entered the mouth of an enormous stone hearth at the far end of the hall, where it promptly vanished.

The mysterious allure of the wolf beckoned her into the grand hall. A wooden table, thick as an anvil, ran the length of the room. Roan was struck by the glittering orange and yellow hues of the setting sun shimmering through a profusion of tiny glass panes on her left. They were too thick to see through, though sufficiently translucent to set the wall aglow. The light cast a moody warmth over the hall, dulled only by an ubiquitous layer of dust.

Benches and chairs were sequestered underneath the table. The hall had been made for another time, a time when visitors must have filled the house. Could an old forsaken manor such as this have been regaled with cheer? If it boasted such evenings, those days were long gone. From the crossbeams iron chains hung, the ends of which bore broad chandeliers. The chandeliers themselves were made from the antlers of stags, the kind of noble beasts one only hears about in tales of old. On her right sat a large cabinet. The upper half was open, and upon the top shelf, a line of blue-and-white platters faced the hall. Below these were two smaller shelves of pewter plates. Then came a shelf filled with an assortment of earthenware

bowls and drinking crocks with handles and lids, apparently
orphans waiting for their person to return and claim them. At
the end of the table, Roan could see a semicircle free of dust,
an arc the length of a person's arm. The dark hardwood shone
through with some of the merit of its dignified past. *Minol,*
thought Roan. Apparently, he was human after all.

Inspecting the hearth, Roan could see the fireplace was
a traditional Ilyrian design, with river stones set in mortar.
However, it was much larger than any she had ever seen—certainly an entire boar could roast therein. Two metal cranes
used for swinging pots over flames were attached at either end.
Stepping into the hearth, Roan looked up the chimney. There
was a smidgen of sky far above. She then spotted the obvious,
an opening where a flat interior stone had gone missing. It was
tall and wide enough for a reasonably sized person to pass.
Beyond, Roan could see the beginnings of stone steps curving
sharply down into darkness. Instinctively, she felt the knife on
her waist. For a moment she thought about removing it, but
decided to wait. The Yatu teaching was abundantly clear on
this matter. "Never draw your knife unless a fight is imminent
. . . and you can see the eyes of your enemy." Her chest tightened as she began making her way down, turning in a tight
spiral. The atmosphere below felt stagnant. She felt hemmed
in; it reminded her of the Pukka. She reached up to wipe a cob-
web from her face.

When the stairs ended, Roan found herself on a hard, even
surface. There was no telling where the wolf was now, for she
could barely see. To her right came a tame flicker, presumably
from a small fire. To her left, a sheet of blackness. Roan sensed
there was some kind of opening beyond, but she was not about
to step into the tenebrous pit. How she would have preferred

a proper welcome, even a meager "Hello" would have sufficed. Roan called out, but only the sodden, plaintive echo of her voice came back, sounding a bit too much like the girl who wandered lost in her grandfather's house.

Moving toward the firelight, Roan found herself standing at the edge of a spacious room, much larger than she had anticipated. What she thought would be a fire turned out to be an expanse lit with torches in sconces and candles in varying degrees of expiration. The entire floor was covered with a most intricate tile mosaic. Eight carved stone pillars stood equidistant from one another at the center of the room forming a sort of inner sanctum. Where the columns reached the ceiling, they split apart, their thick ends twisting like vines. Everywhere she looked the craftsmanship was remarkable. As Roan passed between two of the central pillars, she came to the innermost area. Here sturdy tables were set in two orderly rows. They were polished and clean but with absolutely nothing upon them. Roan counted six fireplaces spaced along the walls. Had they all been burning, it would have created a cozy atmosphere. It was then she noticed an odd shape on the farthest wall.

Lifting a torch from a sconce, Roan walked over to inspect it. She discovered the cause of the irregularity was a multitude of boxes built into the wall itself. The embedded shelves started just above her knees and continued up beyond where she could reach. Each box was a polished wood. Each a perfect square, fitting precisely in its niche. Blue rings appeared on the front of each box, with a small symbol in its center. Roan stepped closer to have a better look. The rings turned out to be relief carvings of snakes biting their own tails, each stained indigo blue, with rubies for eyes that glittered in the torchlight.

Roan's skin crawled. As Roan passed her fingers over a ruby, Issa's voice came into her head. "Papa Para Keet Magento. Protector of Little Blue Snake." Just then, she realized that she was not alone. Leading with the torch, she swung about.

Only a few feet away stood a man. He did not step back, even though the torch was held toward his face. "Welcome, Roan. I am Minol," he said in flawless Ilyrian. With the slightest movement of his hand, he gestured downward, motioning to the wolf standing at his side. "And this . . . is Sza. I believe the two of you will be good friends." Roan found his comment odd. The wolf's head came up almost to the man's waist. As much as she thought she should be afraid, Roan felt safe, the kind of ease one feels when one knows there is nothing to fear. Roan lowered the torch. "Please, accept my apologies for not meeting you at the door," said Minol. "I have been busy completing my final tasks. I had hoped to be done before you arrived."

Roan studied him. His long gray hair was pulled back in a ponytail—not unusual for a Pagani man. Minol had no beard, or even a hint of stubble on his chin. She couldn't quite tell how old or big he was. He seemed both large and diminutive. He appeared strong, but he didn't puff his chest. His wide face bore its share of wrinkles, but somehow he seemed ageless. His pale eyes were quiet as a still pool, but not without light. His body, his voice, did not remonstrate needlessly. There was no hostility that Roan could sense.

Minol stepped to the wall and took hold of one of the boxes. "If I am not mistaken, this is what you were looking at." Roan did not answer but watched him pull out a surprisingly long box. He carried it in both arms to the nearest table and slid it across the top. As he was removing the lid, Roan noticed Minol's fingertips were black with ink. Pulling on two silk straps, a layer of panels rose. Each panel appeared to be the exact size and shape of the one preceding it. Gilded markings with elegant sweeping curves slanted across the surface in perfectly straight lines. None of the writing, and this is what Roan assumed it was, meant anything to her. But it did not require literacy to see they were beautifully inscribed in gold leaf. Roan figured each panel had been sealed with a clear resin. Minol passed his fingers along the veneer. "There is no greater treasure in all of Bajarmaland," he said with tenderness and devotion befitting a disciple.

His statement vexed Roan. If these boxes were so important, why hadn't she ever heard of them? *No*, she thought, *the greatest treasure in Bajarmaland was the Ayn Noor!* But Roan remained silent.

"Before the Ilyrians conquered Okomorling, a small number of priests escaped," continued Minol.

"I didn't know any survived," interjected Roan.

"A small group of Gnos, mystics, foreseeing the destruction of Okomorling, fled to mountain caves before the Ilyrians arrived."

Roan had always thought that the Gnos were too meek and mild mannered, and now, if what Minol said was true, and they had actually known of the impending attack, they were worse—they were cowards! "The Gnos should have fought," proclaimed Roan.

"No," said Minol, shaking his head. "The Gnos were not fighters! They believed that it was better to be destroyed than to destroy. After all, to kill another is only to harm oneself. In a spiritual sense, that is." Roan shook her head. "I know," said Minol, "to a warrior it all must seem backward. Eventually, Ule's father, Gustav, invited them to live among the Noumenos. Ule was just a boy at the time, but a more eager and gifted student one could not find. The Gnos priests taught him many things, including how to skywalk. When Ule became the chieftain, he had this house built. Some say it was the first schism between the Noumenos and other tribes." Minol watched Roan keenly. "Regardless of what the Pagani thought of the Noumenos Clan," Minol went on, perhaps having read her mind, "they kept coming to see Ule. After all, there was no greater healer in Bajarmaland." Minol motioned around the room with a sweep of his hand. "Even as they came to the house, underneath, in this very room, the surviving priests were writing down their teachings."

Roan noticed Minol's face had become a touch sad. Roan looked at the rows of tables. In her mind's eye, she could see the priests carving, painting, and sealing the tablets. "It must have been quite a workshop."

"It was. And I have spent the last twenty years translating their teachings into Ilyrian." Minol pointed to a small bookshelf on a far wall with an array of leather-bound books she hadn't noticed before. "It was their wish."

"Why would they leave their teachings to their destroyers?"

"Contrary to what one might think, the priests felt no antagonism toward the Ilyrians. They did not think in terms of one life. That would be a far too limited view. Neither language nor the color of hair or skin meant anything to them. What they were concerned with was preserving the teachings. They felt strongly that they should not be lost to humankind." Minol stood there waiting. It seemed he was expecting her to say something, but she had nothing to say. Minol continued, "I prepared a room for you in hopes that you might stay the night—there is much to talk about."

She considered traveling back to her tsik at this hour. She would have to sleep in the woods, which was fine, but what would be the point in coming all this way without getting proper answers? "I will stay," she replied.

"Good," he said with a smile.

Roan waited as Minol went around the room blowing out candles and extinguishing torches. When he was done, she followed him back up the stairs, out the fireplace, and into the great hall. Going to the far side of the hearth, Minol lifted a metal wheel. Roan was surprised she hadn't noticed it and chided herself for not inspecting her surroundings better. Minol stuck the wheel onto the side of the stone chimney. Against her expectations it hung there without falling. He then turned it. Roan could hear the bright clink of rolling chains. "There is a hidden shaft and a pulley within," explained Minol. "From this crank, the stone at the back can be raised and lowered." Roan watched as a flat stone came down, sealing off the passage. When the stone settled into place, she could see that it was equal to the other parts of the fireplace, besmirched with streaks of charcoal and smoke residue. Roan stepped closer to inspect it. The seal was precise, there was absolutely no visible fissure or crack. The fireplace appeared as ordinary as any other.

When Minol was done, he removed the wheel and pulled a square metal shaft out of a hole. He motioned for Roan to have a look. There was a tiny gap between two rocks. If one didn't know better, one would notice nothing except where a small stone may have gone missing. "In the morning I will show you where I hide them." Roan was taken aback; she could not comprehend why he was showing her the secrets of his house.

Nor did she want to know them. But before she could protest, Minol excused himself.

A couple of minutes later he returned with a bucket and a cloth. He wiped down a spot for her to sit. "So few guests these days," he said. He then departed again and came back with an armful of firewood. He refused to accept any help, saying, "It's time for you to rest." Roan noticed that her legs did feel ragged. After Minol had the beginnings of a fire crackling, he gathered a pot from a nearby room, set it upon a crane, and steered it over the flames. The pot and the fire seemed like a child's toy inside the mouth of this giant hearth. Roan couldn't help but wonder about the secret passage. Never in her wildest dreams would she have guessed the magnificence that lay beneath the flames.

Minol put two bowls on the table, a basket of country bread, two large cups, and a pitcher. Minol filled Roan's cup. "Try this," he said. "It will refresh your limbs." Roan tasted it; she liked the concoction straightaway and proceeded to drink it down.

"It's good!" she said, setting it back on the table.

Minol leaned forward and refilled her cup. "Do you want to know the secret?" he asked, raising an eyebrow. Roan nodded.

"Water!" he blurted and then began to laugh, so much so that he bent forward until he was through. Roan smiled, not that she thought what he said was particularly funny, but rather that he found it so. Sza was curled up in a ball by the fire. Roan noticed the near imperceptible expression a canine makes when it is content. Gazing out the window, she realized that the sun was gone—the entirety of night had been exhumed from the easternmost quarry.

"You live all alone?" inquired Roan, as Minol uncovered a basket of bread.

"Yes," he said, sitting up straight, "if you don't consider Sza, and the other animals of the forest, companions." Roan felt embarrassed. She did consider animals companions. In fact, her horse Hanoomé was as close to family as Tieg and Farwah. She nodded sheepishly. "Time has become a short rope," Minol continued. "Great changes are upon us." He looked up. "Since the theft of the Ayn Noor, have you noticed any changes in your tsik?"

Roan's brows scrunched together as she nodded firmly. "But if that is why you have called me, you've chosen the wrong person. I know less than most."

"I do not choose, Roan . . . I follow." His words made her uneasy. It did not bode well, for if spirit guided him, he might not even know himself why she was here. "The theft of the Ayn Noor has set in motion certain configurations," continued Minol. "New actors are being summoned, new deeds will hasten a new era. The past will be set aflame. The real question becomes, what will rise from the ashes?"

"At least we know where the Ayn Noor is," stated Roan. "I am sure we will win it back."

Minol's eyebrows pinched together. "Where is it?" he asked.

"In Okomorling! Where the thief took it!" Roan stated with emphasis.

"Maybe that's what the Ilyrians want you to believe, but the Ayn Noor has already left. It's on its way to Jesut Edin as we speak."

Roan shot to her feet, sending her chair crashing to the floor. "Then we must stop it!"

12

MINOL'S HOUSE

Roan's chair remained on the floor where it had landed. Without the slightest degree of alarm, Minol opened his hands. "Even if we could win the Ayn Noor back, *should we?*"

Roan felt her blood surge. "They stole the Ayn Noor!"

Minol brought his elbows to rest on the table and interlaced his fingers. "That's not the catastrophe I see," he stated.

Roan wasn't about to sit there and politely discuss the loss of the Ayn Noor as if it were something trivial. Minol was sounding more and more like a traitor. "You speak of the talisman as if it is of little importance," she declared.

"You want to fight me on this, don't you?"

"*Yes,*" she answered frankly. "How you speak is . . . *wrong.*"

"Ahhh, Noumenos, the great traitors!"

Roan kept her eyes on Minol but said nothing that would excuse him—he would have to prove otherwise. Regardless, she needed to be careful not to react to his every word and say something she would regret later. Roan took a deep breath, righted her chair, and sat back down.

"Do you know where the Pagani came into this world, Roan?"

"Farwah says it's somewhere in the south," she answered, crossing her arms.

"That's correct, and to be precise, in Jesut Edin." Roan remained silent, but her attention was piqued, for she didn't know anyone who claimed they knew its exact whereabouts.

"Have you heard of the gates?" he asked.

"Yes, of course," she answered. Every Pagani knew of the opening to the underworld.

"The gates were formed when Iana sealed the opening to prevent Bardor's flood from filling the upperworld. In the storm, Bardor destroyed the Spiral Path, leaving only the Chasm of Eternity. Do you have any idea where the gates are?" Roan shook her head. "They are also beneath Jesut Edin!" he added.

Roan frowned. "Is this why the Ilyrians are taking the Ayn Noor to Jesut Edin?" But the moment the words came out of her mouth she knew it was not so.

Minol shook his head. "No, they are taking it to Jesut Edin because it is a magnificent jewel!"

"Well . . . if what you say is true . . . then the Ayn Noor *must* go to Jesut Edin," she said, measuring her words carefully.

"Yes. It's going back to the only place it can be returned."

"But I don't understand. If this is true, why weren't we taught this?" said Roan, her voice quavering.

"Some choose to forget; others pretend they never knew," said Minol.

The crickets were wallowing like drunks in an Ilyrian tavern. Roan turned and looked at the darkened windows. Turning back to face Minol, she spoke. "We should return it—not the Ilyrians. It's our responsibility. Besides, we can't rely on them. They know nothing of the power of the other side."

"They will learn soon enough," Minol said. "But trust me when I tell you, if the gates opened up before the council of Pagani elders and the Ayn Noor was in their possession, they would not throw it back! They would argue amongst themselves that the gates were not the *true* gates.

"For centuries, the Pagani have told stories about the Ayn Noor. Over time, these stories have become our myths. The myth of the Ayn Noor is trapped in the fabric of our minds. Giving the Ayn Noor back would be akin to chopping off one's arm to cook meat for supper. It goes against our most basic instinct! The Ayn Noor has a better chance of being returned by an Ilyrian than a Pagani."

Roan didn't particularly like Minol's steady eye contact, but she held his gaze, if for nothing else than to show him she was not afraid. But she was also studying him. If Minol betrayed even the slightest deception, she would leave. Changing the direction of the conversation, Roan asked, "What is a Blue Snake?"

"Ah, the symbols on the boxes!" he said, slowly nodding. "Does the Blue Snake mean something to you?" Roan said nothing, for she felt nothing needed to be revealed—certainly not her naming ceremony. "Perhaps this is why spirit brought us together," he added.

Roan's brow deepened into a furrow. "You really don't know why I am here?"

"I have my suspicions."

"That's not reassuring," she said.

"Spirit never gives reassurances," answered Minol. Roan thought she caught sight of a mischievous sparkle in his eye. "But . . ." he added, holding up one finger, "I can tell you about the Blue Snakes."

"That would be a start," said Roan flatly, trying not to sound hopeful.

"The Blue Snakes were a group of Gnos priests who foresaw the arrival of the Ilyrians and prophesied the destruction of Okomorling."

"So the Blue Snakes were the Gnos that ran away?"

"Yes, Roan, the Blue Snakes ran away. But not how *you* think of running. They were not cowards; they did not fear death. They simply were not as obliging as the other priests. They felt strongly that certain teachings should not be lost to the world, so they smuggled as much as possible out of Okomorling before King Teufel's arrival."

"So the Blue Snakes were smugglers!"

Minol's head went back as he expelled a hearty laugh. "It seems you have a great dislike for the Blue Snakes?" Roan shrugged. But it was true, she hated everything about them, and in particular, her own secret association. "The Blue Snakes," Minol went on, "were a small sect within the Gnos priesthood. Their temple sat at the center of the Lake of Mirrors at the very top of Okomorling. The Blue Snakes were responsible for all burial rites and cremations . . . as well as identifying reincarnations. But the most important aspect of their learning was centered on entering Bardo Fey."

Roan's throat became tight. "They entered Bardo Fey?"

"Well, not in body, but yes, they frequented the spirit realm."

Roan suddenly felt cross and irritable. How on earth did she come by the name Protector of Little Blue Snake! Perhaps Issa was wrong? Or maybe it was a different Blue Snake? *That's what it has to be,* she concluded. Minol sat quietly staring at her. "So the Blue Snakes *really* entered Bardo Fey?" she asked, unable to curb her curiosity.

"And returned!" added Minol. "To them, death was more important than life."

"That's just backward!" said Roan, shaking her head. "It makes no sense. It's like putting the fire *inside* the pot."

"It does seem that way, from where we stand. But to them, both life and death were simply . . . different states of one ever-changing reality. Only, in death, there is no body, thus consciousness is much shiftier, making Bardo Fey more difficult to navigate. In the spirit realm there is no solidity, no physical matter to anchor us. In an instant, one's spirit can travel great distances, and a single thought can create a mountain or make it disappear. This is why it is called the Land of the Dreaming Dead. What you see in the afterlife appears very real, even though *everything* in the death realm, as in this realm, is just an illusion—a dream. Visions of angels or demons loom large, and if the spirit doesn't recognize them as illusions, the spirit will feel compelled to react. Some spirits may get caught in blissful encounters, others in fearful ones. Regardless, these visions are simply images created by the spirit's own mind. When one dies, it is similar to falling asleep and entering a night dream . . . but it is a dream few will ever wake up from. Most never realize they are dead! For the Blue Snakes, to wake in death was considered 'the great achievement.' Only by remaining fully awake could they explore the other side."

"Why would anyone want to do that? Life is enough for me!"

"I understand, I understand," agreed Minol. "But think about it this way: the only thing certain in life is that death will come. That we will enter the spirit realm, at one point or another, is a foregone conclusion. Whether we want it or not, whether we die old or die young, one day, each of us *must* pass through the veil! So would you rather have a map, or nothing at all?"

Roan considered his words. "I guess I would rather be prepared," she said at last.

"Exactly. That is the warrior speaking! It's good to be prepared. Let me ask you, Roan, what happens when a warrior dies? What do the Yatu tell you?"

"If a warrior is valiant in battle, their soul will be taken to Mount Kalisha."

"What happens then?"

"The warrior feasts with the gods and other warriors who have died courageously in battle."

"So, I ask you this. What if the great Mount Kalisha is not true?"

"But . . . it is true."

"For a moment, all I'm asking is for you to imagine it wasn't. How would that be?"

"I . . . I would feel betrayed."

"Of course you would! Think about all the religions and beliefs the world over. The Yatu say God is a woman, the Ilyrians say God is an old man with a gray beard, and the Moohady believe there are many gods, some with animal heads. How can they all be true? How is it all possible?" Roan shrugged. "It's the fallacy of plurality!" he added quietly.

"The what?" said Roan.

"Never mind that, but let me ask you, what if each god *is* real, as each of the aforementioned peoples believe? How then is it possible for there to be so many *true* gods? Let's say, for the sake of argument, they are all valid . . . Wouldn't it follow that each particular image of god must then be the subjective creation of those people . . . and not some objective fact? Only beliefs solidified through repeated storytelling become accepted as truth. But mind you, only for that culture, and those people.

"Over time the story becomes their religion . . . and over time, their religion becomes historical, with its own holidays and rituals that further validate their beliefs. They become so sacred that no one dares to challenge them. After all, no one even remembers who made them up in the first place.

"But what's important is that such a god would no longer be an objective, independent god but a belief, developed by a specific group of people. So if they insist that by some miracle their god is *the* one absolute God, then wouldn't it follow that such insistence itself would undermine the legitimacy of their claim? For if all images of God arise out of our subjective imaginations, then only an ignorant and deluded person could claim their version is somehow superior, or more valid, than any other people's vision of God."

"Why would anyone make up Mount Kalisha?" said Roan; there was a hardness to her voice.

"I see this makes you angry," said Minol.

"Well, if what you say is true, then Mount Kalisha is something made up. And that would be unacceptable! Imagine all the Yatu that die fighting . . . for some *lie!*"

"True, and what's more, you would be left with a hole in your understanding, where before you were confident in how life and death unfolded. Suddenly, you would feel unsure and confused. Without Mount Kalisha, you would be left staring into the crack of uncertainty. Nothing to believe in. No Kalisha! How awful!"

Roan stared at Minol. She wasn't sure what she thought of him. He seemed sincere, but he was also saying such bizarre things . . . and making her very uncomfortable. "So you invited me here just to confuse me?"

"No! Not at all," said Minol, waving his hands. "What's most important are the Blue Snakes' teachings. They taught us that death cannot be defeated . . . but ignorance, on the other hand, can!" There was a bright spark in his eyes.

"I don't follow you," confessed Roan.

"Ignorance can be defeated by *waking up* and seeing the world as it truly is. By waking up from the dream! The maelstrom of ignorance is very strong, always pulling us into it, lulling us to sleep. It is not so unlike when you dream at night. Let's say you dream you are riding in a boat with dark water all about you. You even dip your hand in the water—it feels wet, so real! But the moment you wake, the boat, the water, are all gone. How can that be? What was so real suddenly disappears! So we look back from our daylight eyes and laugh and say, 'That was just a dream! Goodbye dream!' But what if life is the same? What if we wake upon death and look back on this life and realize it, too, was just a dream?"

"If we are asleep, then this is the most real of dreams," said Roan.

"Dreams within dreams," said Minol, almost to himself. But then his eyes bore intently upon her. "Think about what happens when one dies. The dream that was your life is gone! But that doesn't mean we don't take life seriously," he continued. "Life is an important dream, for it's the one we are in. But we must work hard and recognize it for what it is—a passing phenomenon.

"What the Blue Snakes discovered looking through the eyes of death was that one lifetime is short, and that only by looking further could one begin to properly see. The Blue Snakes saw that everything moves in one continuous flow, similar to sitting in a boat and watching the riverbanks pass. What happened to yesterday? Where did those last moments go? If you look at it honestly, we are trapped in our little boats, looking out the caves of our eyes, while the changing scenery, changing bodies, and changing people flow on by. The only time we feel safe and untroubled is when we come together with friends and family who agree with our illusion. 'Yes, yes,' they say, '*that* is your boat. And *this* is my boat. This is our god. That is Mount Kalisha.' Only by looking at death does one come to see the ephemeral nature of life. This is why the Blue Snakes studied corpses."

"I don't care *what* you say; *that* is *not* normal."

Minol shook his head and laughed. "No," he agreed. "Truth is abnormal! What is normal is only normal to a deceived, ignorant person! After all, normal people think of themselves and the world as solid. They stand up in their boats and shout, 'I am, I am!' But who are they? They are only make-believe stories, the dream of themselves. But how could this be? Everyone else seems so real. They all seem to be having fun eating and drinking. If they are real, then we must be real too! Besides, we can't miss out on the fun. So we join them singing, 'Me . . . me

... me ... you ... you ... you.' But it's only ignorance singing its own ballad, the ballad of ignorance!"

"I can feel myself. I see myself. How can I not exist?" stated Roan.

"Shut your eyes and stop thinking about yourself . . . even for one minute. Can you?"

Roan shut her eyes. After a little while, she opened them. "No, I cannot," she said with an exasperated look.

"Exactly. But if you could stop your mind for long enough, you just might see *through* the illusion. If you could stop your mind, there is a chance you might wake up and enter the pure land of the Ayn Noor."

"The Ayn Noor? Our *talisman*?"

"Yes and no. It's a contradiction of sorts, for even the Ayn Noor cannot be considered an object. The real Ayn Noor cannot be touched, smelled, or seen. It's not of the physical world. This is why it must be returned—to rid us of the temptation to make it an object.

"The real Ayn Noor is the essence of consciousness that extends beyond time and place. It sees everything, but it can never be seen. If a person rests in the Ayn Noor, there is no 'I' and there is no 'you.' As long as there is an 'I' and there is a 'you,' there is ignorance. As long as the Pagani make the Ayn Noor into an object, their talisman, it will remain something to possess. It becomes another god. And this is why the Ayn Noor must be returned.

"The Gnos understood that the Ayn Noor is pure awareness itself. It has always been and will always be. But ask for proof, and there is none! It's the most simple phenomenon and yet the most difficult to comprehend. The Ayn Noor is everywhere but nowhere. It is the most abundant thing in the world but the hardest to grasp. The true Ayn Noor cannot be measured by our hands, nor by any tools, no matter how fine or accurate, not now and not ever. The moment we look out *there*, we'll just keep finding new images, new realities, new stars. Out *there* no one will ever find the Ayn Noor." Roan shook her head slowly.

"Once we believe ourselves and the world to be separate," continued Minol, "we are trapped. This is why the Blue Snakes felt compelled to save the teachings, so people would not have to discover these slippery truths all over again. And that's why the writings *are* the greatest treasure in all of Bajarmaland."

"Why don't I feel grateful?" said Roan with a sardonic smile.

Minol roared with laughter, his voice filling the room. "It's hard to appreciate, but would you rather remain ignorant . . . or know the truth?" Roan kept silent. More laughter ensued. She thought back to the Blue Snakes. "So what happens if a person doesn't wake up when they die?"

"An unawakened spirit will eventually fade. The luminous body disintegrates just like everything else. When all that is left is a seed of consciousness with no name or identity, passing through Bardo Fey, it seeks the only outlet left available to it, rebirth . . . and the story repeats itself . . . birth and death, birth and death, and so on, until one wakes up and says, 'I *see*.'" Roan thought back to her naming ceremony. Suddenly, Minol's face lost all its mirth. Roan was about to speak when Minol raised his finger. "There's something else," he said. "And I now suspect this is why spirit summoned you." Roan became highly attuned. "The Blue Snakes," he said, "not only learned to navigate the realm of death, but some masters went on to manipulate their own rebirth." Again, Roan thought back to her naming ceremony. As strange as this seemed, she somehow knew that what Minol was talking about was indeed possible.

"Rebirth is not exact," he went on. "A lot of things can go wrong." Now it was Minol's turn to become silent; it appeared he had suddenly been pulled inward by a secret worry.

"Is there a problem?" Roan finally asked.

Minol's head shook, and he lifted his eyes to focus on her. "Perhaps . . ." he whispered. "You see, Roan, choosing birth is not as simple as saying 'I want this body. I want to be born in this location . . . on this date . . . at sunrise.' On top of this, when a person chooses rebirth, they forget their past. Anyone born in Jesut Edin would be born in the cauldron of ignorance. They would be hard pressed to remember how to locate their past knowledge. Yet their soul would be rattling its chains, wanting to break free and wake up! I have good reason to believe that one such person is there now."

"Are you saying that there is a Blue Snake in Jesut Edin?"

"Yes! They have chosen rebirth in these times . . . for a reason. I fear this soul will be hard put to it. Even a master's soul has to find its way out of its cage. Their eyes will have to open, but opening them is fraught with danger, for reality, as I have just described for you, is tricky. But time is moving fast, much faster than anyone expected."

Roan had a sudden awareness. She knew, without a doubt, the answer to her next question but asked it anyway. "You think this is why I am here?"

"The more we talk, the more I believe this is why spirit brought us together. I don't pretend to know the details . . . but I will help you in any way I can."

It was late into the evening when the two of them were finished discussing the particulars. When Minol suggested they rest, Roan had no objection. "Both of us will need strength tomorrow," he said. Roan was too tired to be bothered by yet another one of his cryptic statements. Minol showed her to her room. As he closed the door, Roan dropped on top of the bed.

But sleep did not come immediately. She thought back on the course of the evening. It seemed a mountain had slowly grown up over her, and now the mountain was sitting squarely upon her shoulders. She remembered Minol saying that in Bardo Fey, a mountain can appear before you, but with a single thought, it can also disappear.

Roan shook her head. There was so much to consider.

13

The Garrison at Grebald, Jesut Edin

Lines of consternation cut across Weeks' forehead. He was in a standoff with a pair of boots. His had been stolen off his feet two nights before. He had borrowed this pair from Chunsey, only they were too small. Weeks had already ditched his socks and smeared bacon grease on his toes. Grabbing the first boot, he pushed and pulled until he got his foot in. The second boot was a bit easier as his left foot was smaller. Standing, he grimaced and then called out, "Bossun, give me somethin' to drink."

Bossun held the bottle out for him to take. High-stepping across the room, like a cat when its paws get wet, Weeks grabbed hold of it and spun the bottle around, a habit he had for measuring the contents before he drank. As they stood over Marius, who was asleep on the floor, they passed the bottle back and forth. Bossun pulled at his mustache between swigs.

"Was there a more 'ansome man than Cap?" said Weeks, shaking his head slowly. "An' a darn good shot."

"Excellent horseman," added Bossun.

"No horse to carry 'im now," continued Weeks, whose mood was already on the mend.

"No gold to line his pockets," said Bossun. "And nary a woman to fancy 'im I reckon."

"Nary a woman," repeated Weeks, as if this were the captain's final epithet.

Chunsey, in his perfectly pressed shirt and collar, pushed back the wooden shutter that opened onto the garrison courtyard.

"On about a year 'go," Weeks went on, his voice permanently hoarse, "Marius here comes riding into the stables. I'd been mucking the stalls when I looked up an' seen 'im. I nearly pissed myself. Cap'in Marius Proudst! Course, I'd seen 'im from afar, but never had a proper looksie. He was even more 'ansome in 'is jacket an' shiny buttons." Weeks motioned with his fingers to the front of his shirt. "*He* was a *propah* cap'in!"

"I wonder what he thought when he seen you?" asked Bossun.

"Prolly thinks 'e's looking at the King of Manuuure!" said Weeks, and at that they laughed. "Mind you, I didn't even salute 'im."

"Cat got yer tongue?"

"Somethin' like that. I figure that was 'bout the time he went north and got 'em soldiers killed an' started this rebellion."

"I reckon," agreed Bossun.

"Tell you what, an' I'll guess what you're gonna say, but I'd 'ave done the same. I'd 'ave followed 'im anywheres. He just made you feel that way," said Weeks, shaking his head. "You don' suppose he remembers anything 'bout what happened?"

"Dunno," said Bossun. "Battle changes a man."

"Diamonds change 'em, too, or so they say," added Weeks.

"Wouldn't know a thing 'bout diamonds," concluded Bossun.

Weeks crouched down as low as he could manage. He pushed the bottle under Marius' nose. "'Ere you go, Cap. It'll wake ya!" Marius groaned and pushed the bottle away. "Too good for lubjok, are we?" Weeks shook his head as he stood back up.

"Suppose it's against his religion!" said Bossun. The two of them chuckled.

"The colonel," muttered Chunsey, as someone does when they swallow their words.

"Whad'ya say, Chun?" asked Bossun, his ears perking up.

"The colonel," he repeated louder.

"The colonel? Where?"

"On his way!"

"*'Ere?*" squeaked Weeks. His eyes bulged. "Duns should have told us Radavan would be coming hisself!" he whined.

"Quick! The bottles!" responded Bossun bending low, with his arm and hands outstretched. He moved towards the empty bottles as if he was going to herd them back under his bed. Weeks opted for another swig instead. "Put that darn thing away!" commanded Bossun.

"Where's the stopper?" queried Weeks, looking around frantically. Bossun wagged his finger toward the table. Weeks fumbled for the cork, knocking it onto the floor.

As he turned to face the door, Chunsey straightened his shirt and adjusted his cap.

"*Weeks!* The *bottle!*" whisper-shouted Bossun, just as the door sprang open. Chunsey saluted, followed by Bossun, and lastly, Weeks.

Colonel Radavan paused. Each man waited, the atmosphere brimming with expectation for the inevitable bright clink of rolling bottles.

The colonel's remaining black hair was no match for the emerging grays, but his brows remained bushy and dark, rivaling his eyes. A purple scar clipped the corner of his left brow. Colonel Radavan could have been a general a few times over, but had turned down every promotion—unwilling to join the "gentleman's club," as he referred to the coterie of generals who opted for talk and leisure. With his hands interlaced behind his back, he looked over at Marius. "Why is the captain on the floor?" he asked.

"He refuses to sleep 'n a bunk, sir," provided Bossun, his hand remaining in a salute.

"Where is his uniform?"

"He removes it, sir," answered Bossun, taking a small step forward but mostly keeping his distance. He was masterful at stepping without really moving.

"Take him as he is, then," ordered Radavan. "We're due at the palace at the top of the hour," he said before departing and leaving the door wide open.

"Sir!" the three soldiers called out after him. Bossun then stepped forward and closed the door and leaned against it.

"Did you 'ear that, Bossun," exclaimed Weeks, giddy as a schoolboy. "Goin' to the palace! Always wanted to see the palace."

Bossun pushed off the door. "Not like that, you ain't!" he said. Weeks gazed downward to see a small portion of his belly protruding through an opening in his shirt. Bossun frowned. "And where'd you 'ide that bottle?"

Reaching into his pants, Weeks yanked it out. "I didn't know where else to put it."

Bossun's jowls shook vigorously. "Fifteen years in the army and you've never been promoted. Don' think that's 'bout to change."

"Don' reckon," agreed Weeks.

"At least you know yer place, unlike Chunsey here," said Bossun. "Come, help me get Cap."

• • •

Emhet was enjoying watching the soldiers work. Weeks had been his personal assistant on the way up to Okomorling. For days, the most simple request was met with a vacant look. At first, Emhet thought perhaps he didn't hear well . . . or didn't understand the king's Ilyrian. But soon he realized that Weeks actually understood just fine but was simply obligating him to make every request twice—sometimes three or four times.

Keeping Marius from running off was proving to be quite the task, and watching Weeks huff and puff was a joy to behold. Every time Marius opened a window, they would have to close it. But it was when Weeks tripped and fell that an unexpected laugh erupted from Emhet's mouth. Afterward, the colonel put a stop to the comedy, ordering the soldiers to leave Marius and take a position against the wall. Wandering unsupervised, Marius promptly flung all the windows open before settling on the floor. The breeze was welcome, but a harrowing dullness returned to the room.

Emhet rued making haste to leave his house so early. His coach had arrived late last night, when Costa was already asleep, and he left for the palace before Costa had risen. He hadn't seen his son in over three months. Emhet chastised himself for not heeding his better judgment—everyone knew that Julian was night friendly and morning shy. Truth be told, he left early because he wanted to get the day over with. He wanted to part with the peculiar diamond.

Emhet nervously glanced over at the wooden box on the table. He hadn't opened it since leaving Okomorling. The box was varnished a deep cherry red with large brass hinges. He'd had it made before he went north. Ornate boxes were de rigueur for his big customers, and there was none bigger than the crown prince—hopefully, he would become a patron for the length of his reign.

Normally, he hovered over his gems like a proud hen her eggs. But this diamond was deviant! He had never seen anything like it. It appeared to have its own internal source of light. To test his theory, he'd had the windows in the governor's palace covered. Without an external source, the jewel should have remained unseen. But not so! The light seemed to come from within. It was beyond baffling. Emhet had attempted to study its enigmatic depths for imperfections, but truth be told, he couldn't look at the diamond for more than a minute. Each time, he would inevitably lose his bearings. And what was most inconceivable was that instead of being the examiner he felt as if he were being examined. And the more he looked, the more his points of reference wobbled—his mastery and knowledge of jewels, his memories of his wife and son, even physical characteristics like the solidity of the table under his hands or the seat of the chair became less and less distinct. Suffice it to say, he had placed the diamond in its box, closed the lid, and locked it.

Emhet could feel his heartbeat. What if Julian blamed him for bringing the nefarious jewel back to Jesut Edin? Or worse, what if he blamed him for the rebellion in the north? Emhet wiped his brow. Maybe he should have been more careful and advised the governor to return it. But it was, without a doubt, the most magnificent specimen he had ever seen. Julian had implored him to find a gemstone befitting an emperor—and this was it! Just then Emhet noticed Weeks leaning against the wall. The audacity of the lazy fellow was boundless! How a soldier of such low rank could get away with such insolence was stupefying.

• • •

Weeks, Chunsey, and Bossun stood against the far wall. A large chandelier hung down from a plaster medallion at the center. As beautiful as the room was, the novelty was wearing off. Weeks' feet were aching. For the first hour he ignored them, for they had been busy keeping Marius from running off. But ever since Colonel Radavan ordered them to desist, the throbbing had become intolerable.

Weeks' toes were numb. He had to do something, so he leaned back. Colonel Radavan was too busy talking with the lieutenant and his staff sergeant to notice. The only one paying attention to him was the nasty little merchant. To remedy that, Weeks sent him eye daggers. He had been responsible for Emhet Turan all the way up to Okomorling. Thirty-five days of putting up and taking down his tent, heating his water, cleaning his clothes, emptying his piss pot, making sure he had enough pillows, bringing him food, taking it back to the cook for one reason or other, and so on and so forth. He hadn't joined the army to be someone's chambermaid! On top of that, he had his soldiers' duties to attend to. The days were long and the nights short.

Fortunately, the lieutenant's ears were not completely stuffed with cabbage, and on the return trip he assigned Chunsey to assist Emhet, while he and Bossun were given the task of looking after Marius. At first, their task seemed simple: keep him from wandering off. One moment Marius would be peacefully relaxed, so much so that they would soften their vigilance, but a moment later he would be gone! The day before their departure south, they found him in Okomorling's public market. A large crowd had gathered around him, and Marius was preaching. "God is love! Nothing but love I tell you." At times he would even embrace the onlookers. "You are God, just as I am God," he would tell them. Many were left smiling; after all, how often did the hardworking frontiersmen and women get a hug from a member of the royal family? Of course, everyone had heard of Captain Marius Proudst. His entrance into Okomorling was legendary—riding half-naked across the plateau, chased by the Pagani, holding the diamond in the air like the north star.

Compared to Emhet, serving Marius was easy. Not even ten days of rain had dampened Weeks' mood. Marius spoke maybe once or twice daily, if only to say "thank you"—a simple phrase that seemed to have gone missing from the merchant's vocabulary. It didn't matter if it was blowing wind or rain or both, if he was wet or caked in mud, Marius never complained. More often than not a serene contentment would blanket his face, and he could remain in this state for hours. He ate whatever they gave him, and slept where they told him. He never asked for special favors. Weeks soon found himself going out of his way to make sure Marius got hot soup and bread. He would clean his dirty clothes, and always gather fresh straw for him to sleep on at night. At some point along the way, Marius started calling him and Bossun his fishermen.

"Fishing, we like fishing, Cap" was Weeks' rejoinder. "You going to take a couple of lowly foot soldiers fishing?" he would ask.

"I will feed you the most glorious of fish," Marius would answer.

"I don' know," Weeks would chide him, grabbing two fist-fuls of belly, "I can eat a lot."

It was hard not to chuckle, thinking back on it all. And now he was in the palace! It was as spectacular as he had imag-ined. Weeks recounted to himself all the things that he would later tell the missus: the enormous gold-leaf frames and the painted ceilings, the chandeliers with a thousand crystals, the woven rugs without boot-mud and sand, and the waxed floor that reflected tall windows that went the entire length of the rooms. And, of course, the footmen at every door with their gloves and white stockings. He found the fragility of the palace almost haunting. If a platter fell, would the palace shatter like a fallen mirror?

Weeks turned and looked at Bossun. "Is this the throne room?"

Bossun, who himself had never been to the palace, grum-bled, "For the last time, Weeks, do you see a throne?"

"No."

"Well, it ain't the throne room, then." Bossun was in a foul mood—the liquor was wearing thin. Chunsey stood between them. They were accustomed to his silence, so they spoke around him as if they were a couple of farmers gabbing across a fence post.

"I was hoping to get a look at the throne to tell the missus 'bout it. You know, she always wanted me to be a palace guard and all."

"You? A palace guard!"

"Why not?"

"And I should be a general . . . and Chun here a bishop. But seriously, does yer missus fancy the king?"

"Whad'ya mean 'fancy'?"

"Is she one of 'em people who wants to know everything 'bout the royal family? Like what they ate fer dinner and the color of d'er socks?"

"Yeah, sure, why not," replied Weeks.

"Then it's her lucky day; the prince will come, and you'll be able to tell her all 'bout 'is stockings."

"Nah, 'e won't come hisself! He'll send 'is 'visors."

"Nothin' doin'. He'll come hisself, mark my word. He'll want to see his jewel in person. Besides, Marius being family and all. It's not the type of thing he would leave to 'visors, if you know what I mean?"

"Whad'ya getting at?"

"Let's say that something went badly at 'ome while you were gone."

"Like what?" asked Weeks. His eyes narrowed; he didn't like such speculation.

"Well, let's just say the side gate was left open, and the ducks got out. Who would be the best person to tell you?"

"Nobody!"

"But somebody has to, so who would it be?"

"I reckon the person who left the gate open."

"Exactly."

"But what if it was the missus who left the gate open?" added Weeks after a moment of consideration.

"That's not the point," answered Bossun flatly.

"Yes, it is!"

"Well, then your missus would 'ave to tell you."

"She'd say the kids left it open."

"That's between you and the missus. All I'm trying to say is that Julian is going to be 'ere."

"Why?"

"Forget it," growled Bossun, crossing his arms over his chest.

"No, no, I see," insisted Weeks. "Julian's comin' 'cause he wants to see who let the ducks out."

"Something like that," Bossun concluded with a scowl.

Weeks thought back to the many days he had been with Marius on their way down from Okomorling. He was pretty sure all of Marius' ducks had flown. Sometimes, at night, when he had gone to relieve himself, he found Marius watching the night sky, still as a frog. Once Weeks joined him just to see if he could pinpoint what was so captivating, but there hadn't been anything unusual, only stars.

One night, a week out of Jesut Edin, Marius escaped again. They had set camp just as a dense fog came drifting across the steppes. Not long after, a flock of not-to-be-seen ravens descended upon them, cawing and squawking, their foul cries echoing about camp like feral ghosts. It was as eerie a night as he could recall. Even the night watch sat in their tents that evening. In the morning, the birds were gone, but so was Marius. They eventually caught up to him twirling with his arms out and his head and palms raised upward. After that, the lieutenant ordered them to chain him to the wagon at night.

The hardest part for Weeks to understand was this—all Marius had to do to change his miserable living conditions was to stand up and claim, "I am Marius Proudst." Immediately, he would resume his princely status and all the comforts that it entailed. But for some inexplicable, baffling reason, Marius would not . . . or could not.

As Weeks considered all this, the gilded doors opened. Two courtiers in blue velvet jackets with long tails stepped into the room, positioning themselves on either side. "All rise, the crown prince," they said in unison. Weeks surged off the wall, hauling in his paunch and lifting his chest. This was the moment he had been waiting his entire life for!

14

FLEEING MINOL'S HOUSE

Roan woke with a start. She dreamt she had been in battle and was standing amidst clouds of dust and black powder. There had been a volley of musket shots fired. Roan could still smell the discharge in the air. She had been in hand-to-hand combat. Bodies were lying all over the ground: the wounded were crying for help. It had been near impossible to tell friend from foe. Looking down, she watched a fresh stream of crimson blood trickle into her palm and off the tip of her little finger. She was wounded. It was so fresh she didn't yet feel pain.

Clutching her hand she turned over to have a look. To her surprise, her hand was not wet from blood but from where Sza had been licking it. Roan pushed herself onto her elbows just in time to see the wolf's tail disappear out the door. "What is it with this wolf?" she wondered. "He's always been a step ahead of me."

Glancing around the room, a fresh light was upon the world. Roan was about to drop her head back but suddenly felt a clasp of horror. She had overslept. Only novice Yatu slept late, *never* warriors! Roan leapt out of bed. She was still in her clothes from yesterday. Embarrassment, hot and spiky, prickled across her brow. Even though Minol had set a basin of fresh water in a pitcher and a towel in her room, Roan decided to go outside. She found her way to the well she had gone to the day before. She washed her face and drank. When she returned, Roan found Minol sitting at the large table with her belongings gathered next to him.

"We don't have much time," he said. "I took the liberty of gathering your things." Minol's face was drawn tight. The twinkle that was in his eyes yesterday was gone, replaced with dark crescents. "I put some food in your satchel," he said. "If you choose the path we discussed last night, once in Torbeshacken, find the shop called the Red Lantern. Ask for the matron, and give her this letter." He held out a white piece of parchment with a burnt-orange seal. Sensing Roan's hesitation, he added, "You can trust her. She will help you."

Tentatively, Roan took it. She had not held paper in a very long time. She brought it to her nose; it had no odor. Taking her satchel, she tucked the paper inside just as she recalled Minol's earlier words. "What do you mean 'not much time'?" she inquired.

"The Red Bows will be here soon," he replied.

"Red Bows!" exclaimed Roan, her eyes blazed.

Minol nodded. "Which is why you had to come quick . . . and without being seen."

"How do you know?"

"A raven."

"But what have you done?" Though, even as she asked, Roan knew there were plenty of reasons.

"When Patrig learned of Skadje's innermost twisted desires, he knew he had no choice but to betray her, and ultimately, the Pagani."

"But that was a long time ago."

"To them, I am dangerous. There are things I know that they don't want others to know—much of which I told you last night. Skadje wants the Yatu and the rest of the Pagani to go to war alongside the Red Bows. She wants to rise up against Ilyria. She knows that the Ayn Noor is the one thing that unites all Pagani, and she is using the theft to forward her selfish ambitions. I am pretty certain it was *she* who revealed the whereabouts of the Ayn Noor to the Ilyrians in the first place."

"Skadje?"

"Yes!"

"Then she is free?"

"No, she is still a prisoner. She leads from the dungeons of Grebald. Sometimes prisoners are more dangerous than those that freely walk the streets."

Roan's mind could not fathom what Minol was saying. It took a moment before words could form in her mouth. "She would give the Ayn Noor to the Ilyrians?"

"It makes sense, does it not?"

"But if the Ilyrians have the Ayn Noor, she won't get it!"

"She's a sly one—the Ilyrians, after all, are bringing the Ayn Noor to Jesut Edin."

"But the Yatu could stop this!"

"Let me ask you, Roan, do you trust Ruus?"

Roan hadn't yet put words to her deepest feelings, but if she were honest, she did not trust Ruus at all. She *had* trusted Ferja, though.

"Ruus is rotten," continued Minol. "These are dangerous times! But all is not lost. The Turtle Clan survives. There are others that are on our side, ones you would never suspect—like the matron at the Red Lantern. What is important, in this moment, is that *you* are not here when the Red Bows arrive."

Roan's mouth went dry. "We should leave together! Come with me!" pleaded Roan, motioning with her head.

"I cannot," answered Minol. The timbre of his voice was grave. "If I am not here, they will track us down, and you will be caught in their net, too . . . and that *cannot* happen!"

"What are you going to do?"

"My work is almost done."

"What do you mean?"

"I took tincture of kalactraq an hour ago."

"Kalactraq reverses the course of one's blood. You will die!"

"The Red Bows are barbaric. Either way I will die."

Roan couldn't believe what she was hearing, though the haggard look on his face and the grayness of his skin made more sense. Just then Sza's ears perked up, and the hair on his back rose. "You must go!" Minol said, pushing himself to stand. With his arms and hands he ushered her out of the great hall.

"I . . . don't . . . understand," she protested. Roan felt utterly confused—this was happening much too fast. Last night it had all made sense. She had felt the truth of her purpose. Today, it wasn't so clear.

"There is no more time left to discuss!" said Minol, guiding her to the front door. Before opening it, he pulled out a small glass vial and held it up for Roan to smell. She recoiled.

"It will protect you," he said. Roan wanted to vomit. "It won't be so strong in a couple of minutes, I promise." Conceding, she bowed her head, allowing him to rub some on her neck.

"Make no mistake, Roan, you have a difficult choice to make. Remember all that I have told you."

Roan raised her head and nodded. "How could I forget?"

"Good," said Minol. He reached forward and turned the handle.

As he pulled the door back, Roan glanced outside. She was half expecting to see the field full of Red Bows, but there was not a soul in sight. There was not even a grain of wind in the air. The morning sun was shining upon the tips of the trees, and dewdrops were hanging upon gossamer strands like glittering diamonds.

"Sheets of glory and shades of gray," said Minol, quietly clasping the doorframe to support himself. Roan's throat felt swollen and her stomach tight. They stood in the doorway, saying nothing. Both of them were imbibing the verity of the morning.

Roan felt as if she were straddling a great mystery—that somehow the eternal and enduring sadness of death equaled the grandeur and magnificence of life, that sadness and beauty were entwined. It was life's most delicate recipe. Without one, there could not be the other. A tear sprung down Roan's cheek. She turned to look at Minol who was smiling back at her.

"We didn't have time for me to show you where I hid the chimney wheel. I placed it in the cemetery, next to Ule's gravestone. If they burn the house, you alone will know how to get below." Roan nodded. He then motioned with his head for her to go. Roan took her first step out, but then stopped. Minol remained in the doorway, waiting, as if expecting a question.

"Aren't you afraid?" she asked.

"I do not fear death," he said, shaking his head. "I am prepared, but you are not . . . *You* had better run!"

Roan found herself bounding across the field, her speed born out of both fear and adrenaline. She was headed straight for the woods. Suddenly, she noticed that Sza was running alongside her. Minol must have sent him away as well. It felt strange to be running for one's life without being chased. Normally, one ran away from danger, but in this instance, she didn't yet know where the danger was coming from.

Out of the corner of her eye, she noticed Sza peel away to the left. Roan did not know whether she should follow him but opted to stay her course—a choice she would soon regret. Branches slapped her face as she crashed through the trees and bracken at the edge of the woods. Once in the forest, instead of feeling safe, Roan felt an immediate sense of peril. She dove for a fallen tree. Wriggling under the giant trunk, she pressed her body against its rotting underbelly where fungi and beetles foraged. Breathing through her mouth, she rationed her breath in order to silence it.

A few moments passed, and still nary a sound could be heard. As Roan lay there wondering if her actions had been unnecessary, a subliminal plink reverberated out from the subterranean realm of innermost instinct. She was not alone. In stark silence, sometimes it is the *absence* of sound that is loudest. The little forest noises came next, the faintest crunches and cracks that Pagani warriors mimic when hunting. It was no surprise to Roan when bodies began to appear around both sides of the log. The men were shirtless, their upper bodies covered in streaks of reddish clay and black ash. It was a war party of Red Bows! Roan stopped counting after ten. Slowly she undid her sheath, readying her knife. *So many warriors for one man!* thought Roan. *They must fear the shaman.* A couple of the Red Bows held axes, but most carried muskets. Muskets still surprised Roan—such a new phenomenon in Bajarmaland.

As she watched them gather at the edge of the clearing, a Red Bow jumped on top of her log. Flakes of dirt landed in her eyes, but she didn't dare wipe them away. He stood on the log for what seemed to be an unbearably long time. When he did jump off, he landed on the ground not more than a couple of feet away. His deerskin leggings were open at the back, exposing his sinewy muscles. If Roan dared, she could have lashed out and cut the tendon at his ankle. Fighting a male warrior in hand-to-hand combat was the ultimate test for a Yatu, but it was a test Roan preferred to postpone for as long as possible.

The man turned and sniffed. Even the streaks of black war paint could not conceal his face. It was Jagr. He had a crooked nose, and the brow bone above his right eye was depressed from the beating he had received as a boy when fighting his mother's attacker—his father. Even so, he was bewitching to behold. The line of his jaw was sharp and bold. Jagr was one of those people you just wanted to stare at—if you dared. A craziness churned from his eyes, which made staring risky. One had to be careful not to become the subject of his focus.

Jagr's sadistic tendencies were well known. There were warriors who fought for honor. There were those who were willing to die for what they believed to be the greater good. There were some who sought the warrior lifestyle, the camaraderie, and the discipline. Some simply fought for loot. But there were a small number who fought because they *enjoyed* killing, and these persons could be divided into two categories: those who killed for hate and the subsequent pleasure of ridding the world of the target of their derision, and those who killed because they liked how it felt to take a life. Hatred Roan could understand, but those who killed for pleasure . . . with no reason, no need or purpose other than pleasure . . . confounded her.

The first time she saw Jagr was when the clans had gathered after the theft of the Ayn Noor. He rode bareback through their tsik without any greeting and speaking to no one. He accepted no hospitality, choosing to camp away by himself, keeping his own company at night. The only time anyone heard him speak was at the council when he demanded the execution of Ferja. Fortunately, the council did not heed his advice and chose exile instead. Roan now understood why Minol had rubbed such a potent oil on her neck. Jagr could smell fear—that's what fed him.

Surely, he sensed her presence. But as Roan's fortune would have it, Jagr could not break Minol's scent. He turned away and continued to the edge of the forest. The other warriors made way for him. Roan realized that they, too, were afraid of him. Raising his hand, he held his fist in the air. When he dropped it, there was a piercing cry as the Red Bows charged out of the woods. Shivers coursed up and down Roan's back. Even after they disappeared, Roan found it hard to move. Fear gripped her body. She had to force herself to stand up. Her arms and legs were shaking. Roan suspected that Minol would do everything he could to delay them, if only to give her time to get as far away as possible. Still, Roan withdrew her knife in case any had stayed behind. As she ran, Roan kept as low to the ground as possible. When she was a good distance from the house, she put her knife in its sheath and ran without restraint. Only when she reached the Great Northern Road did she stop.

Taking a moment she leaned up against a tree. Her heart was hammering. Her body felt drained—the adrenaline was gone.

"Some kind of warrior you are!" Roan berated herself. But soon another voice came to her defense. *Only a fool would not be afraid of a party of Red Bows.* She knew well the peril she would have been in if they had captured her. They would have bound her and had their way with her—only a rock would not be terrified. Besides, the Yatu teachings were on her side. "All warriors feel fear; what they do with that fear is what matters."

Looking up and down the road, Roan could see no sign of people. She began to run again, stopping only when she was high over the plateau. She glanced back and saw smoke billowing out of the sea of trees. Minol's house! She wanted to scream but instead chose to keep moving. As she went, she thought about the hidden stairs at the back of the fireplace, the basement, all the ancient tablets, the engraved boxes, the teachings, and all of Minol's translations. Roan suspected what he said was true; the secrets stored below would be untouched by the fire—they were her secrets now.

Had he passed into Bardo Fey? Was he on the other side? Was Minol able to stay awake in the afterlife, like a Blue Snake? Maybe he was watching her now? She spotted an eagle not moving its wings, as if stationary, riding the currents coming over the ridge. Was it him? Suddenly, a fierceness returned to her with vengeance. Roan began to charge up the hill. She hopped over boulders and sped up the mountainside like a bear. If Minol was watching, he would see what a formidable warrior she was!

It wasn't long before Roan was back at the narrows. Her next marker would be Little Guanyin. Her mind scuttled forward. A dread came over her—never before had she felt reluctant going back to the tsik. In only two days, she had plunged into dark and perilous waters. All she knew was she had to make a choice: to heed Minol and go south into the unknown or to stay with her tsik and live the life she was accustomed to. If she left, she would be seen as a traitor. There would be no going back. She would enter a world full of strangers. "A warrior's path leads through the darkest of dark woods. No warrior enters the forest where another has gone before. A warrior's path is a solitary path with no guideposts. If it were marked, it would be easy. If it were easy, one wouldn't need courage. If courage was not needed, there would be no use for warriors."

Roan felt dread like hard, cold ice filling her belly. She would have to make a decision soon. Ruus had ordered her to report back to her upon her return from Minol's, even before going to her own lodge. If she didn't report, Ruus' fury would be forthcoming—that was a given.

The question became whether she would risk going back to the lodge to say goodbye to Tieg, Farwah, and Gynn. Though Minol had advised her not to, how could she leave and not say goodbye to them? They were roots that had grown around her heart. It would be impossible to tear them out without damaging her own. Some things men did not understand, like how a woman's fortitude was built upon the foundation of relatedness. Most men seemed to think dependence was a kind of weakness, but connectedness was what gave Roan strength.

Roan wasn't so concerned about Tieg, mostly Farwah and Gynn—for different reasons. Farwah was old. Roan doubted she would live through another winter. She had been an old mare when Roan arrived six years ago! Now she was ancient, like a grandmother tree in the forest with its scraggly branches full of bearded moss. Farwah had been slowing for some time.

That is not to say she didn't work; she did small tasks all day long. When she wasn't gathering sticks for kindling or tending the fire, she was weaving mats and baskets. But with war upon them, surely, it wouldn't be long. Hardships were coming. Food would soon be scarce. As it was, Roan had been doing twice the amount of hunting to make sure Farwah's slowing wouldn't be noticed by others—and most of all by Farwah herself. If an elder deemed themselves no longer useful to the clan, if they sensed they were holding the tribe back in any way, they would take "the long walk" to the bardo grounds. When an elder entered the grounds, there was no returning. No more intake of food and water. To enter the gate was to surrender to death, to climb the platform was to prepare for departure. For months, Roan had feared she would come home and find Farwah gone, but now, of all ironies, it was not Farwah who would be leaving.

And poor Gynn! There was nothing in her that was a warrior. It simply was not in her constitution. Without Roan to protect her, she would become an outcast among her peers. Not because the Yatu were inherently mean, but because weakness could not be tolerated. The Yatu survived on strength. If one could not compete, there was no hand holding. Roan enjoyed the physical demands, but Gynn wilted under duress. She gave up far too easily, she had no self-belief. It was frustrating to watch. Tieg was too busy, too important to the tsik and lodge to pander to any one individual. The only hope for Gynn was if Droogie took her under her wing. Droogie was a fearsome opponent; even Surl wouldn't cross her. All of the senior warriors already treated Droogie as an equal. If she made it known that Gynn was in her care, she would remain safe. But how would she find Droogie at this hour? For all she knew, Droogie was off scouting the Ilyrian army.

With these thoughts spinning in her head, Roan arrived at the split in the trail. The northern path led toward Ruus' lodge, the other, her oikos. Roan could no longer put off the decision. *The darkest of dark woods,* thought Roan. She closed her eyes and let her body choose. For better or worse, a choice had been made.

15

THE ROYAL PALACE, GRAND HALL, THIRD FLOOR

Julian claimed he could smell an assassin. It was purported that as a child he could point out a liar in his mother's court—which made for an uncomfortable gathering when he happened to appear. But for all the virtues of intuition, it is an imprecise form of knowledge, and to base one's opinions and beliefs upon hunches, without the stone foundations of fact and reason, is risky, as more than one soul curled up in a corner of Grebald could attest. Julian was infamous for ordering his coach to change directions on a whim. Premonition or paranoia, no one would ever know. Not even Julian, for beneath all of his exuberant confidence was a forceful river of fear and suspicion that people were speaking poorly of him, laughing at him, maybe even wishing him dead.

Julian marched briskly into the room ahead of Lucius and Woefus. He had been waiting months for this day. He wore a bright blue velvet jacket with yellow lining, chosen by Lucius for this very occasion. Its long tails went below his knee-high stockings. His pale pink cravat was perfect. Julian's knee-length britches were of the same color as his jacket. His shoes were a lizard skin from somewhere beyond the Swaran Sea.

Lucius almost always accompanied Julian. If there were such a thing as a government appointment for a socialite, it would be him. He was a youth of slight build and a daring shock of black curls. Joviality and sarcasm were his natural inclinations. He knew most everyone's business, and the more salacious, the better. He was masterful at abstracting toxin from the plant, teasing out people's buried secrets, rationing out the correct portion of poison to pound of flesh, titrating the venom in just the right doses to keep people's tongues wagging. Careers tumbled, and reputations soared, bitter enemies and lovers were made, just by flushing a few juicy berries out from the bushes.

Woefus, on the other hand, had little tolerance for social occasions. He was chief of the Black Coats, and Julian's liaison to the queen. He was as tall as he was thin. Mostly, he was careful. Careful not only in the manner he moved, but in the way he talked. He didn't touch anything, or anyone, unless he meant to—and then only begrudgingly. With words he was parsimonious. If he weren't so chilly to behold, he might be considered refined, maybe even handsome.

If Lucius was the hot wind blowing through boughs, filling the air with the sound of chatter, Woefus was the silence of dirt, irreproachable and pragmatic—a terminal substance. He had the ability to gather information by muted, functional methods: threats, payments, and finger-snapping for starters. In gathering information, he was even better than Lucius. Signed confessions were his forte. He rarely attended social functions, so if he was present, it ensured the meeting was not merely social, but an affair of the state.

"Mister Turan," Julian declared. "This diamond better be worth all this trouble!" If lightning could strike where no storm brewed, where not even a cloud roamed, it might—for a sudden thunderstorm, dark and brooding, crackled within Emhet's skull threatening to send a lightning bolt down his neck and smote his heart. Julian watched as Emhet nervously tugged for the handkerchief in his pocket—sweat had begun to accumulate on his forehead.

"Gentlemen, sit!" implored Julian, motioning downward as he continued into the room. Out of the corner of his eye, he spied a man sprawled on the floor with his bare feet up against the wall. Julian halted. He had to look twice, for at first he didn't recognize his own cousin. He put his hands on his hips as a bemused grin spread across his face. "Marius, Cousin, is that you?" There was no reply. Julian looked over his shoulder at Lucius. "Is it my imagination, or is Marius dressed like a shepherd?"

A laugh popped out of Lucius' mouth. "Yes, he is rather poorly dressed, sire."

Julian shook his head. "Please, Marius, remain as you are, don't bother standing, or bowing, for your future king." Marius didn't so much as even turn to look at Julian. "And did you open all the windows?" Julian inquired. Again, there was no answer. He turned to face Lucius. "Do you think 'it' can even speak?" he asked. "Or has it lost its mind completely?" Julian twirled a finger beside his head.

"Perhaps it's best if it doesn't speak," said Lucius. "A wordless beast is a blessed beast . . . for it cannot offend."

"Right," agreed Julian. Clearing his throat, he addressed Marius once more. "Cousin, if you cannot greet me properly, then why not at least acknowledge me? There could be no harm in that." Marius lowered his feet and came around to sitting. He looked straight at Julian but said nothing. Turning once more to Lucius, Julian spoke. "So tell me, wise Lucius, when *does* silence become offensive?"

"Oh, maybe just about now."

Julian took a step toward Marius. "Dear cousin," he said, "I understand you've been through many travails. I do not see any harm in coming to you." Taking a few more steps toward Marius, Julian put out his hand. "Here, kiss my ring, and all shall be forgiven."

"I will not kiss your ring," stated Marius.

"Oh," said Julian, quickly withdrawing his hand.

"I will not place any man above God . . . nor any man above another."

"It *should* have remained silent," piped Lucius.

"No, Lucius," countered Julian. "If it had not spoken, we never would have known where it stood. But now we know. If it is mad, it's the dangerous kind! Cousin Marius, I do not claim that I am above God, but I am certainly not just any other man."

"Is there a difference?" inquired Marius.

Julian then looked to Woefus. "What does one do in such circumstances, being that he's Proudst and all?"

"Send him to Grebald . . . for his own safety."

"I like that!" Julian said. "'For his own safety.'" Julian swiveled to face Marius. "Pray tell, what on *earth* did you do with your shoes?"

"This is all I have need for."

"Are you not a captain in the Ilyrian army?" continued Julian.

"Never again will I fight for a man's worldly ambitions."

"'Tis a shame; he was rather handsome in a uniform," added Lucius.

"What about defending your queen and country?" asked Julian. "Surely, there must be exceptions to your lofty ideals."

"A leviathan may have many heads, but it is still a solitary beast."

"What on earth does that mean?" asked Lucius.

"I believe he's referring to the monarchy," clarified Julian. "So, Captain"—Julian's voice became stern—"you may believe your words are noble . . . but do you forget that you left your command and *stole* this . . . this diamond?"

"If I stole, I did so out of the ignorance of a deluded man."

"'If I stole,'" repeated Julian. "Did you hear that, Lucius? He's already absolved himself!

"Since you don't behave as my cousin, maybe I should treat you like any other captain. Desertion is a serious offense, not to mention needlessly putting your men in harm's way. Surely, you are counting on the military tribunal being lenient with a Proudst."

"A court should favor no one man over another. If it does, it is a tribunal of fools."

"A fool that calls others fools is either the king of fools . . . or no fool at all," injected Lucius.

"Do not waste your time with things that cannot be undone," continued Marius.

"'Things that cannot be undone,'" hooted Julian. "You are going to lecture me on what cannot be undone? Do you know what it costs to send two regiments north? I'll remind you in case you forgot—a small fortune!"

"Don't stand before the gates of heaven and worry about worldly possessions."

"Marius, I receive sermons from highly educated, religious men . . . not soldiers derelict of duty, dressed as shepherds."

"God does not want any man to stand between him and his people."

"Heed my warning, Cousin—even my dear mother will not come to your defense if you speak badly about the church."

"One should not throw pearls to a swine."

"Sir, do you refer to the queen as *swine*?" Julian's eyes burned into Marius.

"Set down your crown, Julian. You burden yourself needlessly."

"I am beginning to feel mad myself," said Lucius.

"If I put down my crown, Marius, who will pick it up? *You?*"

"I do not want your silly hat."

"'*Silly hat?*'" Julian bellowed. "Did you hear that, he calls the crown a silly hat!" Julian's face turned red.

"It doesn't exactly provide much shade for gardening, now does it?" added Lucius.

"Hush, Lucius!" admonished Julian, holding his finger up. "This is proving difficult." Turning back to Marius, he spoke. "Cousin, why pick a fight with me? That alone makes me think you *have* gone mad."

"Julian, the vines are full of grapes. Choose the grapes of wrath or the grapes of love, both hang before you."

"Perhaps he only feigns madness," said Woefus, stepping closer to Julian. "He seems to have all his faculties."

"Feigning madness to avoid consequences?" inquired Julian.

"We could find out."

"We wouldn't want to alarm anyone."

"Of course not," said Woefus. Lucius giggled nervously.

"For the time being," said Julian, "just make sure we aren't bothered by his sermons." Woefus motioned for the palace guard, who rolled Marius onto his belly, tied his hands and feet, and gagged him.

Julian smiled, rubbing his hands together. Looking over at the jewelry box on the table, he proclaimed, "At last! Before the sun goes down, I want to see this bloody diamond!"

Emhet maneuvered across the far end of the room on wobbly legs. "This box hasn't left my side for days," he began. "I locked it with this key." He held the brass key up for Julian to see.

"Just open it," said Julian, shaking his head.

But even as he spoke, a commotion came from the entrance. With a flash and a whirling shock of black hair, a voice called out, *"Marius!"*

"Someone . . . is going . . . to be . . . mad!" hummed Lucius.

All eyes were now upon Colette as she pulled Marius upright and flung her arms around him. After a tight embrace, she pulled the cloth out of his mouth. Then upon seeing the ropes around his wrists and ankles, Colette sent Julian a scalding look. "How dare you tie him like this!"

"Go on, Emhet," instructed Julian, returning his attention to the box. "I cannot be bothered with brotherly love."

Emhet inserted the key into the lock just as the footmen announced, "All stand, the queen."

"*My God!* What *now!*" growled Julian.

An ensemble of people began pouring into the room. At the center of it all was Queen Beatrice, carried upon an open sedan chair hoisted by six strapping porters. Most days she did not venture out of her living quarters. And although the sun had dropped below her proverbial horizon, light still suffused the skies of her mind—her authority remained undimmed. The queen was well loved by the Ilyrians. She had not gained territory during her reign, but neither had Ilyria lost any. It was said if she had one weakness, it was that she had overindulged Julian.

As the porters set the litter down, a livid Colette steamed toward her. "Look what Julian has done!" she yelled, pointing back at Marius. A palace guard stepped in front of her to prevent her from barging into the queen.

"Calm yourself, Colette," said the queen. "And be mindful; it's not proper to shout in public."

"Mother," said Julian, making his way next to her. "This is horrible timing . . . We were just about to take a look at my diamond. Can we not have this family reunion later?"

"I . . . don't *care* about your diamond, Julian!" she barked, giving him a tempestuous look. "I came to see Marius."

"Look what they've done to him!" exclaimed Colette, pushing people out of the way so the queen could see Marius tied on the floor.

"For heaven's sake, Julian, is that necessary?" asked the queen brusquely.

"It's inexcusable," added Colette. "What next? Send him to the prison tower?"

A smile pushed up the corners of Julian's face. "Perhaps," he confessed.

"Julian, Grebald? Really?" said the queen.

"He's not well, Mother," he pleaded. "In his condition, it would be the safest place for him. At least he would get three good meals a day!"

"That he would have to share with rats!" added Colette.

"Let's not forget ourselves," said the queen sternly, warning both Julian and Colette. "Take those ridiculous ropes off him," said the queen with a wave of her hand. The queen's guards removed the restraints.

"Marius," said Colette, kneeling next to him. "The queen made a big effort to come see you." Marius said nothing. "It's the queen, Marius," Colette persisted. "She's here to welcome you home!"

"I have no home, unless you mean among the birds of the field . . . and the destitute."

"But we will care for you, Marius. We're your family."

"'Whoever loves the mother more than me is not worthy of me, and whoever loves a son or daughter more than me . . . is not worthy of me. Whoever does not take up the cross and follow me . . . is not worthy.'"

"You are tired, Marius," added Colette. "You've been under much duress; you don't know what you say!"

"No, Sister, my eyes have been opened. And I say, why kings and queens? Why does a man raise himself higher than another when all are equal before God? Men bow only because they fear swords. But I say, 'Do not fear those who kill the body, for they cannot kill the soul.'"

"Marius, you must not offend those who are trying to help you," said Colette. "Julian wants to put you in Grebald."

"Is there a difference between a palace and a dungeon? Not in the eyes of the Lord."

Julian chuckled. "Oh, Marius, you are cruel, indeed. You're hurting your poor sister. She is trying to help you, yet you throw darts at her heart."

"He does not!" snapped Colette. "He's allowed to speak his mind!"

"See, Mother, this is not Cousin Marius, it's Jesus Christ."

"Our Lord and Savior," quipped Lucius.

The queen raised her hand. "Dr. Oppensky," she summoned.

The good doctor stepped forward. "Yes, my Queen."

"Tell me, what do you make of my nephew?"

Dr. Oppensky's arms were clasped behind his back. "Well . . ." he began, "when a person goes through a traumatic experience, such as losing one's comrades in battle, a reaction sometimes takes place in the substratum of the psyche. One might say a solution is found to assist with the shock of imminent death. It's a clever tactic really, a means of survival. In difficult circumstances a person *may* take on a different personality in order to compensate, most often a person from history with powerful attributes, like a great emperor, or in Marius' case, Christ. In this manner they adapt to protect themselves, perhaps to lessen the trauma. If he is cared for properly, Marius may find his way back. A person's defenses have a natural cycle, or as my colleague Alber Hoffe was fond of saying, a pattern of lessening."

"So what then is your diagnosis, Doctor?" inquired Julian with a tired look.

"Of course, I wouldn't be able to give you one until I do a thorough examination, speak to him, observe him, and take a full history."

"Dr. Oppensky," asked the queen, "are you suggesting Marius may never again be the same?"

"It's hard to say, but one should adjust one's expectations. Certain individuals may never again fit *our* criteria of 'normal.' We frequently see it in the fifth ward. Yet perhaps they can, with the right attention, live good lives, and be as dear in their own way, as any of those we regard as highly functional, especially if they are treated with respect and kindness."

"Respect! I'll make sure he gets respect, Mother," offered Julian.

"In Grebald?" said Colette, looking at Julian with disbelief.

"Not as a prisoner!" clarified the crown prince.

"That seems heavy handed, Julian," said the queen. "My wish is for the good doctor to help him. Have Marius delivered to Malador Hospital! Dr. Oppensky, see to it that he gets the very best care."

"Fine, Mother, let Marius feast with the loons!" said Julian, waving his hand in dismissal.

"That is my desire. And spare no expense, Doctor."

"Yes, my queen," said Dr. Oppensky, bowing.

"Oh, and Colonel Radavan, where is he?" asked the queen.

"Your Highness," said the colonel, stepping through the courtiers and bowing.

"I want you to see to it that Marius gets to the hospital and that he remains in the care of Dr. Oppensky until either the doctor releases him, or I tell you otherwise."

"I will see it done," said the colonel with another bow.

"I am tired," said the queen. Turning to Colette, she held out her hand. "Come, my dear, keep me company."

"I will stay with Marius. I don't want Julian to treat him badly again."

"Suit yourself."

The queen waved, and her entourage departed. And as soon as they were out the door, Julian lifted his hands and shook them in the air. "Finally, some peace!" Turning toward Emhet, he commanded, "Just open the box before there's another interruption!" As Julian neared the table, Emhet promptly lifted the lid.

Emanating from its bed of purple velvet, the Ayn Noor radiated to the four corners and beyond. Even a mere glance left no doubt in anyone's mind—this was indeed the emperor of diamonds. Julian's jaw dropped. He could find no words as he stumbled toward the table. Emhet gently put his hand up, intercepting him. "Your Highness, please be careful," he said, holding out a pair of white gloves. "It's highly recommended you wear these."

Julian stopped, but his face remained blank. It took a moment for him to hear what Emhet had said. "Yes, yes, of course," he replied in a distant voice but then frowned. "I want to see what happens . . . if one *does* touch it." Looking around the room, he noticed the three foot soldiers against the wall. Snapping his fingers, he motioned for them to come forward.

♦ ♦ ♦

Weeks reached across Chunsey and tagged Bossun on the arm. The three of them began to approach the assembly, but as the crowd parted, Chunsey stayed back. Weeks and Bossun proceeded without him. From the wall all they had been able to see was a glow. But as they rounded the table, Weeks found himself slowing down, not so much from his own volition but

rather a response that overtakes the body when one is awe-
struck. Bossun was close at his heels.

When they reached the table, Prince Julian pointed to
Weeks. "You, fat soldier. Pick it up!" Lucius giggled.

"Me, sire?" asked Weeks, his fingers gesturing to his chest.

"Yes you! Pick up the diamond!"

To disobey Julian would be unpardonable. Taking tiny
steps, Weeks neared the refulgent orb. Seeing the gloves in the
merchant's hand he reached for them.

"No gloves!" commanded Julian. "Pick it up with your bare
hands!" Emhet withdrew the gloves with a smirk. Weeks' eye
twitched. He had heard of the diamond's supernatural powers.
His pudgy fingers edged forward like the tentacles of a nervous sea creature. Weeks could feel Bossun's hot breath on his
neck. As he scooped it up, he shrieked, "Ayy-eeee," and flung
the Ayn Noor up into the air as if he had grabbed a hot, hot
coal. Instinctively, Bossun reached out and caught it. His body
immediately went rigid. Bossun hit the ground like a slab of
granite. Yet the Ayn Noor miraculously remained cupped in
his hands. For those in the room, Bossun looked not so unlike
a knight whose sword had been placed upon his chest in death.
His eyes remained open, but through them he was not seeing.
Weeks stood next to him on one leg like some exotic bird.

• • •

As all of this was transpiring, ravens began pouring into the
hall through the open windows. Hundreds of squawking birds
flew into the room, flying around and around in a giant circle. An ever-increasing mass of black feathers and caws filled
the chamber. Everyone who wasn't Weeks, Bossun, or Marius

covered their heads, shielding their faces. All light seemed to have suddenly left the world.

But as fast as the birds came in, they began to leave . . . going out the windows they had entered. Before anyone fully grasped what had just happened, the room was empty! Feathers and greasy white excrement lay splattered about—if evidence was needed.

Colette broke the silence. *"Look!"* she exclaimed, pointing at the fallen soldier. His cupped hands were empty. The diamond was gone.

Julian ran to the window. He could see the birds trailing into the distance. *"My diamond!"* he screamed. "Those birds stole *my* diamond!"

Just then, a great guffaw erupted. Spinning around, Julian gazed down at Marius, who was leaning against the wall, laughing hysterically. Julian's ashen-white cheeks flushed red. He reached for his dagger.

Colette threw her arms over her Marius. "Radavan," she shouted. "Come! It's time to take Marius to Malador."

"I'll deal with him later!" snarled Julian. "Let's go," he said, motioning with his head to Woefus. "Let's hunt those fucking birds!"

16

IN THE FORESTS OF BAJARMALAND

Farwah handed Roan a steaming bowl. The initiates and the warriors who were not out hunting were huddled around the fire. The mood was somber. Those gathered took cues from Tieg and Farwah, who remained silent. Roan put her nose to the broth. She could smell the qamas leaves and pitsana root. Farwah rarely gave out pitsana—it was hard to come by and only given to a warrior who had fought in battle or had pushed themselves to extreme physical limits. The aroma was relaxing, and the chunks of venison and bear fat were welcome too.

In silence, she sipped and chewed. Roan wondered if the others could see the mountain sitting on her shoulders. Maybe they did, for no one asked her any questions. They were wise not to ask! If they had, she would have had no choice but to lie. After all, she could not have told them the truth. Surely, Ruus would be interrogating them come morning. It was then Roan realized Tieg and Farwah were leaving it up to her to speak

first. Roan could feel the youthful, unsure part of herself wanting their advice. She wanted them to tell her what to do, to
relieve her of the burden of making her own decisions. Perhaps
this is why Minol advised her to stay away.

No longer able to remain quiet, Roan framed her question
carefully. "I am needed here?" she asked out loud to nobody
in particular. Her question was met with more silence. When
Tieg did look up, she did not say a word. She simply moved her
head from side to side—a Pagani expression meaning "maybe
. . . and maybe not." Her answer was as ambivalent as one could
give. Roan felt a hot rush of frustration come over her. It was
an unsatisfactory answer. But as she sat there, and the more
she thought, the wiser it seemed. For if Tieg had said, *Yes, you
are needed,* it would suggest that Tieg did not truly understand
Roan's dilemma and would have placed an even heavier burden
upon her by obliging her to stay. But if she had said, *No, we
don't need you,* that also would have been untrue. Every warrior was needed in these perilous times.

Roan lifted her bowl to take another drink. As she did, she
noticed a number of the younger initiates were watching her
every move. Only Gynn remained still. She had not even looked
up. Roan could see that she was trying to be brave. Guilt began
to drive into Roan's heart. So when she heard Droogie's whistle
from outside, she almost jumped to her feet.

Roan went straight over to her bunk, and began gathering
her belongings. She took a few things: her bow and quiver full
of arrows, her pouch of tools, her bow drill for fires, her long
knife, and various medicinal herbs, including her hunting poison. Placing what she could in her satchel, she paused for a
moment, looking at her leather helmet and body armor. She
decided against it—they would be too burdensome to carry

and would be needed by the others when the Ilyrians attacked. Tieg would give them to someone worthy. Roan grabbed her large bear fur and placed it in Gynn's lap—it was a formidable gift. Gynn pulled the skin around herself. Her blond head was all that was visible underneath the mound of fur. From the wooden frame above the fire, Roan gathered a couple of strands of dried meat. Not nearly enough to make it all the way to Torbeshacken, but it would give her a few days, enabling her to flee without having to take time to hunt.

Roan then went over to Farwah. She knelt before her and took her soft, wrinkled hands and brought them to her nose. She breathed in deeply, taking in Farwah's sweet smell for the last time. Looking up, she peered into her eyes and searched. Roan could not locate any sadness. There was only the steadfast quality of love. Roan smiled. Farwah's cheeks pulled upward followed by a bevy of wrinkles. Roan kissed her hands and let go. Tieg was standing by the entrance. They embraced quickly before Roan pushed the door open. None of her training had prepared her for this moment, crossing the threshold, stepping into the wilderness, the darkest of dark woods.

The night sky was a pool of blackness. Only the glint of the buoyant stars kept her innermost being from drowning in the watery abyss. Roan felt consumed by a multitude of contrasting emotions. But the fresh air did something to soothe her, as did the silhouettes of the pointing trees.

When Roan heard the stomp of a horse's hoof, hope ignited inside her. She marched toward the sound. Had Droogie fetched Hanoomé?

"Over here," came Droogie's voice. Roan found her perched upon a horse. "Congratulations," she proclaimed, "you have done something very bad!"

"What makes you say that?" asked Roan.

"Because they've taken Hanoomé." Roan's heart sank into her stomach. "I saw Surl leading him away. I came to see what you could possibly have done!"

"All I can tell you is that I must leave tonight . . . and I am in great need of a horse."

"You can have this one," said Droogie, dismounting.

"I cannot take yours. If they find out you helped me . . ."

"But this is not my horse!" interrupted Droogie.

"Whose is it?"

"Surl's," she said dryly.

Roan burst out laughing. Droogie was a black magician of the best sort. "A horse thief! I believe you have found your calling, Droogie!"

"No," said Droogie, "when I saw Surl riding Hanoomé, I knew what my destiny was."

"Which is?"

"To make Surl's life miserable."

Roan's head went back as she expelled a hoot. "I am grateful, Droogie," said Roan, "although it troubles me to leave without Hanoomé!"

"Why don't you politely ask Ruus for him back?" she answered.

"I suppose Strasi will do," said Roan.

"Look at it this way, if you need fresh meat on your journey, you can eat him . . . and you don't have to feel too bad."

Roan could now see the dark pits that were Droogie's eyes. There had always been an unspoken closeness between them. Roan could tell her anything—except today. Surely, Ruus would be demanding answers. "I must go!" she said, for she couldn't think of anything better to say.

"Is that so?" said Droogie sarcastically, but then her voice changed. "These northern Yatu are like old leather, impossible to work with."

"Why haven't they come for me already?" asked Roan, perplexed.

"They underestimate you. Ruus is arrogant. She thinks all of the warriors in this tsik are soft. She thinks Ferja didn't train us properly. She expects you will come groveling, begging her to give you back Hanoomé."

While Roan thought about it, Droogie reached forward and touched her cheek. "You are my great friend!" she said. "And you will always be." Roan was surprised by the sudden tenderness. Affection was rare from Droogie. Roan dropped her forehead against Droogie's shoulder and squeezed her hand. After a moment, Roan pulled away. Placing a hand at the base of Strasi's mane, Roan threw one leg up and over his back. Sitting up high, she spoke. "If I don't see you at sunset . . ."

Droogie finished her sentence. "We'll feast on Mount Kalisha at sunrise!"

"Droogie," said Roan suddenly remembering. "Can you do me a favor and look after Gynn?"

"Of course," she answered.

Roan's eyes welled up with tears. It was as if a weight had been lifted off her heart, allowing the groundswell of emotion to rise. Gynn would have a formidable ally.

Roan leaned slightly forward. Strasi was off like an arrow, almost taking her by surprise. Roan decided to head south. The fastest route to Torbeshacken would be to ride across the open plateau, but Roan thought it wiser to go along the foothills and stay in the cover of the trees for as long as possible. Surely, Ruus would send a party after her.

The cold spring air filled her nostrils, invigorating her mind. Roan had only been riding for a few minutes when she heard a shrill whistle. Strasi abruptly reared. Before Roan could clasp his mane, she found herself hurtling through the air, landing flat on her back. *Uuuugh!* came the long exhale. Roan felt paralyzed as she waited for the course of her breathing to reverse. She heard Hanoomé whinny nearby. He must have just recognized her! As she lay there, a rider came out of the trees. Roan recognized the oafish figure, the rounded, muscular shoulders, the mountain that was Surl. Dismounting, she came and stood above Roan, dangling a rope in her face. Roan's long exhale had yet to reach its end. "You thieving bitch," hissed Surl. "You think Strasi would let a traitor ride her?" Just as Roan began to breathe, Surl put her foot against her throat. Roan reached up with both hands and took Surl's foot, but she had no strength to push it away. Surl could easily crush her windpipe. "I could kill you," said Surl, "and nobody would blame me." Roan wanted to move her head, but doing so would only cause damage to her windpipe. She forced herself to remain unmoving, trying to bring air quietly through her nose.

"What does it feel like to die?" asked Surl, touching the rope to Roan's cheek. If she could have spoken, perhaps Roan would have told her about the speckled light forming at the periphery of her vision . . . or the excruciating pain in her lungs as they cried out for air. But before Roan had a chance to further consider, she heard a terrifying growl. Surl screamed and spun away. Roan rolled onto her stomach and clasped her throat. Immediately, she began gasping and coughing. As her senses coalesced, she could hear a battle raging a couple of feet away. Surl's grunts were mixed with the sounds of a snarling canine. Amidst her own gravelly rasps, Roan forced herself onto her hands and knees. Looking up, she saw Sza's mouth locked around Surl's arm. Surl had grabbed him by the scruff with her free hand. Sza was pulling downward, using all his weight to keep her from gaining leverage on him, but it wouldn't be long before Surl would lift him up and pummel him to the ground. Roan frantically rummaged around, searching for something heavy. She grabbed hold of the first thing she came to—a thick log. It was much bigger than she would have chosen under normal circumstances. She grasped it with both hands, and with all her might, she hoisted it above her. Roan let it fall on top of Surl's head. Surl dropped to the ground. Roan relieved her of her knife and flung it into the woods. She then leaned over to feel for Surl's life pulse. Whether she deserved to live or not, she would . . . albeit with a throbbing headache.

Roan looked for Sza, but the wolf was gone. Retrieving the rope, Roan tied Surl's hands and feet behind her back. This would give Roan some needed time. She quickly gathered her belongings strewn about, then whistled for Hanoomé. He would not have gone far. Hanoomé whinnied. As Roan stumbled in his direction, she palpated her throat. It appeared that nothing was broken, nor could she taste blood. Surl had been foolish to come alone.

Roan marveled at the mystery of Sza's appearance. He must have been following her since leaving Minol's. What good fortune! Minol did say they would be friends. When Roan caught up to Hanoomé, he threw his head up, greeting her. Roan stroked him as he put his muzzle against her and nibbled affectionately. "I hope you still feel this happy in a few days," she croaked. It hurt to speak. She threw her leg over him, and with the slightest turn of her head, she gave Hanoomé the direction she wanted him to go. "Tali! Tali!" she called out.

Let's go! Let's go! Hanoomé surged forward, barreling into the open maw of night.

Hanoomé was regarded as one of the finest, if not *the* finest horse in the tsik. Many warriors had made Roan offers, but what was the price of priceless? Tieg had brought Hanoomé to her when he was just a colt. Tieg was known in the mountains for her equine knowledge. Many Pagani called on her when their horse was sick or lame. She even assisted with difficult births, or assessing injuries, and provided general horse care and training. Sometimes she would be gone for weeks. After one such call, she had returned leading a leggy chestnut colt. "I have something for you, Roan," said Tieg with a mischievous smile.

All Yatu were given care of a colt when they turned thirteen, and the arrival of Hanoomé auspiciously coincided with her birthday month. Roan loved him from the first moment they met. With assistance from Tieg she looked after him with the greatest of care. And as Hanoomé grew older, Roan trained him in the way of the warrior.

• • •

It was late afternoon, and Roan had been riding since the night before. She couldn't stop, for she was being followed. Three riders had been on her trail since midday. They hadn't been gaining, but nor had they been losing ground. Roan knew she couldn't keep this pace forever. Soon she would have to rest and, perhaps most importantly, let Hanoomé rest. As great a horse as he was, he was not Papilon, the immortal horse with wings. No, he was a horse with real legs, and real legs tire. And Sza! He would need to rest too. Roan had been catching glimpses of him running alongside them. Hanoomé appeared to have grown accustomed to his presence.

Roan wondered who Ruus had sent to bring her back. Obviously, the lead tracker was good, for they had been surprisingly quick to pick up her trail. Would she risk sending an elite tracker such as Ussuri when the tsik was preparing for war? Roan looked across the open plateau. If she had panicked and ridden across the plains, they would have probably caught her by now. After all, there is nothing quite like the sight of prey to spur the hunter onward. In the foothills, out of sight, she could instill doubt in their minds. At this point, it was her only advantage. It would slow them down some, for they would have to remain vigilant in case she ambushed them. However unlikely, they would have to consider that possibility. Roan reached up and stroked Hanoomé. He was a powerful horse . . . and proud. He would not readily let another horse overtake him.

When night came, Roan lit a fire but promptly abandoned it. She hoped that her stalkers would rest themselves, thinking she had stopped for the evening. Walking Hanoomé deep into the night, Roan hoped she might gain some precious time. At the break of day, she stopped and rubbed Hanoomé's legs before resting herself. She put some meat on a nearby rock for Sza, who was still keeping his distance.

As the sun's fortitude grew, Roan kept her eyes behind her. Riding for over an hour without sighting them, she began to think that perhaps her plan had worked . . . that is, until the three riders appeared in the distance. Her heart sank. They *had* tracked her through the night. It had to be Ussuri!

By midday, darkening clouds were hemming in the horizon. Surely, rain would be forthcoming. Roan had two days' worth of meat left. At some point she would have to hunt. It would be near impossible to do so and simultaneously flee. *They're too good,* she thought as she glimpsed one of the riders cresting the ridge. *Watch your gloomy thoughts, Roan. One can lose a battle even before it starts.*

An hour later rain began to fall, and with it, an errant cold front had come. Her breath became visible. In the distance, she caught sight of a river. *Hanoomé and Sza could use a drink,* she thought. Roan made her way down through the trees. At the bottom of the hill, she found an old trail. She had never been this far south. The Pagani used to live in these parts before the Ilyrians came north. She considered the trail might lead to an abandoned village. After watering she would have to make a big decision.

Coming around a bend, the view of a stream opened up before her. However, the trail continued along the hillside, winding through boulders and trees. She could hear the river clearly now. Roan was certain the trail would eventually lead to a crossing as the curvature of the land suggested. After cresting a slight rise she suddenly found herself gazing upon a rider sitting in the middle of a ford. Roan tensed. She wondered if one of her pursuers had somehow gone around her. Or had she mistakenly gone in a circle? Whatever the case, it was too late to turn away. She urged Hanoomé forward.

Roan dropped her shoulder and took hold of her bow. She fitted an arrow on the string. As she neared the stream, she could see it was a woman, but as of yet, the rider made no movement to lift her weapon. Roan lowered her bow. The rider's feet dangled on either side, relaxed and unthreatened. Just then, Hanoomé and the other horse let out a couple of friendly whinnies. Roan squinted. Could it be? Yes, it was! "Ferja!" declared Roan with a surge of excitement.

Ferja raised her hand in a welcoming gesture. Hanoomé stepped into the stream and threw his head back slightly; both horses were happy to see one another.

"Greetings, Roan," said Ferja.

"Greetings," she replied.

"I've been watching you since yesterday," said Ferja. "Ussuri is tracking you!"

"I wondered if it wasn't her."

"You still have a chance if you listen to me."

"I thought you were banished."

"Which means I make my own rules. And if you are fleeing, then the rules don't apply to you either. And as the saying goes, 'The enemy of my enemy is my friend.'"

"What do you suggest? We are only two, and they are three."

"Not good odds given who it is," said Ferja. "If I am not mistaken, Eorl is with them. If I were younger, we might stand a chance, but as it is, we must use our wits. They are only tracking one horse. So only one horse must leave this river."

"But they will see your tracks and know a second horse has joined up with me."

"But they won't! I rode downriver suspecting you would come to this ford. When they reach this point, they will have no reason to think another rider met you here. So, if only one horse leaves, they will believe it was Hanoomé and will follow my tracks. They must be tiring, too, and I doubt even Ussuri would have the presence of mind to see the slight difference in hoof marks . . . at least not until it's too late. Meanwhile, you must stay in the river for as long as you can. It runs east until it joins the Sombol. Am I right to believe you are headed south?"

"Yes."

"Good. Then I will ride west. I will lead them farther into the mountains. Compared to theirs, my horse is rested. It will take time for them to catch this old fox, and by that time, you will be far away."

Roan was about to speak, but Ferja raised her hand. "I have watched you for a long time, Roan. I knew your mother well. I don't know how this became your path, but I trust it is a good one. The Yatu are in disarray. There is no proper leadership anymore. I suspect it is Skadje who leads now."

Then Minol was right.

"It's a pity, but such are our times."

Ferja flung a string of smoked rabbits that were tied by their feet. Roan caught them. In her tiredness she hadn't noticed them hanging over Ferja's shoulder. "May the huntress always be at your side!" With this, Ferja's horse splashed up the bank on the far side of the ford. Roan watched her gallop away, but she didn't wait for her to disappear. She directed Hanoomé down the middle of the stream. Roan was careful to avoid all branches; she would not risk leaving even a single hair. When she was about to disappear around the first bend, she looked back to see if the riders had yet reached the river. There was no one in sight—perhaps Ferja's plan would work.

17

The Hoffe Residence, Jesut Edin

With his head in one hand, Brill tapped the fingers of his other against his desk. An hour earlier his mother had left the house with Liis and Pola. They were off to meet Monsignor Iraneous. Brill glanced over at Costa. His face was drawn long, and he was slumped down in the chair like a spineless toy. With his head flopped against the wing of the chair, Costa gazed absently at Brill. After a longish pause he professed, "I'm bored."

"Let's go onto the roof," said Brill, sitting up.

"The roof? What about my crutches?" he said, motioning toward them.

"You can stay here if you want," said Brill.

"No," said Costa, shaking his head vigorously, "I can do it."

"Okay," said Brill, "but first, let's go to Liis' room."

"Why?" queried Costa, squinting at him.

"You'll see."

The two of them carried on down the hallway. When they reached the third door on the right, Brill put his ear up to it. After a moment, he turned the knob and pushed inward. It was a large rectangular room that mirrored his own, except that Liis had only a single window looking out onto the courtyard. Brill walked up to her armoire and pulled it open. Costa waited at the door. "Come over here," said Brill, waving for him.

"What are you doing?" asked Costa, crossing the room.

Brill held up one of Liis' uniforms. "This would fit you!" he said.

"There's no way in hell I'm going to put on that dress!" declared Costa.

"It's no big deal," said Brill. "Just put it over your pants." After putting one on himself, Brill stood in front of the full-length mirror and smiled.

Meanwhile, Costa was opening and closing Liis' drawers. Glancing up, he sneered, "You really are maladapted, Brill. But look at these!" He held up a pair of Liis' underwear.

"*Costa!* Put those *back!*" Brill's face reddened.

"You're no fun," claimed Costa, stuffing them back in the drawer.

Brill frowned. "Come on, let's get out of here!"

"I'm not going with you like *that!*" trumpeted Costa.

"Why not?"

"What if Hanna sees us?"

"She won't. She's in the kitchen."

Vigorously shaking his head, Costa added, "Maybe you should be a . . . nun, Brill."

• • •

"Wait up!" shouted Costa from below.

Brill hustled up the ladder and onto the ridge; he was desperate to have a moment to himself. Looking out over the city and beyond always relaxed him. Up here, his eyes could travel loose and free as a kite on a gamboling wind, reaching all the way to the meeting place of land and sky, where vision can go no farther.

A moment later, Costa pulled himself up next to Brill. His lips were pasty. Costa's countenance reminded him of how one's face appears just before discharging something disagreeable from the belly. He was breathing hard, but it didn't stop him from grumbling. "This is dumb. I can't even see the park from here."

"This is as far as it is safe to go," instructed Brill. "Besides, my mother could come home any minute." Even before Brill finished speaking, Costa began scooting down the tiles feet-first. "Don't!" Brill called after him.

"Oh, come on, you big baby!" said Costa, steering himself toward the most exposed section on the roof. Brill reluctantly followed. "Much better," said Costa, arriving at the abbreviated cornice wall that doubled as a drain. "If you don't want to go to seminary, Brill, you must show your mother what you're made of."

"What do you mean?"

"Do something . . . stupid," said Costa, flashing a cynical grin.

"What, like falling off the roof?" clamored Brill.

"Something like that."

"Just don't stick your head up too high, Costa. If you can see people's faces, then they can probably see yours."

Costa leaned forward. Brill held on to the back of his shirt. "Oooh, that *is* far," he said, his eyes widening.

"I told you," replied Brill. Just then he caught sight of a dog sauntering toward the park, its curved tail lowered to half-mast—the summer sun was a brutal master. The dog was headed across the street, probably hoping to find some shade, perhaps under the lemon tree that had survived by the charity of a housemaid's bucket of dirty water. The jacolandis hadn't been so lucky. Brill missed their tiny green leaves that used to blanket the park. People from all over Jesut Edin would make the long pilgrimage up the hill, not only for the park's cloistered promenades and their shady benches but for the splashing fountain at the center of it all. More than anything, what Brill missed were the jacolandi blossoms. This time of year, the violet flowers filled the air with a fragrance that could only be described as the smell of purple itself.

Costa's shrill voice brought Brill out of his musings. "Look!" he said, pointing. Brill turned to see strands of black birds streaming toward the park. Brill couldn't recall seeing so many birds before, except maybe in the wintertime when they left the city at dusk. Pola used to tell him that the reason the ravens journeyed west in the evening was because they roosted in the sun at night, which was why they were charred black. A smile broke across his face—for so long he had believed her!

"Those birds are the devil's own," proclaimed Costa. Brill watched the early arrivals find their places among the barren branches atop the trees. Their cawing, combined with the torrid heat and the incessant buzz of cicadas, cast a morbid spell over the park, filling the remaining cracks of day with a sticky sort of lethargy.

Lately, an idea had been forming, and Brill began to wonder out loud. "It seems to me," he said, holding a finger to his bottom lip, "that *everything* is born from something before it." Costa's eyes remained fixed on the park. "But each moment," Brill went on, measuring his words carefully, "is so close to the next that nobody can really tell if the new moment is any different than the preceding one."

"Ugh," groaned Costa with more than a little hint of exasperation. "What *nonsense* are you going on about now?" Momentarily he took his eyes off the park.

"Remember how almost every afternoon we used to have rain? Now we have none, but did anybody see the changes? No, they happened too slowly for anyone to notice. And now we're in the middle of a drought."

Costa sent Brill a look of incredulousness. "The only changes I know of," said Costa, wiping his forehead with his sleeve, "are the ones I see in the servants' quarters. Have you seen Mallory lately?" Brill shook his head. "This winter she didn't have any tits, and now she has these." Costa snickered as he cupped his hands to demonstrate. Brill shook his head. There were some things Costa said that he doubted, but spying on servants was not one of them.

"All I am trying to say," continued Brill, "is that change happens . . . because of something before it . . . *something* . . . invisible. Take water, the vapors rise off the ocean . . . and when there is enough, they become clouds . . . and when the clouds get full, they can't hold any more and it rains. But all we see is the rain . . . We don't see the vapors. We don't see what came before, what made the clouds in the first place."

"Of course not, vapors are invisible!"

"That's what I'm saying!"

"No, you're not."

Frustration came over Brill—it was an effect Costa had on people. Trying not to get pulled into an argument with him, Brill continued as calm as he could. "What would it take to *see* the cause . . . before the changes take place? Take those birds, what *caused* them to come to the park today? We only see them arriving, but there's got to be a reason—an invisible reason!"

"What I want to know . . ." said Costa, jutting his chin forward. "I want to know what that man is doing over there? Look at him! He doesn't move! And that damn bird on his bench is making such a ruckus!" Brill shaded his eyes and squinted toward the park. He noticed a couple of servants hurrying in earnest, their arms stretched long from the weight of their satchels.

"No, stupid! Over there," said Costa, wagging his finger. Brill followed his direction to a man sitting on a bench. He was surprised he hadn't seen him. A hood covered most of his face. He sat alone, except for a large raven on the spine of his bench. The black bird was shuffling sideways, going a few paces one direction, then shuffling back the other way. Occasionally, it paused long enough to snap its beak and send out a couple of chortles skyward. Brill could even hear the bird over the dissonant buzz of the cicadas.

"What I really want to know . . ." said Costa, holding a finger up to his lip, mocking Brill. "Is the man a bum . . . or a beggar? And what's his problem? And why doesn't he chase that bird away? If I were him, I would hit it with my stick!"

"I don't know . . . Maybe he's dead," offered Brill.

"Dead!" Costa's lips tightened. "A bit drastic, *that!*"

"Why? We're all going to die . . . someday."

"Oh, is that so," said Costa, rolling his eyes. A moment passed before Costa spoke again. "I bet if we went down there, he'd smell like lubjok. He's probably been drinking all morning! That's what bums do! He's probably too drunk to lift his head. See, it's not *so* hard to find your invisible reason. Drink a bottle of lubjok, and sure as the sun rises, you'll dumb pass out!"

"When I've seen people passed out, they're usually lying on the ground."

"And people die sitting up," countered Costa.

"Maybe. Have you ever seen a dead person?"

"No, but neither have you."

"I saw my father."

"No you didn't."

"Well . . . Liis told me about him."

"Yeah, yeah," Costa mumbled something Brill couldn't make out.

Brill gazed over at the birds gathering in the branches. Maybe the ravens had come to feast on cicadas—was *that* the invisible reason?

"Maybe you're right," said Costa. "That old man is dead . . . and that's why the ravens are here, to eat his eyeballs. It's a delicacy to them you know."

Brill then noticed a gang of youths gathering nearby. With their arrival, the big raven leapt off the bench, flapping its greasy wings hard enough to join its cohorts. A shirtless boy lifted a stone and whipped it into the tree after him, sending the flock into a cawing frenzy.

Costa pointed at him. "The one without the shirt. I can't believe his family lets him go about town like that. He looks like a rat!"

"His parents probably don't care," said Brill.

"Well, they should! And what do you think they do all day?" asked Costa.

"I don't know . . . play cards," answered Brill.

"Play cards!" shrieked Costa. "Steal is what they do," he declared. "That bum, if he's not dead, would be wise to push off." Just as Brill opened his mouth to speak, Costa smacked his arm. *"Your mother!"* he barked. Brill dropped flat against the roof. After a couple of moments, he chanced a look up. Sure enough, he could see his mother dressed in black, still in her mourning attire, bearing down the avenue, returning home with Liis and Pola. For a moment, he thought she looked a bit like a raven herself.

When Brill figured they were beneath the roof, he scrambled up the tiles. "Wait here," he told Costa. Passing over the ridgeline, he shimmied down the other side, descending the ladder onto the upper balcony of the courtyard. Brill crouched behind the wall of the upper terrace. Before long, he heard a door shut. Seconds later his mother barreled into the courtyard. She was followed closely by Liis and then Pola, who was clad in her usual linen garment that concealed all but her hands and ankles. Liis wore a light blue dress that stopped below the knees. At first his mother headed straight for the chapel, but at the last minute, she veered toward the well. *"Haannaa,"* she called out.

"Coming, ma'am," came a reply from within the house. Brill watched Hanna run through the open door holding her skirt up slightly. She was a broad-shouldered girl, a half a year younger than him. At the well, Hanna dropped in the bucket. A second later Brill heard it smack the water.

"Have you seen Brill?" his mother demanded.

"No, ma'am," she replied, keeping her eyes lowered. Brill exhaled. Hanna hauled up the dripping bucket and placed it on the edge of the well. Dipping in the ladle, she carefully poured a cup for his mother, then Liis, and then Pola. When they were done drinking, Lisbeth marched toward the chapel. The other two dutifully followed. Just as Brill was going to turn away, Liis' head spun around, her eyes hooking his. Brill slid down the wall. With their footsteps buried behind the wooden doors of the chapel, Brill hurried back up the ladder.

"Did your mother see us?" asked Costa, not bothering to take his eyes off the park.

"I don't think so, but Liis might have."

"Watch this," said Costa, whipping a silver terkel toward the park. The coin glittered as it arced, catching slices of the sun. Ricocheting off a trunk, it rolled to a stop on the ground near the youths. A tall kid whose head hung off his neck like an overripe gourd saw it first. A second later they were all pushing and shoving to get to it.

"Look at 'em," declared Costa, chuckling. After the short melee, the shirtless boy held the terkel overhead in victory. Before Brill could say anything, Costa threw another. The coin hit a kid in the shin. As he rubbed his leg, the shirtless youth grabbed the second. Prancing around the others, he displayed one in each hand.

"The rat got 'em both!" he bemoaned. Costa and Brill leaned back in order to avoid their searching eyes. Brill was reminded of the story he learned from Father Bartholomew about the Hebrews who were showered with manna from heaven on their journey across the desert.

"Do you have a terkel?" asked Costa. "I need another one."

"A . . . *ter*-kel?" repeated Brill slowly, trying to give himself some time.

"Yes . . . a *ter-kel*!" mimicked Costa. "Do you have one?"

"No," Brill lied, unable to think of something better to say.

"Just give it to me; I know you do!" Costa stuck out his open palm. "I want to see if I can't get it over to the bum. I bet he'll move if he sees a little money."

"If you really want to give him some, why don't you go down and hand it to him," said Brill.

"That's no fun!" said Costa. Brill shrugged and scooted back up the roof.

"You know, you really should be a priest," Costa called out after him. Once over the top of the ridge, Brill waited just to see if Costa was following. Upon hearing his curses, Brill made his way down the ladder to the upper terrace. When Costa arrived, Brill held out his crutches for him to take. Costa snatched them out of Brill's hands. Brill hopped down the steps into the courtyard, taking a moment to peek into the chapel. His mother, Liis, and Pola were kneeling in prayer, as still as egrets.

Brill scooped a ladle of water and poured some into a wooden cup for Costa. Holding his crutches under his armpits, Costa took it. His hands were shaking so much that water splashed out. Brill picked a crock off the top of the well and filled it. Puffing a series of shallow, rapid breaths, Costa labored to speak. "Who's . . . that . . . for?" Costa tended to wheeze when he exerted himself.

"The beggar," said Brill.

"Oh . . . I see . . . now . . . you're the . . . patron saint . . . of beggars?"

"No! Just thought I'd see if he was thirsty."

"You . . . just want to see . . . if he's *dead*," said Costa with a smirk. Brill shrugged. There was little use arguing with Costa. "Well . . . you better get . . . that dress off first . . . unless you want to get beat up."

"I suppose you're right," Brill agreed.

Once he'd changed, they headed through the kitchen toward the carriage yard. A big pot of water was boiling on the stove. A cluster of limp hares lay flat across the counter, their legs outstretched as if still springing away from the hunters. Sisal was preparing food for dinner. Hanna was nowhere to be seen.

Once in the carriage yard, Brill could see that the wagon was gone. Gasol must have left on an errand. He took care of the stables and the carriages. Passing the servants' quarters, Brill caught sight of a big horse next to the stalls. He had never seen this horse before, which in itself wasn't unusual, but the large dog resting on its haunches and forepaws next to it was. As soon as Brill laid eyes on the dog, it stood up and trotted up the steps, disappearing into the servants' quarters. Brill stopped and turned toward Costa. "Did you see that *dog*?"

"It looked more like a wolf to me!" said Costa.

"A wolf! Here in Jesut Edin!" retorted Brill. Just then he noticed a woman looking at him through a half-open shutter. Her hair was straw blond. He had never seen her. But before he could point her out to Costa, she was gone. Brill knew they didn't have the money to hire a new servant; Emhet had been very clear that he would not pay for any more help. *Perhaps she's visiting Pola and Gasol,* he thought. Brill looked around, hoping to catch another glimpse of the dog. Just then, Costa hooked his arm with his crutch. "Come on, Brill," he said. "I want to get my money back . . . and you need to see if that old man is dead!"

Figuring he could find the dog later, Brill headed across the carriage yard. Costa tried to kick a couple of ducks. They squawked and waddled beyond his reach. The carriage gate itself was massive, but a smaller door had been built inside the gate for foot traffic, though it was large enough for horses to pass. The door emptied onto the backstreet. Brill and Costa journeyed around a pile of fresh dung, "road apples," as Gasol liked to call them. Every house had thick stone blocks situated below the doors, enabling people to avoid the muck when stepping in and out of their carriages. Above the street, on the second and third floors, were tall doors with small iron balconies that used to boast potted geraniums.

Turning the corner of his house, Brill could see the park. The flock of ravens were still atop the trees filling the branches like leaves. They were cawing loudly and sometimes hopping into the air, trading places.

As he and Costa entered the park, Brill realized the youths were bigger and tougher than they had looked from the roof. They had returned to their card game, although every now and then one would glance around, making sure another coin was not to be had. Costa headed straight for them, swinging his legs forward with urgency. "I'm going to get my money back," he declared. Brill shook his head and made his way toward the cloaked figure.

18

The Beggar in the Park

As Brill approached the man, he noticed a gnarled walking stick leaning against the bench next to him, a twisted root he must have picked up in a ravine somewhere. His hood came over his eyes. Nonetheless, Brill could see he was ancient by the grooves encroaching his mouth. The man's clothes were ragged, barely held together by poor stitchwork and patches. Stopping a few feet away, Brill detected the acrid smell of dried urine.

"Excuse me," said Brill, announcing himself. "I brought some water. Would you like some?" The man didn't so much as move let alone reply. Inching closer, Brill asked, "Are you thirsty?" Again, there was no response. *Perhaps he is dead,* he thought. As Brill leaned low to have a look under his hood, a white flash seared his vision. For a split second he could not see. When the colors of the world returned, to his surprise, the man's hood was off.

Brill recoiled. He was an aberration. His eye sockets were empty sunken craters, and the slits where his eyes should have been were caked with dried pus. His skin was dark red from exposure to the sun, and his hide was as thin and taut as an underfed beast's. But even so, there was something unnervingly familiar about him.

"Why're you afraid?" croaked the beggar.

"Who me?" asked Brill. "I'm not afraid."

"Mmmm," murmured the old man, moving his head ever so slightly from side to side.

"Well, you did startle me," confessed Brill.

The beggar pushed a wooden bowl forward. Brill stayed as far back as he could while still being able to pour. After the bowl was filled, the beggar brought it to his mouth. Sucking loudly, his cheeks pumped in and out. Brill noticed small ink marks crossing his sunbaked scalp. When he was done drinking, the beggar set down his bowl and raised his hand to where Brill had been looking. His thumb appeared frozen under his palm and his crooked fingers were all but stuck together. He raked his knuckles across his head where his hairline would have been if he were younger. A series of dotted lines retreated over the top of his skull. "Each is for an enemy I killed," he said.

"Killed!" proclaimed Brill. "You?"

"Once, I was fierce as a lion."

Brill tried to imagine him as a younger man but couldn't. "That must have been a long time ago," said Brill.

"Pagani chieftain," he said, lowering his hand.

"Chieftain!" repeated Brill. He wasn't sure whether to believe him or not. His mother had always told him that even when you don't believe someone, it was not polite to disagree with them, at least not to their face. But he questioned the man anyway, for he was unduly curious. "If you were a Pagani chieftain, where's your tribe?"

"So few left," he replied.

"What happened to them?"

"Perished during the uprising."

"My father's family was Pagani," said Brill, feeling sympathy for him.

"Mmm," he murmured. "Your father was Noumenos . . . like me."

"Nooo," replied Brill. "I've never heard that name before." The old man's face turned up, as if to look into his eyes. Nervously, Brill gazed away.

"Tell me . . ." said the old man again. "How old are you?"

"Thirteen," said Brill. "But soon I'll be fourteen," he added quickly.

"As they say in the mountains, you're almost big enough to carry a small wife." At that, his face lit up with a toothless smile.

Brill shook his head, unsure what the old man meant. "So what happened to you, being chieftain and all? You must have done something terrible to end up . . . like *this*!"

"Depends who you ask," the man answered.

"What happened to your eyes?" Brill continued, feeling bolder.

"The Red Bows cut them out."

Brill's heart skipped. "You're lucky you didn't die!" he declared.

"Died? I died . . . many times," the old chief replied, nodding his head.

"That doesn't make sense!" added Brill.

"Mmmmm," he murmured.

"Why don't you go back to the mountains? Back to your people," asked Brill. "Are you afraid?"

"Not afraid, no. At first, ashamed. But then I lost all idea of who I was. When I remembered, it was too late. I had no interest in being that person. So I kept wandering, living off mushrooms and grubs and green shoots . . . when I could find them. But one day, my mind became clear as a high mountain lake. It was then I heard her voice."

"Whose voice did you hear?" asked Brill.

"*Her* voice," he repeated.

"Didn't you ask her who she was?"

"When you hear such a voice, there is no need to ask."

"What did she say?"

"That it was time."

"Time? Time for what?"

"For the gates to open."

"Gates?"

"What do they teach you in school?"

"They teach us history and math . . . and about the Bible."

"What's your name?" said the old chief.

"My name?" repeated Brill, although he had heard his question.

"Yes!"

"Uh . . . My name is Brill . . . Brill Hoffe."

"Hoffe." The old man coughed as if he had gotten something stuck in his throat. The chieftain then spit a glob of phlegm onto the ground. Brill looked down—it was disgusting! "Come closer," said the old geezer. Brill didn't move. He had no idea what the batty old man might do or say next. Then the old man's eyelids began to flutter. Brill could see the tiniest bit of red-and-white pith beneath them.

"I see death," he started. "I see lots of death. You have the Eye of the Orlach, Ule's gift! You could see all this for yourself, but you choose to hide."

"Wha-what are you talking about?" stuttered Brill. Just then the crock slipped out of his hand and shattered on the ground.

"Fear prevents you from seeing!" continued the old man. He waved his hand in the air in a dismissive gesture. "Fear . . . the great thief of life!"

Brill's breathing became shallow. "Wh-whose death do you see?" he asked, ignoring the broken pot.

"Maybe yours . . . maybe someone you know. The wheel of fate is always spinning . . . always spinning . . . never stopping to ask permission. What a shame!" He clucked his tongue. Brill bit his lip. He wanted to leave, but his feet would not carry him. Unknown things that he *knew* but did not want to acknowledge were hanging before him like ripe fruit. "Go on," said the old man, "don't be afraid."

Brill's eyes widened. "Mister, I really don't know what you're talking about!" was all Brill could think to say.

The chieftain lifted his hand and waved his fingers at Brill. Brill suddenly felt nauseous. For a minute he thought he was going to retch, and he bent forward over the ground. When the nausea passed, he straightened himself. "You . . . you really *must* be talking to the wrong person," he stammered.

"If you want to hide, I cannot help you. But I will tell you a great secret!" Brill was about to protest again, but the chieftain spoke first. "Stay to the center of the wheel. That is the only place that does not move. There you will find the Ayn Noor!"

"I *have* heard of the Ayn Noor," offered Brill.

"Who told you?"

"Pola, my governess," said Brill. "She told me that the Ayn Noor is the Light of the Inner World. That it comes from the beginning of time—and can heal all wounds. She also said that if one touches it," he added after a short pause, "one will either become mad . . . or see the bright shores of eternity!"

"You know about the Ayn Noor but not about the gates?"

"Well, I have heard of *those* gates . . . if that's what you mean."

"Yessss," the old man hissed. "Through the gates . . . a mortal man can walk . . . in *flesh* and in soul . . . into the Land of the Dreaming Dead and return what doesn't belong! Free Queemquesh from the underworld."

"What doesn't belong?" asked Brill.

The chieftain did not bother answering. "Changes are coming," he warned. "It's time to grow up and become a man!"

"But I'm just a boy. I live over there," Brill protested.

"I know where you live," replied the old chief. "Raven was telling me everything. You and the other boy were on the roof throwing shiny things." With this his head went back, and he expelled a wicked sort of laugh.

Brill's blood froze. How was it possible? He had no eyes to see with! Had he really been speaking with the raven? Brill concluded he must have overheard the youths talking about them.

"Ravens are Noumenos' friends," he said. "They will help you."

"I don't need help," stated Brill.

"Mmmmm," came his reply.

"You're the one who needs help, being blind and all," said Brill, but even as he spoke, he heard shouts erupt. Looking over his shoulder, he saw Costa gathered with the youths around a lemon tree. Brill considered sneaking away quietly, but decided he better clarify for the old man who he was. Brill spoke loudly and enunciated carefully so that he would not be misheard. "Listen," he said, "my name is Brill *Hoffe*! My father's name was Alber *Hoffe*. There are no Noumenos in my family. You *have* the wrong person."

The old man shook his head. "As sure as the sun rises, you are Noumenos."

Brill couldn't believe someone could pretend to know things about another person better than that person knew themselves. "What do you do? Go around scaring young people?" he inquired.

"Good!" said the beggar.

"Good? What's good?" asked Brill.

"You're angry!" stated the old man.

"I'm not angry!" Brill shot back.

"You are. That's good. That's good. Fire burns water! You have too much water. Once, I did not know my own anger."

"You speak to me as if you know me, but you *really* don't."

The old man chuckled. "We'll call it even," he said.

"Even? How are we even?"

"A laugh is worth a bucket of truth . . . I tell you truths . . . You make me laugh. We're even."

Brill shook his head. The old codger was as frustrating a person as he had ever met. There was another roar among the boys. "I've got to go," said Brill. He paused to see if the chieftain would say something, but he didn't. It was then he noticed the man's bent toes. They looked as if they had been broken, countless times. Dry mud was caked between them from the foul slop he must have mistakenly walked through. Looking up, Brill could see a couple of flies were now digging in the corners of the old man's empty eye sockets. He didn't even bother to brush them away. Sympathy slowly won Brill over, and he reached deep into his pocket and found a silver terkel. Dropping it into the beggar's bowl, he could hear the coin settle at the bottom as he turned and walked away. Before he arrived at the tree where the boys were congregated, he took one last look over his shoulder—the old chieftain had disappeared back beneath his hood. Brill shook his head.

◆ ◆ ◆

Brill found Costa at the center of the youths, perched on a stone. They were all staring at a small lemon tree. Brill located what looked like a piece of white yarn, no more than two inches long, hammering back and forth on a leaf. At first he thought it might be some kind of trick until he heard one of the boys say, "The worm's giving it a right fight!" Brill now understood it was not a string but a living creature. It was using its body as a club, frantically beating one end of itself against the leaf, while on the outside, skirting the edge was a wasp. The wasp's big, bulging eyes fused with its striped yellow-and-black helmet and its massive viselike pincers made for an otherworldly foe. One could search the entire earth and not find two opponents more unevenly matched. The squidgy, gelatinous worm, with no appendages and seemingly no defensive capabilities, was in battle with a being whose entire body was itself a weapon. Nonetheless, the wasp moved cautiously . . . that is, until it engaged, clasping the worm with its pincers, causing the worm to cavort wildly into a knot.

"He got 'em," shouted a boy with excitement. But as quickly as the wasp attacked, it disengaged. The worm promptly rolled off the leaf, dropping to the ground like a pebble. As soon as it hit, it spared no time fleeing, moving as fast as its legless body could, coiling and uncoiling across the ground. The boys instinctively scooted back, unnecessarily so, given that it would be a whole minute before it reached them.

Meanwhile, the wasp scoured the leaf. Not finding its prey, it took to the air. Searching up and down the branches in ever-widening circles, the wasp increased its perimeter. The worm had crossed a meager portion of earth when the wasp alighted next to it. Brill's heart clenched. The wasp's orange wings were drawn straight into the air, poised like an assassin's blades. Unwilling to lose the worm a second time, it grasped its prey once more. Buckling, the worm wrapped frantically around the wasp, and the two rolled in a ball across the dirt. As they tumbled, the wasp managed to lift its abdomen enough to inject its stinger into the worm's flesh. If its gyrations had been wild, now they were frenetic. Brill could not help but wonder whether the convulsions were the manifestations of pain or the desperation that precedes when the black curtain of death is being slowly lowered. Brill couldn't decide which would be worse.

"The worm will win," shrieked Costa, his voice cracking. There was a howl of disagreement. "I swear he will," he insisted.

"I'll bet you," said the shirtless youth.

"You don't have anything to bet!" rebuked Costa. Digging into his pocket, the boy pulled out the two silver terkels. "Where'd you get those?" Costa asked.

"None of your business. Do you want to bet or not?"

"No," whispered Brill, pushing his way up next to him.

"I'll bet you both," said Costa.

"You're on," said the boy, and he reached out his hand.

Spurning the handshake, Costa returned his attention to the battle. The wasp stood nearby, perhaps waiting for his prey to tire. In one motion, Costa reached out and struck the wasp with the butt of his crutch.

"Hey!" the shirtless youth shouted, shoving Costa onto the ground. But Costa had already delivered a lethal blow. The wasp turned in a semicircle like a rudderless ship. The shirtless boy went over and stomped on the worm. "There, yours is dead now too!"

"Fine," said Costa, pushing himself to his feet. "But yours died first. So I win." Costa maneuvered himself away from the tree to the open area. As the boys pursued him, Brill reached into his britches and pulled out a piece of crumpled parchment. He picked up the now flaccid worm and, by the wing, the wasp and delicately laid them side by side in their candy-paper sarcophagus. He then returned them to his pocket. He could hear Costa arguing. "All I bet you was the wasp wouldn't win."

"No you didn't, you said the worm would win."

"Same thing."

"No, it isn't. You're a cheater," said the shirtless boy.

"You're a sore loser," replied Costa.

Walking forward, Brill tugged Costa's arm. "Come on, Costa! Let's go." Another youth grabbed Brill by the shirt and held him back. "Costa, just apologize so we can leave!"

"No! I'm not going to say sorry to this riffraff," he declared.

"Then I'll say it for you."

"No," said the shirtless youth. "I want to hear it from him." With this, he poked Costa's chest with his finger.

Just then a rather striking blond youth stepped forward. He was tall and had been mostly watching. He took the shirtless kid by the upper arm. "Deet, let's go. They're just stupid boys!"

Deetmar yanked his arm free. "They're old enough to know better. We'll settle this another way," he said. "Show me your coins."

"No!" refused Costa.

"Show me your coins, or else," he said as he made a fist and put it in front of Costa's face.

Costa turned to Brill. "Hand me your coin."

"I gave it to the beggar," whispered Brill. Costa shot him a salty glare.

"Go get it back."

"I can't do that."

"You don't have any?" stated the boy. "You're worse cheaters than I thought."

"Do you know who my father is?" asked Costa.

"Do I care?" answered the youth.

"My father's Emhet Turan."

"You're lying!" he scoffed.

"I think it's true, Deet," interjected one of the youths. "I've seen 'em together."

The blond kid spoke up. "All the more reason to leave, Deet. Let's go!"

"No, these little rich finches need to learn a lesson. They need to know they can't go around cheating people and getting away with it." He moved closer to Costa's face. "If your father really is Emhet Turan, then everyone knows where to find you." He motioned to the city with one hand. "But nobody knows where to find me. Your dad might own the city, but he will never own the streets. And you know what? I *am* the street. My first name is Street, and my last name is Wasp. And do you know what your name is?"

"Let me guess . . . *Worm*," answered Costa sardonically.

"That's right," said Deet with a bob of his head. "Look, he knows his name." There was mild laughter among the boys.

"Just give me the money you owe me," ordered Costa.

"Owe you! You rich worms owe us!"

"Come on, Deet, they're not worth the trouble," said the blond youth, tugging at him once more.

"No, Klempt! I'm going to teach them a lesson," he said, pushing him back.

"We can get you two silver terkels," promised Brill.

"*Two?* Now it's *six*! Two that you owe me, and one for each of my friends."

"Never," said Costa, and he swung his crutch as hard as he could into Deet's shin. Brill was immediately struck across the side of the head, which was followed by a harder blow to his gut. Brill's knees gave out, and he dropped to the ground. Toppling onto his side, Brill soughed as he curled into a ball. As every morsel of oxygen exited his body, two of the youths kicked him. But he didn't feel the blows. In fact, time seemed to have slowed to a crawl, and beyond the silent ticks of the invisible clock, Brill watched a curling wisp of a cloud floating in the larger field of blue above. Turning his head, he looked toward the chieftain. The old man's lips were moving silently. Brill's belly suddenly let go. *Uuuuugghhh!* came the gigantic sound as he sucked air back through his windpipe like some dying hag.

"Birds! Birds!" shouted the youths.

Brill rolled onto his back. He could see ravens whirling down like falling leaves. The youths were bumping into one another and tripping as they scrambled to get away. It felt to Brill that he lay at the center of a most beautiful symphony—a swirling black universe. It was grand, almost operatic.

Shortly thereafter, time boomeranged forward. The youths were gone, and the birds were few and far between. Brill's ribs ached something awful. He could barely push himself up. Standing, he patted the dust off his pants. Costa was sitting with his legs sprawled out in front of him, crutches scattered. Blood was running like a river out of his nose, and his lower lip was busted open. A crimson delta fanned over his shirt. Brill retrieved his crutches. "Pinch your nose," said Brill. "It'll stop the bleeding."

"Bunch of cowards," declared Costa. Brill reached for his own head and felt a large welt near his temple. "Give me a hand," said Costa. Brill did so. As Costa stood, a gob of blood swung precariously from his nose. He wiped it on his sleeve. Brill glanced over to the park bench. The old man was gone, although there was something on the bench where he had been sitting. Brill looked around for the old chieftain. He was nowhere to be seen. Holding his ribs, Brill walked over and picked up a pouch. It was nicely made with soft leather, although dark with stains. The straps were pulled tight. It was surprisingly weighty—it obviously contained something substantial. Brill gave it a squeeze. It was hard as a rock. Again, Brill looked around for the chieftain. Gazing up into the trees, he saw a few ravens scattered here and there. The park now seemed solemn and morose.

Costa was leaning on his crutches when Brill approached him. The blood was already fading to a dullish red.

"What did the old geezer forget, his teeth?"

"No," replied Brill, "he didn't have any to forget. But he left his pouch." Brill held it up for Costa to see.

"Probably a stale piece of bread," concluded Costa.

"I don't think so," said Brill. "It's too heavy."

"Just leave it. He'll be drunk on the same bench tomorrow."

"He wasn't drunk," said Brill, "just odd."

"Then let's see what old geezers keep in their pouches."

Brill shook his head. "It's none of our business."

"Of course it is; we found it!"

Just then there was a voice calling from across the street. "Brill!" They both turned and saw Hanna running toward them.

"Hurry! Open it before she gets here," said Costa.

"No," said Brill, shoving the pouch into his pocket.

"Come on!" moaned Costa, throwing back his head.

"What happened to the two of you?" said Hanna as she approached. "It looks like . . ."

"Like we've been beaten up?" said Brill.

"Yes," said Hanna, making a weak attempt to hide a smile.

"What do you want?" said Brill.

"Your mother's looking for you!"

"Am I in trouble?"

"What do you think?"

"*Please*, Hanna, no games."

"You should be . . . but you're not! Nikolas' ship arrived. He's on his way home. She wants you to be ready for his dinner tonight."

"Nikolas' ship! Where?"

"In Goyer. It arrived yesterday."

"How long will it take for him to get here?"

"I don't know!" said Hanna, frowning.

"It takes about sixteen hours," said Costa. "He could be here soon, depending on when he left." Hanna departed. Costa wiped his face. Brill thought he looked like a rag that had been used to clean a horse's stall. "You're a mess, Brill," said Costa, who obviously had been thinking the same thing. "Why don't you give me the pouch and go get cleaned up for dinner. I'll find the beggar and give it back to him."

Brill considered for a moment, but then thought against it. "No, that's all right, Costa," he said, "I'll find him myself."

"Just give it to me," insisted Costa, putting out his hand.

"Why do you want it so badly?"

"I just want to give it back to him," he said, trying to sound innocent.

"No, you just want to open it. But I'll walk you home if you like."

Costa frowned. "Now *that* I can manage myself."

19

TRIPE TOWN

With his shirt pulled up over his head, Klempt ran for a bush. Ravens swooped down one after another, sometimes two at once, their raspy caws piercing. The birds seemed determined to have flesh. The last thing Klempt heard before the attack was Willit's scream. Klempt had laughed out loud as he ran; hearing him bleat like a baby lamb was beyond precious.

Klempt scrambled under a nearby bush, while the ravens continued to pelt him with their cries. He imagined they were saying, *We see you. We see you!* He pulled his shirt back down and rested his head on a couple of branches. He was still breathing hard when Deetmar came scampering under the bush. "One of 'em got me," he declared, his voice boiling with emotion. Blood was dripping through his fingers.

"Let me see," said Klempt, moving Deetmar's hand aside to inspect his ear. "Jesus, Deet!" he exclaimed. "They darn near ripped the whole thing off."

"Knock it off, *Klempt!*" said Deetmar, pushing him away.

"It'll be fine," said Klempt, but he could see that a raven had punctured it clean through. "Here," said Klempt, offering a threadbare handkerchief from his pocket. Deetmar yanked it out of his hand. He was in a foul mood. Klempt didn't know how the others had fared, but surely they couldn't have done worse than Deet. He had never seen a flock of birds of any kind attack humans. Although once he did see a pair of hawks go after a meddlesome boy that got too close to their nest.

"Why did they attack us?" asked Deet.

"Maybe because you started the fight," proposed Klempt.

"Me? That crippled boy started it. You saw him hit me with his crutch. And why would those birds defend those rich finches anyway?"

"Suppose they figured you were picking on them."

"Birds don't figure. Where are the others?" asked Deetmar, his dark eyes darting around.

"Just listen for the bushes with the squawking birds; that's where they'll be," said Klempt.

"Give me a rock," said Deetmar, searching the ground for a stone.

"Wait," said Klempt, reaching for Deetmar's hand. "Just stay out of sight, and they'll go away. I promise."

"Is that country wisdom?" asked Deetmar.

Klempt shrugged.

"I'll tell you what," continued Deet. "That old man sent those flying rats. He was being friendly with that raven when we first came to the park. Have you seen him before?"

"Me?" said Klempt, his voice betraying bafflement.

"I thought maybe you'd have seen him in the hills where you come from."

"Have you ever been out of the city, Deet?" Klempt asked, looking at him with renewed interest. Deetmar's lips pursed as he shook his head. "Do you have any idea how many villages there are?"

"All I can say is that the codger's got backward written all over him."

"Well then, maybe he's Pagani, come down from Bajarmaland. Trust me, he's not Hutsu if he speaks with birds."

"Whatever hole he crawled out of, it don't matter. Next time I come 'cross him, after I kick his scrawny ass, I'm going to steal his walking stick . . . and that's just for starters." Klempt knew Deetmar's threat was a promise sealed. He suspected that even if his grandmother crossed him, he would stick it to her.

"If he's really a Pagani witch, that would be foolish," said Klempt.

"He's not in the country anymore; his magic don't work here," said Deetmar, nudging his chin forward to make his point. "But what I want to know is why you stayed out of the fight?"

"It wasn't a fair fight," said Klempt. "My sister could have licked 'em. Maybe you should have stayed out of it, too, especially if that *was* Emhet Turan's son." But before Deetmar could respond, Klempt put his hand on Deetmar's shoulder. "Listen!" he said. "The ravens. They're gone."

"Let's get out from under this damn bush," growled Deetmar as he began to crawl. Only a few ravens remained, sitting high up on the very tops of the jacolandi trees. Deetmar scowled at them.

"Don't let them see your face," said Klempt. "I *swear* they remember faces." Deetmar turned his head down, for once not arguing. They trudged down Queen's Avenue. Klempt marveled at how the streets in the affluent part of the city were so clean. He started to whistle. Occasionally, he studied Deetmar, who strode slightly ahead of him. He noticed dried blood was caked to the side of Deet's neck. Deetmar rarely expressed emotion, but the ravens' attack had unnerved him. It showed by the quaver in his voice when he had asked Klempt to look at his ear. It was the first time Klempt had ever seen a hint of fear about Deet—the city boy wasn't used to dealing with animals. Animals were Klempt's lot, though more and more, farm life was becoming as distant as the stars.

Klempt noticed that Deetmar's face was drawn tight—he was smoldering inside. He was probably already plotting revenge. Deetmar was the most vengeful person Klempt had ever met. Every slight he suffered he paid back double—that was his rate of return.

Just then they heard the thunder of galloping horses. They quickly turned their backs to the road. Deetmar always said it was a bad idea for a thief to garner attention. A group of soldiers galloped past, speeding toward the park. When they were gone, Deetmar motioned with his head for them to continue. But as they started walking down the avenue, they noticed a rider in a black coat, sitting upon his mount watching them. "Come over here!" demanded the man in a commanding voice. Deetmar's shoulders immediately rounded forward, and his gait became slow and rigid. "Well, if it isn't Deeet-*mar*!" said the rider, in a tone denoting both familiarity and disdain.

"I didn't do nothin', Woefus," said Deet. Klempt recognized the name, but had never seen the infamous chief. Klempt could see that he was of Hutsu ancestry. His frosty eyes were not so unlike a raptor's.

"I'll be the judge of that, Deetmar. Empty your pockets."

Deetmar's jaw screwed tight. To Klempt's surprise, Deetmar managed to pull out his pockets and at the same time conceal the two silver terkels between his thumb and his palm. "You're such a weasel," declared the man. Deetmar shot him an unfeeling grin. "How long have you been in these parts?" he asked.

"Oh, not too long," answered Deetmar.

"Don't play with me," warned Woefus.

Deetmar's face screwed tighter, bottling all emotion.

"Have you seen a flock of ravens?" Woefus asked.

Deetmar stuffed his hands back in his pockets and tilted his head upward. Squinting, he nodded slowly. "I seen 'em."

Woefus reached into his coat and pulled out a coin bag. Reaching into it, he pulled out a silver terkel. If minutiae could be measured, Klempt thought he heard Deetmar's voice soften. "We were sitting there, playing cards, not bothering nobody. All these birds were in the trees, 'cept one; it was on a bench with this old man."

"Did you know the man?" asked Woefus.

"Never seen 'im before. Besides, he was all covered up, with 'is hood."

"Go on."

"That's the way it was. The raven on the bench was jabbering away. At first I figured it was checking out the old man for scraps. But now I think maybe it was speaking with him. Then a crippled boy with crutches came over to bother us."

"Who was the boy?"

"Emhet Turan's son."

"Are you certain?" Woefus' eyes narrowed.

"Yep," said Deetmar. "He knew something 'bout them birds too." His voice began to get animated. Klempt realized Deetmar saw his chance for revenge. "The crippled boy an' the old man were in cahoots, of that I'm sure. Emhet's son started the fight, and the old man sent them ravens after us!"

Klempt wondered why Deetmar was leaving the second boy out of the story.

"Emhet's son, the cripple, started a fight with the likes of you! *And* he was in league with this old man who was talking with ravens?"

"I swear," said Deetmar in an almost submissive voice. "That's exactly what happened!" Woefus' horse backed up and stomped its hoof. "Look!" Deetmar turned his head to show Woefus his bloody ear.

Woefus' face remained unmoved. "You're a liar and a thief, Deetmar." He put the coin back in his purse. "I know where to find you," he said, spurring his mount onward.

Deetmar spit on the ground after him. "I hate that man!" he said. "He thinks I'm his boot boy."

They hadn't gone more than a city block when another rider came toward them. Deetmar didn't bother moving aside this time—nobody could be worse than Woefus. The rider with the aubergine cloak maintained his horse's position, coming right at them. When it was a mere ten feet away, they quickly stepped aside to let the horse and rider pass, but the steed came to a halt. Klempt could hear the air passing in and out of the horse's nostrils. Behind the cloak, to his astonishment, was a striking woman. Her black hair was tied back, but it was her stabbing blue eyes that made him uneasy.

"Have you boys seen a flock of ravens?" she asked, despite not looking much older than them.

"Maybe," said Deetmar. Reaching inside her coat, she produced a silver coin and held it up. "Give it to me first," said Deetmar. He wasn't going to be gotten twice. The girl tossed it up, and Deetmar snatched it out of the air like a hound a morsel of meat.

When he was done telling her everything he had told Woefus, the girl looked over at Klempt. "What did he leave out?" she asked.

Deetmar whined, "I told you everything." The girl kept her eyes planted on Klempt. "You'll have to pay extra if you want him to speak to you," added Deet. A flash of anger passed over her face, and she steered her stallion toward him. Deet backpedaled.

"You are the second person who asked us about them," chimed Klempt.

She reined back her horse. "Who was the first?" she asked.

"Woefus," added Deetmar—he couldn't stand not being in charge.

"What did you tell him?"

"Everything we told you," he said.

"Except," added Klempt, "there was another boy, with Emhet's son. He was talking with the old man before the birds attacked us."

"And you didn't tell Woefus about this other boy?"

"Noooo!" said Deetmar.

"But you don't know who he was?"

"Noooo," Deetmar said again.

Klempt could see there was a hardness about her, a quality that made him uneasy. She gazed sharply down at him. He held her gaze. Without another word, she turned her horse and galloped back the way she had come—apparently, she had all she wanted.

"Colette!" Deetmar announced.

"The *princess*?" inquired Klempt.

"None other."

Klempt nodded slowly. Meeting her in person did not disappoint.

"You have a lot to learn," stated Deetmar, frowning. "First, *never* tell anyone more than they ask, *especially* the Black Coats. Even if you didn't do anything, they'll turn everything you say 'gainst you, and before you know it, *you'll* be guilty. And always . . . *always* keep secrets. That's your only currency. If they have everything, then we become nothin' to them." Klempt shook his head and stayed quiet. In a way, he was surprised Deetmar wasn't in a better mood, for he now had three silver terkels.

Deetmar began fidgeting. Klempt suddenly realized what it was: Deetmar knew there was something he was missing out on—something bigger. People didn't pay for information unless there was a more valuable prize lurking in the shadows. Oftentimes, Klempt imagined that a waterwheel with a crank and a shaft was lodged in Deet's head. The gears propelled the shaft, causing Deetmar's legs to bounce and his hands to tap incessantly. The only time the gears stopped turning was right after Deetmar won at cards, or after he stole something. For a brief instant, all movement would cease, and a fragile peace would come over him.

"One of those boys has something," claimed Deetmar, raising his eyebrow at Klempt.

"Emhet Turan's house should be easy enough to find," answered Klempt.

"He doesn't have it. It's the other boy. I tell you, you should *not* have mentioned him!"

"How do you know?"

"I just now saw it." And Deetmar tapped his head.

Klempt nodded. Sniffing secrets was Deet's domain. He came from the Clan of Gilbert, one of the oldest lineages of thieves in Jesut Edin—as close to royalty as one could get in Tripe Town. Deetmar was teaching Klempt the trade. The mystery was lessening by the day. Knowing where and whom to sell stolen goods to was important, as was knowing how to study a house without being noticed. But this was not what made the Clan of Gilbert successful. Their ability to read people was a high art, for sure. *See that man,* Deetmar would say, *he has nice clothes, and a beautiful watch, but everything else about him tells me he's poor. He walks as if he owns the world, but he probably owes the world. Now, take that fellow with the saggy britches and little ol' bum. He's hiding something . . . I guarantee it. I bet he's sitting on a mountain of gold. Waste your time going after the first man, and you will be broke in a week, but take a month to pry loose the fingers of the second man, and you will have food for the year.*

But even as sensible and well discerned as these observations were, it was also not what made the Clan of Gilbert successful. It was nothing that could be imparted through words, but rather passed unknowingly from one generation to the next. The secret was simply the way they carried themselves—a silent bearing, their dull, flaccid, but faraway countenances, the solemn way they moved, how they held their jaws, their shifty eyes that ceaselessly followed you. Everything conveyed one thing . . . meanness! And it was true. Even the slightest allegation could provoke them, but not necessarily into a fistfight. It could also be vicious words and threats, and they were not afraid to make a commotion in public. One had to be strong to stand up to such an assault.

Most people were trained from an early age to be polite, not to make a spectacle of themselves. Your average citizen had too much to lose. Any confrontation on the street was out of character, for they had been taught to walk sensibly among their peers. Rarely would someone accuse Deetmar outright, even if seconds before they had seen his sticky fingers in their purse. Most victims would hesitate, preferring to doubt than believe. Five, maybe ten, seconds were all a thief needed to disappear.

Klempt saw the meanness running through Deet's entire lineage. They were all marked, imprinted with the same ancestral scar. One had only to linger in their hideout for a short while to see it. Their sullen faces never perked up. They moved like ghosts floating through a world without souls. Even their jokes were not meant to provoke laughter, but rather to make one feel small. From the young to the old, they all lived in a land that bore no spring.

In this respect, Klempt felt handicapped. As fast as he was learning the trade, it just wasn't his nature to be mean-spirited. He knew he lacked this one indispensable trait. He came from a lineage of farmers who for generations measured things like the goodness of a milking cow, the honesty of a workhorse, and the fertility of a plot of land. In growing things, there was basic goodness. Farm life was about nurturing living things. Street life was about taking. Klempt knew firsthand that a crusty old farmer wasn't any fun to be around, but by the very nature of the profession, their outlook was different. Visiting the Gilbert compound, he could plainly see that all goodness was absent.

This was not to say Klempt felt unchanged. On the contrary, he felt the farmer inside him fading daily. He found himself measuring each person he met for their worth—he was slowly forgetting to look for the good. A month earlier he had gone back to the country with his father to complete some business; it was his first visit since their departure. He found himself walking into old friends' houses and wondering which cupboard he might look in first and which window would be best to enter through. The visit caused his heart to beat fast and his palms to sweat. Afterward, Klempt swore he would never return to the country again.

This hadn't been the life his father had wanted for them when he gave up the farm and moved their family to Jesut Edin. If his father had known what was to come, surely he would have stayed in the foothills and scratched the earth 'til death. But life doesn't come with a preview of one's choices. And now the farm was gone, the plow and the horse sold, and the ink on the deed was as dry as late-summer grass—that most important piece of paper now filed in a rarely touched book in a far-away office, sitting on some forlorn shelf in a basement corner of some decaying provincial courthouse. It was now survive or die in the city, and for better or worse, Deet was his lifeline.

"Hey," said Deetmar. Klempt looked up just in time to see a shimmering object coming toward him. Catching the terkel, Klempt protested weakly, "Are you sure?" Deetmar winked. Klempt mumbled, "Thanks," but it was hard to get out. Perhaps the terkel was a payoff for seeing his vulnerability earlier, and Deet was just making sure that Klempt remained tight-lipped about it. Or maybe it was a payment for fealty. When he looked back up, Deet had already disappeared behind a passing cart.

Klempt turned and went the other direction. He would go to the grocer to buy food for his family.

After filling his basket with groceries, Klempt gave the man his silver terkel. The grocer handed back one copper klat. "That can't be right," said Klempt, looking at the coin in his palm.

"The farmers!" claimed the grocer, looking at him through the thick lenses of his wiry eyeglasses. "The farmers keep raising their prices," he said, shaking his head and pursing his lips. If Klempt hadn't known any better, he would have thought that the farmers were ruthless money grubbers and that the poor grocers had no choice but to pass on their criminally high prices.

Klempt's first impulse was to laugh so hard that spittle landed on the grocer's glasses, but he couldn't find an ounce of laughter within him. Just then the grocer's pockmarked face morphed into a vile entity, a rotting pumpkin that had been caught out in a hard frost. He had become so accustomed to telling this lie that he had misplaced the better part of himself. Klempt was certain he had just seen him counting his profit through the poppy-sized holes that were the portals to his shriveled soul.

Perhaps it was Klempt's accusatory silence, but something made the grocer go over the purchase. "Four grams of sugar, a loaf of bread, a quarter round of cheese, and a crock of milk. You're lucky, young man, to have gotten anything back at all." Klempt dropped his eyes to the floor. The man's shamelessness was unbearable. Klempt quickly departed.

Heading straight for home, Klempt found his Clara near the entryway. She looked up and smiled faintly. Klempt put the food on the table and then looked over her arms and legs—the red marks seemed to be fading, and she felt less hot to the touch. Perhaps the medicine Liis had administered was working. Klempt felt a surge of relief. Clara's eyes were still dull. "You hungry? Is that it?" he asked. She nodded faintly. Just then, Penelope stepped through the door. The sweetness of dodgy perfume wafted ahead of her. Klempt wheezed. "Hooo-wee, Pen," he exclaimed. "What are you wearing?"

"Who's asking, the family thief?"

"Why don't you go down to the river and help Mother?" he prompted.

"Why don't you? You've got hands too, Klempt."

"Shut up, Pen!" Just then Clara coughed. Klempt and Penelope looked at one another and dropped their fight. Truce for Clara had always been their unspoken agreement. Klempt ripped a chunk of bread off the loaf and broke the cheese. After placing it on a saucer, he went down on one knee, handing it to Penelope. "M'lady of the nightly charms," he cooed.

"Rise, good knight of swift fingers," said Penelope as she took the plate. Penelope held out her other hand for him to kiss.

Klempt obliged. Clara giggled at their theatrics. Klempt rose and picked up a bowl, put some milk in, added sugar, and stirred. Taking the loaf of bread, he pulled off small pieces, then put them in the saucer and placed it all in front of Clara. "Eat, my little Albu," he said. Klempt then tore off a piece for himself and was about to bite into it when a groan came from the other room.

"Has Father even gotten up today?" Klempt asked.

"How should I know," answered Penelope.

Klempt changed the subject. "Pen, did you see Clara's spots are lessening? As is her fever!"

"Liis is very nice," interrupted Clara. "Klempt is going to marry her." Penelope rolled her eyes.

Klempt smiled halfway. "Now, Clara, you don't know that."

Their father appeared in the doorway, scratching his backside. His hair was smashed upward on one side of his head from lying in bed. "How'd you come by the food, Klempt?"

"An honest day's work," he answered. From his father's grunt, Klempt surmised disbelief. Each of them followed him with their eyes as he pulled off a hunk of bread. He didn't even bother to look up. After drinking from the crock of milk, he put it down and disappeared back into the bedroom.

"Why doesn't he at least try to be nice?" said Penelope.

"Shut up, Pen!" snapped Klempt.

"It's his fault; he dragged us here," she said loudly. Penelope was a big girl whose moods were like giant boulders that teetered on steep mountainsides. When they did come rolling down, they took everything in their path.

"He thought we could do better for ourselves here," Klempt answered, lowering his voice so as not to agitate the boulder.

"Well, he was wrong!" said Penelope, reaching up and wiping her eyes. With this she turned and burst out the front door.

Klempt pursued her. "It wasn't all good there either!" he shouted after her.

Penelope kept walking down the street. Returning to the table, he took a seat next to Clara. "How's the bread?" he asked.

"Good!" she answered, looking up at him with her lazy blue eyes.

"Now, that's what I like to hear."

20

Nikolas' Homecoming

Brill could barely reach the handle on the front door; his ribs hurt from where the youths had kicked him. He looked down at his clothes. What would his mother say? *She best not see me,* he concluded. Gingerly turning the brass knob, Brill pushed the door in. The foyer was empty, but he could hear voices within the house. He closed the door, taking great care to turn the handle so the latch would not click. Removing his shoes, he lifted them into his hands. As he neared the intersection where two corridors met, the voices grew louder. Sneaking a peek to his left, he peered through a rounded arch that led to the dining room.

The blond girl he had seen earlier in the day, the new servant, was on her knees scrubbing the tiles. Behind her, Liis stood with her back to him—she held a streamer in one hand and was pointing at the wall. Brill guessed his mother was at the other end. As he tiptoed into the corridor, the servant girl looked up. Their eyes met. With a quick look over her shoulder, she motioned her head for him to continue. Brill hurried on past. He was grateful for her help but also surprised.

In his bedroom, clean britches and a white button shirt awaited him, neatly laid at the foot of his bed. There was also a basin of fresh water, a pitcher, and a towel. Pola must have come. At his desk, Brill removed the parchment with the worm and the wasp and set it down. He then tugged on the leather pouch. It was hard to get out of his pocket. When he finally had it in hand, Brill inspected the pouch more closely. The leather was stained, as one might expect belonging to a beggar, but its quality was not in doubt. He opened the top drawer of his desk and dropped it inside.

Taking off his shirt, Brill found he could barely raise one arm. His entire torso was red and painful to the touch. His skin was hot and swollen. It even hurt to breathe. Brill took the cloth and ran cold water over his ribs and then pushed his head into the basin. The cold was paralyzing. When he was done cleaning, he changed into his fresh clothes and tossed the dirty ones into his armoire. He figured he might rest, just for a moment, before going to help.

When he woke, a mangy dusk filled the courtyard. Brill's body felt stiff. He managed to sit up, but his stomach felt hollow and his legs flimsy. Teetering, he made his way to his desk where he picked up the parchment with the day's casualties and put it back in his pocket. He was headed down the hallway when he heard voices coming from Liis' room. His brother's voice seeped into the hallway. Brill could see the flickering of lamplight through a crack in the door. He leaned in closer to listen.

"There's so much more I could tell you, Liis . . . but tell me about you! How are things here?"

"Now that you're home . . . we can all finally stop praying."

Nikolas let out a laugh. "God answers the faithful, Liis. And there's none quite as faithful as Mother." He laughed again. "But look at you! You grow more beautiful by the day!"

"Flattery will only buy you a few cheap smiles, Nikolas."

"Speaking of smiles, Lalot keeps asking about you. I believe he's smitten! What? Why the long face? Most girls would be over the moon."

"I'm not most girls."

"What makes you so special?"

"It's not that I am special, I'm just not interested."

"Come, Liis! He must capture a little of your fancy? It's Lalot Gingham! He's fabulously wealthy!"

"I thought he was engaged to that other woman . . . What's her name?"

"That's his mother's agenda; she is always meddling in his affairs. He assures me it's not a foregone conclusion." There was a pause. "What?"

Liis finally spoke. "Am I supposed to be impressed?" she asked.

"You really *are* cynical," derided Nikolas.

"That's what men say when they don't get their way. But do me—and really Lalot—a favor, and don't encourage him."

"Tell me, Liis, who are you interested in? Science? Are you going to marry a book?"

"If I could, I would. Unfortunately, Mother has been scheming."

"How so?"

"She wants me to marry Julian."

"Julian? As in the crown prince. Are you kidding me?"

"Apparently, the queen has involved the archbishop."

"You mean, to speak with Mother on her behalf?"

"It's worse; it appears there are nefarious incentives being dangled in front of her."

"Unbelievable!" said Nikolas. "That would solve all our problems in one go. It's good, right?"

"Julian! Are you being serious? He's the biggest lecher of them all!"

"He's young! He'll grow out of it."

"He's in his thirties, Nikolas! Can you imagine having that man for a husband? I feel *nothing* for him, and honestly, I'm not sure I feel *anything* for men. The fact of the matter is, I have little appetite for romance at all."

"Blasphemy, Liis! You just don't have the experience. You cannot speak of what you do not know."

"By that logic, you are suggesting one cannot know without experience."

"Exactly."

"So a newborn should not know to suckle, and a baby bird should not know how to fly?"

"Don't try to trap me in your scholarly games." Nikolas' voice became fierce. "Just heed my warning, Liis: a woman's soul can wilt from lack of pleasure! I *have* known such women. Their blood runs cold, their skin becomes pasty, their eyes fill with scorn. Simply because they deny their bodies. The culprit? Their minds! Their minds are like stoic generals that command them to march forward with no feeling. They refuse their instincts with moral arguments. And many of these women, like you, are quite beautiful . . . What a pity."

"I suspect you'd fancy yourself to be their hero."

"Not you, of course . . . but others? Sure, I could help them."

"How kind of you, Nikolas. You *are* truly selfless."

"You mock me, Liis, but without virile instincts, one walks the earth like a ghost!"

"Sounds fun."

"You don't know what you say. You haven't been with a man. Or are you one of those who look upon men with the neutrality of a butcher?"

"Nikolas, do you always have to be so crude?"

"You should hear the sailors talk."

"Nikolas, all I am telling you is I feel no *love* for Julian . . . or Lalot. It's not their fault. And I doubt in the end they would find me very satisfying. I am far too serious for them."

"*Love!*" Nikolas snorted. "Love is for children. Of all people, I would have thought you would know that. You've just got to get to know them; maybe then you can speak of love."

"Now you've caught yourself in your own web, Nikolas."

"Speak plainly, Liis."

"I know where you go for love."

"What are you talking about?"

"Do you not see eyes and ears on my face?"

"Don't be silly," he said gruffly.

"There's even a nose, if you look closely."

"What's your point?"

"I just wonder why you think your actions are unknown to the rest of us."

"Stop it, Liis!" said Nikolas, his voice becoming stern. "Already we are arguing, and I have only been back two hours." There was a moment of silence as they both considered how to proceed without fighting. "So tell me about Brill?" asked Nikolas.

"He keeps climbing onto the roof," said Liis. "It worries me."

"Is he still putting on your old uniforms?"

Liis said nothing.

"He needs to grow up! I will take him out and teach him a thing or two."

"Don't you dare, Nikolas!" said Liis. "Your idea of being a man is never going to be right for Brill. So spare me and the rest of us the trouble!"

"What can we talk about that doesn't lead to an argument?"

"Probably nothing."

Nikolas let out an exaggerated exhale. "You are just so very stubborn."

"Just don't expect me to be one of your women who doesn't speak her mind."

"What are you talking about? They speak their minds!"

"No they don't! And if they do, it's an act. They're pretending to be sophisticated and independent, but all the while the little girl fiendishly struggles to garner the handsome sailor's attention."

"Enough! Just tell me, how did Brill do on his exams? Did he pass?"

"No."

"For God's sake, why not?"

"Brill's plenty smart . . . You might even say he's a deep thinker—like Father. I just don't think he's being challenged in the right way, which makes him not interested in school. Thus, he doesn't do well."

"What does being interested have to do with anything—it's school!" stated Nikolas.

"And *you* really should be talking," said Liis.

"I did fine." An accusatory silence followed. "Not every-body can be like you, Liis. Wait, I know, the navy is looking for midshipmen," said Nikolas, his voice rising with excitement.

"The navy?" repeated Liis.

"Why not?"

"That would be the *worst* place for him."

"Nooo, it would toughen him up."

"Well, it's too late. Mother arranged for his admittance to seminary."

"If he doesn't like school, seminary will be worse. Does Brill know?"

"He does not . . . not yet."

"Would he have to board?"

"That's the sweetener. Brill also gets room and board cov-ered for my hand in marriage. Both ways, Mother is happy."

"When does seminary start?"

"It's not yet decided. Mother thinks she might wait until after his birthday."

"Oh, then I'll definitely have to take him out on the town!"

"Nikolas, you're impossible!"

"What did I say this time?"

Brill stepped quietly away from the door. It was awful news, but perhaps it served him right for eavesdropping. In the dining room, blue and white streamers crossed the rafters. The long table was covered in a satin cloth with a handsome array of silverware. Gazing into a spoon, Brill's face was upside down; it made his curly brown hair look even more wild.

Brill wandered out the double doors and into the court-yard. The remnants of the day had been obliterated. The heat had bequeathed a sumptuous evening. As he passed under the latticework that surrounded the doorway, he felt as small as a field mouse. But there was some pleasure from being so small and unimportant, for unimportant creatures get overlooked. Yet the more he thought about it, the more he thought that really it was just the opposite. The truth was he was *supremely* visible, a mouse in an empty ballroom, running left and running right. It didn't matter what he thought or wanted; the big decisions were always being made for him.

As he approached the well, Brill had a sudden desire to climb down. He wondered how long he could hide down there, but before he could give it any more thought, he realized he was in his dinner clothes. He looked up, catching sight of the chapel doors. He felt aversion crawl up the back of his neck—he would never go in there again. Climbing up the stairs, he made his way to the upper terrace. He went slower than usual, for his side hurt each time he lifted a leg. Eventually, he reached the ladder. When he arrived at the roofline, Brill placed his hands in his pockets and cast a forlorn eye toward the park. What a strange afternoon it had been. His lonely childhood seemed to be careening like a runaway carriage. Across the street, an irregular patchwork of windows and curtains were illuminated by lanterns. Brill heard the breeze whistling through the jacolandi branches. A burst of air caught his feet and swirled up his midriff. He followed the wind as it rose into the night sky. The stars were popping like daisies out of a field of black. He took a deep breath—the mouse was definitely not alone.

Just then a movement caught his eye. He wasn't able to see much in the premoon darkness, but he knew there was something on the chimney. He couldn't tell what it was until it croaked. A raven! Brill had never seen one on the roof before. "What do you want?" he asked out loud. The raven cackled and flapped its wings. "Go away!" said Brill, but to no avail.

Ravens are Noumenos' friends. They will help you.

Had he known the old chieftain was going to say such bizarre things, he would *never* have brought him water. "Go *away*!" Brill ordered. "I am Hoffe," he asserted. "Hoffe! We are not your friends!"

"*Caw! Caw!*" said the bird as if in response. *Tomorrow,* he thought to himself, *I will find the old man and give him back his pouch and be done with this nonsense.*

Just then he heard his mother call his name. "*Briiill.*" The mouse was being summoned. Placing each foot carefully so as not to be heard, he made his way off the roof and down the stairs. Only upon arriving in the courtyard did he reply. "Yes, Mother."

She came forward from near the well. "Where've you been?" she asked.

"In the chapel," he answered.

Cupping Brill's face firmly in her hands, she spoke softly. "You *need* a father . . . and I . . ." But she did not finish her sentence. For a fleeting second she looked upward, then wiped her cheek. Returning her gaze to him, she spoke. "We must be strong, Brill. God wants us to remain faithful."

"Yes, Mother."

"Ohhh, Brill," she said, squeezing his cheeks. "At times, I don't know where you came from."

"You don't?" he inquired, perplexed.

"I have some news to tell you . . . but not tonight. Tonight we celebrate Nikolas' homecoming."

"Yes, Mother," he answered, his head still in her clutches.

Moving her hands to his shoulders, she turned him toward the house. "March in there like a man and greet your brother!" she said, nudging him.

The chandelier, with its paper streamers, gave the chamber a festive glow. Brill stopped in the entrance. Liis was seated to the left of Nikolas, who was standing behind their father's chair. He had one hand on the back of the chair and the other in his pocket. Brill wasn't sure what to do. His brother seemed like a stranger to him. He did not look like the baby-faced youth who used to wrestle with him. He wore a deep blue officer's dress coat with tails and a stiff yellow collar. His skin was even darker and his hair lighter, perhaps from salt air and long days in the sun. Brill felt a distance between them as considerable as a vast ocean separating two shores.

Nikolas was pontificating. "We are cursed by Father's ancestry. I am *by far* the superior sailor among the lieutenants in my class, but I get no promotion. The rest, with their dark hair and wide cheeks, they receive promotions with no reason whatsoever. Lalot was just assigned captain of his own vessel! It's infuriating!"

"Father always said we Hoffes have to work four times as hard as one Ilyrian to achieve half the recognition."

"Ah, but not you, Sister, beauty . . . always has its privileges."

"Can we talk about something else?" pleaded Liis.

Nikolas had yet to notice Brill, or if he had, he hadn't let it be known. "You can't imagine what an honor it is to serve with Rear Admiral Ferentz. If it weren't for his skillful maneuvering, we would have lost at least two galleons."

"Nikolas," said Liis, her shoulders sagging, "you know I have little interest in such matters."

"But you should! Ilyria is afforded its quality of life for one reason alone, the navy!" Nikolas motioned to the food on the table. "There is no more serious threat than losing control of the Swaran Sea."

"Is it more serious than spotted fever?" asked Liis. "Or the drought?"

"There will always be casualties, Liis. But we can overcome anything as long as we rule the Swaran Sea. So to answer your question directly, yes! But let's talk no more politics." With this, he lifted his wineglass. "Since when has worry ever solved a single crisis? Never that I know of!" He downed the glass. "I am home, and I am in dire need of a good time!"

Liis shook her head. Nikolas was a master of obfuscation, avoiding all topics he did not want to discuss. It was a skill that was as natural to him as breathing. "You mean it's time to bury your head in potions and women."

"If that's what it takes, sure."

Liis threw him an olive branch. "At least you have returned home safely," she said. "Mother hasn't been this happy since before you left."

"Ah, she does dote," he said, taking his hand out of his pocket.

Coming up behind Brill, Lisbeth whispered, "Go on, don't be shy! He's your brother." As Brill skirted the table, he patted the tops of the empty chairs. Nikolas' dark, smoldering eyes beamed from above his gaunt cheeks. He seemed much more powerful than Brill remembered.

As Brill approached, Nikolas turned toward him. Out of his eyes came a sparkle. "Brill!" he said, grabbing him under the arms as if to lift him. Brill winced. "Forget it!" Nikolas said. "You've grown too much!"

"A little bit," said Brill, looking to the ground.

"No, a lot!" said Nikolas. "Wait, I have something for you." He searched a couple of different pockets until he pulled out a cloth bundle. He placed it in Brill's open hand. Unfolding it,

Brill found himself holding a black figurine. "Just a little thing," said Nikolas, winking. The figurine was of finely polished stone, a sculpture of a woman—although Brill only recognized her from her ample breasts. She was holding two snakes, one in either hand, but her head was the strangest. It was that of a lion, and behind her arms were the wings of an eagle. "Not something you can get around here," Nikolas added.

From the other side of the table, their mother cut in. "Nikolas! What did you bring him?" she asked, handing a steaming lid to Sisal.

"It's just a little gift for Brill. Something I bought from a Sulkid. Nothing to worry yourself about."

"Nikolas, you *did not* bring one of their trinkets into this house, did you?"

"It's harmless, Mother."

"If it's Sulkid, then it's idolatrous. I don't want such a thing in *my house!*" she said, sending him a fierce glare across the table.

Brill dropped it back into Nikolas' open palm. "Don't worry," Nikolas whispered, "I've got something better in mind for you."

"Let me help you with that, Sisal," said Lisbeth, searching for a spot on the table for a long platter.

Brill turned toward Liis, reached into his pocket, and pulled out the rumpled parchment. As he opened it before her, Liis leaned in close to inspect. "What do you have here?" she said, moving the worm over with her fingernail. "A bit ruined, this one," she added.

"A boy stepped on it," confided Brill.

"Not so helpful for identification purposes, but it's definitely the order of Lepidoptera . . . and this one . . . Hymenoptera. They're cousins."

"Cousins!" exclaimed Brill, astonished. "But the wasp was trying to kill the worm!"

Nikolas threw back his head and laughed. "Then they're definitely cousins, just like you and Costa."

"It's not a worm, Brill," said Liis. "Look closer." Brill leaned forward. "See, there are small protuberances. A worm would not have them. It's a hairless caterpillar, definitely cousins." Liis patted his hand.

"But how could they be cousins if they look so different?" he asked.

"In the same way birds and reptiles are related, but we can talk more about this later." Nikolas strode over to his mother's chair and helped her to the table.

"Nikolas," she said, "lead us in prayer, will you?"

"Of course, Mother," he answered, returning to the head of the table. Brill observed him closely. Nikolas was something like their father in looks. Both were tall and thin with wavy blond hair. But in character, they couldn't be more different. Their father had always been more labored. Every move seemed cumbersome, as if he were carrying something he could not put down. Nikolas carried little. The only weight Nikolas seemed to bear was his resentment at having a Pagani father. Alber had always been cautious with his words. There was no bravado, unlike Nikolas.

Alber had never been a strict disciplinarian; he was far too busy to involve himself in the day-to-day affairs of the house, which he left to Lisbeth. Although if he made a rule, Brill dared not break it. Not that he feared his father would touch him in anger, but the thought of disappointing him was demoralizing. If he would lay his kind eyes upon him, Brill would melt. But if Brill wanted to talk to his father, he had to pursue Alber and engage him on topics that were of interest to *him*—namely science. He was never openly affectionate and gave scant praise, but then, neither did he criticize.

Sometimes, after long trips abroad, their father would bring him gifts. One time, he brought him a bright green beetle with a massive horn! The beetle was so large it filled Brill's entire hand. On another occasion, Alber brought him a wooden horse. But the best, by far, was when he brought home a songbird. Its hood was bright blue, and it had a tuft of red on its chest and streaks of yellow and orange on its wings. It was the most beautiful creature Brill had ever laid eyes on. He named the bird Ermil. With a string tied to one leg, Ermil lived with Brill for weeks, chirping loudly from the window that opened onto the courtyard. Brill faithfully caught insects for him to eat. Eventually, Ermil attracted visitors, and not just their family guests, but one of his own. She was not nearly as striking as he, but what she lacked in feathery zeal, she made up for in patience. She would sit in a nearby bush, listening to him prattle on and on. One day Pola told him they were in love. After deliberating an entire afternoon, Brill decided to let Ermil choose. Brill untied the string from his leg. Ermil hopped along the windowsill, cocking his head one way and then the other before simply flitting into the bush. A few moments later, the pair took to the air, disappearing over the roof. And just like that, his father's gift was gone.

In the last few years of his life, Alber rarely came home, even for dinner. He had always avoided social events. To him, there was no greater waste of time—much to the chagrin of their mother. Society itself was at best an obligation, at its worst, a necessary evil, a relic, an appendage of humans' evolutionary past that somehow festered into an aberration of cronyism that only guaranteed the rule of the cretinous. He believed that society, more often than not, hindered individual brilliance by not permitting individuals to achieve according to merit. In this manner, Nikolas and Alber were in agreement, for Nikolas knew too well the limits forced upon him by the color of his hair. Once societies became rigid, Alber argued, they would resort to laws governing courtship, shelter, and the distribution of wealth by despotism rather than genius.

Alber's views were mightily unpopular in Jesut Edin, and few people had any interest in debating him, for Alber was clear and concise. And he preferred this anyway, choosing instead to delve into science, where proof of facts spoke for themselves. Alber's life mission became furthering his discoveries of animalcules, or "invisible creatures" as he would sometimes refer to them. Once he showed Brill his animalcules through a microscope. According to him, they were the causation of all manner of phenomena, such things as fermentation and the leavening of bread. Alber believed his animalcules could also be malevolent, causing disease and rot. His primary research was to solve the riddle of disease. The dysenterus epidemic had been his brightest moment, and the spotted fever his last battle. Nikolas had chosen to be a sailor, far from the long shadow cast by their father's genius. Of the three of them, only Liis seemed to thrive in their father's sunlight.

Nikolas' fingers splayed on the table. If their father had been reluctant to fulfill his duties as head of the household, it seemed Nikolas relished the chance. He bowed his head. The rest of the family followed his lead. "We give thanks for this fine Ilyrian wine, for the tender victuals before us, and for the queen's good health. Long may she live! Amen." A burst of air escaped from Liis' mouth. Nikolas glared at her.

"Amen," said Brill, although he was pretty sure he was the only one who spoke.

When his mother cleared her throat with some force, he, and everyone around the table, bowed their heads for a second time. "Our Holy Father," started Lisbeth. "We thank thee, O Lord, for the safe return of our son, Nikolas. We thank thee, O Lord, for repaying our faith and for answering our prayers. We heed your Holy Sacrament, and we abide by the Scriptures. Forgive those amongst us who trespass against you, for yours is the glory of heaven, forever. Amen."

This time the "amens" echoed around the table in unison.

"You may eat," said Lisbeth. And just as the tinkle of silver on porcelain was reaching its crescendo, Gasol stepped into the entryway.

"What now?" cried Lisbeth, clearly exasperated.

"A group of sailors are outside asking for Nikolas, madam."

"Tell them to come back tomorrow," she replied curtly.

"They don't seem to be listening, madam."

"Show them in," said Nikolas. Gasol didn't move.

"What is it, *Gasol*?" demanded Lisbeth.

"They've been drinking, madam, and . . ."

"Quite right, Gasol," said their mother. "Show them through the back entrance."

"I offered, but they said they would wait out front for the master of the house."

"Master of the house," repeated Liis, shaking her head.

Nikolas wiped his mouth with his napkin, trying to hide a smile. Putting it down on the table, he stood. "I'm afraid they will not leave until I make an appearance, Mother. I thank you for this most lovely homecoming dinner." Nikolas bowed and departed.

For a time, the dining room was eerily quiet. They all were listening for the door to open, which was confirmed by a roar of voices. As the door closed, an even deeper silence crept back toward them. Brill and Liis looked over at their mother. Lisbeth's eyelids flickered, but she said nothing. Then her lip twitched, but still she said nothing. Brill could see the impending storm about to make landfall. Her thick eyebrows gradually bore downward. His mother's face was like a fortress built upon the rocky shores of her jaw. Although Lisbeth's family lineage was Proudst, her features were more suited to a peasant than an aristocrat: broad nose, wide shoulders, hardy cheeks—she was no teacup. Lisbeth looked as if she were born to carry buckets of water and bushels of barley, not sit in parlors commanding servants with a flick of her blocky wrists. A good thing, for she would need all her peasant fortitude now. Lisbeth's chair pushed back, and she threw her napkin upon her plate as she shot upward. Turning, she briskly walked out of the room.

"Mother!" called Liis. With this she promptly chased after her. Brill listened to their feet on the tile. When the footsteps had faded, all that was left was a "ree-ree-ree," the pulsating thrum of the crickets coming in from the courtyard. If the house felt empty before Nikolas' arrival, it now seemed a treeless plain. As Brill sat there, he contemplated the table of food spread out before him—much of which was still steaming. Picking up a server, he began loading his plate, adding a helping of braised rabbit, a mutton ball or three, a scoop of potatoes, a couple of spoonfuls of gravy, and on top of it all, a large lump of butter. He even reached for the decanter and poured himself a glass of wine.

When he had finished eating, he teetered toward his room—he couldn't remember ever having eaten so much. Weaving crookedly down the corridor past the lamps, he braced himself against his door. He hung upon it for a moment before pushing. Brill didn't bother to shut it. He noticed that the walls were not behaving properly. As soon as he came within reach of his bed, he lurched forward, flopping on top. Turning over, he lay there unmoving.

21

First Visitor

When Brill woke, he did not know how long he had been sleeping—it could have been ten minutes or five hours. He was lying on his bed, still in his dinner clothes. His room was impregnably dark, so dark that he could see nothing. It was like floating in a referenceless abyss—no armoire, no desk, no tapestry or chest, not even his arms or legs were discernible—none of the familiar objects that helped define his world. On a normal night, Pola would have come and lit a couple of lanterns and talked with him before sleep. But due to the fiasco at dinner, Brill suspected she was preoccupied with his mother.

It was so dark in his room that he couldn't see the walls, or the ceiling. Brill found himself wondering about the blackness. Could the objectless darkness itself be considered an object, like his trunk or his desk? Could something as obscure as blackness be a *thing*? It was hard to imagine. It felt so expansive and intangible. The only real touchstone amidst the nothingness was his body: the sensations of his breathing, the rising and falling of his chest, the pain in his ribs from where he had been kicked.

If objects helped define him when he could see, what defined him when he could not? Besides the feeling of his moving chest, there were the sounds of the crickets coming from the courtyard, and a slight sour taste left on his tongue, perhaps from the wine with dinner. Besides the internal sensory cues, what distinguished him from the external environment?

In that moment, it seemed to Brill he was more like a stage, a sort of platform upon which the world came to him. But what was this platform? Was it his skin? Where did the sounds of the crickets land? He could hear them, but as the sensory world entered his awareness, he struggled to locate the exact point where they landed. There was a frustrating lack of certitude and exactitude. Maybe it was not an actual place, but more of a decentralized arising in a nebulous field of awareness, not so unlike a cornfield that sits waiting for the crows to come or the farmer to till.

And what about his own thoughts? Were they any different than hearing the crickets? Did his thoughts land in the same field of awareness like the rest? Perhaps most mysterious was the actor, commenting on it all. At first he assumed this voice *was* himself. But the more he reflected on it, the more he felt that this was not so, for he was talking to himself as if he was two different people. He seemed to use "I am" and "you are" interchangeably—as if he was both a subject and an object. What's more, there were moments when all the comments stopped, when nothing remained—no actors, no voices—just the same open platform, an alert nothingness.

For a fleeting moment he considered that perhaps he was little more than a mathematical formula, not so unlike the transitive law. *If* a *equals* b, *and* b *equals* c, *then* a *must equal* c. Thus, if the feeling of his hand was equal to the sounds coming to his ear, which was equal to the taste on his tongue, and none of them were any different from the voices inside his head . . . all had to be separate but equal, interchangeable parts. The only thing that was *not* part of the law seemed to be the act of experiencing. In this manner, experiencing was very much like the darkness—undefined, open, expansive.

And all this just because his eyes were of no use in the dark. And just as he thought this, Brill realized *how* he knew the old man from the park! He had been in his dream a few weeks before! The blind chieftain had asked him, "Why do you need your eyes to see?" Brill was dumbfounded. It was the *same* man he had met this afternoon! As he contemplated the impossibility of such a bizarre occurrence, there was a loud knock on his door. Slowly, he turned his head. "Who is it?" he called out. His voice sounded distant, even to himself.

A flickering light appeared, casting aside the shadows and blackness, bringing back the usual points of reference: his armoire, his desk, the sight of his hands, all the usual me-and-you-ness of the world. "Brill, you have a visitor," said Pola, holding the lamp.

"A visitor?" he repeated. The words made little sense. No one ever visited him besides Costa, and never at this hour.

"You had better get up," she said as she scurried to pick up some of the clothes abandoned on the floor.

"Who is it?" he asked.

"Colette Proudst."

"Colette? Maybe she wants to see Liis; they're old classmates."

"No, she was very clear. She asked for you."

"Why me?"

"She wouldn't say, except that it is important. She insisted on following me in; she is waiting outside your room."

Brill stood up. "Uh . . . well . . . uh, have her come in, then."

Pola opened the door. In stepped a woman in a long cape and hood. Walking directly at Brill, she stopped just a few feet away. "Were you the boy in the park earlier with Costa Turan?"

"Yes," he answered.

Colette removed her hood. She looked at him intently. "Was there an old man talking with a raven?"

"Yes," answered Brill, glancing over at his desk.

"Did he leave anything?"

"Why do you ask?" said Brill.

"Can I have a seat?"

"Sure," he said.

Colette chose the chair nearest his desk. "Sit down and speak with me a minute," she said, motioning for him to take a chair.

"Do you know of the story of Queemquesh and the Ayn Noor?" she inquired.

Brill nodded his head.

"If you had been Kurul, what would you have done?"

"I would have thrown the Ayn Noor back!"

Colette leaned forward. "Have you heard of the Gates?" Brill nodded slowly. "Try not to think of me as an adversary," she said, leaning back in the chair. "I believe we want the same thing."

"What is it that you want?" Brill asked.

"I want to enter the spirit world. I want to pass through the gates and leap into the Chasm of Eternity. Give me the Ayn Noor, and I promise you that I will return it—just as Kurul should have done."

"But . . . I don't have it," he replied.

"Listen," she implored. "I won't force you to give it to me, but I very much doubt I will be the only visitor you will have tonight. I warn you; the others may not be so friendly. There are people who will hurt you to get the Ayn Noor. Are you prepared?"

"Prepared," Brill repeated, but his throat was so dry he could barely get the word out.

Colette raised an eyebrow at him. After a long moment of silence, she stood up. "Very well, then. In the morning I will return. If you're lucky enough to still have it, perhaps you will be more agreeable."

"Okaaay," was all Brill managed to say.

"Good luck," she said, and she pulled her hood back over her head and walked out of his room.

After she departed, Brill opened the drawer where he had placed the pouch and began searching his room for a better hiding place. He opened his armoire but decided against it.

Just then Pola returned. "I don't know *what's* going on, Brill," she said, "but now Emhet and Costa are here to see you. Emhet says it's very important. I told him you were in bed, but he said to wake you."

Brill wiped his brow on his sleeve. "Are you sure he didn't mean Mother?"

"No, he specifically asked for you!" Brill's shoulders slumped. "I'll go fetch Liis," said Pola.

When she was gone, the door pushed back, and in stepped Emhet Turan followed by Costa swinging his legs forward in earnest. Brill dropped the pouch on top of his desk. Costa's crutches scraped over the tile like a wounded spider. "I can't believe your servants make me wait in the foyer like some vendor," said Emhet. "For all I do for this family!"

"Hi, Uncle Emhet," said Brill, attempting to smile.

"There it is," screeched Costa. Brill followed his finger past him to the old man's pouch.

Emhet didn't bother with pleasantries. "Costa tells me you have something that is not yours," he said, walking up to the desk and scooping up the pouch.

"It belongs to an old man," answered Brill.

Emhet squeezed it. "I am pretty sure it didn't belong to him either," he said as he tucked the pouch into the large pocket of his overcoat. Costa sent Brill a toothy grin, made more peculiar by his trampled mug. Brill had to look twice, for his face appeared to hang to one side like an unhinged door. His fat, busted lip was juxtaposed against a giant welt poking out of his forehead like a budding horn.

Just then Liis stepped into the room. "Uncle Emhet. What a surprise to come at this hour . . . to visit Brill of all people. How was your journey?"

"Glad it is over. Now, Liis," he said as if beginning a lecture. "Brill has something . . . well, actually, *had* something . . . how do I say this . . . that was not his."

"Couldn't this wait till morning?" asked Liis.

"It's a long story, and I am tired, as you can well imagine. Not really a social visit. Margarithe will have you all over soon, and I can tell you about my travels north. Nice to see you." Emhet attempted to raise his lips in a smile.

"At least let me show you to the door, Uncle," offered Liis.

"That will not be necessary. I know the house as if it were my own. Good night."

"Very well, good night, Uncle Emhet."

After they departed, Liis cocked her head at Brill. Her brows knit together. "What was that about?"

"Costa is such a little brat!" stated Brill.

"That's an understatement," added Liis, "but that still doesn't explain the visit, nor what happened to his face."

"It's a long story," answered Brill.

"I've got time."

"Well . . . this morning . . . when you and Mother were meeting with the monsignor, Costa and I went to the park. Me to give this old man some water and Costa to get his money back from these boys."

"How did they get his money? Costa's not exactly one to give things away."

"I can't explain it."

"You mean, you can't tell me."

"I guess," said Brill, his conciliatory eyes darting away from Liis' gaze. "Anyway, Costa ended up getting us into a fight, and during the fight, the ravens that were in the trees came down and attacked the boys who were beating us up. After the fight, when I looked for the old man, he was gone, and only his pouch remained on the bench. I picked it up, but Costa wanted me to look inside. I told him that it was none of our business. He practically begged me to give it to him. He said he would return it for me. I knew he was just saying that so he could have a look inside, so I said no."

"The two of you got into a fight?" asked Liis in disbelief.

"Costa started it," said Brill, shaking his head. He lifted his shirt to show Liis the welts and bruises on his torso.

"*Oh, my goodness!* You're lucky you didn't get seriously hurt."

"We were lucky the ravens came!"

"You *really* think the ravens came to your defense?" queried Liis, squinting at him. "Maybe it just seemed that way?"

"No, they did! They attacked the boys."

"I saw you on the terrace; I figured you had been on the roof."

Brill's head dropped. "Yeah."

"It's a dangerous place, especially for someone as impulsive as Costa."

"I had to get out of the house."

"Why didn't you just go for a walk?"

"I can't think on the streets . . . too many people."

"So what's inside the pouch?"

"I didn't look . . . and Costa doesn't know either. But you know how he is; he always wants to know everybody else's business."

"Emhet wouldn't come over and demand the pouch just because Costa wanted to have a look inside."

"You know what's even stranger, Liis? Do you remember that dream I told you about a couple of weeks ago with the old blind man? He was asking me where my eyes were?"

"Yes, I remember well."

"It was the *same* blind man!"

"Really? That's remarkable."

"And he said some strange things. One thing he kept saying was that our family name isn't Hoffe. He said it was Noumenos."

"That's not exactly wrong, Brill," said Liis.

"What do you mean?"

"That *was* Father's name . . . before . . ." Liis paused.

"Before what?"

"Before he came to Jesut Edin. Noumenos was his birth name."

"Why hasn't anybody ever told *me*?"

"Father was very private about his past."

"So the old man was telling the truth?"

"Sounds like it."

"That's horrible!"

"Why horrible?"

"Because he said some things that better not be true."

"Like what?"

"He said death would be coming to Jesut Edin—lots of it."

Liis' expression changed. "Scary. But that's kind of obvious, isn't it? There already are plenty of deaths. Spotted fever is getting worse by the day. People are coming to the fifth ward faster than we can part with the ones who have died."

"Maybe that's what the blind man meant. But he also said that I had Ule's gift and that I could see all of this myself, but I was too afraid . . . and that it was time to grow up and be a man . . . and that ravens were Noumenos' friends . . . and—"

Liis interrupted. "Sounds like he was from the north country if he talks like that."

"And his pouch!" continued Brill. "It bothers me that Emhet and Costa just came over and took it without asking."

Liis shook her head. "That's the Turan family for you! But I am not sure there is anything we can do about it except maybe ask Emhet for an explanation tomorrow."

Brill shook his head. "They're probably already home."

Liis nodded in agreement.

◆ ◆ ◆

Emhet felt relief but equal parts trepidation. The entire ordeal was bizarre, verging on esoteric—and that was not a word Emhet cared for. But for now, at least the diamond was back in his possession. Passing through the kitchen, he could hear Costa's labored breathing and his crutches smacking furniture as he followed behind. Their carriage was waiting in the yard. Margarithe had taken the coach that evening and, with it, their driver and footman. Emhet had Lukaz hook up two horses to the old phaeton. "Gasol," barked Emhet, stepping into the carriage yard.

"Sir," answered Gasol, emerging out of the shadows. His face glowed orange from the embers in his pipe.

"Open the gate!"

Emhet assisted Costa into the carriage. Scooting to the far side, Costa inquired, "Father, shouldn't we look in the pouch just to make sure?"

"We will, we will, just not here, lest somebody sees us with it."

"What if it's not what we think it is?"

"I promise you, the . . . *aberration* . . . is in the pouch. I spent two and a half months with it, and I can feel its peculiar presence. Besides, I felt it through the leather—it's the exact shape and size."

"I knew it!" exclaimed Costa. He attempted to push his crutches into their usual place, between the seat and the backrest, but he couldn't manage—something was in the way. He shoved harder. The second time proved fruitful as his crutches took their rightful spot. Emhet unbuttoned his coat and reclined back in the seat. Costa held on to the armrest as the horses began trotting forward toward the open gate. The carriage rattled as it passed over the stones. Soon they were heading down Queen's Avenue. Night had cooled the day, and thanks to a late-rising moon, there was ample light to steer homeward but not enough to see the hand that crept slowly through the opening between the backrest and seat, gingerly making its way into Emhet's coat pocket, relieving it of its sole burden.

22

MORE IS NOT ALWAYS BETTER

Liis stopped in front of her door and turned toward Brill. "There's really nothing we can do tonight. I will go visit Uncle Emhet tomorrow on my way home from Malador and ask him about it. But for now, I must get some rest . . . and so should you."

"I'm sorry for all the trouble I've caused," said Brill.

"None of this is your fault," she said, and she stepped forward, took his head in her hands, and planted a kiss on his forehead. Brill turned and limped back toward his room. Liis watched him go.

As Brill entered, he sensed he was not alone. He swung his head to the left. Sitting at his desk was the new servant girl. She held the pouch in her raised hand.

"*Wha*—How did you . . . ?" he faltered.

"I pulled it out of your uncle's pocket."

"Does he know?"

"I don't believe so, not yet anyway."

"Who are you?"

"My name is Roan," she said, setting the pouch down on the desk.

The hot breath of evening air wafted through the open window as Brill sat in the very chair Colette had been in not so long ago. Roan's clothing was Ilyrian, but he was certain she was not. Her demeanor was stern—there was no frivolity about her. Roan's mouth was full, and her cheekbones were high and wide. A seriousness concealed any natural beauty that might have been. Apparently, she didn't seem to think it was odd that she had come into his room without permission and was sitting at his desk in his chair. "Did I hear you speaking Pagani with Pola this afternoon?"

"Yes," Roan acknowledged.

"Are you a servant?"

"Of sorts," she answered.

"Why did you bring the pouch back?"

"It's yours to give, not theirs to take," she replied.

"But it's not mine either," said Brill. "I just found it. It belonged to an old man I was speaking to this afternoon. He left it on the bench. I'm going to try and find him and give it back."

"I know of the old man you speak of—I suspect he meant for you to have it."

"But anybody could have picked it up!"

"No." Roan shook her head. "He may not look like much, but he is a legend in Bajarmaland. Few have seen him over the years, but a couple of weeks ago, coming down from the mountains, I came upon him sitting by a stream. It is rumored that he can take the shape of animals, and as I approached, he changed into a salmon and swam away. I doubt very much that him leaving the pouch and you finding it was an accident. After all, we're not exactly speaking about an old bone or some crusty piece of bread."

"You know what's in the pouch?"

"You don't?" asked Roan, studying Brill.

"No! Why should I?"

"Why haven't you taken a look?"

"It's not mine."

"It is now."

"So you know what it is?" he asked.

"Of course," said Roan, "I looked in the pouch."

"You *did*?"

"Why not?"

"What's in there?"

"The Ayn Noor," stated Roan. Her pale blue eyes simmered.

"The . . . the . . . diamond?" stammered Brill, his jaw dropping. "But that's . . . that's . . . impossible!"

"Impossible or not, that's what's in the pouch. The Ayn Noor was stolen over a year ago from my tsik."

"Then *you* should take it!" he stated, motioning toward the pouch.

"I would never do that," said Roan.

"Why not?"

"It's not my destiny."

"If it really is the Ayn Noor, why on earth did he leave it for *me*?" Brill stood up and started to pace. "I am only thirteen!"

"Those types of questions will only lead you in circles. Trust me, there are mysteries beyond what we can ever know."

"The invisible reason!" exclaimed Brill, coming to a stop.

"What's that?"

"Oh, just something I've been thinking about."

"Surely . . ." said Roan, almost as if to herself, "if Emhet knows you have it, others will follow."

"What do you think I should do?"

Roan shrugged. "I cannot say."

"Did you know Pola from the mountains?" Brill asked, taking a seat opposite Roan.

"I did not. She is much older than me."

"Does Pola know the old blind man?"

Roan nodded. "They were of the same clan. His name is Patrig; he is Ule's son."

"Ule. The old man mentioned him."

"Ule was one of the great Pagani healers."

"Who exactly was he?"

"He combined the Gnos teachings with the practices of the mountain shamans. He was a skywalker."

"A what?"

"Someone who can separate their soul from their body and travel into the spirit realm."

"Why would someone do that?"

"To heal the sick and retrieve lost souls from Bardo Fey. Ule was known far beyond Bajarmaland. People came from all over to see him—even one of your kings. When the Ilyrians were rounding up Pagani shamans and burning them, no one dared lay a finger on Ule.

"Patrig was Ule's only child. But Patrig rebelled against his father. He wanted nothing but to fight and destroy the Ilyrian invaders. He organized the Great Uprising with Skadje, but in the end he betrayed her and the Red Bows. Some say that he is as bad as Kurul. But a few believe what he did was heroic. They feel that if Skadje gets the Ayn Noor, the world will suffer for another thousand years. Regardless, Patrig betrayed the Pagani and took away our victory. It was the end of the Noumenos Clan."

"If my father was Noumenos, how does he fit in with these people?"

"The blind man you met today is your grandfather."

"This can't be true!" Brill exclaimed, dropping his head into his hands. All of this was so confusing. He raised his head. "Are any of my father's family still alive?"

"No," said Roan, shaking her head. "Minol, your father's brother, was the last Noumenos in the north. He died shortly before I came south. Before I left his house, he told me much of what I have just recounted. He showed me many things. If we have the chance, I will show you someday."

Hearing about his uncle's death brought his father to mind. How ironic the two brothers died within a year of one another. "There are no more Noumenos left, then, besides the strange old man?" added Brill.

Roan frowned. "There are at least *three* others that I know of."

Just then, there was a knock on the door. "Who is it?" Brill called out.

"It's Pola," she said, sticking her head inside the room. "You have more visitors."

"Tell them to come back tomorrow."

Pola stepped fully into the room; her face looked flustered. "That is *not* going to be possible, Brill. It's the crown prince, Julian!"

"Prince Julian!" he shrieked.

"And he's not alone. There are soldiers too. They are waiting in the foyer."

Brill's heart began racing. He didn't know what to say or do. He wanted to ask Roan, but when he turned to her, she was gone. Before he could think of what to do, the door swung open. Into the room strode five men, two of them dressed in uniforms. The last one closed the door behind Pola and planted himself in front of it. Brill recognized the crown prince immediately—he had an unmistakable face. He shot to his feet but forgot to bow. Julian stopped in front of him. "I believe you have something of mine."

Brill was too stunned to bow, and only managed to squeak. "Wha-what?"

"My diamond!" growled Julian.

Brill's belly tightened. "D-di-a-mond!" he muttered.

"You *do* know who I am?" Julian questioned, his eyes squinting. Brill nodded. "Then I will ask you one more time. Do you have my diamond?"

"No," answered Brill, shaking his head slowly. His breathing became shallow.

"Would you lie to your future king?" Brill shook his head again. For a second, Julian's face opened with a perceptible expression of surprise before screwing back tight. "When we find it," he warned, "and we *will*, there will be consequences." Brill began to tremble. Julian motioned to the others. "Start searching!"

Suddenly, there was a loud banging on the door. *"Open up!"* Liis' muffled voice came from the other side. Brill could see that the large soldier blocking the door with his arms crossed was not going to move. Meanwhile, the others were pulling the sheets off his bed, turning over chairs, and yanking his clothes and boxes out of his armoire.

"Open this door!" demanded Liis.

Just then the guard yelped as he jumped forward. The inswinging door nearly knocked him to the ground. "What the . . . ?" said Lucius as Liis flew past him, her robe flapping. She had only had the time to throw it hurriedly over her nightgown. *"What is going on here?"* she demanded. The second guard intercepted her, but she gave him a strong elbow to his ribs. *"Don't touch me!"* she bawled. Liis charged up to Woefus, who was pulling apart Brill's bed, and pushed him aside. *"How dare you!"* Brill had never seen Liis so angry. Her face was flush and her eyes torrid.

Julian, who had been rummaging through Brill's desk, stopped what he was doing and descended upon Liis without bothering to look at her. "Do you know who I . . . *am* . . ." His voice trailed off as their eyes met. He bowed abruptly. "Madam," he said politely.

"I demand an explanation! What are you doing to my brother's room?"

"I apologize, my lady, there's been a terrible mistake," said Julian, bowing even lower, perhaps to conceal his face. "Gentlemen, we're obviously in the wrong house. Let's be going . . . *Now!"* he ordered, flashing Woefus a furious look through gritted teeth.

• • •

As fast as they had come, they left, going back down the corridor, through the foyer, and out the front door. When Julian arrived at their horses, he turned on Woefus and Lucius. His face was hotter than a smithy's tongs. *"Why didn't you tell me she lived there!"*

Lucius turned his hands up. "You said we needed to go at once."

"Just an unfortunate coincidence, Julian," added Woefus.

"We never leave things to chance . . . or *coincidence!*" shouted Julian. Then he grabbed hold of a pot of flowers from the stoop and smashed it to the ground. "That fucking boy has it!" he yelled. "He was *lying!* I know it!"

"Sire," said Woefus, as Julian looked around frantically for something else to destroy. "I know someone who could retrieve it, before sunrise—and there would be no connection to you."

Just then Julian caught sight of the guard limping down the steps, supported by the other. "What happened to him?" he asked.

"Someone stabbed his foot, sire."

"How did they do that?"

"From under the door, sire," answered the soldier.

Julian's jaw clenched tighter. "If that house wasn't hers, I would burn it to the ground."

"Julian, what do you want me to do?" petitioned Woefus.

"Before the sun rises, I want my diamond. I don't care how you get it. Hang the boy by his feet until he spits it up. Whatever it takes!"

Woefus put his foot in the stirrup, threw his leg over his horse, and galloped feverishly into the night.

Julian shook his head. "Of all *fucking* houses, it had to be *hers!*" Lucius shook his head in disbelief. "Don't just stand there!" barked Julian at the soldiers. "Take him to the infirmary."

He turned toward his horse, grabbed hold of the saddle, and swung his leg over his steed. "Come, Lucius," said Julian. "Let's find the nastiest lubjok in all of Jesut Edin."

• • •

Brill was aghast. He surveyed what was left of his room. His armoire looked as if it had been disemboweled; its innards slopped mercilessly across the floor. His mattress was overturned. The desk drawers had been emptied and his belongings scattered. The leg of the carved horse that his father had given him was broken. His room was in shambles. And it had all happened in minutes. Brill picked up the horse and pushed the leg back in place—it fell over. Amidst all the chaos, the pouch remained where Roan had left it, untouched on top of his desk!

"What is going on?" exclaimed Liis, turning toward Brill.

He lifted the leather pouch, holding it up for her to see.

"I thought Emhet took it?"

"It came back," he confessed sheepishly.

"How?"

Brill didn't want to implicate Roan. "After I left you at your room, I found it sitting here."

"Pola." Liis turned to her. "Can you explain any of this?" Pola averted her eyes. "You two are hiding something! Give me that pouch!" said Liis, reaching out her hand.

"I'll open it," said Brill abruptly. It didn't take long for his fingers to find their way inside. As he grasped the jewel and felt its innumerable edges, doors within doors of his mind began flipping open in an almost infinite sequence, projecting along a curving line reaching into a boundless collection of distant memories. Lives he had not known, but somehow lived, were falling out of the vastness of his mind into his recollection. When he pulled the jewel out of the pouch, it filled his hand. He held it up for Liis to see.

Her eyes widened. "Put it back, Brill," she directed.

Brill slipped the crystal back into the pouch and pulled the strings tight. The doors of infinite possibilities began to close. Inside he felt hot . . . yet his skin was ice cold. All the while, a strange serenity had come over him, akin to the waters in a calm bay cradled by a sandy shore. All fear and worry left him. If one lived for lifetimes, what did one moment matter? The tapestry of existence was much too large to concern himself with any particular moment.

Liis noticed that tears were streaming down Pola's face. "Why are you crying?" she asked.

Pola wiped her eyes. "I'm sorry," she said.

"Why is everyone apologizing?" stated Liis.

"I never thought I would see the Ayn Noor," said Pola.

"You know this diamond?" asked Liis.

Pola nodded. Brill looked over at her. How often she had told him stories about it. *Wait,* he thought. He had touched the Ayn Noor! Had he gone mad? Would one *know* if they were slipping into madness? The one thing he knew for certain was that his ribs no longer hurt.

With her hands on her head, Liis exhaled. "I can't believe Julian just did this to your room!"

"Maybe we should send for Nikolas?" suggested Brill.

Liis dropped her arms and shook her head. "First of all, he would only grovel at Julian's feet. It would not be prudent for him . . . or us. Besides, I doubt he would come."

"Why? Why wouldn't he?" asked Brill.

"It's hard to explain how his mind works. Let's just put your room back together."

In silence, the three of them did their best and kept their conversation to the task at hand. When they were done, Liis spoke to Pola. "We'll lock the doors tonight. Make sure Gasol

has the gate bolted, and have Hanna sleep in the foyer. If anyone else comes to the house tonight, instruct her to wake me
before letting them in."

"Very well," said Pola. Brill studied Liis. She was his big
sister and always so brave. But there were limits even to her
strength. "We'll sort all of this out," she said, but her face
looked unsure. "You can sleep with me tonight," she offered. It
was the first time in Brill's entire life where it seemed that Liis
was the one that needed to be comforted. He agreed to come,
but as he lay in her bed, he kept conjuring images of the spectacular diamond and the recollections that had ensued—and
the strange sense of peace that had come over him. He wondered about the improbability of it. He considered everything
Roan had said about Minol, and Ule. And the old man, Patrig
. . . his grandfather. The chieftain's voice came back to him.
"Changes are coming. It's time to grow up and become a man."

23

The Last Visitors

When Brill woke, Liis' window rattled. Wind and moonlight filled the courtyard. Brill listened. He was almost certain that he had heard voices. Fear leapt and sat upon his chest. He held his breath. Brill could hear Liis' soft breathing—she was deep in sleep.

He had left the pouch sitting on top of his desk!

"What a fool! I can't be trusted with the Ayn Noor," he berated himself. As he lay there, the door to Liis' room creaked open. The shaky light of a single flame flickered, revealing an unknown number of dark figures.

"What happened to Willit?" came a rather pathetic attempt at a whisper.

"I don't know, Deet. He was behind me."

"He better not be lootin' the house without us. Woefus said we can have what we want but only after we get the pouch from that boy."

"Look! There's two in here."

"Get a lamp, I can't see," said Deet.

As lanterns were held aloft, four youths gathered around the bed. Brill nudged Liis with his arm. Her eyes popped open. "Who are you?" she said, pulling Brill against her.

Brill immediately recognized the one called Deet, the shirtless youth from the park. "Two little birdies cuddling in a nest," he cooed. Drawing a knife, he slashed the gauze canopy. A boy on the far side yanked off the remainder. Deet reached in and grabbed Brill's arm while another took hold of Liis. She sent a swift kick straight for his temple, but he withdrew in the nick of time.

"Feisty," he declared. Liis clasped her arms more tightly around Brill.

"Enough," said Deet. He leaned in toward them with his knife. "Whose face should I carve first?"

"Liis, let me go," demanded Brill.

"No," she implored.

"Let me go," he said, taking her arm and moving it. "I know what they are here for." Liis relented. Deet yanked Brill out of bed.

"If you hurt my brother, I swear I will—" threatened Liis.

"You'll what?" said Deet. "Don't make promises you can't keep," he sneered through his teeth. "Klempt. Janke. Stay with the girl," Deetmar ordered. "Make sure she doesn't leave this bed or make any noise. If she gets sassy, punch her in the mouth real good." Deet cocked his face up close to Brill's. "You know what I am here for?" Brill nodded. "Then lead the way," he said.

After Brill and the two others left the room, Klempt shut the door. Grabbing the shredded canopy from the ground,

Klempt began to tear strips. "Put down the lamp, Janke," he said, "and let's tie her up."

"Good idea, Klempt. I bet she has some nice jewelry in her drawers," he said, setting the lantern down on Liis' nightstand.

"Be careful, Janke, she's a kicker," warned Klempt. But just as Janke gathered the strips of cloth, Klempt grabbed him from behind, putting him in a choke hold.

"Achhhh," gasped Janke as the two of them dropped to the ground. Klempt then brought his legs around Janke's torso and squeezed as tight as he could. As they rolled, the two of them crashed into the nightstand.

"What on . . . earth!" cried Liis, scrambling out of bed and snagging the lantern just before it fell. Janke's legs were swinging wildly. Liis climbed back across her bed. After setting the lantern on her dresser, she seized a tall brass candelabra.

Aa–a–ach! came the sounds from Janke's half-open mouth. With one last kick, his boot sent Liis' small dresser across the floor. Soon thereafter his body went limp. Klempt lay underneath him, panting.

"Did you kill him?" asked Liis, trembling, her eyes wide.

Pushing Janke off, Klempt wagged his finger toward the floor.

"What? What do you want?" she asked, not sure what he was pointing at.

"The cloth," Klempt managed to say. Liis set down the candelabra and gathered the strips for Klempt.

Sweat was dripping off Klempt's chin. His shirt was already soaked. Taking the fabric, he tied Janke's arms and legs as he had done countless times to the pigs and sheep on the farm. Liis had half a mind to rush out of the room, but her feet stayed planted. "He's just passed out," added Klempt, finally answering Liis' question.

"Ugh," groaned the youth on the floor, coming back to consciousness. Klempt stuffed a handful of cloth into Janke's mouth.

"Why are you helping us?" asked Liis.

"Don't you recognize me?" said Klempt, looking quizzically at her.

"Should I?"

"You came to my house in Tripe Town. Then Clara and I came to see you at Malador . . . remember . . . the little girl who loves Papyri so much. You gave her medicine."

"Ahhh . . . yes," said Liis, nodding slowly. "How is she?"

"Better! Much better! Thanks to you," he added.

"We had such a small amount of biotica left, but I figured with her being so tiny it might work."

The youth on the floor groaned. Liis looked gravely over at Klempt. "You will be in *serious* danger for crossing them."

"You know, this is the first time in months that I have actually felt like a proper person. I'll take my chances."

"Brill!" gasped Liis, remembering. She grabbed the brass candelabra and rushed for the door.

"Wait, I'll come with you," said Klempt.

◆ ◆ ◆

It was dark and quiet when Brill stepped into the corridor. The two boys were on either side of him. One was carrying a lantern. "Ovi, where the *hell* is Willit?" asked Deet, looking around.

"Don' know, Deet," replied Ovi as they marched Brill down the hall.

"It's in there," said Brill when they arrived at his door.

"Open it, Ovi," ordered Deet. The thick-boned youth stepped around Brill and pushed the door open—it scraped to a halt two-thirds of the way. When they were all inside, Deetmar lit another lantern. He motioned with his chin to Brill. "So, where is it?"

"It's right here," said a woman's voice.

Startled, they all looked across the room at Roan, who stood in front of Brill's desk with the pouch in her hand. "I believe this is what you came for?" she said.

Deetmar raised the lantern to see her better. "Is that it?" he asked Brill.

Brill nodded.

"Ovi, go get it from her," ordered Deetmar.

Not one for words, Ovi set down his lantern on a small table and approached Roan slowly.

Roan held up the pouch for him to take. Ovi took a step forward and reached for it. But as he did, she pulled it away. Ovi swung for Roan's face with a right hook, but his knuckles passed uneventfully through the air as she ducked. Underneath his arm, Roan stepped forward and using her legs and hips as Eorl had taught her, she brought her fist, with all its momentum, against his nose. There was an audible crack.

"Aaahh," bellowed Ovi, reaching both arms to grab her. His eyes were so full of water that he couldn't see, and Roan easily avoided his grasp.

Just then the door to Brill's room opened. In stepped Liis and Klempt. Gasol and Pola were right behind. Gasol was holding a pitchfork, Liis a candelabra.

Deetmar looked at the party. "Klempt? You're with *them*?"

"I am done being a thief, Deet."

Brill ran to join them. Liis stepped forward. Deetmar shook his head, taking measure of what stood before him. "An old man, a boy, and two *women*. That's quite an army you got there, Klempt!" Turning, he hurled the lantern in his hand at Brill's armoire. As it crashed against the door, flames immediately sprung upon it. Stepping over to the table where Ovi had set the other lantern, he grabbed the second and threw it against the tapestry on the opposite wall. Gasol handed Klempt the pitchfork. "I'll go fetch some water." The familiarity of the pitchfork felt good in Klempt's hands.

"After all I done for you and your family, this is how you are going to repay me?" said Deetmar, calmly pulling out his knife. "You know what we do to traitors 'round here," he continued. Klempt did not bother answering. Watching the flames go up the tapestry toward the wooden beams, Deet's face lit up. "I am going to enjoy watching this place burn."

"Hey, skinny boy," a voice called out. Turning, Deetmar watched Roan as she moved over to the bed and laid the pouch on top of it.

"Ovi, stop crying," he ordered. "An' go get that pouch."

Ovi's nose was bleeding, but at least he could see now. Walking toward the bed, he moved cautiously. As he approached, Roan leapt forward and struck him in the nose a second time. *"Aaaggh!"* Ovi howled, twice as loud as before, lifting both hands to his face.

Deetmar lowered his head like a bull and sprinted toward Roan, who swiftly darted for the open window. Jumping out, disappearing into the courtyard. "You little bitch!" he shouted out the window after her. He then went over to the bed and grabbed the pouch. Pulling back the strings, he squeezed the bottom and pushed the Ayn Noor upward until he caught a glimpse of the diamond—he had been instructed by Woefus *not* to touch it.

"That girl broke my nose—twice!" whimpered Ovi as a crimson river trickled through his fingers.

As he pulled the strings tight, Deetmar looked around the room. The odds had turned against him. "Fucking Klempt," he snarled. Gasol and Pola returned with buckets of water just as flames were beginning to nip the ceiling. Liis ran forward and yanked the tapestry off the wall.

Gasol unloaded his first bucket onto the armoire. There was a loud hiss. Brill took the second bucket from Pola and emptied it onto the tapestry while Klempt stood his ground between them, pitchfork ready. Deetmar spit toward Klempt. Swiveling, he ran for the open window. In one hand he held his knife and in the other, the pouch. As he jumped out, a foot came up from below, hooking his leg. Instinctively, Deet secured his blade with one hand while the other braced for the fall—letting go of the pouch. Scrambling to get up, he searched the ground frantically.

"Why is this so important to you?" asked Roan. Looking up, Deetmar could see she held the pouch in her hand.

He walked toward her, slashing the air a couple of times as if to sharpen his blade. Stuffing the pouch into her shirt, Roan backed up slowly. At the well, she grabbed the wooden bucket and threw it at him. He dodged it, and it went clanging past. When he came within striking distance, he feigned as if to slash but stopped and lunged, going straight for Roan's heart with the point. Roan pivoted onto her back foot at the last second, swiveling to the side. As the knife passed in front of her, Roan grabbed his wrist with both hands, and using his momentum, she lowered his arm as she stepped behind him, locking his wrist and elbow. Deetmar fell to his knees—it was his only recourse to prevent his arm from breaking. Lifting his arm higher, Roan forced his face into the ground as she had been drilled to do countless times. With a bright *Chink!* his knife hit the ground. Roan kicked it into the shadows. Holding his wrist in one hand, she placed a foot against his face. With her free hand she withdrew her own knife, reached down, and sliced his cheek. Then she hopped backward, leaving him on his stomach. Deetmar sat up slowly. He said nothing as he felt the cut on his face. "Now you will have the mark of a thief," said Roan.

"Fucking Hutsu!" he said.

"Not Hutsu—Pagani—you idiot."

"Whatever you are, you're stupid. You should have killed me. Next time we meet, you're dead!"

"Promise," replied Roan.

Pola was hustling into the courtyard with two empty buckets as Deetmar walked by. He shoved her against the wall. Once inside the house, he yanked a linen off the table, sending the silver candlesticks flying. He pressed the cloth against his cheek. Roan followed him, shouting directions whenever he was about to take a wrong turn. Blood dripped copiously onto the tile. Roan stopped at the threshold and watched Deetmar until he disappeared down the cobblestone street. She looked up at the morning sky—an aquamarine sheen was building in the east.

When Roan turned back into the foyer, she found Hanna in a corner in a ball, her arms wrapped around her knees. "It's all my fault," she whimpered. "They said they'd burn down the house if I didn't let them in."

"Get up, Hanna. You did . . . the best you knew how," said Roan, pulling Hanna to her feet. "Go . . . get some rest." Hanna sniffled as she stood with her head down. "Now!" ordered Roan. Hanna wiped her nose on her sleeve and ran out of the foyer. Roan then went to the linen closet where she had tied and secured the first youth, the one called Willit. Roan showed him her knife. "Will you be good?" The youth nodded. Roan cut the binding on his legs. She grabbed his bound hands and hauled him up to standing. Directing him through the foyer from behind, she shoved him unceremoniously out the front door. He stumbled and then fell. He got to his feet and weaved down Queen's Avenue in the same direction as Deetmar.

Even though the fires were extinguished, the walls were stained black, and the door to the armoire was charred. Ovi was sitting against a wall. His nose had doubled in size. Someone had stuffed a piece of cloth up each nostril to stop the bleeding. Klempt kept the pitchfork at the ready. "Where's Deet?" he asked, seeing Roan. Brill looked up from the floor. "Did you kill him?"

Roan shook her head. "It would have brought the wrong people to the house."

"Wise," stated Gasol.

Roan walked up to Brill's desk, reached into her shirt, and set the pouch down, back where it apparently belonged.

Returning to Klempt's side, she ordered, "Get to your feet." Ovi obeyed. Klempt and Roan led him out of the house as well. Afterward they gathered Janke from Liis' room. Once they had set him loose, Roan looked over at Klempt. "What are you going to do?" she asked.

"I heard the army is desperate for recruits, what with the defeat in the north and all."

"Defeat?" inquired Roan, her eyes narrowing.

"News came yesterday. The Pagani ambushed the regiments sent to put down the rebellion."

"They won?"

"It was a rout."

Roan couldn't believe what she was hearing. "The Pagani won," she uttered, trying not to sound too happy.

"They're saying," Klempt continued, "the governor has fled Okomorling. They're all headed south, headed to Torbeshacken. The army is seeking recruits for the war."

"War?" repeated Roan.

"They say the Pagani will march on Torbeshacken next."

It sounded strange to hear someone refer to the Pagani as if they were foreigners. It made her somehow feel different from what she was.

"Watch out for Deetmar," said Klempt. "He is a bad person to have as an enemy."

"You better heed your own advice," replied Roan. Klempt nodded. With this, he started down the avenue. At one point, he turned back and waved.

Klempt was still in sight when a woman on a large black horse galloped up to the door. The rider swung her leg over the horse, quickly dismounting. "I am here to see Brill Hoffe."

Roan said nothing, nor did she budge from the door. The woman came up the first step. "Do you know who I am?" she asked. Roan shook her head that she did not. "I didn't think so. Have you heard the name Colette?" Again, Roan shook her head. "Do you speak Ilyrian?" Roan did not answer. "Will you take me, or should I call on someone else?"

Roan motioned with her head for Colette to follow her. She didn't particularly like this woman, but at least she was better mannered than the previous visitors—besides, Roan somehow suspected the saga had not yet played out.

Roan and Colette moved to the side as Pola hurried past them with dripping towels. "Oh, Colette," said Pola, bowing. "You're back."

"That I am," she said.

Entering Brill's room, they found Liis and Gasol gathering all the broken and burnt belongings together. Brill was on the floor helping to clean up the water.

"Brill," announced Roan.

Brill looked up and so did Liis. "Colette!" she exclaimed, surprised. "What brings you here?"

"I was hoping to speak with your brother."

Brill stood up. Liis looked over at him. "It's okay," he said, walking toward his desk. Colette followed. Brill pulled a wooden chair over for her to sit on and picked up one that had been knocked to the ground for himself. "I warned you," said Colette, alluding to the disarray.

"Yes," agreed Brill. "You did."

Roan took up a position nearby, against the wall. "An interesting housekeeper you have," remarked Colette.

"What do you mean?"

"She has the markings of a Yatu, not exactly your common housemaid."

"The mark of what?" asked Brill.

"On her wrist . . . All Yatu have them."

"What's a Yatu?"

"A Pagani warrior—some of the best."

Brill looked over at Roan. That explained her bravery and skill, but it also added to the mysteries that seemed to be growing by the hour.

"So you survived the night."

"Barely," he said.

"Is the Ayn Noor still in your possession?"

Brill nodded. Colette shook her head. "Impressive! But you know Julian will come back. You have only poked the lion. I doubt there are three hundred of those." Colette jutted her chin toward Roan. Brill shook his head. "Only one Yatu—that's a pity. But Julian can't directly attack me, you know. He would have to answer to the queen."

"What if I *did* give it to you?"

"I will return it, like I said."

Brill looked around the room. Gasol. Pola. Liis. He did not want any of them to get hurt. "I will give it to you under one condition," said Brill.

"What's that?"

"You let Julian—and everyone else—know that *you* have it. I don't want people to come here anymore."

"Let me see it," said Colette. Brill picked up the pouch and handed it to her. Colette pulled back the cords. When she looked inside, Brill watched her eyes change three shades of blue. She tightened the cords. "I accept." Colette reached into her cloak and handed Brill a card. There was a large red dot on the front. "Turn it over," she said. Brill did so. On the other side was an address. "If you need me, show the person at this address the card. Tell them you want to speak with me."

At that moment, Lisbeth and Emhet stepped into the room. Costa was at their heels.

"Brill!" his mother shrieked as he fell, clasping her head in her hands. "What have you *done*?"

Liis rushed to her side. "Come, Mother," she said, putting her arms around her. "It's not Brill's fault."

Lisbeth shoved her away. *"No!"* she shouted. "I am sick and tired of you all coddling him." She raised herself off the floor. *"Pola,"* she called out.

"Yes, ma'am," replied Pola, putting down the towels.

"Pack Brill's bags. I am sending him to seminary—*today*!" With this, she turned and charged back out of the room.

There was a stunned silence. Colette looked at Brill. "Well, you know how to find me." She promptly walked over to Emhet and held the pouch in front of his face. "Is this what you came for?" she asked.

"Um . . . I believe so," answered Emhet.

"Can't have it," said Colette, lowering her arm and continuing past them.

"But . . . it's not yours; it's Prince Julian's!"

Colette expelled a twisted sort of laugh and kept walking.

Emhet looked toward Brill. "How did you get it back?"

Brill knew only a lie would suffice. "Colette showed up with it," he said. "She came here to ask me what the old beggar and I talked about."

"Damn!" exclaimed Costa.

"How did that witch steal it from me?" Emhet declared.

Costa's face was drawn long; it looked as if he were about to cry. "So we're too late?"

"Yes, Son," said Emhet, raising both palms upward.

"Well, at least *I* don't have to go to seminary," Costa scoffed in Brill's direction.

After Emhet and Costa departed, the rest of them transported the ruined furniture to the stable. As they were returning to the house, Brill dropped away from the group to speak with Roan. "Are you disappointed in me?" he asked.

"No," said Roan firmly. "Here, it would not long be in your possession. It seems to me your choice was best. How this will end is a mystery—I'm not so sure you won't see it again."

• • •

Monsignor Iraneous had unlocked the gate and waited as Liis strolled back to the carriage where Brill was standing next to his suitcase. Gasol and Pola were beside him. Roan sat on the driver's seat with the reins in her hands.

"There's something that's been bothering me," said Liis, coming up to him. "Something the old man said."

"Yeah?" asked Brill.

"When he told you it's time to grow up and become a man, what do you think he meant?"

"I don't know . . . maybe that I need to be more like Nikolas."

"That's just it," she replied. "Why would you want to be a man like Nikolas? Or a man like Emhet? Or Julian? Sure, they are considered *men*, but who in their right mind would want to be like them! What about being a man . . . like Roan?"

Brill's lip raised in a half smile. It was true: Roan was one of the most admirable and tough people he had ever met. He looked over at her, then back at Liis. "Maybe what he meant was that I need to stop wearing dresses . . . or liking girls' things."

"You know, Brill," said Liis, "I don't think being a man has anything to do with what sex you are, or what you like to wear. I think it has more to do with *knowing* who you are and staying true to that. Which brings me to this—you and I both know your being a priest is what *Mother* wants. But it's not what *you* want. Just as she is trying to get me to marry someone I could never love. This is when we have to be strong, like Roan. When the world is against you, telling you that you have to be someone, or something, you are not, that's when you have to be strongest. And it has nothing to do with how big you are or if you can fire a musket or ride a stallion."

"It's time," Monsignor Iraneous called out. "We need to get his things put away before dinner."

"He'll be right there," said Liis.

Gasol turned to Brill. "Take good care of yourself," he said, reaching out to shake his hand.

"I will miss you, Gasol," said Brill, taking his hand.

"Ah, and I will miss you, Son."

Pola threw her arms around Brill and held on to him tightly. She could not find words, but when she let go, her eyes were filled with tears—as were Brill's.

After she stepped away, Liis spoke up. "I put something in your bag, a present."

"What is it?" asked Brill.

"It's a surprise, but I think you will like it. It was one of my favorites." She winked. Brill nodded. "I love you so much, Brill," said Liis, taking both of his hands. It felt as if his heart suddenly fell out of his chest and onto the ground. "I love you too," he confided, bowing his head slightly.

"Remember what we talked about," she said, waiting for him to look back up.

"Of course," he answered, returning her gaze.

"We'll see you soon," she said.

Brill reached down and picked up his suitcase, leaving his heart on the ground as he walked toward the monsignor. The squeaky gate opened just wide enough for him to pass. Before crossing the threshold, he turned to look back one last time. They were all waiting. Their faces looked so sad. Brill could not bear it any longer. When he had passed into the courtyard, he heard the monsignor's keys turn, followed by the sharp click of the lock. The next thirty yards were the longest of his life. What it meant to be a man was unclear, but of one thing he was certain—his childhood was over.

ABOUT THE AUTHOR

Author with his niece at the Great Sand Dunes
National Park (pre-COVID).

CHARLES LARTIGUE was raised in Arizona, New Mexico, and Haiti. From a young age, he experienced many different views on spirituality and religion, having had the good fortune to witness both Native American and vodou ceremonies. He attended college in California until everything in his life imploded and he dropped out of school. A relentless search for a complex understanding of himself and for deeper meaning ultimately led him to study eastern philosophy and archetypal psychology. The quest continues to this day and informs much of his writing and view on the world. He lives in the woods in Maine on land he shares with a family of beavers, a porcupine, and a passel of feisty chipmunks.